A Promise
of
Fireflies

Susan Haught

Amy —
always remember —
Love's ageless &
enjoy !
Susan Haught

FOUR CARAT PRESS

FOURCARATPRESS.COM

A Promise of Fireflies

Susan Haught

Published by Four Carat Press
Copyright 2016 Susan Haught
Printing History
eBook edition 2016
Paperback edition 2016

Edited by Michelle Kowalski
Cover by Elizabeth Mackey Graphic Design

For Mom
the angel on my shoulder

Dreams die every day

Some drown in the endless churn of a washing machine,
some get lost under an avalanche of responsibilities
and still others suffocate in the wake of a broken promise.
Dreams die—disappearing with the sun in the western sky.

But a sprig of grass will sprout from a blanket of snow,
new life will be born when two become one,
and a phoenix will rise from the ashes left behind.
Dreams reborn—blooming with dawn's radiant new light.
~sh~

Chapter One

SCARRED CORNERS FRAMED the small journal she pulled from the old shoebox. She traced the cover with one finger, dark stains and pebbled leather disquieting, yet as oddly familiar as the stale odor of cigarettes her mother promised to quit smoking and never did. Now the tenuous reminder, void of the peppermints her mother nursed to disguise the smell, threatened to unravel the tethers holding her together.

God, how she wished she could rewrite the last year.

With her legs crossed beneath her, Ryleigh Collins clutched the journal to her chest, leaned against the wall of her mother's apartment—as empty of her possessions as the world was of her—and let the shadows of the waning morning swallow her.

"I can't do this." She grabbed a loose thread in the denim stretched over her knees and yanked hard.

Two feet bundled in thick navy blue socks appeared in front of her. "Can't do what?"

Ryleigh raised her eyes, moist with remembrance.

"Ah." Natalie crossed her feet, lowered herself with the grace of a toned dancer, and placed a firm, yet gentle hand on Ryleigh's arm. "The personal stuff's the hardest."

After a pause, Ryleigh tucked the knot of emotions neatly back where they belonged and turned. "I'm such a wimp."

"You'll get through this." Natalie Jo Burstyn's perfectly manicured brows knitted together in a scowl that masked her usual playful grin. "I intend to see you do."

The lump in her throat strangled the words she'd rehearsed since Natalie had offered to drop everything to help. Of course she would. Her meddling best friend always seemed to know exactly what to do. Or say. She grasped Natalie's hand and squeezed.

Sometimes words got in the way.

Ryleigh released a long breath and straightened her legs. The journal tumbled to her lap.

"What's that?"

She swiped a hand across the journal's cover and then wiped them on her jeans. "An old journal," Ryleigh said, brushing away the dusty handprint.

"Don't just sit there fondling it, open it."

The binding creaked. Timeworn pages fanned in a graceful arch as if her touch had resurrected them. Faded ink swirled across the unlined parchment, and the musty balm of old paper and ink tapped at a recollection, distant and unformed, yet ripe for picking—but couldn't pluck it from her memory. Smudged and watermarked, the words danced across the aged pages. She turned each one with care.

Nat leaned in. "Well?"

Ryleigh frowned. "Looks like a collection of poetry."

"I didn't know your mom wrote poetry."

"This isn't her handwriting," Ryleigh responded without thought, "and my mother never wrote anything more literary than a grocery list."

Natalie peered over her shoulder. "Then whose?"

"Don't know. Just an 'R' at the end of the entries." The pages crackled as Ryleigh turned each one. "And the year. '66. '67 on some." A shiver feathered its way from her neck to the tips of her fingers.

"Want to read it?" The familiar weight of Nat's head settled on her shoulder. "Like old times?"

She'd never considered not sharing something with Nat and quickly harnessed the prickling urge to slam the book shut to prying eyes.

Careful not to damage the pages, she smoothed them flat, the tickle of selfishness nibbling at her consistent, rational side. As she scanned the pages, she muttered lines at random, the only autograph the watermarked scars of blurred ink. *"The air is thick, gray ashen snow, the ghost returns, its presence unfought."* She flipped the page. *"Fireflies flicker against azure skies, frolicking hither in reverent riverdance."* The weight against her shoulder anchored a covey of troublesome thoughts, but Ryleigh continued to pluck lines from the pages. *"Sodden showers of infected rain, across crystal skies littered with fire."* She dragged a finger across an eyebrow. "Intriguing."

"You're mumbling."

"They dance to their reticent song."

Natalie frowned. "Who?"

"Fireflies." She tapped the page with her index finger. "One of the poems is about fireflies. I wonder if they're really like that."

"Seriously?"

Ryleigh tucked a strand of hair behind an ear and closed the book with a finger marking her place. "I've never seen one."

"C'mon," Nat said, crossing her arms. "Kids catch fireflies in jars all the time."

"Not this small-town, sheltered Arizonan."

"Come to think of it, I've never seen one since moving here."

"They're on my bucket list."

Natalie opened and then shut her mouth. "You added to your bucket list without telling me?"

The concentrated effort Nat used to curb her bewilderment caused Ryleigh to forget her grief for a fleeting moment. "I'll see one someday," she said and reopened the book to the last page.

"Read to me, Riles." Nat folded her long legs beneath her, anticipation deepening her eyes to warm chocolate. "Like when we were kids."

Ryleigh glanced sideways at her. "I had to explain them to you."

"So?" Nat said, the short word long on sarcasm. "It's nostalgic."

"Okay." Ryleigh took a deep breath. "This is the last entry. It's called 'Lost.'"

> "*'I placed my love inside your heart*
> *and softly called your name—*
> *I placed a hole inside of mine*
> *as God's heavenly angels came.*
>
> *I placed a kiss of golden tears*
> *upon your tiny chest—*
> *I placed a rainbow at your door*
> *the day you came to rest.*
>
> *I placed a single pure white rose*
> *upon your tiny feet—*
> *I placed my hand against your cheek*
> *and said good-bye, my sweet.*
>
> *I placed a gentle autumn breeze*
> *within your tiny space—*

I placed with you, a piece of me
and let you go in God's embrace.'"
~R~'67

The words stuck in her throat with painful intensity. Ryleigh dragged her finger over the 'R'—the last letter in the journal. "Forty-three years ago."

Natalie picked at a stray thread in the shredded knee of her True Religion jeans. "I'm not very good at analyzing poems, but—"

"Whoever wrote this lost a baby." Careful fingers traced the cover, the stained leather unsettling, yet somehow comforting beneath her touch. Ryleigh's neck prickled. A tear trembled on the edge of her eye. "I feel like I'm eavesdropping," she said and closed the book. Sheer will eased the roiling in her stomach.

"Sounds like something you'd write."

Ryleigh shook her head. "Cozy articles for *The Sentinel* on county fairs, care packages to our soldiers, and Mrs. Grayson's baby quilts don't count. I haven't written fiction or poetry in years."

"You should."

Ryleigh raised the journal. "This is raw passion," she said, sniffing back the telltale signs of her emotion. "Emotion stripped naked."

"Your work is like that. Peeking inside the places of your heart no one ever sees."

"Maybe I don't want anyone to see."

Nat paused, and then wrapped her arm over Ryleigh's shoulder. "Things will get better. I promise."

Nat's words soothed her, a spoken ointment soothing a fresh wound.

* * *

The women sat cross-legged in the empty apartment sorting a mish-mash of items. One scrap at a time, Ryleigh placed the pieces of her mother's life into neat piles, turning each one front to back, puzzled at how little she knew about the odd trinkets, mementos, and letters safeguarded inside worn-out cardboard boxes. With one pile marked "Save" and the other to be discarded, it occurred to her what a parallel her mother's passing was to the death sentence Chandler had given their marriage. Nothing remained but the pompous flashbacks of one and a handful of useless trinkets from the other, and with one flick of the wrist (or philandering penis in Chandler's case), they are tossed aside with yesterday's trash. Yet the part that remained—the part that had wrapped itself around her heart—seemed useless to try to dismiss. Love doesn't stop with someone's absence. Sometimes it grew heavier, the ache deeper, until the hurt no longer gave in to tears.

The gravity of grief had exhausted her, and she felt as overused as the boxes that held her mother's meager belongings. Ryleigh pressed her fingers hard against her temples as if the pressure would numb the ache and quench the niggling urge to leave it all behind and walk away. Yet that wasn't entirely true—the impulse to run bulldozed past any rational thought.

"You okay?"

Ryleigh rubbed the back of her neck. "Just tired." Her hands fell to her lap. "It's just," she said with a sigh, "none of this makes any sense." Ryleigh picked up a patch embroidered with an open-mouthed eagle's head and tugged at the broken threads. "Who keeps junk like this?"

Natalie shrugged.

"Or this?" She held up a single brass button. "Mom had hundreds of orphaned buttons. Why isn't this one with the others?"

"Don't know," Natalie said, straightening, "but I'm curious about the letters."

Ryleigh stilled. "What letters?"

Natalie reached for the stack bound with a rubber band. "These," she said, "postmarked forty-something years ago with no return address."

Fragments of Eleanor's life lingered in Ryleigh's hands—tokens she never bothered to share. Or had she simply not paid attention when her mother spoke of these things? In either case it was a moot point: she'd never bothered to ask. And now it was too late.

The items were meaningless, but an ambiguous feeling tapped at her like the annoying click of a retractable pen. "I don't want to save this crap, but it feels strange to think about throwing it away. Does that sound weird?" She voiced the question with no expectations of a reply.

"Of course it does," Nat said, the usual lilt returning in her tone. She rose and brushed the dust from the backside of her jeans. "But it doesn't surprise me. You *are* weird."

"Thanks," Ryleigh said, reaching for the shoebox. The penciled sketches on the front had faded, but the drawing of the stylish low-heeled dress shoes remained intact. Over the years, the corners had become torn and sloppy and the lid slipped easily free. She placed the items inside and then pressed the lid into place, concealing portions of her mother's life, remnants absent of explanation.

An empty feeling swept over her. "Something isn't right, Nat." In truth, it felt as if she'd been yanked from the pages of a fairy tale and didn't know how to find her way back.

Or if she truly wanted to.

"We're almost done, Riles." Natalie offered a hand up, her deep brown eyes glistening with tiny flecks of copper in the afternoon light. "All that's left is the desk."

Ryleigh's shoulders slumped. "I forgot." She clasped the journal with one hand and grabbed Natalie's outstretched hand with the other. Nat had been her rock when she needed a steady hand, yet waggish enough to celebrate the good times with all-out regale. Always there. No matter what. With an achy groan that migrated through every forty-three-year-old bone, she allowed her best friend to pull her upright.

A photograph fell to the floor between them.

Ryleigh reached it first. They rose together and turned toward the apartment window, light spilling across the photograph. Yellowed and creased, and deckled edges crimped in several places, it wore the markings of time.

"Wait…is that your father?"

Ryleigh nodded.

"Where'd this come from?"

"Must've been inside the journal." She pushed the hair from her eyes. "Why didn't Mom ever show this to me?"

"Don't know, but check out your father's friend. The Kodak is faded, but he's gorgeous. Killer eyes," she said, letting loose an exaggerated whistle.

Ryleigh flipped the photograph over. "Look at this," she said, tracing a finger over faded ink, a ghostly impression of time long passed. *"Today this may be nothing, but tomorrow it may be all that's left."*

"An 'R' and 1967." Natalie raised an eyebrow. "Just like the journal."

"I wonder if my father's friend is still alive? Is he the author?"

"Be fun to find out."

"Fat chance. I'm a fair hand at research for inconsequential feature articles for my column, but I'm no sleuth. I can't find my phone half the time." Ryleigh slumped. "Or keep track of a husband and where he's sleeping. Or with whom."

"Ouch." Natalie paused, cleared her throat, and then pointed to the photo. "The jungle background. The dates. This was taken in Vietnam. It's as good a place as any to start."

Ryleigh tapped the photo three times against her fingers. She worried her bottom lip in a series of successive tugs and slipped the photograph into the shoebox.

Natalie grinned. "Well, Sherlock? Shall we find him?"

Chapter Two

ASIDE FROM THE memories, the garishly carved oak desk was the only thing of value left in the tiny apartment. Preparing to dive into the chore of emptying it, Natalie shimmied her sleeves to the elbow, straightened her shoulders, and turned to Ryleigh who was busy packing the smaller items into bigger cardboard boxes. The kind with cut-out handles. The kind that made it easy to carry the trinkets (memories) of someone's life out the door.

Natalie rolled her head from side to side, each rotation a useless attempt to relieve the underlying tension. "Is there any coffee left, Riles?"

Ryleigh stuffed one cardboard flap inside another and sat back on her heels. "No, but it sounds good. I'll make a fresh pot."

Natalie shifted her weight. "I'll get started on the desk."

"Don't get lost in there." The corners of Ryleigh's mouth turned up but didn't reach her inquisitive green eyes that normally exhibited the passion of a rising sea, and her lips were void of the natural blush that endorsed her smile. Grief-infused exhaustion had its own set of distinguishing marks and Natalie didn't care for the autograph written across her friend's face. Over the past year, Ryleigh had ridden a broken carousel with more downs than ups, and Natalie had to stand by as her best friend's heart shattered.

Ryleigh tucked the flap over the last box. Natalie's heart stuttered. She missed the carefree girl, the silly teenager and the amiable yet determined-to-a-fault woman she'd known most of her life.

Nat leaned against the desk and watched as Ryleigh performed the ritual of filling the coffee pot, spooning ground coffee into a filter, and rinsing their cups while the coffeepot gurgled to life. The automatic movements passed in slow motion. How many times had Ryleigh done this for her? For Chandler? Her hands curled into tight fists. Turning away, she plopped to the floor, her rear end taking the brunt of the sudden drop and dug her hand into the largest desk drawer.

Jammed with recipes, the contents of the drawer were easily removed, and without lifting her eyes from the task, she raised her voice to travel the short distance to the kitchen.

"Hey, Riles—" The sudden appearance of long, slim legs cut the words short.

"I'm not deaf," Ryleigh chuckled, handing her a mug.

Rising steam greeted Natalie with the mellow aroma of glazed chocolate doughnuts. She took an indulgent swallow. "This is heaven. Remind me to order some for the med spa."

Choosing a spot adjacent to the desk, Ryleigh propped a foot against the wall and leaned into it. With both hands laced around her mug, she sipped the hot liquid. "Your clients would love it," she said, the gold band on her left hand snagging the last bit of light from the setting sun.

Natalie nodded, the ring a reminder Ryleigh had yet to face the facts about her husband. A benevolent dreamer, she stretched the boundaries of forgiveness, searching for the tiniest scrap of explanation to justify foolish behavior. And Chandler Collins topped the list of those whose foolish actions had done more damage than a category five tornado.

"So," Nat said turning to her, a mountain of recipes in both hands—some with torn edges, others cut with precision and neither in any sense of order. "There must be thousands of recipes in here."

"Toss them."

"You sure?"

"Positive. Mom rarely used recipes."

"Like mother, like daughter," Nat said and tossed them into a large trash bag. Eleanor had passed her cooking skills to her daughter and it was one thing Chandler never complained about—Ryleigh's cooking always seemed to satisfy him.

Fringed in thick, dark lashes, Ryleigh's eyelids lowered over weary green eyes. A smile tugged at the corners of her mouth, but vanished as her attention steadied on the floor and whatever message lay ingrained in the dense hardwood planks. Natalie sighed, her hands on her thighs. What had happened between them that her husband had sought satisfaction dabbling in someone else's software? Maybe he thought he'd found a sweeter deal. Some people switch baseball teams midstream just because their team isn't winning. A lifetime of loyalty deserted for instant gratification. Wimps.

Natalie crossed her legs and swung around on the bit of real estate she'd claimed with the rear of her jeans. "Stupid, horny old man," she mumbled and smashed another mountain of recipes into a bunch at the bottom of the trash bag.

"Excuse me?"

Natalie pushed the hair from her forehead and slumped. "I was thinking nasty thoughts out loud."

"And taking it out on the trash?"

"I can't stuff Chandler's sorry ass in there."

Natalie stood, brushing the dust from the backside of her jeans. "I thought your husband was smarter than that," she said, and shoved her hand into the back of the desk. More papers flew.

"All he saw was a younger woman ogling him."

"She's nothing but a gold-digger. Said so herself that day at Il Salotto, bragging how she'd been married and divorced. Twice," Nat said and slapped the desk. "Ouch!" She rubbed her palm, hot and stinging and flushing bright red. "How could he not see through that, that—"

"Bimbo?"

"Bitch. Don't give her the benefit of the doubt." The vivid memory of Della Mayfair's dramatic entrance into Il Salotto Salon & Med Spa a year ago still nauseated her. Female clients gossiped. Male clients drooled. "What was he thinking?"

"He wasn't." Ryleigh shrugged. "Except with the part of his anatomy standing at attention between his legs."

"No-o-o, not because of a perfect pair of double Ds and podgy lips men go all stupid over." Nat waved her hands at her mouth, sighed, and then took Ryleigh's hand and gave it a reassuring squeeze. "Sorry, Riles. I didn't mean to bring this up."

"You're merely verbalizing my thoughts." A furrow formed across her brow and deepened. "Damn him!"

Natalie scowled. "Damn that horrid woman," she said and shoved her hand to the very back of the desk. Angry pain shot through her finger and up her hand. "Shit!" she said, poking her finger into her mouth. The tang of wet copper replaced the foul bitterness in her mouth. "What the hell was that?"

The women peered into the corner of the desk. A rapid search of the dark chamber of secrets revealed a splinter jutting from the wood like a tiny oak dagger, poised keenly in its mission. They exchanged a curious look. Beneath a neatly trimmed measure of tape, an envelope hung from the back of the desk.

"That's odd," Ryleigh said, reaching in.

"Watch that splinter. It's wicked."

Ryleigh loosened the tape and with a final tug the envelope came free.

Early evening light filtered through the window. Natalie flipped the switch to the overhead light and touched her friend's arm. "Do you think your mom taped it there on purpose?"

She shrugged. "I wish I could ask."

The short edge had been torn open and Eleanor's name and address were neatly handwritten across the front of the envelope, the postmark's inky footprint smudged across a Yoda forty-one-cent stamp—several years old in postage cents. Ryleigh removed a single sheet of lined legal paper folded into thirds, edges perfectly aligned. Grasping the edges, she unfolded the paper, turned slightly to catch the best light and read aloud:

"'Dearest Eleanor:

The documents are ready for delivery when the time arrives. All is as you requested, and are in perfect legal order. I recognize a binding legal document, and I foresee no complications.   I   have, however, extreme reservations concerning this matter. She must be told—at your discretion—but you are well aware of my position concerning this most sensitive matter.

I am grievously troubled to hear your illness has advanced. I send my heartfelt wishes for your recovery and as always, my unfaltering love. Though I know you will honor my request   in   due time, I implore you do so in the very near future. Please give my love to Miss Ryleigh.

Highest Regards—
Ambrose'"

Natalie watched Ryleigh scan the words again secretly hoping an explanation would seep miraculously from between the lines. She refolded the paper and tucked it inside the envelope, tapped it three times against her hand, and turned to Natalie. "Who's Ambrose?"

"Your mom never mentioned him to me."

"It's like reading a stranger's mail."

"It's kinda creepy, Riles. How does he know you?"

"It's obvious he knew my mother, so I'm assuming that's how he knew she had a daughter. But am I the 'she' he refers to? And the postmark." Ryleigh steadied the envelope. "Ballston Spa, New York."

"Where you were born?"

Ryleigh nodded.

"Someone in Ballston Spa knows you?"

"Mom said her and Daddy were passing through when she went into labor. Couple days and they were on their way to Arizona. I had no idea she knew anyone there, and if I'm the 'she' in the letter, what was she supposed to tell me and what's this about honoring a request?" Ryleigh let out a deep breath. "What request? What documents?"

Natalie's eyes grew wide.

"God, Nat, am I looking at my life hanging upside down from a monkey bar? Who is this guy?" Ryleigh glared at her. "And who's the author of the journal?"

Natalie crossed her arms. "Only one way to find out."

Chapter Three

BY THE TIME Ryleigh arrived home, the purple autumn halo above the mountains surrounding Hidden Falls had vanished. She stepped into the laundry room from the garage, tucked the shoebox securely under her arm, and flipped the light switch.

"Crap."

She tried the switch again—up, down—as if the power of suggestion would repair the faulty switch Chandler had promised to fix. He'd promised to fix a growing list of neglected items. In fact, he'd promised over twenty years ago to honor their vows. And she'd witnessed firsthand how that panned out. Why would she assume he'd fix a disconnected switch? Or the cracked walkway? Not to mention their broken marriage. The muscles in her jaw tensed. The unsavory thoughts burned inside her but she forced them to fizzle before they rekindled the anger.

Ryleigh groped her way along the wall in the dark—and froze. Cold denim brushed against her leg. Fear sucked the air from the room. Her pulse thundered behind her eyes. She tightened her grip on the shoebox, scrambled for the light switch and spun around.

Iridescent cat eyes stared quizzically up at her. His ears, a lighter gold than the rest of him twitched warily. "Kingsley." She set the shoebox on the counter and slid down the wall to the floor beside him. "You scared me," she crooned, stroking his back. "You know I hate surprises, you silly boy." Kingsley pushed his head into her palm, golden eyes sleepy with the sudden attention. With an ostensibly squashed face, she thought him absurdly adorable. And the best of companions, even if he did just scare the piss out of her. A birthday gift a few Septembers ago, the kitten (now a hulking tomcat) had been a surprise from Chandler. Her now estranged husband had beamed the entire day, knowing she'd fake a tantrum at the surprise. But she'd seen his eyes well with tears when he presented her with the ball of fur and she'd begun to cry. He'd said he was allergic. Cedar trees? Yes. Cats? No.

She cupped Kingsley's head in her hands and kissed him squarely between the eyes. The hirsute cat pulled away, flicked his tail, and with an indignant strut, sauntered away. "Off you go, Mr. Arrogant."

Ryleigh pulled herself to her feet, reclaimed the shoebox, and headed for the den. The contents intrigued her. And although it haunted her, the journal had kindled her curiosity.

Glass French doors with amber knobs defined the room she referred to as her den. Aside from the modest desk concocted from yard sale finds, a large padded circular chair filled the area beneath the window, worn just enough to be comfortable. The furniture and stacks of books piled in a reconditioned closet consisted of homeless strays. Her affinity to the orphaned items magnified the sense of being adrift without an anchor.

Across from her desk, she'd stenciled the words *"Liber Dilectation Animae—Books, the delight of the soul."* She pressed her palm to the wall and opened her mind's eye. Locked inside a child's memories, the gravity of her father's rich, deep voice echoed in her mind, the rhythm and colorful words soothing and comfortable in the safe cocoon of his arms wrapped snugly around her five-year-old frame.

This memory was hers alone—one she was certain of. Soap and minty toothpaste. Prickly whiskers, caterpillar eyebrows, and big, comfy lap—the images stamped in her mind as real as if she could reach out and touch flesh and bone.

Ryleigh lifted her hand and the memory faded like a watercolor image bleeding down a wet canvas.

Kingsley strutted into the room and entwined himself in and out of Ryleigh's legs. "I must be absolved of my earlier crime of passion, huh, Kings?" She curled into the pulpy chair and tucked her legs beneath her. The cat leapt, curled up nose to tail beside her, and set his purr motor on high. She placed the shoebox on her lap, careful not to disturb the contented cat.

Once home to a distinctly '50s pair of black and white pumps, the shoebox had been around longer than she had, edges shabby from years of being moved, shuffled, and stored. Opening the vintage shoebox felt exhilarating, yet oddly paralyzing. Her heart drummed between her ribs. A treasure chest? Or quicksand? A moment's hesitation would make no difference in the trash or treasure that lay hidden inside.

She removed the lid.

Stacks of letters lay neatly inside, but she picked through them until her fingers brushed the pebbled surface of the journal. Her eyes lingered on the deep-set stain. She set the journal beside her opposite Kingsley and sifted through the letters for the photograph. Kingsley kneaded her thighs in response.

Two soldiers in military fatigues stood side by side, arms stretched over the other's shoulder. A single dog tag dangled from their necks. One wore a bandana tied around his head and each held out a can in an animated salute to the photographer. "I'm sure this is my father." She hesitated. "Why not try to find his friend?"

Ryleigh rose and set the shoebox on the chair. Kingsley peeked through one partial slit of an eye at the sudden movement. She placed the photo on the scanner bed and held her breath as the device hummed to life. Only when the photo appeared on her computer screen did she dare breathe.

Kingsley lolled upside down in the middle of the chair. The schoolhouse clock chimed nine tones, and Kenny Chesney warbled from her pocket, startling her and irritating the cat. Ryleigh answered Nat's call. "You forget something?"

"I didn't want you to freak out if I rang the doorbell."

"Doorbell's toast anyway. Sounds like a sick bullfrog."

"Let me in before I freeze into a permanent lawn ornament. It's raining." A soft knock followed Nat's voice. Ryleigh rolled her eyes, stuffed the phone in her back pocket, opened the door, and came face-to-face with a sack from Jack in the Box.

"I brought food. I know you don't care for eating artery-clogging junk food, but I'm not much of a chef, and a good burger with extra pickles and fries once in awhile aren't going to kill you." Natalie stepped through the doorway. "And the fries are hot." Dark eyes twinkled.

Ryleigh's stomach rumbled at the mingled aromas of hot potatoes, grilled burgers, and spicy dill pickles. "I hope you ate your own," she said, blowing on a hot fry before popping it into her mouth. "Remember the old photograph we found?" She swallowed a mouthful of potato, dragging Natalie by the arm.

Nat nodded, her mouth busy.

"Well," Ryleigh said, raising an eyebrow, "I found something interesting."

Chapter Four

THE ECONOMY HAD taken a deadly toll on the quaint mountain town of Hidden Falls. Work in the building trades had come to a near standstill since the meltdown, sending most local contractors to the bigger cities of Phoenix and Tucson looking for anything to keep them from going under. Most did anyway. A general contractor for over twenty years, Chandler Collins had seen the good, the bad, and the ugly.

His business ledgers were aligned in sequence, a brown envelope stuck between them—the kind that held important documents. Chandler leaned into the office chair and checked the date stamped across the postmark. Weeks had passed, yet the culmination of twenty-four years of marriage waited for him to sever the ties with the sweep of a pen.

He turned the envelope over, the swish of paper against calloused hands a harsh reminder of the erosion of time and what he once had. The freedom his signature would assure meant nothing to him. The two lives represented inside the envelope belonged together, but the odds of finding his way back after a year of regret seemed insurmountable.

He rolled the sleeves of his flannel shirt and thermal tee together to his elbows. Chandler's jaw muscles tightened and his stomach took a nasty twist as a hint of perfume drifted through the expansive den. The delicate scent preceded her feather-soft touch.

Della wrapped her arms around his neck. "Those papers aren't going to sign themselves," she cooed, dusting the curve of his chin with a lingering kiss. "It'll be easier for both of you once this is over."

Chandler rose, took her hand in his, and released it back to her before shoving the envelope back between the ledgers. "It's not the right time," he said, turning to face her. He took a step, but with a quick shift to her left, Della matched it.

"It's been a year." Della folded her arms across an abundant chest. "You deserve your freedom."

"You mean *you* deserve my freedom, don't you?"

Long lashes fluttered. "For us." Quick with a response—with her body if her tongue failed—Della was unrivaled when it came to manipulating the situation to her own desires.

He turned to leave. "I'll know when the time is right," Chandler said, intent on avoiding another confrontation on the subject either upright or horizontally, the latter her special recipe infused with guilty pleasure.

"Chandler, wait."

"I have work to do." He grabbed the door frame.

She stepped toward him. "Maybe now is the right time."

"The framing inspection came through on the Sommars' house. Electrical and plumbing subs need to be lined up."

"That can wait a few more minutes. Or until morning."

He rubbed his neck, and then dragged his hand slowly through the thick tangle of hair, coarse with sweat and wood dust. He faced her, a single lock of hair falling against his forehead. Leaning against the door frame, he shoved his hands into the pockets of his jeans. The solid muscles of his forearms bunched into a knot. "I told you I'd take care of it."

Della approached him, silver blue eyes chipping at his defenses. "I'm tired of waiting." Her words dripped with provocation, and without breaking eye contact, she reached her arms around his waist.

Chandler's jaw tensed. "Not now."

Ignoring his words, she pressed her breasts against his chest, urging him closer, hinting at what lay beneath the thin barrier of cloth.

He willed himself to fight the involuntary responses his traitorous body summoned from her mere touch.

"It's the right time," she said, her mouth turned in a wry smile. "In fact, it's perfect timing."

"Why?"

"Because we're going to be a family."

The feeling drained from his legs and her words hung in the air, a heavy cloud of idle, misconstrued chatter. Surely.

"I'm having a baby, Chandler," she whispered, fondling the buttons on his shirt. Eyes the color of a cool summer sky rose from beneath wisps of black lashes. "Our baby."

* * *

The anemic squelch of the doorbell interrupted their last swallow of fries. "Needs replacing." Ryleigh rolled her eyes. "Along with a few other things around here."

The women exchanged eye contact and walked together to the door. "You really need a peephole, Riles."

"Distorted faces leering at me through a tiny glass? That's creepy. No thanks."

Natalie shook her head.

"Who is it?"

"Ryleigh?" The voice was muffled, but all too familiar.

Dinner flipped inside Ryleigh's stomach. With a deep breath, she opened the door. "It's late, Chandler."

"Can I come in?" Chandler averted his eyes and shoved his hands deep into his pockets. "Della thinks I'm picking up my allergy meds." He shrugged. "Season's late this year."

Ryleigh acknowledged with a slight nod, having suffered through many an allergy season with him, but she'd never have let his prescription run out.

She straightened. "You could've called."

"She wouldn't understand." The lines deepened between his eyes. "I couldn't think of any other way to see you," he said, pausing, "to see if you need anything. After Eleanor's passing and all." The compassion in his demeanor caught her off guard. "I have some news and I wanted to tell you myself. I still care for you, Ryleigh. I hope you believe that."

Chandler wasn't one to outwardly show emotion for anything except the career-ending injury of an Arizona Cardinal or a disastrous Diamondbacks trade, so this rare display puzzled her. "Come in out of the rain." She relented, drawing the door fully open. "I assume you haven't forgotten the way to the living room?"

Chandler stepped into the entry. "Natalie," he acknowledged with a nod.

Natalie's lips pursed. "Chandler."

"I didn't know you'd be here."

"I didn't know you were coming over."

"Touché."

Natalie spun around, entered the living room, and plopped herself on the smaller of the two sofas.

Ryleigh took a seat next to Natalie. "What's so important it couldn't wait until morning?"

Chandler sat opposite the women. "Is there anything I can do to help with Eleanor?" He raked a hand through wet hair and then across his face, wiping at the moisture gleaming on his skin.

Ryleigh eyed him with sudden longing. Though on the backside of forty, his rugged features, sun-bleached hair, and steely good looks favored his years. He was exceedingly handsome—one legitimate excuse for Della's ploys, though a fifteen-year gap separated their ages. "Mom's been gone two days. Why now?"

Deep furrows creased his brow, adding years to the otherwise graceful face. "I thought you might need some help."

"You're too late." She shook her head adamantly. "Arrangements are made, her apartment is clean and Evan will be home tomorrow. So, no."

A weighted pause hung in the space between them. "Too late," he whispered, glancing around the room. "Thought I'd ask."

Chandler sat on the edge of the sofa, forearms stretched across his knees. He picked randomly at the back of his hands and examined his nails. In detail. He raised his eyes slowly, the summer color not yet faded from a face littered with uneasiness. "I don't know how to say this."

"Try English. My Elvish is a bit rusty."

Natalie glanced from one to the other.

"I wanted to tell you before this whole damn town starts wagging their tongues." Sad sincerity darkened his eyes to steel gray, a battleship amid a stormy sea, and then darted back to his hands as if something terribly interesting lurked there. "Della's pregnant." The words tumbled carelessly from his lips and splashed across her face.

Remnants of dinner burned in the back of her throat and every breath became a concentrated effort not to curl into a fetal ball. Instead, she rose on unsteady knees and walked to the window, arms wrapped tightly around her middle, shielding herself from the reality of shattered hope. Pregnant? How could he? He had a grown son. *Their* son. And dammit they were still married!

Chandler broke the awkward silence. "I didn't mean for this to happen."

She whirled around. "For what to happen? Sleeping with her?" She squeezed her hands into tight fists and choked back the urge to slap him. "Or knocking her up?"

"I didn't plan either."

"What do you think happens when you screw someone?" she said, her voice louder than she expected. "You're forty-eight. Not fifteen."

"We were careful." Chandler stared at the floor, picking first at his left hand and then the right. "I don't know how it happened."

"You stuck your hard prick where you shouldn't have. Doesn't take a rocket scientist to know when to bag it, Einstein."

"She said she was on the Pill."

"That gives you permission to shut off your brain?" Ryleigh raised her hands to stop him from saying anything, but it was meant to stop herself. Calm is strength and she wanted—*needed*—to remain resolute. "Forget it. It's your problem, not mine." She stared at him from across the room, wishing he'd stop that infernal picking—his hands, strong, steady, and the lifeblood of a carpenter—were rough enough.

"I'm sorry." He hesitated. "Ryleigh, I…" He rose and stuffed his hands in his pockets.

"I just lost my mom. I don't want anything from you," she said, ignoring the trite apology. "You know the way out." She turned her back to him.

The thump of his Dr. Martens echoed down the hall. How many pairs had she tossed and replaced for him over the years? The oily balm of new leather passed through her senses as if she held his shoes in her hands.

The distant click of the door cleared the memory and signaled the door had closed—not only to the entrance of the house they had called their home and raised their son in, but to the place in her heart only one man had ever entered. In that moment, her heart broke—the pain crushing and deep, reopening the unhealed wound.

A tear trickled past her nose. She swiped at it, sickened at the prospect of its reminder. It wasn't a tear for the staggering news her husband had delivered, or for the resentment she felt toward the woman who had stolen her life. Nor was it for the bitterness she harbored toward the man who left her for a younger woman and left a gaping hole in her world. A silent tear spilled for what she had known for quite some time.

Her marriage—like her mother—was dead.

Light autumn raindrops merged into little streams cascading down the glass, distorting the reflections in the picture window. Emptiness rooted her to the spot. Moving would surely tear apart the remaining threads of a thin membrane that held her world together. Her mother, whose long fingers stroked her baby-fine hair, whose voice lulled her into slumber when she cried for an absent father, and whose love was warmth enough for them both, was gone. And Chandler embraced another. His dreams, his future, and his love were hers no longer. And his seed—the evidence of their love— ceased to flow inside her. She would no longer feel the connection, the oneness Chandler had provided for nearly twenty-four years.

CHANDLER PULLED THE door shut, and with a doleful click the latch engaged, the sound the signal she was safe from the outside world, something he'd done without a conscious thought hundreds of times. He shouldn't leave her like this, vulnerable and upset. Her body language was unmistakable; the unwavering staunchness, the resolve—the barrier she built whenever threatened. Rain spit in his face and pelted his clothes, yet his throat had dried to a sticky silence. He hadn't counted on invisible fingers reaching in and twisting his gut. It was inconceivable how badly he had hurt her. Again. He sloshed through a puddle where the concrete sank. Why hadn't he fixed it? Standing alone in the rain, he wished he had.

Drenched and hair dripping, he shoved his hands in his pockets and turned back toward the house. He stopped midway. Powerless to see a way back through, he stood in the rain staring at the door. "Dammit, Ryleigh." He tipped his face to the sky and let the cold rain pour over him, her name dissolving into the force of the storm. "What have I done?" He couldn't bring himself to finish walking the few steps to tell her what he needed to. Instead, he made his way through the rain to his truck, heaved the door open, and stepped in. He'd done this to them. He'd severed the ties that bound them as one, and the reality forced him to bear its heavy weight.

They were broken. And though he was one of the best contractors in town, this was one thing Chandler Collins didn't know how to fix.

NATALIE JO BURSTYN felt like throwing up. She'd risen discreetly and left the room. With one of the most forgiving hearts she'd ever known, she knew Ryleigh would have taken Chandler back in a heartbeat. Maybe now she could finally accept the fact he wasn't coming back. Maybe now she could leave her wedding ring at home.

"Hey," Ryleigh said as she entered the kitchen.

"I'm so sorry, Riles."

"You promised things would get better."

Natalie looked away. "I still believe that. God won't give you any more than you can handle." She couldn't keep her words from growing heavy in the weight of sadness. Her friend hurt. And so did she.

"Mom said that when Chandler left. I'm not so sure I believe it right now."

"You'll believe again. Someday." Natalie gave her a quick kiss on the cheek. "I love you, Ryleigh, and you *will* get through this. I'll make sure of it. Mitch and I will always be there for you."

"You're a lucky girl, Nat."

"Mitch knows better," Natalie scoffed. "I'd break his friggin' legs if he ever cheated on me."

A frown curdled what had almost been a smile.

"Do you have any of the Syrah wine left? The one made here in Arizona?"

Ryleigh examined her.

"The bottle your boss gave you for Christmas."

"Coming from Bernadette, I figured it wasn't worth drinking. Why?"

"It's actually an exceptional quality."

Ryleigh reached into a nearby cupboard. "She couldn't have known what she was buying."

Nat twisted the opener and popped the cork with the skill of a seasoned pro. A fragrant fog rose from the bottle and she promptly filled their glasses with the smooth, aromatic liquid.

"To the future," Natalie said, raising her glass.

"If there's one worth toasting."

"There will be." Natalie grazed a finger around the rim of the glass. "Don't you have something to show me?"

"Mmm, the old Kodak." Ryleigh raised her eyebrows. "It's definitely my father," she said, a trace of excitement elevating her tone.

They entered the den and Ryleigh picked up the computer print she'd made of the photograph and handed it to her.

"It's a little blurry," Ryleigh added with a vague smile. "I enlarged it on the computer."

Shock widened Natalie's eyes. "All by yourself?"

"Bite me." She pointed to the picture. Although somewhat blurred, *I-C-O-T-T* was clearly visible on the uniform near the pocket.

"Your dad was a nice looking man, but this other guy is seriously handsome. Gorgeous eyes."

"His name is hidden, but military buddies sometimes kept in touch. If I only had a name."

Natalie's insides leapt at her friend's sudden enthusiasm.

"He probably doesn't remember or care. Otherwise why didn't Mom ever mention him?"

Natalie set the snapshot on the improvised desk. "Okay, Sherlock. Grab a bug detector, a magnifying glass, and cell phone spyware and start investigating."

"What?"

"I read John Grisham. Once in a while."

"Nat, I don't know—"

"Your eyes speak louder than words, Ryleigh Collins. Your curiosity just shifted into overdrive."

Chapter Five

EVAN'S WHITE CIVIC was parked in the drive and the house brightly lit, a sure sign her son—one with little sense of utility costs—had arrived. Ryleigh closed the garage door and Kingsley pranced around the corner, greeting her with a hearty meow, followed by footsteps.

Kingsley darted as Evan approached."That cat hates me, I swear," he said as he wrapped her completely in a hug. College life had added a few pounds to his lean frame, and at an inch over six feet, he'd matured into his father's features, the line of his jaw as strong as his will. But his blue-green eyes were hers. They too smiled when he spoke. A lump welled in her throat. When had it happened? When had he crossed the delicate line between boy and man? "Damn cat disappears every time I walk into a room. Should have named him Houdini."

She smiled at Evan's cheeky comment. "I'm glad you're home. And Kingsley doesn't hate you."

"Kingsley hates everyone except you, Mom." An artful smirk curled his mouth. "His face is squashed, he's fat, ferociously finicky and arrogant. And he sheds."

"Animals can sense how you feel about them."

"Now that we've established your cat officially hates me, how are you holding up?"

"I'm okay."

Evan turned his head a fraction in silent question.

"Really." The words stumbled from her mouth. She swallowed and took a seat at the dining table. Evan followed. "Gram's apartment is clean, your friends will be here Sunday to drop off the desk, and once the funeral is over tomorrow, maybe things will return to normal."

"What about Dad?"

Discomfort inched its way over her skin at the memory of the previous night's encounter, and she rubbed her arms. "He stopped by last night."

Evan considered this with a dramatic raise of his eyebrows.

"Don't even go there." The glimmer of hope in his eyes extinguished itself. "And there's something else." She shifted her weight. "He and Della have been together for awhile now and things are bound to happen."

Evan stiffened. "Don't expect me to congratulate him if he's dumb enough to marry that nympho."

God, how she wished it were that simple. "They aren't getting married. We have to be divorced first."

"That's a positive on top of a negative. So, if not that then what is it?"

Her internal voice screamed it loud and clear, but the voice she relied on to form the words vanished. She smiled a little, only to have it shrivel before it had a chance to mature. It hadn't been easy for her to hear, and there was no easy way around telling him. The words burned past her hesitation. "Della and your father are going to have a baby."

Evan shot to his feet. The chair flew backward. "This is bullshit." He plastered his hands to his hips. "What a fucking idiot!"

She bristled. "Evan!"

"Sorry."

"He's still your father."

"Doesn't make him any less the idiot." His nostrils flared. "He's almost fifty years old. Doesn't he know what causes that?"

"That's the only thing that makes this almost comical. He should be thinking about grandchildren—don't get any ideas," she said, pointing a critical finger at him, "not having one of his own."

Mischief peeked through the anger that moments ago smoldered in his eyes. "No worries, Mom. I've got too much on my plate and I *do* know how not to make a kid." He paced a few times, shrugged, and grabbed the back of the chair. "Looks like I'm going to have a half-brother or sister."

Even in anger her son seemed to find a positive, and she relaxed.

"I'll talk to Dad after the funeral. Has he mentioned anything about divorce?"

"Nope. He came by to personally deliver the headlines. God, I can't imagine her being a mother."

"Hell in heels with a diamond-studded shovel."

Ryleigh pressed her fist to her mouth but failed to stifle a snicker.

The haggard croak of the doorbell interrupted their discussion, and Ryleigh met the waiting courier at the front door. He handed her a large envelope with her name and address typed neatly across the front. Her heart stuttered.

Though she'd been expecting it for weeks, she hesitated, turning it over and then over again, the unbound paper, ink, and words a heavy weight in her hands. Conflicting thoughts wrestled with her better judgment. A few swipes with a pen and it would be over. Or there was the option of using it for kindling. Or toilet paper. Accidents happen.

She opened the envelope to documents dated weeks ago.

Evan sat next to her with his palm glued to his forehead while she signed her name where indicated—the shaky squiggles dissolving their marriage. She prepared the return envelope in the artificial light of her kitchen and in the presence of the somber stare of her only child—her tiny family of two.

With a funeral looming, a divorce imminent, her soon-to-be ex's girlfriend pregnant, and questions without answers surfacing from a small shoebox, Ryleigh counted along with the ticking second hand like the condemned walking the Green Mile.

Chapter Six

R‌YLEIGH COULDN'T DECIDE which was worse—burying her mother or burying her marriage—as if it mattered which one took top prize. By the end of the day she would finalize one life and begin another.

Both terrified her.

Morning broke with a menacing layer of dark clouds suspended over Hidden Falls, a Thursday bleak enough to match the slow churn of dissidence inching itself through her belly. The drive through the mountains seemed to take forever.

An hour and a half later, Evan took hold of her arm as they filed past the gates of Pinewood Cemetery toward the plot where Eleanor Endicott would rest.

Cemeteries fascinated her. Covert clues engraved on the headstones offered glimpses into the mysteries of those buried beneath the stone. Where most people found sadness and apprehension crossing from one grave to the next, Ryleigh's curiosity heightened.

Today promised something different.

A light breeze rustled through the trees, and bronzed in red, orange, and gold, leaves fluttered from above and stirred underfoot. An odd uneasiness plucked at her as she crossed the cemetery, but Ryleigh's eyes remained glued to the casket perched next to a mound of soggy dirt. Simple in style, the casket seemed overly large for a body diminished by a silent, arbitrary thief.

Not far from here, Ryleigh had brushed through her mother's hair as white as the roses she so loved and held her misshapen hands for the last time. It seemed peculiar how quickly the memory had become engraved on her mind like the names carved in granite.

Evan guided her as they approached the gravesite, his grip unwavering. Natalie and Mitch stood arm in arm under the scarlet umbrella of two immense white oaks and the couples nodded to each other, their somber message understood.

Artificial grass covered the soggy earth and leaves speckled the white casket with the burnished shades of October. A small wreath rested against it and ivy formed the word "Mom" across a circle of wildflowers and two perfect white roses. Fireflies danced among the flowers. It seemed an odd choice to her, but her mother had been specific in her wishes. The roses and "Mom" part she was sure of, but more in the forefront of a growing list of questions was why there seemed to be so many pieces missing from a simple woman's life. Fireflies? Why? Why didn't she know?

The pastor excused himself from a small knot of people and took his place across from Ryleigh and Evan. He scanned the gathering and then nodded modestly to her. He blew a breath across his fingers and opened his Bible, tucking the frayed ribbon into the binding. A familiar melody murmured with the voice of the breeze as a small choir of ladies quietly sang "Amazing Grace," and Pastor Edwards spoke fondly of one of God's children—a wife, mother, and grandmother.

* * *

The service was short and thoughtful, yet uplifting, exactly as Eleanor would have wanted. The small crowd filed past and conveyed their condolences before moving on to pay their respects to loved ones. Ryleigh didn't envy them. On any normal day, imagining the lives of the deceased was fascinating, but she didn't take much pleasure in visiting her family here. One had been too many. Now there would be two.

"Excuse me, Ryleigh?"

The pleasant voice pulled her from her thoughts. Ryleigh turned. "Pastor Edwards." She smiled and extended her hand, and he accepted it warmly with both of his. With round cheeks flushed from the October chill and ears that took up more space than they should have, he wasn't a particularly handsome man, but his expression was compassionate and kind, his handshake warm and comforting. Prerequisites that surely came with the territory. "The service was lovely and I appreciate the kind words about Mom."

"Your mother was quite explicit in her wishes." The pastor reached inside his jacket. "And she left this for you," he said as he handed her a worn, yellowed envelope.

Ryleigh frowned. "What's this?"

"It's an insurance policy your mother asked me to keep until after the funeral."

"Life insurance?" She glanced at Evan, and then back to the pastor. "I'm afraid I'm finding there's a lot I don't know about my mother."

A subtle smile crinkled the corners of his eyes. "Some folks aren't comfortable sharing their lives," he said, still holding the envelope, "and some want only to protect those they love." The pastor pressed his Bible to his chest. "And she valued her privacy."

Ryleigh nodded. "Thank you, Pastor. You've been most helpful."

Pastor Edwards smiled and tipped his head in thankful acknowledgement. "Eleanor was special to God and to us." He patted her hands politely and offered a firm handshake with Evan. "She was a strong woman and I sense her strength in her daughter as well. Yours will surface, Ryleigh, once healing has surpassed your grief." Pastor Edwards took her hands, his engulfing hers in a warm cocoon. "If there's anything I can do, you have my number." He gave her hands a squeeze and then turned. The questions he'd raised disappeared with him into the crowd of mourners.

"You ready to go, Mom?"

She glanced around as the last of Eleanor's friends filed through the entry gate. "Can you give me a minute, Son? Alone?"

He squeezed her arm. "I'll wait with Nat and Mitch."

The unpeopled silence filled the cemetery. Grief's darkness pulled at her, yet life penetrated its thickening fog. Birds chattered. Tires splashed on wet asphalt. Wind murmured its song. A child laughed in the distance. Time passed in lethargic motion, stalled in the air heavy with the musty dampness of rotting leaves, and weighted in sorrow. To remain in the shadows of grief seemed effortless. To move forward, an unwelcomed burden. Yet life drifted by—air, light, and sound.

Only she stood lifeless.

Ryleigh blinked and the mental fog lifted. She removed a plastic bag from her purse and brought the roses to her nose, the scent a promise of sunshine and warmer days. Placing one white rose on top of the casket, she kissed her fingers and pressed them to the wood. "Sweet dreams, Mom." With the second rose in hand, she turned to her left and paused.

Two white roses lay at the base of the headstone. She spun in a slow circle, searching. Who else knew of her mother's affection for white roses? She turned back, knelt, and placed the last rose next to the others at the foot of Benjamin Endicott's headstone. She kissed her fingers and pressed them to the engraved name. Cold rippled through her, choking her words. "You're together again, Daddy."

Light snow settled on her shoulders. Ryleigh rose and removed her gloves, tucking them neatly under her arm. With her palm facing the ground, she held her bare left hand in front of her and twisted the gold band, the metal a warm comfort—a reminder of the close family circle it once stood for. She removed it from her finger and clenched the ring tightly against her heart. The urge to run trembled in her legs. To reconsider. To forget. Then with a mix of grief and purpose, she straightened her shoulders and tossed the ring into the black hole of her mother's grave. Never before had it left her finger.

THE GNARLED TRUNK of an aged oak forked at the base, their girth twice that of a grown man. Chandler stood behind the tree, his head between the forks and eyes focused on his wife standing near the casket.

He adjusted his view to watch, longing to take her in his arms and hold her, protect her, and shield her from the pain. But he couldn't force his feet to move and simply watched from the shadows of his blind.

She raised her ungloved left hand, tugged on her ring finger and hesitated—just for a moment—and tossed something into the grave. No light glinted from it, but he knew exactly what it was and what she'd done.

Gripped in the unbearable straightjacket of self-torment, his six-foot-two-inch frame slumped against the tree as if its strength could take the weight of regret from him.

Chandler shoved his hands deep in the pockets of his jeans, the collar of the lined denim jacket pulled up against the icy fingers of remorse. His eyes remained dry, yet his heart wept as he grieved the loss of someone he should never have let go.

Chapter Seven

RYLEIGH SHIVERED, BLEW into her hands, and then pressed them against the vents in the cab of the Tahoe.

"So," Evan said, turning onto the highway, "what's the plan for the weekend? I don't intend to spend the next three days studying."

Evan's exuberance lifted the tension. She leaned into the seat and studied the concentration seeping into his features as he settled into the drive. "Do you know how to locate someone? You know, someone you don't know anything about. Or who they are or where they live?"

"Thinking of joining a dating service?"

"God, no." Warmth flushed her cheeks.

He glanced at her with a sly smile. "You sure?"

"Positive. But I do need to find someone."

"Who?"

She lingered on the thought. "Nat and I were going through your grandmother's desk and we found a letter signed by someone named Ambrose."

"Got your curiosity up, did it?"

"You'll help?"

"What do you expect to find?"

"Nothing, probably. But your grandmother never mentioned this person, so how does he know us?" She waved her hand to dismiss the silly thought. "I can't figure this out," she said and turned to look out the window.

"I'm not into investigative reporting, but I am taking a media research class and this sounds intriguing."

She studied her son with renewed interest. "I'll show you the letter when we get home. And there's something else I want you to see."

"Look out, Jessica Fletcher."

"Not hardly. But I have so many questions."

Evan kept his eyes glued to the winding mountain highway, but concentration pinched the muscles of his jaw. The telltale sign confessed his absorption in deep thought, a mirror of his father's. "Now I'm curious."

"It would've been so much easier to just ask your grandmother."

Evan agreed in a methodically slow nod.

Ponderosas passed in a blur. Sleet splattered against the windshield as they navigated the curves through Arizona's Mogollon Rim. The more miles that separated her from the cemetery, the closer she was to a life alone. To answers she didn't truly want to know. Though warm inside the Tahoe, she shivered. Ryleigh's right hand swept to her left and she twisted a ring no longer there. The automatic gesture twisted nothing but the ghostly shadow of what once had been.

* * *

By dusk, the temperature had dropped dramatically. The wind skipped through town in fitful gusts depositing whirls of leaves in heaps. Intermittent waves of nickel-sized snowflakes feathered the sky and the shades of evening fell over Hidden Falls. Kingsley was curled contentedly at the end of the sofa engrossed in a cat bath.

Ryleigh retrieved the envelope Pastor Edwards had given her and sat next to Evan. Annoyed at the jostling, Kingsley peered at Evan, jumped off the sofa and strutted off.

"I didn't do it, you poor excuse for a cat. Go do something constructive like puke up a fur ball."

Ryleigh glared at him.

"Okay, okay." Evan raised his hands in resignation. "I'll try to be nice to the mangy critter."

Ryleigh removed the policy and skimmed the information, Evan reading over her shoulder. Ryleigh's hand flew to her forehead.

"I guess Gram wanted to take care of you."

"Mom didn't have any money for things like this. She barely made ends meet."

Frowning, she returned the papers to the envelope and removed a sheet of stationery. She ran her finger curiously over the embossed fireflies.

"What's wrong?"

"Nothing, it's just fireflies…" She rose. "Come with me."

Evan followed her to the study. Ryleigh retrieved the journal from the desk and motioned for Evan to pull up a chair beside her. Without thinking, she pressed her palm to the stained cover. Her stomach fluttered.

"Looks old."

She handed him the journal and watched his eyes move rhythmically through the verses and duly noted his expression, a reflection of hers.

When he'd finished reading, he looked at her with a deer-in-the-headlights stare. "Who wrote these? Fireflies are significant, there's no doubt," he pondered. "But why?"

"Don't know the answer to the 'why' *or* the 'who.'"

"Want to give another one a shot?" Evan's eyes shone with anticipation. She understood the feeling. "Aloud?"

She nodded. "You read. I'll listen."

Evan turned a few pages and stopped. "This one's called 'Beside You.'"

" 'When raindrops dance upon your windowpane
or turn to a blanket of new-fallen snow—
and transform the earth to tranquil hill and vale
I'm there beside you, as the stillness quietly grows.

When a seedling emerges with the first breath of spring
or trees once barren burst forth in budding grace—
and the breeze wafts warmly against your skin
I'm there beside you, in subtle embrace.

When you hear the symphony of summer birds
or listen closely to the flutter of butterfly wings—
and hear the harmony of a wind chime's notes
I'm there beside you, as the soft breeze sings.

When the wind whispers and gently graces your cheek
or whips golden autumn leaves upon the ground—
and chases chasms of sunlight into the dusk
I'm there beside you, just take a look around.

When you feel the last kiss of sunlight on your face
or as twilight beckons to steal the day—
and fireflies dance to their reticent song
I'm there beside you, a heartbeat away.' "
~R~ '66

Evan set the journal in his lap. "Fireflies again."

Ryleigh nodded and tucked a wisp of hair behind her ear.

"And it's about separation. But Mister R comforts the recipient by telling her she can feel him with her in everything around her."

"How do you know it's a man?"

"I don't. Just sounds like a guy." Evan shrugged. "And you have some investigating to do."

Ryleigh raised her eyebrows. "That's the second time I've heard that."

The corners of Evan's mouth curled into a suspect smile. "This will drive you nuts until you figure it out."

* * *

Murky afternoon skies slipped into the quiet shadows of night. Ryleigh curled into the round chair in her den, an unexplained edginess pushing its way through the part of her that begged to settle into some sort of calm, but clashed in a duel of wills. Pouring over loose papers instead, she couldn't help but think how ironic it was an entire person's life boiled down to two cardboard boxes stuffed with what amounted to little more than junk.

Kingsley curled next to her with a flick of the tail. "Hey, big guy," she said stroking the sweet spot under his chin. His purr-motor reacted loudly, paws kneading her thighs.

"I didn't see Dad at the funeral today, so I thought I'd go see him." Ryleigh turned to see Evan standing in the doorway. "Don't wait up. You look tired."

Ryleigh acknowledged with a slight nod. "Please be careful."

The door closed after him with a benign shudder. Ryleigh took a deep breath and giving into the relentless debate, tossed the papers aside and turned to the journal. An odd familiarity swept over her as she rested her palm against the dark stain. Sinking deep into the chair's embrace, she turned to the first page. "Enchanted" spoke of wizards and fairy tales, shooting stars and fairy-dust kisses—a lover's magical language. But it was "The Shadow" that caused the hair on her arms to stand on end.

> *it clings to my heels*
> *follows me close*
> *it clings to the earth*
> *i think it knows*

it's there in the light
cloud or rainbow
it's there in thunder
i think it knows

it trespasses thoughts
larger it grows
it devours dreams
i think it knows

it pollutes the mind
plague of souls
it taints my tears
i think it knows

under mask of fear
the shadow grows
under destiny's guise
i'm sure it knows

it is the shadow
ever present still
it is the shadow
it is God's will
~R~ '67

She felt an inexplicable connection, of déjà vu, as she read the words. But there were no notes—nothing to hint at the writer—except the sole "R" and the year closing each composition.

Ryleigh let the journal fall to her lap. The pages hesitated, and then stood at attention—a silent plea to re-enter their world. She hesitated, yearning for more, yet sidestepping the urge to toss it back from where it came.

Instead, she turned to the last entry. Though she'd read this one before, the words begged her back inside them.

Encased in the fragile world of grief, every word seemed to settle in her heart as an ache, a growing abscess threatening to explode in a rush of anguish.

Reading the disturbing verses unleashed the anger, pain, and guilt she'd kept locked away. The barrier she'd built around herself as an impasse to a year of pain had shattered and it gushed from her, a flood of emotion for the decimation of years built on trust. Tears stung her eyes, and deep, aching sobs shook her shoulders.

Minutes ticked by. Her tears ran dry. In her forty-three years there had been tears, of course, but there had been happiness, and fun, and love. But late into this October night, she couldn't see past the pain that had overtaken her tiny slice of the world. He'd been unfaithful once. How many other faceless ghosts would emerge? He'd never reeked of anything but sawdust and sweat, but looking back, she swore she felt the ghostly whispers of unnamed women stroke the inside of her mind. But what did it matter? One time or twenty, he'd still broken their vows. She would forgive, eventually; but contrary to popular belief, it was impossible to forget.

* * *

Evan turned the corner into the swanky neighborhood. The Civic's headlights pierced the dark façade and portico, casting shadows in the stone crevices. As impressive as it was, he never felt comfortable here. In fact, it gave him the creeps and embarrassed him to think his dad couldn't see through the motives of someone as superficial as Della Mayfair. She was hot, but come on, even someone his age could see through the false layers. Like a rotten onion. The deeper the layers, the deeper the spoiled flesh.

God, he hoped he never proved to be that shallow.

Light spilled from the open garage, the familiar white Ram parked in the furthest stall. Della's Mercedes wasn't there. He couldn't have timed his arrival any better, and allowed himself to breathe as he killed the engine and stepped from his car.

Chandler stepped from the house carrying an armload of books and ledgers and when he looked up, he stopped, balancing the pile on his knee.

Evan waved. "Hey, Dad."

The sincerity of Chandler's smile met the corners of his eyes as he raised a hand before he tossed the books through the Ram's window with his other. At the sight, a sense of dread swallowed Evan's elation. They slapped each other on the back and his father pulled him into a vigorous embrace.

Evan pushed himself away, hands on his hips. "What's with the business ledgers?" Recognizing the scene from a year ago, he searched his father's face for the answer he already knew.

Chandler adjusted his ball cap, the Diamondbacks logo obscured by the upward tilt of the bill. He cleared his throat. "I rented an apartment on Frontier."

"You're leaving her?" Resignation rendered the part of Evan's brain that controlled movement useless. "She's pregnant."

"I see your mother told you about that."

"First you dump Mom." He shook his head. "Then you knock this woman up and now you're turning your back on her?"

"I take full responsibility for the baby."

"*Your* son or daughter," Evan said, clenching his jaw, "and my half-brother or sister. This makes twice you've walked out on your family."

Anger narrowed his eyes. "Don't make insinuations you know nothing about." Chandler released a long breath and Evan took a step back. "At least let me explain."

"This is bullshit." Evan stuffed his hands in the pockets of his jeans and took several more steps backward. "It was a mistake coming here," he said, eyes fixed on his father.

Chandler stepped toward his son. "Evan, wait."

Evan matched his step with another backward. "Why should I?" He turned his back to his father.

"I'm still in love with your mother," he said, his voice a faltered version of the usual deep, steady tone.

Evan froze and then turned abruptly. "You have an epiphany between yesterday and today?" He teetered between the urge to cry like a little boy with a skinned knee and standing up to his father like the man he was and punching him.

"You don't understand."

"What's not to understand about divorce?"

"I had to file."

"Or what, Dad? What catastrophe would have happened if you didn't? Except maybe putting our family back together?"

Chandler raked a hand through his hair. "You don't know Della."

"I've got a pretty good idea, but go ahead," Evan said, raising his hands in frustration, "explain her to me."

"I don't need to explain her or myself to you. I'll take care of this baby. That's all you need to know."

"How fucking sweet." Sarcasm dripped from his words.

"And I've taken care of your mother. She'll understand when she reads the decree." Chandler paused, searching the ground with his eyes. "I was a fool."

"You're just now figuring that out?" Evan yanked the car door open. "And by the way, Dad, you still are."

The engine whined to life and he shoved the gearshift into reverse. Chandler motioned and then hollered after him to stop. Evan ignored the gesture and gunned it. Glancing in his rearview mirror, his father's outline grew smaller as the distance grew wider. Hands in his pockets and head down, the silhouette of the man he had always looked up to seemed lost and somehow broken. Evan navigated the last curve in the subdivision with a twinge of regret.

Chapter Eight

RYLEIGH SLID INTO the Tahoe, her teeth chattering as she turned the key. While she waited for the car to warm, she tapped a message to Evan on her phone. Fairly adept at the simple technology of texting (a desperate lesson in keeping up with the times) she'd refused to master the art of butchering the English language and wrote the message in full. "Going to Nat's. Don't wait up."

She had barely left the driveway when Evan answered. *'take divorce papers to uncle mitch.'*

She tapped her finger three times against the phone. The suggestion seemed a good one, and although Mitch wasn't an attorney, he wore money and business like a second skin. She replied and then backed up to retrieve the envelope from inside.

A crescent moon severed its way through the lingering clouds as Ryleigh started down the street on the other side of town to Nat's house. The house backed the Tonto National Forest and overlooked a trickle of water they loosely called a creek.

The house wasn't expansive, but it had a den. A *real* den, not a converted bedroom decorated with misfits. With a bay window overlooking the almost creek and shelves and shelves of books, Nat's den had everything Ryleigh dreamed of. The trickle of water gurgled over river rock in the summer and cool breezes sweetened with evergreen and jasmine blew through the open windows. Chandler had promised to build her one of her own someday—isn't that what contractors were supposed to do? She stacked this promise on top of all the other broken ones.

Natalie met her at the front door with an embrace meant for a mother shielding her child.

"You look awful."

"Thanks."

"Get your butt in here. I'll make us a latte."

Ryleigh followed her to the kitchen and threw a leg over a barstool. "I brought the divorce papers." She plopped the envelope on the counter. "Think Mitch would take a look at them for me?"

"Of course he will."

"I didn't read them," Ryleigh said and tucked her misbehaving hair behind an ear.

Natalie glared at her over the top of the espresso machine. "What?"

"I'm not contesting anything."

"You should know what's in there."

She shrugged. "I just want this over and the quicker the better."

Natalie handed her a goblet, the espresso rich and dark with a thick layer of frothy milk, a sigh of caramel rising with the steam. "C'mon." She waved and grabbed the envelope. "Let's sit in the den. Mitch turned the lights on by the creek."

The double doors invited them inside; nubuck the shade of a newborn fawn covered the window seat and overstuffed pillows lined the perimeter. Natalie set the envelope on Mitch's desk, stepped to the window seat and removed two throws. Ryleigh curled up next to her and drew her knees and the blanket to her chest, the sweet spice of cedar lingering in the fleece.

A smile softened Natalie's face. "It's been a long time since we sat together like this."

Ryleigh nodded, the echoes of forgotten memories surging to the forefront of her mind.

"You'd recite poems I didn't understand. We'd plan the future. Not a care in the world."

Ryleigh sank into the childlike whimsy—magical carefree times wrapped in the frayed ribbons of time. But little girls grow up and dandelion wishes and fairy tales rarely turn out the way of dreams.

"I'm glad you're here, Riles. I've been worried, wondering when you were going to finally break."

Ryleigh's brow creased into a daring accusation.

"Get over it." Natalie raised her index finger. "You have to let go of Chandler before you can begin to heal."

"Don't bring him into this." Ryleigh sipped her latte.

"He left you. And though it was a different kind of separation, so did your mother."

She took a deep breath. "I thought I buried the hurt. And doubt," she said, lowering her eyes. Then she took another breath, raised her eyes and straightened her shoulders. "The self-pity pool is empty." As she spoke, the heartache eased as if the air had filtered the pain. "Time to crawl out from under this nightmare."

Mitch tiptoed across the hardwood floor in his stocking feet.

"We're here for you, Riles," Nat said and caught Mitch's eye as he left the room with the envelope. He winked, an unspoken reply to her comment.

Ryleigh leaned into the cushions. "I know I can count on you."

"Hey, we've been inseparable since we were five years old. You're pretty much stuck with me."

* * *

The grandfather clock chimed once, marking the half hour. Huddled like schoolgirls at a slumber party, the women talked until Mitch poked his head into the room.

He cleared his throat. "Excuse me, ladies." He held the envelope in front of him. "Ryleigh, we need to talk."

Ryleigh straightened, a flush of warm dread pushing aside the thin veil of serenity.

"What's wrong?"

"Nothing." Mitch scratched his temple. "In fact, it's a little puzzling."

Ryleigh pushed the blanket aside and dangled her legs over the seat. "What do you mean?"

"Chandler's attorney drew these up and since you've already signed them, it means you own everything. Including the business."

"That doesn't make any sense. I don't know anything about building houses. What was he thinking?"

"In my opinion, it's his way of creating a shelter from Della. I don't know what's going on behind closed doors, but I think he may have finally figured out what makes her tick."

"Took him long enough," she said, frowning. "But we—he—doesn't have any money. It's all tied up in investments, right? And the business is stable, but it's never been overly profitable."

"He's good at what he does and the business has been more profitable than you think. And you're right, a lot of money is tied up in investments. They're worth a hefty chunk of change in spite of the economy and they'll continue to grow. We aren't going to let anything happen to the spa and that's what Chandler invested in." He held up the documents. "Everything is yours, including every penny of the investments."

"You're serious?" Confusion flooded her mind.

Mitch shrugged.

"We had enough to live on so I never asked. As long as he was happy, so was I."

"Chandler must still care about you or he wouldn't have done this."

"Don't go there. He was thinking of Evan's future, that's all."

"Evan is written in as a contingent beneficiary."

"Which means?"

Natalie's head toggled between the two to keep up with the conversation.

"If something happens to you, everything will go to Evan. Chandler had his act together when he came up with this."

"He had it together all right. Knew exactly when to unzip his pants and parade his junk when the circus came to town," she said, her tone as sharp as the point of a lead pencil. She pressed a palm to her forehead. "I still don't understand why he did this."

Natalie caught Mitch's eye and nodded. "I can't say I don't harbor resentment toward Chandler," she said, "but I think I understand his motives even if you can't see what's happening here."

"See what?"

"Della foolishly underestimated him, Riles."

"Takes one to know one."

"He'll have to start over. He must still love you to give up everything."

"This is ridiculous," she said, shaking her head.

Mitch raised a finger. "There's one more thing."

Ryleigh pressed a hand to her forehead. "Do I want to know?"

"Evan called earlier. Chandler's leaving Della."

The blood that had risen to angry cheeks drained in a cool rush. "Mitch, she's pregnant. What the hell is wrong with him?"

"He still loves you."

"Bullcrap." Ryleigh frowned. "He just doesn't want to face up to his responsibilities."

Mitch held up the envelope. "He faced up to this."

"That's different."

"I can't speak for him, but I think I know what he wants."

"He doesn't know *what* he wants."

"His motives are abundantly clear," Natalie interrupted.

"Forget it." Ryleigh glanced from one face to the other. "No," she said, shaking her head. "It's too late."

* * *

The asphalt glistened in the wake of the streetlights as she turned onto her street. One storm had passed with a few raindrops and a dusting of snow, but another bubbled hot and liquid. Pain (or was it resentment?) settled in her mind safely locked away—a place she'd vowed not to disturb, afraid to arouse its slumber.

Mitch's news disturbed her, more than she cared to admit. She'd been on the side of rejection and took no pleasure knowing what Della was going through. Though she couldn't bring to mind one good reason Della should be a mother, the woman was bringing a child into this twisted picture. Chandler's child. Her heart ached for the unborn baby. She once loved Chandler with everything in her and knew firsthand what that love meant in creating and raising a child. Her insides whirled. Did Della love him? Could anyone love Chandler the way she had? Did she still?

Stars littered a clear sky, a sheet of black velvet scattered with tiny diamonds. Turning into the drive at the end of Pinecrest Circle at a little past two in the morning, she guessed it was a moot point.

Chapter Nine

RETURNING TO her weekly column and writing a major feature story about the return of a local Marine for the *Hidden Falls Sentinel* flickered through her fog of semi-consciousness. With everything else in her life upside down, at least she still had a job. Though the post-recession population had steadied, newspaper circulation hadn't, and many of her coworkers had been forced to find other employment.

Sunday morning dawned over the mountains and spilled through the closed blinds, growing brighter on the inside of eyelids still heavy with sleep. Ryleigh stretched and stirred fully awake, tossed the comforter away from her and crawled out of bed. A low growl and look of complete indignation crossed Kingsley's face as he emerged, the heavy comforter flattening his ears. He sauntered to the edge of the bed and shook himself, tossed her a smug look, flicked his tail and jumped.

"Sorry," she said, wrapping herself in a white terry robe. She shook her head at the captious ways of the haughty cat.

Ryleigh finished rolling tortillas with egg, sausage, veggies, and was topping them with shredded cheese and salsa when Evan wandered into the kitchen in rumpled shorts and T-shirt, hair askew and not fully awake. He poured a mug of coffee, yawned, and vigorously ruffled his hair in a useless effort to tame the errant bedhead.

"Breakfast burros," he mumbled through a sleepy yawn.

She smiled, followed him to the table, and sat with a fresh mug of her own. Entirely of his own accord, Evan chose his father's place at the table. Fingers laced and mug halfway to her mouth, she paused at the sight. It was pleasant—Evan sitting in his father's place—yet mixed with a heavy dose of longing. Baby powder. Stale milk. His pudgy hand, fingers dimpled in their youth. But at some point, whiskers had sprouted on his baby cheeks. And Chandler hadn't come home. Steam rose in lazy swirls from her mug and in the still of the moment, she wondered if her life would ever feel normal again.

Evan took a deep gulp of coffee. "You going back to work tomorrow?"

"I should," Ryleigh said, "but I'm not anxious to hear my new boss bitch at me for leaving the paper without a column. Bernadette is about as much fun to be around as Meryl Streep in *The Devil Wears Prada.*

Evan chuckled. "She that bad?"

"She's younger, but I can only wonder how much more cantankerous she'll become with a little more practice. A confrontation is inevitable."

"Confrontation?" he asked, shoving a mouthful of burro into his mouth.

"I need more time off," she said, pushing a loose strand of hair behind her ear. The decision hadn't come easy. She'd wrestled with an ever-multiplying list of contradictory reasons, but every time a perfectly legitimate reason against pursuing answers ended her plans, two perfectly good ones popped up to complicate things. Her decision had been confirmed after a storm had cleared up more than the skies.

"Why?" The word stumbled over pulverized food.

"Don't talk with your mouth full."

Evan swallowed. "Why more time off?" He wiped his mouth with his sleeve and a mischievous smile flickered across his face.

A loud knock interrupted their conversation. Evan jumped up, downed the last of his coffee, and sprinted to the front door. Ryleigh followed.

The door opened to a lanky young man, his hair rumpled as if he'd just crawled out of bed. "Hey, Evan. What's up? Hi, Mrs. C."

"Nice to see you, Hunter."

The two young men exchanged handshakes—the kind that entwined thumbs—and slapped each other on the back.

"I rang the doorbell, Mrs. C," Hunter said, pointing to the doorbell, "but I don't think it works."

Ryleigh nodded and lowered her voice. "It's dead, Jim."

The boys chuckled at the Star Trek reference, and then Evan glanced at his watch. "You must've been up early to be here by nine with the desk."

"Need to get back to Tempe early to see Molly." Hunter wiggled his eyebrows. His smile was warm, and a bit mischievous— one Ryleigh made a mental note not to ask Evan about. These two boys grew up together, and what mischief they got into as youngsters was far different than what they landed themselves into as young men. Frogs and ladybugs versus a young man's hormone-fueled instinct could prove to be rather embarrassing if pressed for details. Some things were better left unknown.

The boys made short order of heaving the desk into place in the den. They moved quickly and without being told, removed the makeshift desk from the study and positioned the oak rolltop in its place.

When the boys left, Ryleigh surveyed the modest den. The large oak desk nearly overpowered the space and contents from the old desk were strewn across the floor.

Evan leaned against the doorway. "Need some help?" He scratched his head as he surveyed the room.

"You can keep me company."

"Sounds fair—I'll sit and you work," he said, the comment layered with sarcasm.

"Nice try."

Evan paused and then dragged a thick block of paper from beneath a mountain of odds and ends and brushed the top of a layer of fine dust. "What's this?"

A prickle of uneasiness grappled with the coffee in her stomach. "Give that to me." Ryleigh wiggled her fingers.

Evan pulled away from her outstretched hand. "When did you write this?"

"None of your business. It's an old, unfinished manuscript that pretty much sucks. Give it to me."

He stepped back, just out of reach. "Can I read it?"

"Of course not—I told you, it's not finished," she said, flicking him the look of exasperation she reserved for her particularly naughty child. "There's no climax. I mean—"

Evan's head fell backward and he laughed, a deep throaty sound so much like his father. Her chin fell to her chest in a desperate attempt to recant the ridiculously inappropriate comment, but rose as a prudish heat from her toes to every nerve she owned. She pulled her lips in on themselves and lifted her eyes to her son.

"That was priceless, Mom."

She raised her palms in resignation.

"I'll make you a deal," he said.

"No deals. I always end up taking it in the shorts."

"I promise I won't let anyone read it but me—"

Her hands landed firmly on her hips. "No," she said, prepared for a battle of wits.

"You always let me read your work."

Ryleigh turned away and busied herself restacking a lopsided pile of resource books. Acutely fond of the story, she'd fleshed out the characters and the plot was solid, but the ending never came together. Out of sight for months, she'd simply forgotten the manuscript. The idea of letting it go and her son reading some of the scenes she'd written left her terribly uncomfortable.

"I don't know—"

"I won't let it out of my sight. I swear."

"That's not the problem and don't swear."

"I'll give it back as soon as I'm done. Thanks, Mom."

"I didn't say you could take it—"

The moment he turned and left the room Ryleigh grabbed her stomach, the groan in her throat a paralyzing reality check. A cursory zip signaled he'd opened his sport bag. Then the shuffling of paper. Her unfinished story. Her manuscript under a pile of dirty underwear in a smelly gym bag both amused and nauseated her, but her thoughts abruptly turned to his leaving. He had to get back to Tempe for classes. And she had to focus on returning to work. And to some parody of normalcy.

The space between heartbeats lengthened, the gray silence as unfamiliar as the curveballs life had thrown her. Lost in anxious thought, she leaned against the wall and listened while her son packed his belongings (and one of hers). The first steps onto that stage both tugged at a ripple of excitement and plunged her into terrifying uneasiness.

Chapter Ten

EVAN PULLED INTO the driveway earlier than expected for Thanksgiving break, the Civic's horn screeching through an otherwise quiet neighborhood. Ryleigh hurried to meet him, arms flailing to stop the infernal noise. Joy split his features into a mildly malicious grin, and he picked her up and twirled her around. "Mom, you're never going to believe this."

"You know I don't care for surprises, so tell me," she pleaded, slapping him on the shoulder. "But first—Put. Me. Down. I can't breathe."

Evan released his death grip and once inside the house, slid into his adopted place at the kitchen table opposite her. "Well?" she asked, her eyebrows arched to match the curl of her smile.

"I landed an internship," he said, a profusion of emotions radiating across his face, "and it's paid."

"Evan, that's wonderful," she said, tilting her head and folding her hands on the table. "A perfect way to spend next summer."

"It's full time." Evan sucked a breath between his teeth. "And it's next semester."

"What about school?"

"I'll earn credits from the internship and I can take classes online," he said and rubbed his hand across a sparse growth of whiskers, "but it means an extra semester of school."

Ryleigh nodded, calculating the added expenses. But the normal spark in his eyes had grown into a consuming passion. Her apprehension seemed trivial, and she bathed herself in the gravity of his exuberance.

"It's a small, upstart magazine publishing company based in Los Angeles."

California. First her husband. Then her mother. And now her son? The emptiness she thought she had abandoned swallowed her, and she lowered her eyes to hide the sudden casualty of her elation. An unbearable weight anchored her to her seat and her fingers clasped into a tight fist squeezing her disappointment into a steeple of white knuckles. Every ounce of enthusiasm vanished, yet she feigned a smile.

"I think it's fantastic."

Evan squirmed. The chair legs dragged across the floor punctuating the silence with a pathetic groan. "You don't look very happy about it."

A deep breath dispersed her misguided jealousy. "I thought I had three semesters to get used to you leaving Arizona." Slowly, she lifted her chin to face him. "This is an exceptional opportunity you can't pass up, and if you're happy, I'm happy. And you can't imagine how proud." She reached across the table and gave his hands a firm squeeze.

"There's something else." His expression turned serious. "I found him."

"You found who?"

"Ambrose."

A hand rose to her mouth. "Oh, God."

"Actually found two. Judging by what little information I could gather, either of them could be the right one. Or neither."

Ryleigh nodded and leaned forward on her elbows, her chin resting on her folded hands.

"And?"

Evan handed her a scribbled note. "Here's the address for Ambrose Thompson. His family's been in Ballston Spa since the 1700s. Says he's a pharmacist at O'Neil's. It's a small town—they call it a village," he said, his eyes trained on her. "Shouldn't be hard to find."

The realization stunned her to momentary silence. "You think I'm going to go traipsing all over the country in search of this guy?"

"There's no doubt in my mind."

"I've got plenty for both of us."

"Why would you ask me to snoop if you weren't going to look for him?" A flicker of amusement turned the corners of his mouth upward. "Be good for you to get out of town. Spread your wings."

"I don't need to spread my wings."

"The other guy's name is W. L. D'Ambrose."

"Wait...." Ryleigh pressed her back against the chair. "D'Ambrose is his last name?"

"Couldn't find much on him. There one minute, then poof—gone." Evan shrugged. "He just vanished off the Internet."

A whirlwind of opposing thoughts saturated her mind and heart, desire and fear grappling with one another. She pressed her fingertips hard against her temples as if doing so would clear the playing field. The points stacked against finding Ambrose far outweighed finding him. Yet a niggling itch tapped at unguarded logic. "I don't have a clue where to begin."

"With an airline ticket."

"Very funny."

He spread his hands in front of him in a self-appreciative gesture.

"I'm anxious for answers…but it's frightening."

"Mom," Evan said, his voice slicing through spoken and unspoken thought, "take the time off and go."

"I had it all planned in my head, but now that it's an actual possibility, it's so far away," she said, cringing.

"It's New York, not the Outer Limits. Besides, you were born there, maybe you have roots you don't know about."

"I doubt if there's any connection at all, except Ambrose, or Mr. D'Ambrose, or whatever he calls himself. This whole thing is rather intimidating."

"Gram must have known someone in Ballston Spa, or why'd they go there in the first place?"

Despite the fact her mother had never mentioned anyone by the name of Ambrose and Ballston Spa meant nothing to her but an unfamiliar town on her birth certificate, Evan had a point. She suspected the restless suspicions would continue to gnaw at her. One question would raise another until she'd be swimming in a tiny universe of unsolved mysteries. At least until she found answers. She guessed it would be no different than digging for the facts for her newspaper column and hoped she didn't drown.

She glanced at Evan. The resultant silence flowed back into the space that seconds ago reverberated with animated conversation. She bit her lip and held out her hands in a mock surrender. "Okay."

"You'll go?"

"Soon," she said, the weight of the word hanging in the air.

Evan glared at her. "Mom?"

"Okay, okay." She twisted a strand of hair around her finger. He'd always been persuasive, but she wondered when he'd become so…*weighty*. "After Thanksgiving I'll tell Bernadette I have plans for an early Christmas vacation."

Chapter Eleven

SANTA CLAUS, SLEIGH bells and pine boughs replaced pumpkins and honeycomb turkeys everywhere and as quickly as Thanksgiving disappeared, Christmas barreled in right on schedule.

So had her flight to New York.

Time evaporated over rivers and mountain ranges as the plane passed from west to east. A recent snowstorm left a blanket of snow over the New York landscape, and from the air the roads crossed the landscape in a spider web of black asphalt. Though her wristwatch ticked slowly past two in the afternoon, the setting sun painted a much different picture as the plane descended into the shadows of New York. At least Evan had reserved a vehicle with navigation, and Ryleigh was fairly certain the GPS wouldn't steer her in the wrong direction, even though she'd already done a good job of doing exactly that without an ounce of help.

A wave of anxiety clutched her chest and whitened her knuckles as the airplane's wheels kissed asphalt with a jolt.

The Albany terminal dwarfed in comparison to Sky Harbor, but departing the plane and stepping into the terminal on the other side of the continent was as foreign to her as an intergalactic space station. She was surprised at the ease with which she claimed her bag and walked the short distance to the Alamo counter. The Tahoe, equipped with all the gadgets a techno-whiz could wish for (useless bells and whistles for the technically challenged), was ready, and a young attendant synced the Bluetooth and briefed her on the navigation. With a smile filled with blue and gray hardware, he assured her the navigation would take her to the Brook Hollow Inn's doorstep in Saratoga Springs without a hitch. He handed her the key fob and left her to navigate an unfamiliar world.

Ryleigh recited the instructions step by step and entered the address. The male voice that answered the instructions surprised her.

She patted the dash. "Nice touch," she said and pulled forward, the man's voice telling her to turn right at the airport exit. "We'll be spending some intimate time together, Mr. Navigation, so you need a name. It's night and vampires love the night. Barnabas." She shrugged and turned right. "Take me to my temporary home, Barnabas Collins. I'll share my last name with you if you promise not to get me lost." Talking to an invisible man in the dashboard seemed awkward, but the company—invisible or not—was more than welcomed.

A half-hour later she pulled into the Inn.

The room mimicked a quaint coastal cottage in weathered blues and white, and flames danced in the fireplace with a flip of the switch. Ryleigh stepped to the deck. She shivered and tightened the pink ASU hoodie. Pearls of moonlight rippled over Saratoga Lake as the moon's drowsy rise took dominance over the stars, the air brisk and pungently fishy. Waves lapped against the shore. Returning to the warmth of the room, she dialed her cell phone.

"You made it, huh? How was the flight? And your room?"

"Everything's perfect, Son. The lake is gorgeous. I just wish you or Nat were here with me," she said with an uninvited note of uncertainty.

"You'll be fine. Ballston's a small town. And if this Ambrose is an objectionable sort, somebody will tell you. People in Hidden Falls would. So many dubious characters wander the streets there." Sarcasm dripped from his words. "Oh, I almost forgot. Dad called. He was pretty upset you went to New York by yourself."

Ryleigh slumped. "Why'd you tell him?"

"Didn't know it was a secret. He said he should have gone with you."

Her heart faltered on the words. She stared out at the black water, moonlight rippling across it like fingers strumming a guitar. "It doesn't matter what he thinks." Her voice wavered and she kicked herself for the lack of control. "Some things can't be changed." A pause afforded her the time to gather her composure.

"Sorry, Mom. I thought you'd want to know."

"I know what you're thinking," she said, rubbing her temples, "but once certain things are set in motion, they can never go back to the way they were."

"I get it."

"I should call Nat. It's late and I need some sleep."

They offered their good-byes and Ryleigh waited for the connection to go silent. She blew him a kiss and hoped the lump in her throat would subside from the news he'd so candidly blurted out.

She hadn't known. And what had caused Chandler's sudden concern? She shook her head. It made no difference now. The dissolution would be final any day.

Dismissing thoughts of Chandler and a life she'd worn like a treasured sweatshirt, she dialed Nat's number. When it went straight to voice mail, she told Nat everything was perfect and she'd call her tomorrow.

With her inner clock set to Arizona time, she ran a bath and sank to her nose into the hot water. The jets chiseled away at the uneasiness. Though an intimation of apprehension remained, she drifted into the conscious daydreams that precede sleep, and a sense of satisfaction bubbled around her, rising with the faint aroma of lemon sage bath salts and the roar of the jets.

Fatigued from the bath, Ryleigh slid beneath thick blankets and let their weight fold around her. As she gave in to the magnetic pull of slumber, she allowed herself to fully grasp the first step into unknown territory. It terrified, yet comforted her—as did the words written in the leather journal. The decision to resist the stagnated state of her life and come here felt right. Yet in the furthest places she couldn't grasp, a small knot remained.

On the first night an entire continent away from home, Ryleigh drifted uneasily over the threshold of sleep.

Chapter Twelve

RYLEIGH WOKE EARLY (Arizona time) with a queasy mix of intrigue and dread. Dressing quickly in a well-worn pair of jeans and a pink long-sleeved cotton T-shirt, she pulled the ASU hoodie over her head, took another glance in the mirror and fluffed her hair. She blew out a breath, the air lifting short wisps of bangs. Her arms dropped to her sides with a slap.

Stalling would get her nowhere.

She opened the satchel and made sure the journal, Ambrose's letter and the drawstring bag containing the patch and button were still there.

Ryleigh slung the satchel over her shoulder and shivered as she stepped from her room to find some breakfast. Or at least coffee. Her stomach rumbled, avidly protesting the lack of food. The ground sparkled with frozen dew, her breaths billowing ahead of her as she headed in the direction of the dot on the Inn's small map.

The breakfast room was nearly deserted, but the aroma of freshly brewed coffee and strawberry jam greeted her like comfortable old friends. She slathered a bagel with jam, grabbed a tall coffee to go and sat at a table by the window. A thin layer of fog hovered over Saratoga Lake. She watched it float across the water and tried to summon the courage sleep had swallowed. She glanced around. Judging by the pamphlets in her room, Saratoga Springs was big on horse racing. During the summer season, the Inn would be bustling with horse racing enthusiasts and bettors would be perusing *The Forum* instead of the lone gentleman hidden behind *The New York Times.*

Ryleigh picked at the bagel, neither tasting it nor realizing she had eaten the last bite. She scooted her chair back, pulled the hoodie tighter around her neck, refilled her coffee, and headed for the Tahoe.

Once inside, she punched the button for the seat warmer. "Whoever invented heated seats should be awarded the Nobel Prize, Barnabas." She glanced around to make sure no one had seen her talking to herself, or to an empty car. She rummaged in her purse for the address to O'Neil's Pharmacy in Ballston Spa, touched the navigation screen, and waited for Barnabas to wake up. "Okay, big guy. Here we go. First stop, O'Neil's." Ryleigh held her breath until the route appeared on the screen.

The burly voice directed her to the route, but her body refused her brain's command to move. What was she thinking? How'd she get to the other side of the continent searching for someone she knew nothing about? She'd rarely been out of Hidden Falls, let alone Arizona, and she was definitely no Sherlock Holmes—she detested pipes. And magnifying glasses (which were much too similar to peepholes) gave her the creeps.

Nothing, excluding the sun (the same one that shone over Arizona) was familiar. The air hung heavier, the sky a murkier blue. Strangers bustled about. Maids knocked on doors. Travelers loaded luggage into cars with unfamiliar license plates. Everyone had a purpose. They knew what they were doing or where they were going. She knew neither. A rapacious urge to flee tingled down her arms and skirted her middle. *Keep it simple, they'd said. Find Ambrose and come home.* She eased the gas pedal. The voice boldly told her to stay on the route around the lake.

At least someone in the Tahoe wasn't lost. Or terrified.

The blanket of fog had lifted. The lake glistened in the midmorning sun along the route, the water mere feet from the road. Boat docks skewered the shoreline and quaint, mostly older homes lined the road, and she soon found the landscape easing the apprehension. Instead of the unpleasant grip of uneasiness testing her coping mechanism, Ryleigh saw the road ahead once again as simply a quest for answers.

She crossed over the Adirondack Northway, and recalled a novel about a little girl lost in the Adirondacks; the little girl had used her favorite baseball player to take her mind off her fears. Chandler wasn't a ballplayer (in the normal sense of the word) but he'd always been there, until he chose to cast aside an entire life for a woman as transparent as a pane of window glass. But he wasn't here. No one was. The seat next to her was empty.

Twenty minutes later, she entered Ballston Spa and slowed. She passed a few businesses and a unique coffee shop when Barnabas announced her destination ahead. She parked the Tahoe and chose to walk the short distance to O'Neil's.

Timeworn and draped in history, the buildings oozed charm and character, frozen in time like a quaint village in a snow globe. If she listened, she was sure she could hear the stories of the souls who once walked the sidewalks.

Ryleigh approached O'Neil's and pulled on the door handle. A bell tinkled. Her heart raced. History blossomed from the store, but bore the telltale signs of modern technology—fingers tapped a keyboard and a young woman giggled into her cell phone. A Christmas carol jingled in the background and the scent of brisk evergreen collided with the pungent twang of Vicks. Ryleigh made her way to the back of the store and approached the counter. Absorbed in the computer screen, a gaunt, balding man in a white coat didn't look up right away. When he did, he spoke through a sterile smile, the eastern accent she'd hoped to hear a vague whisper.

"May I help you?"

Ryleigh cleared her throat. "I'm hoping so." This man didn't look like the Ambrose she'd imagined, and a quick glance at his nametag confirmed her suspicions. "I'm looking for someone," she said and then paused. "My mother recently passed away and she spoke of a man named Ambrose she knew here."

"Sorry for your loss," he replied coolly, "but I can't help you."

"My mother never mentioned a last name, but does Ambrose Thompson work here? I was hoping to speak to him."

"Don't think so."

"He doesn't work here?"

"Nope." The man raised weedy eyebrows and glared at her above half-moon spectacles.

"Do you know where I can find him?"

"Sure," he answered with a fair amount of smugness. "Take this street to the end and hang a left. You'll find him way in the back under six feet of frozen dirt."

"Oh." Ryleigh blinked. "I'm sorry," she said, wondering if all New Yorkers were this flippant. "May I ask when he died?"

"Alfred, are you giving my customers a hard time again?" The squeaky voice belonged to a round-faced man who had shuffled to the counter, his smile so wide his eyes had all but disappeared. "I'm Casey O'Neil. You must not be from around here if you don't know about Ambrose. And yes, he worked here for many years."

"Pleased to meet you, Casey. I'm Ryleigh Collins," she said with an inward cringe. Should she have used an alias? Detectives and sleuths did, but that option died with her opening her big mouth. She extended her hand. "My mother knew Ambrose."

He took her hand in both of his. "Hmmm. Been five years now since he passed." Casey scrutinized her closely.

"It's not him," Ryleigh mumbled, reclaiming her hands. Casey threw Alfred a quizzical look. "This letter," she said, digging in her satchel, "is from him. But it's not the same man. I'm sure of it." She pointed to the envelope. "The postmark is only four years old."

"I'm sorry, Miss Collins," Casey said, his eyes fully visible. "But it seems you're quite correct."

Alfred removed his spectacles and placed them atop his shiny head. "Sorry I was rude."

Casey rolled his skimpy eyes. "You're always rude, Alfred."

"Thank you both for your help." Ryleigh faked a smile. "You don't know another Ambrose around here by chance?"

"It's not a common name." Casey's face contorted in concentration. "I'm the only pharmacist in the village, so if this Ambrose needed meds of any kind, he'd have to come to me." He wrinkled his chin. "Unless he goes to the Springs or Albany." Casey's eyes disappeared once again into his smile. "Good luck, Miss Collins. I hope you find your mother's friend."

"I do too," she said with a shy smile. "And it's Mrs." *...at least for another day or two.* She made her way back through the store, the little bell escorting her outside.

She leaned against the building and made a quick Google search for him. Nothing. Just as Evan had said. The sun had burned through the clouds, warming the afternoon air. The weather had turned for the better, but her day hadn't. Disheartened, she strolled along the sidewalk, pausing at a wide storefront. Bing Crosby's smooth version of "White Christmas" crooned from overhead speakers. Smoke chuffed from a toy train as it circled a quaint village and gingerbread houses lined one end.

"Best gingerbread in New York." The old man had startled her, but his crooked smile was warm and friendly. The aroma of fresh gingerbread wafted through the doorway as he stepped inside the bakery.

Her gaze returned to the window and in the center of the tiny village, skaters whirled in dizzying circles on an icy pond. And then her eyes settled on the crèche and baby Jesus. Where had the time gone when Evan would have stood on tiptoe, wide-eyed at wonders just like these? When had life pulled the plug on the simplicity of everyday things? And the unity of family? Of her family?

She cinched her scarf and kept walking.

Uncertain what to do next, Ryleigh crossed the street to the coffee shop hoping to clear her head and come up with Plan B. With no address or phone number for the second Ambrose on her list, she was lost as to how to find him. But Ballston Spa surely had a newspaper. Or a library. Both were worth looking into.

Within a minute Ryleigh was sitting in the Koffee Kettle warming her hands on a steaming caramel latte. A small, fat candle flickered in its nest of Christmas holly as she watched the locals pass by.

A young barista approached her table. "Arizona State by chance?" she asked, twisting a stiff tendril of jet-black hair between her fingers. A metal-studded headband held the short spikes in place.

"Sorry?"

She pointed to Ryleigh's sweatshirt. "Arizona State?"

"Oh," she said, mildly amused and threw a hand on the ASU logo. "Yes. My son's in school there."

"He's a long way from home," she said, hands perched on her hips. "Can I get you something to go with your coffee? A scone or a warm croissant?"

"Thank you, no." Ryleigh flashed a reserved smile. "My son's close, actually. I'm the one who's a long way from home."

"My cousin's enrolled at ASU and says it's awesome." She scrunched her face. "But it's sort of hot." The crystal stud in her nose glinted. "What brings you to Ballston Spa of all places?" she asked, rolling her eyes. "It's not the mecca New York City is. In fact, this place is one person shy of losing our dot on the map."

Guessing her age as a bit younger than Evan, Ryleigh smiled at the young lady's frankness.

"I'm Ryleigh and it's not so bad. It's loaded with historical charm."

"Megan," the barista replied, pointing to her name tag.

"Pleased to meet you, Megan."

"Likewise."

"Care to join me?" Ryleigh asked, offering a chair.

Megan pulled up a chair, the glitter in her hair reflecting the light from the window. "There's a ton of history here all right. Stuff I don't want to remember."

"Not a history buff?"

"Oh, I like history. Just not *my* history." Her chin dropped into her palms. "Real history is cool. Abner Doubleday was born in the Spa, you know. The guy who supposedly," she said, air quoting the word, "invented baseball."

Ryleigh nodded. She remembered the Doubleday name from something Chandler had told her, but couldn't recall the details. "What do you mean, supposedly?"

"It's folklore—debunked by most sports authorities. He's actually a Civil War hero. His house is here. You should visit. It's on the corner of Washington and Fenwick."

"Interesting," she said, peering over the rim of her mug.

"And, old Georgie Washington is rumored to have come here for the mineral baths. Makes for cool conversation to newbies." She shrugged. "What brings you all the way from Arizona? If I lived there, I wouldn't come here." She wrinkled her nose. "Not deliberately."

"I'm looking for someone," she said after a conscious pause. "It was a long time ago, but I'm hoping he's still in the area."

"The Spa's small. Maybe I know him. What's his name?"

"W. L. D'Ambrose. He is—*was*—a friend of my mother's."

Megan rose, bumping her knee on the table. "Shit." Melted wax spilled over the side of the candle and dribbled down the side. "Never heard of him." Metal bracelets clinked down her arm as she turned and waved a dismissive hand. "Enjoy your stay in the Spa."

"Megan, wait—" Having raised a teenager, she had seen the look before—the one that shouted *'busted.'* "You know him, don't you?" Ryleigh rose to follow her.

Megan disappeared behind the counter, grabbed a dishcloth, and began scrubbing the espresso machine in short, jerky strokes. "It's important I find this man," Ryleigh said as she approached the counter.

Megan didn't look up. "Why?" A long feather earring swung to and fro with each deliberate swipe.

"My mom passed away a couple of months ago and I found a letter addressed to her from him." She'd already resigned herself to begging. "Would you care to see it?"

Megan stopped scrubbing. She glanced around at the empty shop. "Yeah, I know him." Her dark eyes had gone black.

"It's very important I find him."

"If I tell you, you have to swear you didn't find out from me."

"Deal."

"No questions asked?"

"Promise."

She leaned over the counter. "He lives on the outskirts of the village." She hesitated. "You can find out anything on the Internet. Understand?"

Her heart raced. "Got it." It wasn't really a lie; Evan had dug up that much himself.

"No one here knows him by that name."

"Why?"

"You'll have to ask him yourself. He goes by Ambrose."

Megan's face paled even in comparison to the pale makeup and Ryleigh's thoughts churned. "What happened? Did he hurt you?"

Megan shook her head. "Good Lord, no," she emphasized with upraised eyebrows. "He's an old man, ancient—like Stone Age—and he wouldn't hurt a fly. But I don't want to…" she swallowed, "he trusts me."

"I see."

"You do?"

"There's nothing more important than trust." Ryleigh winced. "So why are you telling me?"

Megan licked dark lips. "I can see the determination in your eyes, and if your mom already knew him by his real name, you'd find out anyway. Besides, you seem honest. And desperate. You look sort of lost. Or something."

"You're very perceptive."

Megan gathered her composure. "Ambrose helped me out. God, if he finds out I told you, he'll kill me."

Ryleigh recoiled.

"Shit, not literally *kill* me," she explained with an exaggerated eye roll, "you know, as in 'YOU IDIOT,'" she said, gesturing with both hands, black nails bitten ragged.

"Got it. Tell me where I can find him. Please?"

Ryleigh sat and Megan slid into the seat opposite her, again surveying the store. "He's sort of a recluse. Lives at the end of Nightshade Path. I'll draw you a map."

"I have navigation."

"Sweet. But you won't find it on any Google map."

"Why not?"

"Doesn't exist."

"Excuse me?"

"If you research his address or anything about him, he seriously doesn't exist."

"I don't understand."

"You will," Megan replied, "once you find him." She squirmed in her seat, pulled a napkin from the dispenser, and drew a crude map. "He lives like a hermit and isn't crazy about visitors. Goes to the Springs and Albany to take care of business. Doesn't own a phone. Landline or cell."

"How do you know all this?"

"Like I said, he helped me out."

"How so?"

"Jeez, you're nosy," she said as she tossed Ryleigh a sheepish grin.

"So I've been told. Guess that's part of the reason I'm here."

"I'll tell you, but never ever let on you found out from me. He really will kill me."

"Your secret's safe," Ryleigh said, swiping her pinched thumb and index finger across sealed lips.

"Famous last words." Megan gnawed on a thumbnail. "God, why did I open my big mouth?" She slapped her head in her hands, sighed, and then looked directly at Ryleigh. "Guess it's too late now." She studied the chipped polish on her nails. "A while back I did something really stupid and got myself knocked up. Well, I didn't get *myself* knocked up, but I suppose you know how that works." She fingered the feather earring. "Ambrose helped me with the adoption. He's amazing. Doesn't seem to be anything he doesn't know, or can't do."

Ryleigh's eyes lit up. "How so?"

Megan raised an eyebrow. "Don't interrupt or I might lose my courage. I shouldn't be telling you any of this."

Ryleigh nodded for her to continue.

"Everyone in this crummy village thought I went to visit my aunt in Chicago because I hated school and I look like this." Megan cocked her head and raised an eyebrow, gesturing to her clothing and oddly placed body piercings, pale face, and dark makeup. "But I stayed right here in the Spa. No one knew I was preggers either. Ambrose took care of me and forced me to keep up my studies. He's majorly smart—like way over my head smart," she said, waving her hand over her head. "Anyway, he took me to a doctor in Albany. When the kid came, he was there with me. And the adoptive parents. Everything was cool." She lowered her eyes. "But I don't know where they took my son."

Ryleigh slumped, an involuntary reaction to the sudden disquiet in Megan's tone.

Megan's brow furrowed momentarily. "Doesn't matter now."

Given the circumstances and the young woman's age, she understood, yet her stomach did a dizzying somersault.

"I so want out of the Spa when I graduate next December. Pretty cool, huh?"

"Umm, okay. If you think it's cool…"

She scowled and waved a hand. "I meant graduating early."

"Of course." Ryleigh let out a sigh of relief. "The whole story is incredible, Megan. How did you get hooked up with Ambrose?"

"Whoa, I never hooked up with the old guy," she said, shaking her head.

"Sorry. I forget the idioms of kids even though I have a son a little older than you."

"Right. I hooked up with a sailor. Cute, but as dumb as a box of rocks. But hey, I don't have room to talk. I'm pretty talented at making bad decisions. For every action there's a reaction and my reaction was throwing up for three months."

"Morning sickness isn't fun." Ryleigh twisted a wayward strand of hair. "How'd you know Ambrose would take you in?"

"Didn't. The old guy knows things. He found me. Never did ask how he found out I was preggers, and if I didn't know better I'd swear he knew before I did." She shrugged. "I was glad I could get it past my old man—he *would* have killed me," she said, raking her hand across her throat in a slicing motion, her dark eyes wide.

"Your father doesn't know?"

"Nope. And if he finds out…" she said, pointing a ringed index finger at Ryleigh.

"No worries, Megan."

"After I went back home, my father left me alone. He thought my aunt straightened me up. But it was Ambrose. Told me in order to get out of the Spa, I needed to score not just good grades, great grades. I told my dad what he wanted to hear, that my aunt worked me over to get me to conform to their ways. They're two of a kind, and it ain't no picnic being around either of them."

It was the first time she had used anything but good grammar—aside from the occasional cuss word or teenage jargon—a slip possibly, back to the old Megan. "I'm sorry. I can't imagine."

"It worked out." She sighed. "Ambrose took care of everything—tickets, correspondence, my aunt." She pushed her bangs back with her palm. "Ambrose is a master at hiding people—like scary good." She leaned forward. "I refer to it as witness protection. Sounds cool, sort of FBI-ish." Megan bobbed her head mockingly. "The way he knows things—stuff he shouldn't—is creepy sometimes." Three tiny metal studs rose with one dark eyebrow.

"He should have the answers to my questions then, and I have no plans of ever coming back." She reached across the table and squeezed Megan's hand. "By the way, I'm curious. You seem to have your act together, so what do you want to study?"

Her cheeks flushed. "Thanks," Megan said quietly before perking back into high gear. "International law. I want to travel the world. See and do it all. Maybe do an internship in Italy."

Ryleigh folded her arms on the table and smiled. "Italy's on my bucket list."

"Maybe I'll see you there." The girl with the artificial Goth look stood. "I hope you find the answers you're looking for, Ryleigh. Ambrose is an antique, but he's cool. Just keep it low-key. The Spa is a small town and people like to flap their jaws."

The source of idle chatter was nothing new to her. "Your secrets will go to the grave with me," she said, crossing her heart. "You have my word."

"Good luck."

"Good luck to you too, although I think Megan the Barista will make her own luck. You're a very bright young lady."

Megan blushed. The new color in her cheeks didn't go well with her stark black hair and pale features, but Ryleigh suspected the Goth look was merely a ruse to draw attention away from the young woman underneath.

Ryleigh rose and hugged the teenager. "By the way, what's he look like?" she asked, pushing the door open.

Megan chuckled. "Do you like to read?"

"Yes, why?"

"You'll know him." A sly smile thinned her lips. "He looks exactly like a well-known author." Megan slipped behind the counter. "You'll see."

Looking back through the window outside the Koffee Kettle, Ryleigh smiled. Megan had already struck a conversation with a new customer as she mixed another coffee creation.

Ryleigh hurried the few blocks back to the Tahoe, crude map in hand. The engine came to life. She leaned into the headrest and air-pumped a fist.

Unfamiliar with the area, she studied the map Megan had given her. By the time she found her way (if she didn't get lost) morning would be a memory and she had no intention of finding her way back in the dark. She sighed, knowing this leg of her adventure would have to wait, and instructed Barnabas to return to the Inn.

As Barnabas calculated the return trip, apprehension crept up her spine. Megan had said Ambrose was a loner and didn't encourage company. What if she wasn't welcomed? Maybe he wouldn't know her even though the letter had mentioned her by name. Doubt riddled her thoughts. She locked the doors and engaged the Bluetooth. Chandler's deep, calming voice would reassure her. Should she make the call? She shook her head and dialed Natalie's number instead.

Natalie picked up on the first ring. "Hey, Riles—everything going okay?"

Nat's soothing voice eased her apprehension. "I found him."

"See? That wasn't so hard. What's he like?"

"I haven't met him yet, but it's too late today."

"Good grief, it's only noon—oops. Forgot the time change. It's probably afternoon there."

"It is and I'm not familiar with the area, so I asked Barnabas to take me back to the Inn and get a fresh start in the morning."

"Who the hell is Barnabas? Have you taken in a stray vamp?"

"No, you goof—he's my navigation."

"You need to be a little more specific when you mention vampires. I don't want to have to charter a jet and come rescue you."

"If by chance I had taken in a stray—vampire or not—I don't need rescuing. Especially if he looks like Johnny Depp. And besides, Barnabas shares my last name, and I can take care of myself. I think. Who knows? Might be fun."

"Oooh," Natalie purred. "Perfect age, perfect male specimen."

She pictured Natalie's naughty grin. "You know what I mean, vampires…never mind."

"You read way too much fiction, Ryleigh Collins. Sometimes I think you have your head stuck in a fantasy world."

"Maybe I do."

"Okay, what gives?"

"I met a girl at the coffee shop who knows Ambrose. She says he's a loner and doesn't care for visitors. What if he won't talk to me, Nat? What do I do? What if he's got a gun or something?"

"You're overreacting. Your mother wouldn't have made friends with a creep. He wrote her—and called you by name. I doubt he's a serial killer, nor do I think he'll turn you away."

"Megan says he has secrets."

"Who doesn't? Some are a little scarier or more embarrassing than others, so take a deep breath, go back to the Inn and relax. Then tomorrow when you find him, have your cell handy. He's not going to do anything stupid. Trust me."

"Easy for you to say, you're thousands of miles away. Twenty-five hundred to be exact."

Natalie laughed. "You'll be fine. Go back to the Inn and leave the *Dark Shadows* vampires to Victoria, okay?"

"Not a chance," she teased. Excitement was beginning to overpower her trepidation.

The two women embraced their smiles, though neither could see the unspoken expression.

"I'll call you tomorrow, Nat."

"Sleep well."

Ryleigh pressed the disconnect button, sent Evan a quick text and then proceeded through town and onto the highway. The panorama of the village dwindled in her rearview mirror, and Ryleigh turned up the volume on the radio to fill the silence. The day had left its unexpected imprint—a dead end, and then an intriguing young lady and a route roughly scribbled on a paper napkin—her very own lost highway. She hummed along to the radio. Maybe Bon Jovi knew their life was clearer and where they were headed on their "Lost Highway," but she had merely turned the corner of her own.

Chapter Thirteen

CHANDLER PULLED TO the edge of the property on Juniper Ridge Road and cracked his window, the gritty idle of the diesel truck mixing with the drone of the backhoe. Permits to begin construction had been processed and he'd wasted no time in scheduling subcontractors. Work was scarce with the housing industry at a near standstill, and subs practically begged for any kind of job, big or small.

He shoved the gearshift into park, laced his arms over the steering wheel, and scanned the property. Over the years he'd kept a close eye on the secluded piece of land and couldn't remember how many times he'd stood on this spot, waiting for the right opportunity. As fate would have it, he was able to purchase the land at nearly half the appraised price—one bright spot in the housing slump.

Earlier, with the morning sun barely over the treetops, he'd laid out the dimensions of the house in chalk lines placed precisely where the den would overlook a craggy bank of rock and a creek—no wider than a man's exaggerated stride—that ran along the edge of the shallow rock canyon. Over the last months, as an orange western sky swallowed the sun and dragonflies hovered over the inconsequential trickle of water, he'd contemplated the placement of the house. On one overcast day, a doe and her twin fawns gathered near the water at twilight as a bald eagle circled overhead. It landed on the stone cliff, a sentinel regarding his surroundings. In that moment, he decided this would be the view from the bay window of the den he'd promised her.

God, why hadn't he built it sooner?

The gentle slope from the creek's bed opened into a clearing where the house would stand no more than six or seven months from now when the air was warmer and spring wildflowers bloomed. The bay window would frame the view, a constantly changing seasonal landscape. She would love it for its natural beauty. He loved it for the warmth and beauty of her smile.

The engine idled loudly, and a sudden fog of diesel fumes blew through the window on a cold burst of October wind. Chandler closed the window, unfurled the blueprints, and checked the foundation elevations. Though winter had embraced the mountains of Arizona, the ground was frozen only through the topmost layer and the backhoe teeth, worn slick from the abrasion of rock against steel, dug tirelessly into the earth blazing a trench for the footers. He pushed the hair from his face, repositioned his Diamondbacks ball cap and mentally calculated the old man's maneuvers. He stepped from his truck to the dirt road and pulled the collar of his lined denim jacket a little tighter around his neck.

Chandler paced the perimeter, gestured to the operator to continue, and then hopped back into the warm truck and grabbed his cell. Footers were ready to be poured.

Before he could dial the concrete subcontractor, his phone chirped. He frowned at the unfamiliar number.

"Collins Construction. Chandler speaking."

A momentary silence ensued. He glanced at the number again. "Hello?"

"Hey, baby," she said, the familiar voice sending an involuntary shudder through him that had nothing to do with the weather. "I like the new company name. How are you?"

Chandler grit his teeth. "Della," he said as his free hand clamped the back of his neck. "Everything okay?"

"That's what I want to talk to you about. But not over the phone."

He straightened. "The baby okay?"

"Everything's fine. Can we meet where we can talk privately?"

"Not a good idea."

"Jesus, Chandler. People already know I'm pregnant with your child. I don't think anyone is going to think twice about it. Please," she pleaded, "it's important."

His jaw clenched. "Where?"

"My place? I promise I have no plans except to talk."

"Pick someplace public."

"My place. Twenty minutes. You won't be sorry."

The line went dead. He gripped the steering wheel and dropped his head to his forearm. "Dammit," he mumbled, and bundled the blueprints.

Chandler started toward the house he once shared eagerly with a woman he thought he loved and it had cost him dearly—a mistake he wouldn't repeat.

Della's sporty black Mercedes was ahead of him by half a minute. The scene was familiar, having been in this situation on a brisk autumn night over a year ago. On that particular night, he'd hidden his truck in the garage away from prying eyes. Today, he parked in plain sight. Guilt tightened his chest.

The garage door opened. The Shelby was gone, the garage empty.

A realtor's sign wagged in the breeze as he slipped from his truck and went inside. He briefly celebrated the possibility she was leaving town, but his gut objected. Along with her possessions, she would be taking his son or daughter.

Blonde hair fell in soft waves over Della's shoulders as he approached the kitchen, and she brushed one side to the back, exposing the long lines of her neck and the birthmark she wore as the unmistakable kiss of the Devil. Chandler coughed and crossed a knuckle under his nose to hide a smirk. Della Mayfair didn't need a set of plans to execute her immutable strategy.

"Like old times, isn't it, baby?"

Chandler raked the hair from his face. "What's this about?"

"Let's talk in the den. It's more comfortable." She reached for his hands, but he was quick to deny what he had no intention of giving and pulled away.

"I don't need a guide, Della." The muscles in his jaw tightened. "And the den is the other way." He nodded in the opposite direction and motioned for her to go ahead of him.

Her mouth curled, only to have the rudimentary beginnings of a smile shrivel. "What a difference a few weeks and a pregnant belly make. You can't stand the sight of me," she said with a pout and slumped into a leather chair.

He lagged behind, removing his jacket.

Della's perfectly groomed eyebrow raised.

"Don't get any ideas," he said quickly. Throwing the jacket over the twin leather chair, he leaned against the doorframe. "So what's with the For Sale sign?"

"You noticed?"

"Pretty hard to miss."

She approached him and leaned into the curve of his arm.

He fixed his eyes on hers and stared into a fathomless blue sea of misplaced infatuation; he stepped away from her attempted embrace. He knew the game. She'd toy with him, twist his thoughts, and play on his emotions. "Your games may work with the next guy in line, but not with me. Not anymore."

Della turned her back to him and stared out the window.

"What do you want, Della?" Chandler widened his stance and crossed his arms. "I have work to do."

"You look great, by the way. I like your hair long, it's—"

His voice rose. "Get to the point."

She raised her arms, and then let them fall to her side. "I listed the house a couple of weeks ago. There's no reason for me to stay."

"How can I be a father to my child if you leave?"

"I'm not going far. I bought a place in Scottsdale."

Chandler acknowledged the comment with a nod. True, the drive took less than an hour and a half.

"The movers will be here next week. A friend drove the Shelby for me."

"What's his name?"

"You don't have to be so cheeky."

"C'mon, Della. I've been in his shoes. I know what goes on in that pretty head of yours, and you don't hang with women."

"He's just a friend."

"For now," he said curtly, adjusting his feet in the doorway. "I guess Scottsdale won't be so bad. I can take him to Diamondbacks and Cardinals games when he gets a little older. Introduce the little guy to the mountains on weekends."

She smiled, tilting her head. "You think it's a boy?"

"Thinking out loud. He's my flesh and blood. I want to be a part of his or *her* life."

"You really care about this baby, don't you?"

"Evan is the best thing that's ever happened to me." Ryleigh was too, but he kept the thought to himself. "It wasn't hard to fall in love with this kid, either."

Della turned slowly and crossed the room. "Here," she said, placing his hand on her abdomen. She smiled demurely and leaned in closer, guiding his hand. Their hands circled her belly. He held his breath. Did it seem rounder than he remembered? Was his child moving yet? Della was so petite, surely she'd show soon and he'd feel the life growing inside her. Della's free arm slipped beneath his untucked shirt, and she sank into him, sobering his thoughts.

Chandler pulled himself away and held her at arm's length, her persistent wiles striking a note of irritation beneath an unyielding armor. But pouring gasoline on an ember wasn't likely to douse a fire that once burned with intense heat. With one hand, he lifted her face and watched the way her smile softened the faint lines around her mouth. He spoke softly, the words forming from the deepest part of his being, the place no one but him knew what resided there. "You're carrying my child—a child I already love. I will honor that. I will be there for this baby."

Anguish moistened her eyes. "Chandler—"

"But I'm not coming back. I don't love you." His eyes penetrated hers as if to engrave the words in her mind. He smoothed a length of golden hair away from her mouth and dropped his hands to his side. "I'm sorry. And I can honestly say I never did."

Resigned, she stepped away and fell into the chair. "It doesn't make any difference anyway," she said, pulling her legs to her chest and folding her arms around them.

"What's that supposed to mean?"

"It just means it doesn't matter." She stared at the floor. "There is no baby, Chandler."

Her words sliced through the air and struck him hard. "What happened?"

"Nothing happened."

"God, Della. Did you miscarry? When?"

She hesitated. "I didn't miscarry."

"Then what the hell are you telling me?" He raised his hands in surrender.

"Men can be so gullible sometimes." She stood and faced him. "There never was a baby. Do you think I would do something that stupid? Look at me," she said, displaying her body with outstretched hands. "I used it as leverage." Angry tears welled in her eyes. "I'm pretty good at getting what I want and I wanted you."

The lie simmered in his blood. Was she lying to him now? He'd felt her belly. Small and round and firm. He gripped the doorframe tighter.

"You were different," she said, pacing the floor. "I couldn't break you no matter what I did. Then I watched you with your son."

He opened his mouth to speak, but no words formed.

"It was stupid and childish, but I had to try." Tears streaked her face as the confession rolled from her lips. "It almost worked." Her lip trembled. "I'm not sorry and I'd do it again if I thought there was a chance. But I can't pretend. I don't want to be pregnant. Not with your child, or anyone's, Chandler. I'm not cut out for the 'mommy' thing."

Her words settled coarsely inside him and he couldn't form his own. He had accepted and embraced the fact he was going to be a father again. "You didn't do something stupid, you didn't..." the words stuck in a throat gone paper dry.

"No! God, Chandler, I'm not as heartless as you think." Her voice rose. "Don't you understand? I made the whole thing up. I wanted you, not some kid I would be stuck with changing diapers and raising for the next eighteen years." She cringed. "Not happening on my watch."

Chandler couldn't look at her except with what amounted to nothing but pure contempt. How could he have been so blind? Without another word, he turned his back to leave.

"Chandler, wait," she begged, "you—you forgot your jacket."

He tensed. With every nerve on the edge of short-circuiting, he forced himself to pause. Without turning around, he slapped the doorframe. "Keep it, Della. Someday you may need it to keep yourself warm."

He left through the laundry door and fled down the stairs in two strides. Icy December air stung his face as bitterly as her words had his heart.

Still, the echo of what she'd confessed wouldn't settle, as if the lie itself had been a lie.

Chapter Fourteen

RYLEIGH FOUGHT TO decipher reality from broken dreams, but the night passed and she rose to full consciousness the next morning. Excitement and dread snaked through her veins in equal measure, settling into a knot in her stomach. She welcomed a hot shower, a host of questions teeter-tottering in her head as she stepped beneath the spray. Warm water ran through her fingers and soaked her hair. The disconcerting thoughts slowly dissolved, and she allowed them to swirl with the soapy water into the dregs of the sewer.

She dressed in jeans, a comfortable long-sleeved T-shirt under the hoodie, and laced her shoes over thick socks. She took a deep breath, draped her scarf over her shoulder, and then walked to the breakfast room for some much needed coffee.

The lakeside vista embraced her from all sides of the panoramic windows as she entered the breakfast room; the disquiet of the morning vanished with the fog drifting across the lake. Her eyes settled on the only person in the breakfast room—same solitary man, same seat as yesterday—but he screened his face with today's *Wall Street Journal* in place of yesterday's *New York Times*.

Second thoughts sprouted like weeds. A late morning hiding under the blankets of the Inn's downy bed with a novel and crackling fire seemed more tempting, if not prudent. She'd come to investigate questions she hoped Ambrose could answer. And if he could, would he? Before doubt overpowered her courage, Ryleigh grabbed a large coffee, dressed it with the usual spoonful of creamer and packet of sweetener and snapped the lid into place. She wrapped her scarf twice around her neck and stepped into the brisk morning air. Coffee trailed down her throat as she sipped, replacing the apprehension with brief comfort.

* * *

With Megan's crude map etched in her memory, Ryleigh entered the outskirts of Ballston Spa and slowed. She followed Megan's directions through the village, hands clutching the steering wheel as visible signs of civilization disappeared. One at a time she wiped clammy palms on her jeans.

Patches of snow blanketed the ground. Overcast in shadow, the forest camouflaged splashes of sunlight that crept through dense pines, and leafless oak and maple trees. She braked hard, nearly missing a stop sign covered by overgrown limbs. Glancing in both directions, she crossed the railroad tracks.

The road turned to dirt and the outstretched fingers of three unmarked dirt roads beckoned her. Instinct (or was it fear?) insisted she turn right. Megan had instructed her to turn left; she eased the Tahoe over a run-down swell of decomposed wooden planks to a suggestion of a road—two ghostly ruts with tufts of undisturbed brown grass covering the middle. A bridge of tangled tree limbs hovered overhead. *Intruders beware.* Gooseflesh pebbled across her skin as if a ghost had brushed its arctic fingers over her arms.

She scanned the road ahead of her. "Get a grip." She clenched her teeth, engaged the four-wheel drive, and eased onto Nightshade Path.

The shadows deepened. Sprinkles of light seeped through the trees. Images of Fanghorn Forest and frightened hobbits in *The Lord of the Rings* sprang to mind. The forest seemed to have linked arms and swallowed the curve in the road ahead until she felt as small and creeped out as the little hobbits. If she had a magic ring like Frodo, the temptation to use it and disappear far outweighed any reason not to. *Ents and Orcs belonged in Middle Earth. Not New York.*

As suddenly as the forest had closed itself around her, branches yawned and stretched to the sky. Sunlight trickled in. The forest opened to an expansive meadow and a rather unpretentious house on the furthermost fringes of trees. Cattails jutted from beneath the frozen surface of a pond and a lone sugar maple dressed its far bank.

Ryleigh crossed the meadow on the left edge of the forest and pulled the Tahoe into a packed dirt driveway leading to an open garage. Parked inside was an older model wood-paneled Wagoneer covered with dirt and dried mud. The house appeared deserted with the exception of a wisp of silver-blue smoke rising from the chimney. Ryleigh took one very slow, final drink of her coffee. She turned the key and the tic, tic, tic of the cooling engine resounded in the stillness keeping time to the thumping of her heart. The urge to flee threatened to overwhelm her. She glanced around, and then stepped from the Tahoe, purse in hand. Her legs trembled. Her hands shook and it took two swipes at her satchel to grab it. She pushed aside the rising panic only to have it push back harder. She straightened, tightened her fingers around the purse strap, and then walked to the entrance.

A porch ran the length of the house, fully enclosed in glass. A host of wind chimes dangled from the rafters, their songs silent. Dozens of prisms cast their rainbows across the porch, and the faint odor of wood smoke hung in the damp air. She stepped to the door, hesitated with two phantom knocks, and then rapped her knuckles on the door.

Silence answered her.

"Hello?" Taking a step backward, she nearly tripped on a wooden plank leaning against the house. The elements had rutted deep indentions in the soft grain, the handwritten letters nearly illegible. Ryleigh bent to see it more closely. "Firefly Pond," she murmured, glancing across the meadow to the pond.

Before she'd gathered enough courage to knock again, the inside door groaned. Her nerve wilted. A tall, lanky man stepped into the light, his stature bent with age. Copious amounts of long, unruly white hair framed a haggard face, and wiry eyebrows jutted profusely above a pair of steely blue eyes. Tiny rainbows danced across his deeply lined face.

Ryleigh's mouth spread into a spontaneous smile. Megan had been spot on. The man limped across the porch, wooden planks protesting under his weight. As if he had just stepped off a riverboat in a high-collared starched white shirt, pinstriped vest and overused plantation tie, Mark Twain's mirror image opened the storm door. Though the cautious part of her remained on alert, her fear vanished.

"Ah, yes, Miss Ryleigh. We meet at last." Adoration spilled from the roadmap of his face. "I have anticipated your arrival for some time." Old, spotted hands engulfed hers, and his eyes shone with a keen, elderly reverence. He led her up three short stairs and across the spongy porch, but she hesitated to enter the house.

"Please do not be alarmed. If your mother were among the living, she would attest to the fact I bid you no harm." Dark, heavy pillows hung below the pallid blue eyes. Though arthritis twisted his hands and his teeth bore the yellow, uneven signs of age, a bushy white mustache cloaked a genuine, boyish grin.

"Ambrose, I assume?" She hesitated. Swallowing her apprehension, she took the last step into the house—surprised, yet pleased to discover her legs held firm. "You knew I was coming?"

"At your service, madame," he said, and to her befuddled surprise, he clamped one arm around his waist and bowed deeply. "For all intents and purposes, I am, indeed, the one called Ambrose. And though my eyes have paled and my ears have grown past my chin, little encroaches past me." A faint smile curled an abundant mustache and she saw both the whimsy and cleverness hidden in his eyes. "Knew you were coming before you knew it yourself."

She eyed him quizzically. "I'm sorry for my rudeness," she said with a wary smile, "but your resemblance to Samuel Clemens is uncanny."

"Ah, yes. So I have been told," he said with a chuckle. "And I cannot refrain from admiring you as well. Your mother warned me your pictures do not do you the justice you so deserve. And your father's stunning green eyes are most captivating on you," he added. "The color of the inside of an ocean wave, as Eleanor used to say." With a courteous nod, he closed the door behind them. A fire crackled in an antiquated cast iron woodstove, the room small but cozy and the faint redolence of old books a quiet comfort. "I told your mother the day you were born you would have his eyes."

"Please," he said and motioned for her to take a seat.

"You were there?"

"I was indeed." He sighed and settled himself into a worn recliner. "Ah, yes, I can see we have much to discuss." He peered at her above skimpy half-glasses, one eye lively, the other lazy and distant. "Your mother told you very little," he said and raked a gnarled hand through an abundant mustache.

"I never asked about the past." Ryleigh dipped her chin, eyes fixed on the floor. "I trusted there were things she didn't want to talk about or didn't think it important enough for me to know." She took a seat on an old sofa, obviously exquisite in a previous life. "I had my family and her. That's all I ever needed." She shrugged. "I think what little I did know was by accident, and when she died I discovered things."

"Your mother warned me of your voracious curiosity," he said through penetrating, benevolent eyes as strangely perceptive as an old seer's.

Her nerves quivered beneath her skin. "When?"

"Such things are neither here nor there," he said, waving off the question. "She simply could not reveal any more than she did, so I allowed you to find me. So I could."

"Reveal what?" She tilted her head at the curious stranger. "How'd you know I would come? And what do you mean you allowed me to find you? And who are you to my mother?"

Ambrose rose, limped to the window, and stared outside momentarily before answering. "I am Ben's—your father's—" he turned and said with a deliberate pause, "friend. However, I've known your mother for more than forty years and knew without a doubt you would come when you found the letter."

"Why didn't my mother ever tell me about you?"

His eyes sparkled. "Ah, yes," he said with a wink and pointed a knotted finger at her, "you are an inquisitive one, indeed."

"And what's your full name?" Ryleigh scooted to the edge of the sofa. "Why do you go only by part of your surname?"

"We need not rush." Ambrose's smile crinkled his eyes. "One question at a time, the last of which is quite an easy answer." He sighed. "It was my misfortune being christened Wilford Langhorne D'Ambrose." He grimaced. "Quite reprehensible, indeed. I dropped the first two names and dispensed with the futile 'D' and became simply Ambrose." He steadied himself against the windowsill. "For all intents and purposes."

"Why'd my mother never tell me about you?"

"You have an abundance of questions, Miss Ryleigh, and I have more answers than you are prepared for I am sure." Ambrose started toward the doorway and pulled a jacket from the brass coat rack in the corner. With a large quantity of upraised, wiry eyebrows, he nodded for her to follow. "Come. Join me in a walk. To the pond. A most appropriate setting to begin." Ambrose buttoned his jacket and took the steps off the porch one at a time, his limp pronounced in the cold air.

Hesitating only a moment in the wake of his unspoken command, she tightened her scarf and followed.

A path wound its way to the edge of a large pond. An enormous sugar maple hugged the edge, its girth easily that of several men and whose roots dove abruptly into the frozen water. Boulders staggered along the shore merged water and earth and last summer's cattails stood frozen in their upright stances.

Ambrose continued to the other side of the massive tree. "This way, Miss Ryleigh." He stopped and turned to her. "There. Do you see?"

She glanced around, puzzled. "The bench?"

"Your mother's bench."

To be excited over something so inanimate seemed curious. "Why show me this?" She shielded the sun from her eyes.

"Oh, the fireflies, of course."

"Fireflies?"

"You do not know about the fireflies?"

She shook her head.

"Come," he said, rubbing his right leg, "sit with me."

The bench was cast of wrought iron and intricately molded with dragonflies and weathered nearly white, the black iron luster deceased for years. Ambrose patted the seat. "It is not abundantly comfortable for brittle old bones, but when I brought it here," he said, tightening his collar and gazing thoughtfully across the pond, "your mother was younger than Evan is now. It served its purpose quite well."

The mention of her son startled her, but she assumed because he knew her mother (and her) surely he knew of Evan. She swallowed a growing list of questions. "What purpose?"

As if climbing from a distant memory, Ambrose turned to her. "Hundreds of fireflies frolicked about the pond that summer," he said, waving his hand over the expanse of frozen water. "She loved them so, and came every evening to sit and watch. To remember. To embrace your father again. To be alone with him in her dreams."

Ryleigh's hand shot into the air. "Hold it," she demanded. "She came here every evening? Where was my father? I thought they were together, passing through town when she went into labor." An indignant laugh escaped her. "You're mistaken."

"Ah, yes, indeed. It would seem so," he said, rubbing his leg. "You must remember above all things, your mother loved you beyond life itself. She would have used any means to protect you, shelter you, and give life to your desires."

"She proved it every day, but I didn't need anything but her love." Ryleigh swallowed back a lump that threatened to pull the plug on her emotions. "But I have so many questions," she said, her voice surprisingly steady.

"Before I reveal what you wish to know, and most certainly things you will wish you did not, you must promise me one thing."

"I don't make idle promises and I don't care for surprises," she replied, an unwanted edge of annoyance slipping into her words.

"Your reluctance is certainly understandable. However, you must listen carefully and make no judgments until my story is complete." Ambrose sighed deeply, his palms pressed to his thighs. "Life's earthquakes rattle our lives—sometimes they are mere tremors that moderately rock your world. Sometimes they split the earth beneath your feet and swallow you into hell. Then there are tornadoes—dust devils that stir the dirt a bit," he said, his hands twirling in the air, "then quickly die. But sometimes they pick you up, spin you around, and toss you to Oz. Life is not about how to survive, Miss Ryleigh—it is how you weather the storm and your actions in the wake of the aftermath," he said, eyes intent. "You must learn to dance in the rain."

Though skeptical, Ryleigh bit her lip to control a rudimentary response.

"Do I have your promise?"

She nodded once.

"Excellent," he said rising with a firm grip on the bench. "We must return to the house. The colder the days grow, the deeper the ache settles in these disintegrating old bones."

"Please." Ryleigh stood. "Can you tell me about the fireflies? Here, by the pond?"

Ambrose smiled broadly, easing himself back to the bench. "If we do so, we will have circumvented a good portion of the story."

"You can fill in the details later."

"Ah, yes. Many details, indeed."

Ryleigh studied him carefully. "Go on."

"Your mother was with child when I took her in." Ambrose grimaced, a deep furrow appearing between tangled eyebrows, wiry silver hairs nearly meeting in the middle. "What do you recall of the Vietnam War?"

Ryleigh shrugged, wondering what this had to do with fireflies, or anything for that matter. "Only what I learned in school. Why?"

"Your mother and I did not learn about the war from a textbook. Our generation lived it. Your mother—a civilian—remained on the home front, but your father served, as did his best friend, Ryan. I believe you have an old photograph of the two?"

She leaned forward. "How'd you know about that?" she asked, her brow bunched. "The other guy—he was my father's friend?"

"Inseparable. And I shall answer all your questions," he said with a deliberate pause, "in good time."

Familiar with the bond of friendship he spoke of, her heart swelled. The desire to connect with her father's friend stirred her interest even more and she so hoped he'd share his memories from a past she never bothered to ask about, and her mother never offered to share.

"Continue, Ambrose. Please?"

He drew in a deep breath. "When the boys turned eighteen, they enlisted in the Army—the buddy system—in the summer of '66. Both were sent to Vietnam. 101st Airborne Division. 327th Infantry. So proud to serve their country." Ambrose sat straighter, his chest puffing slightly. "Do you recall after 9-11 so many souls enlisted to help defend our freedom and the freedom of others?"

Her chin dipped and she nodded. "Vividly."

"The same was true of Vietnam." Ambrose shook his head. "The objective of the Vietnam War was to rid the country of communism. The media distorted the truth and italicized the atrocities," he said, a solemn severity in his voice, "and not far into the campaign the cards turned and Vietnam became a most unpopular war. Yes, indeed," he whispered. "Freedom is never given freely, but our soldiers came home to jeers instead of cheers." He inhaled and let the breath out slowly. "I beg your forgiveness. I become a bit impassioned when I speak of Vietnam. Or the War on Terror. I have an appreciable respect for those who serve our country." Ambrose rubbed his hand over his face as if to wipe away the memory.

Ryleigh allowed a pause to rebalance the disquiet. "No apology necessary."

Ambrose cleared his throat. "They left for war in January of 1967. How those boys remained together is quite the mystery. Same division, platoon, shared the same missions. In February, they received word Eleanor was going to have a baby. In the sixties, a pregnant unmarried young lady carried the weight of a considerable stigma. Eleanor came from a prominent family, and when her father learned she was with child, he legally disowned her. A travesty. I had the unfortunate task of reviewing the papers with her."

"You're an attorney?"

"Once upon a time." He waved a hand in dismissal. "Her family's reaction devastated her. This is when I stepped in, quite unannounced, but welcomed nonetheless." Ambrose smiled distantly. "Ah, yes, she told me stories of how the three of them watched the fireflies that summer in St. Louis before the boys left for war and when the fireflies appeared here that summer, their presence helped her through the isolation and loneliness."

Vivid pictures formed in her mind. She clutched her scarf, but made no attempt to tighten it. Instead, she dug the toe of her Asics in the frozen ground, and a smile drifted across her face.

"The fireflies raised her spirits. She named the pond for the fireflies, you know," he added with a breathy chuckle.

"Firefly Pond?"

He nodded. "Ah, yes, indeed. It seemed silly, but it made her happy. So many years ago it was." The old man stared blankly as if in recollection. "She spread a blanket every evening and sat by the pond's edge waiting for the fireflies to emerge. As you grew inside her, she found it difficult to rise and it was then I gave her the bench." He leaned back, stroking his bushy mustache. "A unique summer it was. The fireflies remained into September. Never had before or any summer since. There is no doubt they returned each summer night for your mother."

"Fireflies aren't around all summer?"

"No more than a month. Two at best." He shrugged. "That summer was magical."

"Touching story."

"Trust me, Miss Ryleigh, this story is far from over."

Her eyes met the penetrating blue of his, ones that somehow knew her. "I do trust you, Ambrose."

He nodded courteously. "I am, indeed, honored."

"Please finish."

"As you wish," he said, and cinched his coat tighter around him. "Our paths were meant to cross, but I was none too pleased about harboring a visitor, especially a pregnant one." His smile broadened as he took a deep breath. "But it was not long before I too fell in love with her."

Ryleigh shot him an accusatory look.

He laughed openly. "I loved her for her elegance, her grace, and undeniable courage. Quiet and smart. And she loved you so from the moment you were conceived." His face softened as he spoke of her.

"She stayed with me until you were four months of age and Ben returned from Vietnam. He took you in his arms and you were his baby girl, without a doubt."

"Four months?" she asked, every pore screaming in protest at the divergence of what she knew as truth.

"Yes, indeed."

"That means—"

"It simply means your father took you in his arms for the first time when you were four months old."

She leaned into the bench. "I don't remember much, but that's one thing I do remember, Ambrose—I would crawl into his lap and he'd hold me close and read to me."

"He did, indeed."

"Why didn't you keep in touch?"

"That is neither here nor there and is quite another story. I remain, as always, under the radar, so to speak. I am highly proficient at what I do. Stealth in its purest form." He twisted one side of his profuse mustache, and then the other. "You failed to see me at the Inn."

She considered the statement. "That was you behind the newspaper in the breakfast room?"

"Ah, yes. But did you *see* me?"

"I guess I didn't actually see anyone."

"Indeed."

Ryleigh regarded him quizzically. He raised one bushy eyebrow in response, as if anticipating the question. "And you knew Mom passed?"

Ambrose nodded.

"How?"

"It matters not. As I have said before, little gets by me that I care to know about."

"This is incredibly…weird," Ryleigh said under her breath.

"This story will become much more incredible as it unfolds, Miss Ryleigh. Now, we must return to the house. It is cold and these old bones ache dreadfully." Wincing, he rubbed his leg vigorously. Steadying both hands on his thighs, he boosted himself up.

Shadows hugged the woods, a jagged silhouette against the deepening hues of winter's watered-down blue sky. Ambrose led the way along the path, his breaths coming in shaggy spurts to match his labored steps.

Ryleigh cinched her scarf a little tighter, unsure whether to cling to the temptation of knowing, or run from the fear that the past may devour more than it had already.

Chapter Fifteen

RYLEIGH FOLLOWED THE white-haired man, his steps deliberate, bracing his hand against a thigh as if doing so would ease the pain.

She tucked her mouth inward and looked away. "Forgive me for keeping you so long by the pond. I didn't realize you were in so much pain."

Ambrose shifted his weight to his good leg and waved for her to go ahead into the house. "Ah, yes, you have your mother's compassion."

"No," she said, awakening the guilt at her reluctance to see her mother in her final days.

"Your words speak the contrary," he said, pitching his jacket on the rack. "The pain will ease a bit with warmth." He shook his head and sighed. "Do not worry."

With a knotted finger, Ambrose released the top button of his collar, pulled at his tie, and eased himself into the recliner. Broad but thin, his weary shoulders relaxed, as did the deeply cut lines of his face as he closed his eyes.

Ryleigh unwound her scarf, pulled the hoodie over her head, and clasped her hands loosely in front of her. "Is there anything I can do to help?"

"Acting as hostess in a stranger's home. Indeed. Allow me a few minutes to warm up. We have only skimmed the surface and have miles of tales to tell."

Ryleigh eyed him curiously, quite sure skimming was far less dangerous than digging a trench you could fall into. "I'm pretty handy in the kitchen. Let me fix you something—a sandwich or coffee—while you warm up, if you'll allow me to rummage through your kitchen."

"Insistent. As was your father." He chuckled. "Stubborn, if I am to be honest."

"My father was stubborn?" Ryleigh's gaze fell to her clasped hands. "But I wouldn't know that, would I?"

"Indeed."

"I was only four when he died."

"Ah, yes. You were very young, indeed. And yes, he was quite stubborn. When a notion popped into that boy's head rarely did he hesitate. Simply took off running." Ambrose laughed aloud, a twinkle accompanying the sound. "A wild, benevolent dreamer. Wanted to write songs." He grimaced. "The afternoon has faded and I have been a most unaccommodating host. You must be famished. I think food is a marvelous idea, Miss Ryleigh. Please, make yourself at home." Ambrose waved a twisted hand toward the kitchen.

"Okay, then," she said, clapping her hands together. "Let's see what I can find."

The kitchen adjoined the living room, and upon entering, Ryleigh swept her hand along a perfectly groomed counter. She gathered her bearings and spun in a slow pirouette. She spotted a coffee maker and started a fresh pot, the filter and gourmet coffee stored conveniently next to the appliance. With plenty of lettuce, tomatoes and freshly sliced turkey she dug from the fridge, she built a fair representation of two turkey club sandwiches. She sprinkled her own blend of spices into the mayo and called it good. When the coffee pot sputtered, she poured two mugs, choosing the chipped one for herself, set the sandwiches and mugs on a china tray she found in the dish drainer and returned to the living room.

Ambrose had fallen asleep. The highway of lines defining his face had eased under the frowsy mop of white hair and repose of sleep, the roadmap whose destination and origin remained a mystery. She smiled uneasily, unsure whether either would ever be revealed.

The plate clinked when she set it down and the old man's eyes twitched under paper-thin lids. She borrowed a fleece throw from the sofa to cover him, but his thin frame caused her to hesitate. His body, taller in stature than she realized, was nothing more than a boulevard of blue veins beneath a sheath of pale skin stretched over a thin frame. With the care she'd used so many times with her mother, she covered the gaunt frame.

She stepped back and glanced around. Many of his possessions—modest by today's standards—were but a snapshot of a former life; it was quite obvious he'd once been a wealthy man.

Pitch sizzled in the woodstove and the spicy scent mingled with the musty bouquet of old paper and ink. An entire wall was devoted to books—Dickens, Crane, Dostoevsky, Steinbeck, and Hemingway paraded across the shelves. Raised gold letters of *Gone with the Wind* gleamed in the dim light and she couldn't resist pulling it from its niche. The binding crackled as she opened the cover to an inscription and a hand-torn paper heart. She looked away as if she'd happened upon something intimately private, closed the book and returned it to the shelf. She glanced at her peculiar host. Ambrose remained undisturbed.

Unlike her collection of books where mismatched paperbacks mingled with worn hardcovers, these books were masculine, bold, and quite old. Ryleigh dragged a hand along the spines of timeless best sellers and massive sets of leather-bound law books. They stood erect, a line of timeless soldiers, and she felt the image of the man mirrored in them—old and oddly comforting, yet unique and curiously disconcerting, each with its own story crying out from within their covers.

Careful not to wake Ambrose, Ryleigh took her mug from the coffee table and sipped the cooling liquid as she stepped to the window—the afternoon sun a pink tinge across the meadow. Lacing her fingers, she tapped a finger against the rim as she thought of the light fading from pink to orange to rust. Evening came early in winter and would plunge the meadow into hues of purple, the only light a three-quarter moon in a brooding New York sky. A pang of uneasiness crawled through her belly at the thought of returning through the tunnel of trees. Sitting comfortably safe at home reading a Stephen King novel was one thing; living it with a strange man in an eerie forest that seemed to rise from the pages of *The Lord of the Rings* was entirely another. She sat, crossed her legs and pushed aside thoughts of Black Riders and a magic ring with which to disappear.

With an exaggerated stretch, Ambrose woke. "I see you have managed in the kitchen."

She turned to face him. "I did, but the coffee has cooled. Can I warm it for you?"

"Ah, yes, most appreciated." The old man spilled two pills into his palm and raised the mug of cold coffee in a mock salute. "The intelligent thing would have been to take the pain pills before I slept." He returned the mug to the table. "You must excuse my despicable manners and accept my sincere thanks. Many days have passed since anyone has graced this house to share in conversation or the simplest of chores."

Megan. "Really?"

"Ah, yes. I presume you are thinking of Megan?"

Averting the obvious surprise that widened her eyes, Ryleigh said nothing.

"Megan," Ambrose chuckled, the sound deep and unassuming, "is an exceptionally bright young woman. Spunky little thing, actually. She will make an excellent attorney someday."

Ryleigh had no intention of reneging on her promise. "Who's Megan?" she asked, picking at a shoelace.

"My dear Miss Ryleigh." He removed his glasses and looked down a long, crooked nose at her. "I have no need for pretense. Little that concerns me remains unknown because it is I who allows it. You needed Megan. Megan confessed her secrets. The dribble of facts Evan discovered on the Internet—it was I who made it possible. The letter in the desk?" Ryleigh's head jerked up. "Strategically placed. My life is a puppet show and I the puppet master. I alone control the strings. The time had come for us to meet." Puffy pillows of skin underscored an intent steel-blue gaze. Ambrose lifted an unruly set of robust eyebrows and raised his mug in salute. "And here you are."

Ryleigh's face was obscured in vacillation. "Who are you?"

Chapter Sixteen

CHANDLER PULLED UNDER the arches of Il Salotto's entrance, the smoky growl from the diesel engine echoing off the stone pillars. Two years ago he'd spent months on the remodel and yesterday Mitch's message had urged him to stop by concerning another project. The thought of more work on top of the spec home didn't pique his interest, but Mitch's messages weren't to be ignored—if he had any sense at all. Lengthening his stride, he plowed a hand through his hair and entered the spa.

Expansive glass doors opened to quaint Tuscan architecture. Life-sized photos of the hillside vineyards of Tuscany, the enchanting Amalfi Coast with its red-capped roofs and the romantic fishing village of Marina Grande near Sorrento graced the walls.

Chandler approached the front desk.

"Hey, Mr. Collins," Hillari chimed from the check-in counter. "Good to see you. It's been awhile."

"I guess it has been awhile." He glanced around at the changes the Burstyns had made since he'd last been here and chuckled at the obvious signs of Christmas. Unseasonably warm for December he'd forgotten the season. "Nat's been at it, I see."

Hillari leaned over the counter, craned her neck and peered down both halls like someone itching to tell a juicy tidbit of gossip, but afraid of being caught. "She's a bit anal about holiday decorating," she whispered.

Chandler leaned forward. "I see what you mean," he whispered back.

She pointed to a decorative tray of Italian bread, dried figs, candied almonds, and marzipan fruit. "Grab a slice of authentic Italian panettone." A steaming urn of cappuccino stood next to the tray. "My idea," she said, waggling dark eyebrows.

Chandler smiled. "And the art?"

"Yep." She beamed. "My idea too." The statuesque blonde flipped her hair over her shoulder. "They're Mitch's photos from Italy two summers ago. He's got a great eye."

Chandler chuckled at the bubbly young woman. "Keep up the good work."

"I plan on it, Mr. Collins. Mitch and Nat are expecting you in the back office."

He took two steps backward, tipped his ball cap, and took off at a steady clip down the north hall.

Massive double doors stood ajar, the office boasting the same Tuscan feel. Mitch stood staring at a computer screen with his hands plastered on his hips, suit coat open. Nat stood next to him in a sleek white tank top and black workout leggings that hugged perfectly toned legs, hands resting loosely on her hips.

Chandler knocked lightly.

They turned in unison, Mitch motioning for him to enter. "Come in and have a seat." He and Natalie took a seat at the conference table, a set of blueprints curled across the top. "We're glad you came."

Chandler sat opposite the couple, set his elbows on the table and clasped his hands. "What's up?"

"We wanted you to look at a new project we've got coming up," Mitch said. "It's a big one, but we know you can handle it."

Chandler pushed his hair from his forehead and frowned. "The setbacks on this property won't allow for another addition."

"It's not an addition." The couple smiled at each other. "It's much bigger."

He looked first at Mitch and then to Natalie, calculating the implications. Framing of the Juniper Ridge house was already penciled in. "How big are you talking?"

Mitch nodded at his wife to continue. "We're expanding— starting another spa. We purchased a building in Scottsdale and we want you to handle the conversion."

"Scottsdale?"

"It's a great opportunity." Mitch unfurled the blueprints. "We heard Della has her house for sale and is relocating. You'll be close to the baby. And Evan's in the Valley."

"You don't have to decide right now." Natalie slid the blueprints toward him.

"We also want you to reinvest in the company. The timing's excellent," Mitch said.

Chandler leaned back. "I don't have a penny for investments," he said, wiping a hand over a few days' growth of beard. "I gave Ryleigh everything."

"We know about that." Natalie's face dropped. "We have a suggestion." She squirmed. "Part of your salary would buy into the company."

Chandler threw his hands up. "I'm barely scraping by and you want me to take partial payment in stock? Besides, I haven't done anything commercial in years." He rose to leave.

"Take the plans, Chandler," Mitch said, the acidity in his tone duplicating the aversion in his tightly clenched jaw. "Look them over. The money's good and we need you to do the work. This fishbowl is populated with shitty contractors and at least we'll know it's done right."

Chandler sat, but studied the plans with little enthusiasm.

Natalie leaned across the table. "We need you to take this job."

"Do you want me out of town that badly?"

Natalie's eyes narrowed. "I can't say I don't want you to rot in hell for what you put Ryleigh through and I'd just as soon slap you as look at you. But that's not what this is about. You're the best contractor for the job. Period. And whether I like it or not, your baby is going to need you. We thought—"

Chandler shot to his feet. "Stop." He gripped the back of the chair, balking at the urge to fling it across the room. "There is no baby."

Mitch broke an awkward silence. "What happened?"

Natalie grabbed Mitch's hand and squeezed. "She didn't do something stupid, did she?"

Chandler thrust his hands on his hips and paced the room. He turned to face them, and then looked away. He couldn't stand the indignant stares that mimicked the turmoil bubbling inside him. "She made the whole thing up and I was stupid enough to fall for it," he continued, stuffing his hands in his jeans pockets. "I had no intention of marrying her but I wanted to be a father to our baby."

Mitch slammed his fist on the table. "Unscrupulous bitch."

"My sentiments exactly." Anger flushed Natalie's face. "I didn't think anyone stooped to that trick anymore. It's an unnecessary, evil thing to do." She placed her hand on Chandler's arm, the angry lines softening. "You're human, Chandler. The Dellas of the world are not easy women to resist for anyone with an XY chromosome," she said, and shot Mitch an *I dare you glare*.

"There's no excuse for what I did. Baby or not."

"Oh, I don't condone your actions. Not for one minute."

Chandler raked a hand through his hair. "I have to make it up to Ryleigh. I have to fix this."

"Oh, God." Natalie's shoulders collapsed. "I've known her a long time, Chandler. She's moving on and you should too."

The words seared across his heart. He preferred not to think about it, allowing the days to pile up and avoid the truth of what he'd done. Chandler shook his head. "I won't believe it until she tells me herself."

"Take the job," Mitch interjected. "It'll be worth it."

"I'll think about it," he replied, rolling the plans tightly, "but I can't start right away, I've got a house to build." Tucking the blueprints under his arm, he started for the door.

"That works," Mitch said. "Perfectly, in fact. Construction won't start for a while—summer probably." He and Natalie stood to see him out. "Where's this house you're building and who's it for? Anyone we know?"

He looked first to Mitch and then to Natalie. "Juniper Ridge Road."

Natalie's mouth fell open and she glowered at her husband. "Mitch?"

"I know. Shit."

"Chandler?"

Chandler had crossed the room and was turning down the hall when he heard Natalie call after him, but had no intention of answering. No intention of explaining. He had his reasons. And a plan.

Chapter Seventeen

"**Who am I?**" Ambrose sipped his coffee, steam rising in swirls over an abundant mustache. "Ah, yes, I ponder that question myself," he said with a chuckle. "I am who I need to be at any given time. Today," he said, taking another sip, "my story is yours—an ambiguous one. Remove your shoes, Miss Ryleigh. Get comfortable. This story is not a comfortable one, but you might as well be."

Ambrose rose from his chair, the kinks releasing in pops and cracks. He paced. Years of a continuous back and forth shuffle had worn a faded path across an already threadbare carpet. "I shall start from the beginning, some of which you already know."

Ryleigh kicked off her shoes and curled her legs under her. "I'm ready."

Ambrose twirled the generous tendrils of his mustache. "This will not be easy for you to hear, Miss Ryleigh. Do you remember earlier when I spoke of storms crossing your path?"

"Yes." Riddles were tricky and she placed them on her mental list of aversions one notch below surprises. "Earthquakes and tornadoes." Ryleigh visibly relaxed, allowing her doubts to settle in his trust.

"Ah, yes. This will be one of those earthquakes that will split the earth beneath your feet. Be strong, Miss Ryleigh." He bunched his hands into knotted fists. "You are your mother's daughter and of your father's loins. However," he said with a deliberate pause, "before I continue, this old man must get some air and stretch his legs before he tells an old story that has been preserved." He pointed a crooked finger to his temple and said, "The truth unchanged as there have been no storytellers but I. It will be told as it occurred forty-four years ago."

Reservation crept into her thoughts as Ambrose massaged his leg, short steps obviously branded with pain.

"I shall not be long."

Ambrose threw a knee-length black coat over wide slumped shoulders and removed a walking stick from a peg by the door. As gnarled and twisted as the fingers that gripped it, the carved haft and mahogany and maple staff was as weathered as the man it bore. Exquisitely honed, it was another testament to the man's prior status. "I'll freshen the coffee," she said.

The lines of his face deepened with each step, etched as much from the pain as from the unforgiving years that preceded him. Deterioration into pain was no stranger to her, having watched a silent thief destroy her mother day by day. She identified with the pain—not the physical kind—but the kind that pierced the heart. The kind that steals your air. Like drowning. Though she barely knew him, her heart ached with each step the old man took, each one a promise of the wisdom of time passed beneath his feet. How old? She could only guess: as ancient as an eighteenth-century gentleman if she were to guess by the formality of his speech, as seasoned as a riverboat captain by his whimsical attire, yet as youthful as the twinkle in kind, blue eyes.

The storm door groaned and the faint tap of the walking stick mingled with the cold night air. Ryleigh paused at the window surprised to see the shades of evening had slipped into the deep purple of night and if not for the three-quarter moon's silver spotlight across the pond, the meadow would have been a canvas of black.

The silhouette of the bent figure's silver-white hair gleamed in the moonlight, his staff by his side. Ambrose raised and then slowly lowered the staff. A flicker of light died in the distance and the right side of an overactive brain kicked into overdrive. *Gandalf.* The subdued, introspective wizard sprang from the pages of *The Lord of the Rings* and into her head. Her fingers gripped the window frame, but nothing moved but a wisp of his breath. If not for the peculiar old man's trustworthy, quiet nature, he and this place would give her the creeps. Ryleigh rubbed the gooseflesh from her arms and stepped away, content to put the misguided images to rest. For now.

Ambrose had warned her it would be a long night. Her nerves begged for caffeine, and she headed to the kitchen. While the coffeepot gurgled, she sent a short text to Evan that things were going well and she'd call him later. He answered quickly, and she wondered if his phone was permanently glued to his thumbs. She threw him a cyber-kiss and dialed Natalie.

Nat picked up on the first ring. "It's about time. Well?"

"It's going okay, but it's kind of creepy here. Especially since the sun went down and it's dark. Ambrose is, well, I don't know exactly how to describe him."

"You're a writer. Take a stab at it."

"He's a bit…eccentric." She shrugged. "And he resembles Samuel Clemens."

"Who?"

Ryleigh smiled into the phone. "Mark Twain, silly. You know, *Tom Sawyer* and *Huckleberry Finn?*"

"Oh. But I can't say I know what he looks like."

"Look him up on the Internet," she said, twirling her hair around her index finger. "The resemblance is uncanny."

"So, has he told you anything good?"

"My mother was pregnant before her and Daddy got married. Quite the scandal back then."

"Wouldn't make much of a splash in today's world, would it?"

"No." Ryleigh rubbed her arm. "Had that scenario play out in my living room. But I guess it wasn't as common in the sixties. Nat, I need to go. The coffee's done and Ambrose will be back soon."

"He left you alone?"

"He went for a walk. To stretch. He's pretty crippled up. I'll call you when I get back to the Inn if it's not too late."

"It won't be late in Arizona. Call me."

The coffee finished with a sputter. Ambrose returned, rusty hinges protesting his entry, and stepped gingerly inside. Ryleigh filled their mugs with fresh coffee.

"Good timing," she said. "Coffee's done. I'm a coffee junkie, but I prefer it sweetened."

Ambrose dipped his head. "Ah, yes, Miss Ryleigh." He hung his coat and returned the staff to the corner. "A steaming cup of coffee to soothe one's soul on a chilly night." Though he smiled, pain pierced his steely eyes. "Unfortunately, I do not keep the ingredients to make the caramel lattes you so enjoy," he replied with a wink. "I trust your son and dearest friend are well tonight?"

She sputtered, and the sting of hot liquid shot through her sinuses. "How'd you know I spoke to Evan and Natalie?" She wiped her chin with a finger. "And that I enjoy caramel lattes?"

"It is my business to know."

"You must have a connection to every phone in the country and every link on the Internet. What's your story?"

"My network," he said, air quoting the words, "is, indeed, extensive. However, that is neither here nor there. It pleases me they are concerned. However, you are never more protected than when you are with me. Come. We have many mysteries to explore."

Ryleigh threw him a disconcerted look and brushed past. "You become more complex with every tick of the clock. You're a parallel to Gandalf and Asimov and Dumbledore rolled into one," she said, sinking into the cushions of the sofa.

"Your imagination is unequivocal," he mused as he sat opposite her. "I'm afraid the confusion you feel right now cannot be helped. However, this is not about me. This is your story." Ambrose stroked his substantial mustache several times, twisting the bristly ends. "I think we shall back up and fill in a few blanks. Shall I continue?"

"Please," she said and drew her knees to her chest.

He smiled. "You know, of course, your mother was raised in St. Louis?"

"I do," she said, "but she never told me anything significant about her childhood or spoke of my grandparents." She frowned. "She said they died before I was born, so I never pursued it. Is this true?"

"Partly. Your grandparents did not pass until several years after you were born."

Ryleigh's mouth flew open, and Ambrose immediately raised a hand. Bushy eyebrows quirked up. "A seed planted requires patience in its nurture."

Ryleigh closed her mouth in answer to his ardent stare.

"Eleanor attended private school. The civil rights movement was at its pinnacle, the Vietnam War escalating, and racial turmoil caused tremendous unrest and bitter rivalries among schools. The sixties," Ambrose said, shaking his head, "turbulent times, indeed.

"Ben first saw your mother in the spring of nineteen sixty-six. Eleanor tagged along when her friends left their school dance to create a little mayhem at a rival school. Ben's school. Tempers flared, and when they decided to kick some ass—pardon my language," he said, peering down his crooked nose, "Eleanor put herself between Ben and another boy most anxious for a fight. A brawl was averted, in part to Eleanor butting in, but mostly due to the arrival of the police. Ben was smitten. Before they parted, your mother slipped him her phone number. A few days later, he introduced her to Ryan and rarely were the three seen apart after that night. Ben told Ryan quite frankly he would marry her some day."

The absence of a past tugged at her heart and the void these few words filled clogged her throat with renewed emotion. Why had she been so stubborn and not asked her mother about this? "She never told me any of this."

"She would not have done so."

"But why?"

"Eleanor was severely private and mindlessly compassionate— and she loved Ben with all her heart," he said, raising a distorted fist over his heart. "And she wanted to protect you most of all."

Ryleigh circled her finger around the rim of the mug, avoiding the small rough chip and tried to imagine her parents so young, falling in love. The image it summoned was heartwarming. A blush warmed her cheeks. Raising her eyes to meet his, she urged him to continue.

Ambrose rose and positioned himself beside her. "To your mother," he said, raising his mug. Their mugs kissed with a clink. The old man's brow furrowed. Blue eyes bored into her with an intensity that unnerved her. She dropped her gaze. "You must remember. He paused to take a deep breath. "Life throws unforeseen storms in your path when least expected."

"I understand. But so far it hasn't been so hard to digest."

Ambrose adjusted his leg. "The boys enlisted in the Army that summer. The 101st Airborne was an elite group of ground troops, transported by helicopter. It was a bloody war; conditions were atrocious. Regrettably, thousands perished. Nothing in your history books can epitomize the horror." Emotion rose in Ambrose's eyes. "I could elaborate further, but I shall not bore you."

"You tell the story as if you were there."

"A cripple on a battlefield is another casualty waiting to happen."

She could sense the discontent. "I'm sorry."

"Do not be sorry. Our lives unfold the way they are destined. I believe we follow a predetermined path. The one you travel today. Your destiny. Your path."

"My mother's path. Her story."

"Yes and no," he said, his head bobbing from one side to the other. "Your mother so loved Ben, truly and with all her heart.

Remember this above all else." His face went solemn, yet his steel-blue eyes pierced hers. "She never meant to hurt him."

She held his steady gaze. "What do you mean she never meant to hurt him?"

"My words have no other meaning."

Despite the warmth from the wood stove, a cold finger of dread slid down her spine. She took a sip of coffee to wet the sudden dryness in her throat, and then set the mug down. Mysteries lurked in his gaze—dark ones he wouldn't give up, and ones she sensed were leading down a path she didn't want to go. She clasped her arms around her legs, resting her head on her knees, and gave no mercy to a loose thread on the sofa.

"You need to know your story."

Ryleigh bit her lip and nodded.

"After Ben died it became easier to bury the past than to relive it. As time passed, Eleanor lived solely for the present, unwilling to disturb ghosts long buried. I did what I did for your mother and for Ben because of his abiding love for her. I agreed to honor her secrets, but I vowed I would not lie to you if confronted." An awkward moment passed. "It is, indeed, time you know the truth." He spoke calmly and took her hand in both of his. "That is why," he paused, gently lifting her chin, "when Eleanor fell head over heels in love with Ben's best friend, she kept it to herself. She cared for Ben deeply, but she had fallen deeply and irreparably in love with Ryan, the boy with eyes the color of the inside of an ocean wave."

She hurled him a vicious look. Green eyes met steel in reckless hesitation, and his eyes held hers as tightly as he did her hand.

"Your eyes, Miss Ryleigh."

Chapter Eighteen

THE WORDS SETTLED in Ryleigh's stomach like a brick of curdled muck. She jerked her hands free. Ambrose fell silent, the ghost of his laugh erased with the caustic words.

She seized and held his unsettled gaze. Gone was the whimsical riverboat captain and in his place was an old man who had delivered a sickening blow—not with his aged body, but with something more powerful—his words. She hugged herself, squeezing the air from her lungs. A clock chimed, the din a hazy cloud of confusion, unbearable hurt and unanswered questions.

Ripples of disbelief erupted and spread, the way rings radiate from the center when a stone is tossed into calm water. Silence magnetized the air. Background noise ceased. Only the pain of uninvited doubt pulsed in her ears.

"I don't believe you."

"This is not the end of this story."

Ryleigh leapt to her feet. "Yes, it is."

Ambrose stood. "Sit down!" The challenge sizzled with an air of command. "You shall not run from that which you fear."

She turned sharply to face him. "I'm not afraid."

"Our lives are weighted by fear," he said severely and raised a fist. "If you are not afraid, you do not live."

Ryleigh digested his words, raised her chin and reined in the unnamed emotion trembling on the edge of her eye.

"Gather the courage that runs through your veins. You shall hear this story to the end." Deep lines creased his brow. Cheekbones, high and hollowed by age, jutted below narrowed eyes. "You will not run!"

As though his words possessed the authority to overpower her will to run, he compelled her to stay. She hesitated, taking in every detail of his face. The words soured her mouth like poisoned spit. Her legs trembled, ready to flee, but she found nothing but truth written in his expression, nothing but sincerity behind eyes that had smiled at her a short time ago. Her knees buckled and she fell into the cushions. She took hold of her thoughts and met his eyes.

"Shall I continue?"

"Go on." The words echoed from somewhere deep in the hollow cavern where her heart resided.

Ambrose sat and continued in a more civilized voice. "After completing boot camp, they returned home to spend time with their families before being shipped off to war. Christmas of sixty-six. Eleanor and Ryan spent every waking hour together. Shortly after New Year's Day of sixty-seven Ryan and Ben left for Vietnam."

Undone with emotion she couldn't label or contain, Ryleigh wiped a tear with the back of her hand.

"The boys wrote of the splendors of a foreign country and nightmares of a bloody war. Ryan's letters were filled with his love for her and the horrors surrounding him, expressive and graphic. Your mother cherished them. And when she wrote she was carrying his child, Ryan celebrated amongst tracers and spatter of gunfire, and a deluge of rain."

Disbelief rocked the foundation of her core, the ache profound. This wasn't her story, this was fiction. Everything was twisted and wrong. Anger surged through her veins, hot and liquid. She raised her chin, swallowed the anger and met steel-blue eyes. "Ben was my father."

"Beyond any doubt. He is, indeed, the only father you have ever known."

With great effort, Ambrose lifted himself from the sofa and handed Ryleigh a tissue. She dabbed her eyes. The groan of the woodstove door split the awkward pause, and Ambrose slid a log into the yawning cavern, pitch hissing as it met the flames and sent a wave of crackling sparks up the pipe.

Ryleigh watched his calculated movements carefully. "Earlier, you spoke of Ben as my father, and Mom—why didn't she tell me? God, I wish she were still alive." Her hands bunched into angry fists. "I want to shake the truth out of her."

"You are undoubtedly hurt and quite angry. Remember your mother as the extraordinary woman she was and I must emphasize she loved you more than life. And she loved your father—Ryan— with everything in her. But time would become her adversary."

She pressed her palms against her temples. "God, this gets more complicated every time you open your mouth."

"The story is quite simple, Miss Ryleigh," he said, taking a seat beside her. "The imprudent decisions of our lives never go away. They simply add up," he said, strumming his fingers across his knees. "The passing of time complicates matters."

"Stop saying that," she said and jumped to her feet. "This is far from simple. This is my life you're talking about. My life, Ambrose. Me!" She poked a finger at her chest.

"It is simply a portion your mother never shared. She wished to protect you and shield herself from a personal anguish too painful to bear. You are the person you are because of your past and you cannot expect the truth not to exist simply by ignoring it."

His words hit her full force.

"How you choose to embrace this will be the difference. You must dance in the rain—as your father did." Ambrose shook his head emphatically. "Never forget. Not ever."

The compulsion to run crippled any thought of a plausible way to connect the dots of a disconcerting story. Anguish leaked from her eyes, and dread boiled in her belly. She turned away.

"Do you wish for me to continue? The rest can wait if this is what you truly desire."

"No. Yes. I don't know—I don't know if I can hear any more." Her voice rose. "You've shattered everything I believed about my family and dishonored my father's memory."

"I beg to differ."

"How?"

"Ben was the constant, true to his word. He loved your mother more than anyone could possibly love another. I believe more completely than Ryan ever could."

"But she chose Ryan—" Realization hit her squarely as if someone had thrown a brick through her thoughts. She spun around and glowered at him. "The 'R' in the journal. It stands for Ryan, doesn't it?"

"Indeed."

"Where is he?"

"In due time."

"Now! Tell me about the journal."

"If I skip more of the story, we will be swinging back and forth like a pendulum. This story deserves to be told from beginning to end, page by page as it was written."

Ryleigh sank into the cushions, pulled a fleece blanket over herself, and dislodged the urge to fold it over her head and disappear. Bunched into a ball, she wrapped her arms around her knees and braced for more of the clandestine story she didn't know if she truly wanted to hear.

"Before I begin, shall we refresh our coffee? Mine has gone quite cold."

And my heart.

"However," he said rising cautiously, "I do believe a bit of the Godiva liqueur is called for. Mocha. I shall add a splash. Warms from inside out and is quite soothing, like whiskey for a teething baby."

Ambrose returned, the aroma of chocolate rising with the steam from the mugs. He sipped the hot liquid. "Ah, yes. Most delightful. I have a bit of a passion for chocolate. As did your mother."

Ryleigh took the mug in both hands but remained quiet, her mother's fondness for chocolate one of the more trivial things she did know. She took a sip and swallowed, the liquor stout and soothing. The sudden warmth bathed her in artificial courage from fingertip to toe.

Ambrose cleared his throat. "When Ryan and Eleanor began seeing each other Ben never admitted how much he loved her alleging it was merely a passing infatuation. But Ryan suspected. Ah, yes, he knew. In the jungles of Vietnam, Ben would read Eleanor's letters aloud, but Ryan never reciprocated. He knew it would hurt Ben to hear the things Eleanor said to him." He stared at something beyond her, the ghosts of the past rising to meet his gaze. "He called her Ellie, you know." A glimmer of the boy masked behind watery eyes glinted at her. "Ryan was the only one allowed to do so and still own their tongue."

"Mom always went by her given name."

"Indeed," he replied. "I learned the hard way."

"You called her Ellie?"

"Ah, yes. Once." He rubbed his forehead. "The only time I did so."

A hint of a smile rounded one corner of Ryleigh's mouth. *Served him right.*

"Ryan wrote of the horrors of war, the land and people, bugs, disease—even fear and death. Exquisite prose."

"You read the letters?"

"Your mother shared portions. Others were too intimate."

Ryleigh lowered her head and twisted a strand of hair around her finger. It was impossible to picture her mother with anyone other than her father.

"Letters arrived sparsely, the wait excruciating. Eleanor marked the days and saved green M&M's," he said with a lazy smile.

Ryleigh's eyes grew wide. "She never ate the green ones. Ever."

"Indeed."

"All those years. They were for Ryan."

Night chiseled away the hours and though the room was bathed in warmth, a chill raced down her arms.

Ambrose squirmed, the lines of his face deepening.

She wiped her nose with the damp tissue. "I have to go," she said, her voice clogged with emotion.

"There remains much to tell."

She stood. "Not tonight." Although the impulse to flee was seconds from becoming a reality, a ravenous fascination to stay held her captive. "I need to think," she said, tugging on her ear. "Alone."

"I sense you feel my pain. And it is true, I am in pain—but I am unwilling to close the story just yet. Please, Miss Ryleigh. Stay. Other commissions are in the winds when the sun rises."

She frowned.

"Ah, yes. Those which require the light of day." Long, bony fingers motioned for her to sit. The skin thinly covering the spiderwebbed crossroad of veins was wrinkled and spotted with age. She knew hands like his. Her mother's were younger, but distinct with life's scars. Two lives that had not been so dissimilar. Lives filled with secrets. She regarded them both as loners.

Once more, she eased herself into the cushions.

"The night is young. Ripe for stories of truth and honor." Ambrose adjusted himself so he faced her. "This will not be easy for either of us, Miss Ryleigh. Bear with me. Your insatiable curiosity has kept you here, of this I am sure. Now the tenacity that courses through your veins will need to be called upon. You are of your father's loins and he was strong—headstrong as well, as you are at times."

Compliment or insult? Producing nothing more than a hint of a smile, Ryleigh nodded for him continue.

"I was proud of those two boys—barely scratching the surface of manhood, yet beyond their years fighting a war. The days and weeks passed dreadfully slow. It was especially hard on young Ben, waging an inner battle alongside his best friend who was riveted in the heady bubble of love. Ben loved Eleanor with his heart, and he loved Ryan with his soul. But he never understood the darkness that seemed to surround Ryan, an ominous veil, if you will. He spoke fondly of the future with Eleanor and his child, but there were times when he wrote of being pursued by an unseen foe—not those that hunted him in the jungle, but something beyond that of which we see and his outlet was his words in a small journal he kept near his heart."

"The journal." Ryleigh straightened, her eyes wide. "Ambrose, please—tell me," she said, excitement punching through the despondency.

"Ryan wrote during lulls in combat and as tracers filled the skies. He wrote in the black of night and under the vast leaves of banana plants when it rained. And he kept the journal in an inside left pocket for safekeeping and to assure the love inside his heart would seep into its pages."

The stain. "Oh my God."

He pressed a gnarled finger to his lips. "Do not interrupt."

She nodded, eager for details.

"In late September of '67—"

"September 21st? My birthday?"

"Ah, yes—although the news of your arrival came to them late. Still, they celebrated quite earnestly." His voice grew hoarse. But a boyish grin emerged from the tangle of his mustache and then gradually disappeared. "They were Screaming Eagles and I assure you, the two of them lived up to the name. The picture you possess was taken the day Ryan received the telegram announcing your birth."

Realization stunned her to momentary stillness. "The photograph." Understanding bypassed all rational thought and settled as an ache in her heart, a piece of which she gave willingly and without reservation. "One of blood. One of heart."

He nodded.

The significance of his words sucked all feeling from the room. Words failed her. As did her tears.

"This page of the story is nearly complete," he said, rising to his feet. "I shall proceed when I take care of this frog that has carelessly lodged itself in my throat. I believe I could do with one more cup of that delightful coffee."

She reached for his mug. "I could use a refill too."

"Much appreciated." Ambrose paused by the window. "And please, a generous splash of the Godiva, if you will."

Ryleigh returned with the filled mugs.

His nostrils flared as he inhaled the steam, tilted his head back, and downed two more pain pills with a long sip of coffee. He nodded. She answered with a nod of her own, a shared affirmation that needed no words. He took a breath. "The day they celebrated your birth was four months before their tour of duty was to end, but it was also the day they received orders of Operation Wheeler—in the Quang Tin Province in South Vietnam. Their celebration was short-lived and they prepared to be flown out two days later. September 29, 1967. You were a mere eight days old."

Ryleigh sat curled in a ball, her hands wrapped tightly around the coffee mug. Her stomach churned, yet her rapt attention remained on the old man.

"The 327th arrived in full force on the battlefield. Orders were to meet their battalion, but they were already engaged in heavy battle," he said, his eyes distant, the words fading into a monotone as if read from a book. "The air reeked of gunpowder, blood and death." He shook his head. "Massive casualties. Their chopper lurched and dodged in a small clearing surrounded by mangrove trees. Gunfire exploded around them, a circle of death." Misshapen hands drew an imaginary circle. "Planes bombed the VC. Tracers pummeled the ground. Massive firepower assaulted them from all sides when Ryan emerged from the jungle, carrying a wounded Eagle. Ben spotted VC hidden near the perimeter and signaled for him to take cover, but Ryan ignored him and flagged a chopper hovering over a small rise." The old man's hands rose and fell. Talking had become a rusty effort. Ambrose paused to clear his throat, or perhaps needed a moment to swallow the heightened emotion. "He did not heed the warning."

Ryleigh focused on the man whose eyes refused to blink, her breath heavy and shallow, struggling from her lungs.

"The battle raged on. The enemy surrounded them. And then the chopper rose, turned and retreated. Ryan fell. Ben dropped to the ground and crawled to him, then dragged him into the cover of the jungle." Ambrose's voice wavered, but somehow he continued. "He tossed Ryan's helmet, ripped the bandana from his head, and pressed it to his chest. So much blood." He paused to take a breath, anguish distorting the old man's weathered face. "Ryan dug his heels in the muddy ground and all went quiet. No gunfire. No choppers. Not even a bird. The silence seemed as deafening as the sounds of war."

Ambrose had gone quiet too.

Breathe. She released her breath slowly and rubbed the marks her nails had dug into her palms.

Though raspy, his voice remained steady with an air of respect. "Ryan's body arched. He gasped and begged Ben to take care of his baby girl and Ellie and to give her the journal. Ben promised, pleading with him to stay awake. Ryan's breathing slowed. His body relaxed. Tiny dots of tracer fire reflected in his eyes. And then a gradual smile spread across Ryan's face and he asked Ben if he could see the fireflies." Ambrose fell quiet, his gaze fixed, not on her, but perhaps on a land as distant as the memory. He dragged a hand over his face. "With one last breath, Ryan surrendered his body. His life. Holding the lifeless body in his arms, Ben closed his best friend's eyes and wept."

Ambrose turned to her, blue eyes gone gray and moist, his curved mouth masking the grief that spilled from his eyes. "Your father—the boy with eyes the color of the inside of an ocean wave—died in the shadow of fate cradled in his best friend's arms, the flash of tracers—his last vision of fireflies—and Ben's promise the last thing he knew of this world."

Chapter Nineteen

ALL FEELING SEEMED to drain from her body. Ryleigh hadn't expected the shock this man had delivered, nor the queasy emptiness she felt in response. The father she worshipped had been stripped from her like dignity from a rape victim, and the father of her flesh had died a soldier's death mere hours after he'd been born to her.

"The ending," he said, his brow creased in a deep frown, "went all wrong." The withered storyteller rose and stared out the window into the black night, his hands clasped loosely behind his back. "Not the way it was supposed to be." He turned to face her. The pain leaking from his passive gray eyes matched the physical pain. He straightened and raised his chin. "The only thing more difficult than being a soldier, Miss Ryleigh," he said, his voice hoarse with emotion, "is loving one."

The impulse to run overtook the will to stay. Pulling her sweatshirt over her, Ryleigh gathered her purse and satchel. She wrapped her scarf over her shoulders and slipped quietly past the old man, the only sound the cruel objection of the door.

The black SUV was barely visible in the darkness. Without warning, her strength vanished, and with nothing short of sheer tenacity, she crossed the distance and opened the Tahoe's door.

"Come on, come on." The last bit of insulation protecting a mess of raw emotions dissolved in a jangle of keys. Ryleigh crammed the key into the ignition, shoved the gearshift into reverse and backed up. She jammed it into drive. Gravel pelted the wheel wells. Light from the windows grew smaller in her rearview mirror, as did any intention of returning.

Darkness swallowed her as she entered the tunnel of trees. Tears blurred her vision. Headlights bounced over the rutted road. Strange shadows formed along the tree trunks and stood sentinel, the guardians of the night. Adrenaline pumped her heartbeat into her ears, drowning the beep of the seatbelt alarm.

The cave of trees opened. She slowed and eased the Tahoe over the hump marking the road's end. The atmosphere changed. The moon shone more brightly. Trees grew straighter. Stars twinkled. She pulled to a stop at the railroad tracks, leaned against the cold window, and allowed the disbelief, pain, and emptiness to flow from her eyes without pardon.

Moments ticked by. Or had it been minutes? Unaware of time, she drove to the Inn in a fog of confusion. A missed text from Evan explained he was studying for finals, and with a sigh of relief, she replied to say she'd fill him in later. How would she approach the subject? Or could she even attempt it? Her phone chirped again, this time a text from Nat reminding her to call with details. As inevitable as it was, she couldn't. Was it too much to want to disappear? To be alone? To close her eyes and forget? *To run*?

Ryleigh took a deep breath, forced back a jumble of emotions and dialed.

The phone rang once. "I've had the phone glued to my hand like a sixteen-year-old. How'd it go?" Her voice bubbled with enthusiasm. "Spare me no details."

Natalie's familiar voice erased what defenses she'd roused to make the call and she squeezed her eyes shut, desperate to contain herself.

"You there, Ryleigh?"

She couldn't breathe. The woman who thrived on words couldn't form a single syllable.

"Tell me you're okay."

"Please don't worry." *Get a grip.* "I'm okay. I'm sorry. I'll call you tomorrow." She pressed the disconnect button before Natalie could answer and she set the phone to silent.

* * *

Natalie redialed. Voice mail. "MITCH?" She raced through the hall, lugged a suitcase from the closet and mumbled a few choice words. "MITCH!"

Mitch flew from the theater room and caught her by the arm. "What the hell's the matter, Nat? And what are you doing with a suitcase? It's the middle of the night."

"It's Ryleigh. I'm going after her. Something's wrong, and it's not the middle of the night."

Mitch raked her into a tight embrace.

Her eyes filled with tears. "She wouldn't tell me anything, but she was sobbing. And now she won't answer her phone. I have to go, Mitch."

"I know you do. But let's think this through. It *will* be the middle of the night in New York."

"I don't care. I need to go now. Will you call Southwest and book a flight to Albany?"

Mitch caressed her face in his hands. "Don't worry," he said, wiping her cheek. "She'll be okay."

"God, I love you, Mitch."

"I know you do," he said, patting her on her bottom. "Now get moving. I'll take care of the reservations."

Natalie stuffed a couple of day's worth of clothing into an overnight bag and zipped it closed as Mitch walked into the room. "Did you book my flight?"

"Southwest had no flights until morning, so I booked you on U.S. Airways. Eleven-fifty tonight to Albany." Mitch checked his watch. "Just enough time to make it to Sky Harbor." He wrapped his arms around her and kissed her neck. "There's a stop in Philly, and I reserved a car in Albany."

"Thanks, Mitch."

"Do you know where you're going?"

"I know where she's staying and her room number. You reserved a car with navigation, didn't you?"

"Oh, ye of little faith," he teased, nuzzling her neck again. "Only the best for my girl. Please be careful, Nat. It's a long flight and you don't get into Albany until late morning."

She turned to face him, her hands resting on his chest. "It won't be the first time I've gone without sleep. I'll be fine," she whispered. "I have to go to her."

"There's no doubt in my mind." He kissed her forehead. "I'll get a room in the Valley and take care of the loose ends on the Scottsdale deal while I'm there. Kill two birds with one stone."

"Perfect. Let's get out of here."

* * *

From the deck of her room, Ryleigh stared across the lake, wisps of hair lifting in the cold breeze. Pebbles of gooseflesh swept over her, a ghostly draft that refueled the bewilderment.

Nothing had been familiar when she arrived here. Now her entire life seemed so remote, a stranger taking up airspace in a story that had once been simple—painful at times—but simple. Her thoughts battled for their rightful place in a timeline of unforeseen events. In the crossfires of hell. Denial had been but a fleeting distraction and she'd plunged headfirst into anger.

Clapping her hands on the deck railing, she returned inside and downed two sleeping pills.

She showered, the force of the water cleansing her thoughts. The confusion began to clear. Returning to the house by the pond was disconcerting and produced a fresh wave of dread, but going back seemed inevitable. What she really wanted to do was change her ticket and go home. *Run.* To escape the past—or was the past her present? Her future? Juggling the idea, she didn't care which as long as it was as far away from here as possible.

But first, she had to make one more trip down Nightshade Path.

Ambrose was expecting her. Of that, she was sure.

* * *

Heavy clouds clothed the morning sky, yet the passageway through the trees seemed less ominous, partly due to the daylight, mostly because more pressing issues overshadowed her thoughts. Ryleigh parked the Tahoe and walked the short distance to the steps, the satchel tucked securely under her arm.

Ambrose met her at the door. The sunless sky smothered the prism's rainbows, and the pillows beneath his eyes had darkened. The wind chimes remained languid.

"You decided to return, Miss Ryleigh." The old man's greeting matched the overcast sky.

"You knew I would."

"Ah, yes," he said, his voice a whisper. "You were born with your father's spirit and his insatiable curiosity. Your return was inevitable." He motioned for her to come in.

Ryleigh followed him through the screened porch, wooden planks repeating their welcoming groan. Ambrose sank heavier into his limp, and the night's sharp edge had carved the lines deeper into sallow skin. Inside, he waved for her to be seated. She did so without hesitation.

"Would I be correct in assuming sleep did not come easy?" Ambrose handed her a fresh mug of coffee.

"I took a couple of sleeping pills. It helped." She looked away to bury the lie. "You?"

"I did not sleep well either," he said, easing himself to the sofa. "Though much time has passed, I had not fully prepared to relive those events."

"You said you weren't there, yet you told the story as if you were."

"That is neither here nor there."

She raised her hands in concession. "There's more to the story, so I suggest we get started. What happened after Ryan—my father—died?" The words rolled awkwardly from her mouth, unable to wrap her feelings around calling a complete stranger her father.

Ambrose fixed her with a searching gaze. "Pieces of the story remain untold, Miss Ryleigh. Some are significant. Some are not."

"I need to know." She squared her shoulders and her eyes narrowed. "Everything."

"As you wish." He rubbed both hands hard against his thighs, took a deep breath and let it out slowly. "Before the medics took Ryan's body, Ben took the journal—the one you now have in your possession—and as promised, gave it to your mother. He also ripped the Screaming Eagles patch from his shoulder and tore a button from his shirt. Those you also have in your possession. During the Vietnam campaign, soldiers wore one dog tag around their neck, the other tied to their boots in case of—" Ambrose stammered, abruptly looking away. "Ben cut Ryan's laces and retrieved it. His body would be shipped to his parents in St. Louis and your mother would never see him again. He wanted her to have something of Ryan's, besides you of course, to hold onto in order to one day let go."

"I didn't find dog tags in Mom's things."

"It is here."

"Why do you have it?"

"Certain things were too painful for her to keep, though she clung to them feverishly. The dog tag she left with me. It belongs to you now."

Pain skewed his face. The old man leaned heavily on the arm of the sofa. Rising slowly, he limped toward the closed door of an adjacent room that seemed to have been added to the house as an afterthought. Ambrose opened it enough to slip by, shadows rippling beyond the doorway, returned, and handed her a small wooden box.

As if seeking permission, she caught his eye. He nodded. With no locking mechanism, the lid lifted easily, the faint tang of cigar tobacco rising from the inside. The dog tag jingled on its ball chain as she raised it from atop a stack of envelopes. Her fingers traced the letters of his name, *LEIGHMAN RYAN MICHAEL* and his service number. She paused on *A POS*, and then skimmed over *PROTESTANT*.

"Type A positive," she said aloud, but didn't look up. "Same as mine."

A remnant of his life she held in her hand, another coursed through her body. Her fingers lingered on the indentations, cold and lifeless, the name of a man she didn't know, but whose blood flowed through her veins. A vague smile pulled at the corners of her mouth and she closed her hand around the metal. The impressions—hard to absorb yet palpably real—left her fingers and sneaked into a corner of her heart. An odd sensation flowed through her as if her blood had suddenly warmed.

"Are there any other pictures of him, Ambrose?"

"None that I possess. But trust me when I say you favor him, as does your son." The old man's face softened, the gleam in his eyes rekindled. "Your amazing smile, the soft dimple in your left cheek, and those exquisite blue-green eyes—"

"—the color of the inside of an ocean wave."

"Always." Ambrose hesitated, raking a bony hand through a thick crop of unruly white hair. "What pictures remained went to Michael and Allison Leighman, Ryan's parents, who are buried in St. Louis alongside their son."

"Grandparents. Something else Mom failed to mention."

"Ah, yes," he began. "Ryan never had the chance to tell them about you. They knew of Eleanor, but assumed she simply fled when Ryan left for the war, unaware she was carrying their grandchild. Ryan wanted to keep it quiet until the three of you were together. And of course, upon his death, Ben took over the responsibility.

"Your mother closed herself to everyone but you after Ryan's death. You were her entire world. I was but a shadow. Not until Ben returned did she begin to pull herself out of the darkness."

"Daddy? When did he come back?"

"Late January 1968. You were four months old. Ben loved you both and had no reservations about keeping his promise to Ryan. He knew Eleanor would never love him the way she loved Ryan, but it made no difference. He was honoring a promise he made to a dying man and surrendering to his feelings for your mother and you. He was ardently in love with your mother and he adored his baby daughter. He was content."

She pinched her eyebrows.

"Ah, yes, Miss Ryleigh, there was never a doubt in Ben's heart you were his daughter from that day forward. He was by any definition, your father."

"But my birth certificate. And the marriage license—the dates, everything is fake."

"I am considered an expert at what I do. Abstract identities. Alternate worlds. Even providing that which does not exist. I shall not exhaust you with details, but the documents were created exactly as specified."

"You're kind of creepy, you know that?"

A boisterous laugh exposed a bank of crooked teeth. "Ah, yes, a distinct entitlement, indeed. And speaking of documents, you will need to take some of those in your box to an attorney."

"Why?"

"Ryan left several government bonds for your mother. She chose not to take the money, instead transferring the documents to you. Rest assured, everything is quite legal."

"Aren't you an attorney? Can't you take care of what I need?"

"Ah, yes. I have worn many hats throughout time, but that part of me died when the need no longer existed. However, two things remain which I must tell you. The first concerns your name."

"Great. I suppose it's fake, too."

"The name on the dog tag."

Unaware she had been clutching it tightly in her hand, she opened her fist.

"Look at your father's first name. The first two letters."

She shot him a puzzled look.

He pointed to the tag. "Now the first half of your father's last name."

"*Ry-Leigh*." It crossed her lips as a whisper. "My name is his name."

"Ah, yes, indeed. Eleanor chose this so not only would she see Ryan reflected in your beautiful blue-green eyes, but she would hear the sweet sound of his name whenever someone spoke yours."

Ambrose rose slowly and gazed out the window. Banks of heavy, gray clouds threatened snow as morning wore on. "It looks as though inclement weather is settling in, Miss Ryleigh. I best conclude this story so you may return to the Inn."

"Snow?"

"The forecast merely calls for a dusting." His mustache curled around a healthy grin. "However, I believe my guess would be as reliable as any weatherman." The silver-haired man bent to open the woodstove. With a lonely groan, the door gaped wide, and he placed a log atop the embers. "A small fire is a must for cold days and bones as cantankerous as mine." He turned with his back inches from the stove and laced his fingers behind him.

"Ambrose," Ryleigh began, emerging from a collage of conflicting thoughts. "Please, tell me more about the journal. Ryan, my father—I don't know if I'll ever get used to saying that—wrote the poems for my mother?" She opened the satchel and removed the worn journal. Her hand lingered over the dark stain. An odd sensation tickled her stomach.

"He did, indeed. He was gifted. He saw things others did not."

"I think I understand."

"Of course you do. You are of his loins. His heart beats as yours and the words flowed from him as naturally as his breath." Ambrose's eyes drifted beyond a long nose, one eye—the right— seemed to move a fraction slower. "Much as you do—your inheritance and future promise, if you will."

Ryleigh traced the stain with her thumb, the pebbled leather familiar, yet as anomalous as her past.

"The words of your father abound with fear and death, beauty, and unending love. And darkness. The Screaming Eagles' motto is 'Rendezvous With Destiny.' Ryan believed fate followed him through the jungles of Vietnam. He wrote vividly of being in the clutches of something he felt but could not see. His destiny. Do you remember what is written on the back of the photograph?"

Recognition lit up her face. "*'Today this may be nothing, but tomorrow it may be all that is left.'* He knew, didn't he?"

"A sixth sense, perhaps. Some are gifted that way."

Ryleigh shook her head slowly. "I'd call it a curse."

"I think you are, indeed, quite right." His right leg dragged the floor as he crossed the room to the sofa.

"Ambrose," she said, tilting her head, "the words in the journal seem so familiar."

"Ah, yes. As they should," he said, his voice rising. "One thing Ben insisted was you grew up knowing your father's words."

The sullen mask fused to her expression melted. The recollection felt like coming home, finding one spot of comfort in a maze of confusion. "This is the book Daddy read to me, wasn't it?"

Ambrose beamed. "It is, indeed."

"I loved this book." She clutched it to her chest. "I remember crawling into his lap at bedtime. He smelled of soap and warm blankets and summer, and he'd read until I fell asleep," she said, reflectively. "The words were so vivid and soothing. I felt safe curled in his arms."

"Ah, yes. He loved you so, Miss Ryleigh, and he wanted you to know your father. But when Ben died, your mother hid the book. His words were her memories, and I believe they were simply too painful for her to read."

"The stain." She pressed her hand over the darkened leather. "This is his blood, isn't it?"

"I beg to differ. It is your father's love. Do you remember where he kept it?"

Lowering her face, she nodded. "Near his heart." She traced the stain with her fingers. "The stain is his blood—love infused in the leather."

Ambrose stood sentinel, watching her.

Overwhelmed and not quite sure it was permissible to love another as her father, yet knowing he was a part of her, a part of who she was, a frown formed on her brow. Her heart ached for what she had gained and ultimately lost at the hands of fate.

"There's one thing I still don't understand," she said. "There's one poem in here that doesn't make sense." Raising her eyes to meet the old man's, she opened the journal, the pages parting automatically where a frayed ribbon marked the haunting poem.

"Ah," Ambrose said as he lowered his eyes. "'Lost.' Is it not?"

"How'd you know?"

"It is the last missing piece to your puzzle, Miss Ryleigh. Come. We must take a drive before the skies open and spill their tears. I do not believe my leg will handle much cold today. We shall take the old Jeep."

Ryleigh replaced the journal in the satchel and fastened her jacket.

Ambrose stretched leather gloves over his knotted fingers, buttoned his coat against the weather, and hooked his walking stick over his arm.

"She is an antique I'm afraid, but she gets around a bit better than I do," he said, showing her out.

"Who?"

"This old Jeep," he said. "She is old, but in superb shape, unlike her owner I assure you."

She stepped into the vintage Jeep. "It's nice."

"Resurrected her from extinction myself. Ostrich leather. Exquisite."

"Nothing will surprise me about you, Ambrose. And if you don't mind my asking, how old *are* you?"

"Some questions have no sufficient answers. My age is of no consequence. I am as young and as old as love itself. Love is ageless. And true love is priceless."

A million miles of memories were etched into the roadmap of the old man's face. But where had they come from? And where did they lead? She smiled. Maybe he was right. Some questions have no sufficient answers.

The Jeep purred as Ambrose drove to the rear of the house and proceeded down a road concealed from every direction.

Ryleigh looked around. "This isn't the way out."

"My path takes a new direction quite frequently."

"Okay, I have another question. The lights the other night. When you took a walk, I saw tiny pinpricks of light. It made me think of Gandalf."

"Ah, yes. The remarkable wizard in *The Lord of the Rings.*" Ambrose chuckled. "Yes, I supposed it would."

"Are you going to tell me?"

"I am not."

"Some questions have no sufficient answers," they chimed in unison.

She leaned her head against the window. Random thoughts swirled in her head. She had acquired a piece of her past, of who she was, but when would she allow herself to truly embrace the knowledge? Ben was the one who read to her, whose lap she crawled into before bedtime, and who protected her from monsters under her bed. She had danced with him, invited him to tea parties and he had tucked her in at night. And she had called him Daddy.

"I fear you are contemplating things you should not," Ambrose said, breaking the silence.

"You aren't only creepy sometimes, Ambrose. You can be so convoluted."

"Ah, yes, a bit twisted, indeed." He nodded. "I am confident you will make sense of this story, make peace with your past and allow it to dictate your future. Please never doubt Ryan is your blood, but Ben was your father in the truest sense of the word. Without Ben, the words of your father would have remained silent."

Very little traffic milled about the village. They followed Ballston Avenue for a short distance and then turned into a dirt drive. The iron gates were swung wide and twin stone pillars flanked each side. The Village Cemetery stood silent, empty, except for the host of occupants whose brief histories were etched in stone markers.

"Should I bother asking why we are visiting a cemetery?"

"Patience, Miss Ryleigh."

The road wound through fir and maple trees, where generations of Ballston Spa occupants were laid to rest. Near the rear of the boundary, Ambrose cut the engine. "Our destination." He removed a small sack from the seat.

Thick, heavy clouds hung low in the air, still and quiet with the muffled feel of impending snow. Icy winds blew in short gusts lifting Ryleigh's hair and teasing her with the crisp spice of evergreen. *Christmas.* She blew on her fingers, pulled on her gloves, and then tightened the collar of her jacket. Ambrose leaned heavily into his staff, one footprint leaving a faint impression, the other a shallow furrow where his foot dug into the ground. Not far behind, Ryleigh followed.

She perused the headstones, careful not to step where the caskets rested. Patches of virgin snow covered those in shadow as if thick white blankets had been tucked around their resting place. Surrounded by history, Ryleigh bent to read the marker directly in front of her. An early settler in the 1700s. She envisioned her dressed in Colonial apron and bonnet, peacefully at rest. Another an infant, ten months and seven days old, died in 1832. A baby. Gooseflesh prickled her arms. And then a Major. Killed in battle, perhaps?

Following the path, the dates became more recent, the stones not as weathered. The one to her right a Ballston Spa police chief. A simple yet elegant Christmas wreath stood upright against the stone. *Daddy.* Her legs went liquid, knowing how it felt to visit your father in a cemetery.

Ambrose had gone ahead. She quickened her step and together they approached a stately maple tree that rose from the edge of a small pond, frozen and lifeless. Ambrose lowered his head and stared quietly at the grave nearest the pond. She followed his eyes to the headstone and her mouth flew open.

"I thought you told me Ryan's body was taken to St. Louis?"

"He was, indeed," he said, nodding toward the headstone.

She read it slowly, processing the words. "Ryan Michael Leighman II, September 21, 1967." She gasped. "My birthday." She turned to him. "But," she said with a deliberate pause, "he only lived one day? This can't be…"

"Ah, yes." Ambrose opened the sack and removed two pure white roses, and for the first time since they'd met, he placed his arm around her shoulders, as a loving grandfather might. "He is your brother. Your twin."

His words vanished in a puff of mist. Her head swam, thoughts rippling through her mind. The ache bypassed a range of feelings and squeezed her heart. "What happened?"

"He was much too small," he said, his voice small and filled with anguish. He cleared his throat. "Will you do the honor of placing the roses?" he asked, handing them to her. "White. A symbol of secrecy. And of innocence."

Secrecy. Innocence. Her heart skipped as she absorbed their meaning.

"One for your father, the other for your brother. In a cross if you please, as I have done for over forty years as your mother wished. If you read the rest of the inscription, I believe you will recognize the words your father penned after he received the second telegram."

Tears clung to her lashes. She blinked them back and read aloud,

> "'*I placed a gentle autumn breeze*
> *Within your tiny space—*
> *I placed with you, a piece of me*
> *And let you go—in God's embrace.*'"

"The journal," she whispered. *And the roses.*

With a gloved hand, Ambrose embraced her shoulder in a gentle, yet firm grip, and she clung to him as though they held each other up. "Your mother wanted him close to the pond so he would be forever lulled by the fireflies. As she was that special summer."

Stillness hummed through the air, so quiet it seemed even God held His breath. Ryleigh knelt beside the headstone and placed the roses, stems crossed, at the base. The ties that bound her to the boy in the grave tightened around the place where her brother would dwell and fill a portion of her heart where fate had carved a gaping wound.

A baby. Her brother. Another who shared her flesh. And he slept peacefully beneath the earth, nothing but a whisper of what could have been yet more tangible than the granite stone that sheltered him. The clouds huddled together, as gray and heavy as the weight pressing against her heart, as if the December sky had dressed to attend a funeral forty-three years in the making.

Another piece of her past had dropped into place, the tug palpable as if a rope linking her heart to her twin refused to let go. Two teardrops tumbled from her cheek marking the ground where the tiny casket had been placed forty-three years ago. So tiny. And alone.

Ryleigh rose. Lazy snowflakes fluttered around her and settled on her sleeve, blossoming into tiny circles of moisture. The skies set free its tears and the heavens wept.

And so did she.

And she dared to wonder if anything would ever be the same.

Chapter Twenty

FLIGHT 258 ARRIVED ahead of schedule. Under ordinary circumstances, Philadelphia's history would captivate Natalie for hours with its vast assortment of museums and historical sites. But with a delay of nearly three hours before the connecting flight to Albany all she could think about as the sun rose in a sea of pink, was how disgustingly slow time seemed to pass. She was drained from the flight from Phoenix and irritated at the long delay.

Natalie tossed the latest issue of *People* magazine aside and pressed her fingers to her eyes. With a little over an hour left before her flight, she dialed Ryleigh's cell phone. Voice-mail. "Dammit, Ryleigh," she muttered, "why won't you answer your flippin' phone?" The words came out quietly, but what she really wanted to do was scream.

* * *

Several hours later with the last leg of her flight finally on the ground, Natalie dialed Mitch's cell and waited for the beep. "The eagle has landed in Albany and I'm on my way to Saratoga Springs," she said, and then glanced at the airport clock and counted backward to adjust for the time change. "You're probably in a meeting, so I'll call you after I find Ryleigh. I love you."

Natalie followed the navigation's directions to the Brook Hollow Inn. A light snow had begun to fall and a skiff of white settled around Saratoga Lake, as if the edges had been dusted with sugar.

The Inn's parking area was deserted, so she parked near the door to Ryleigh's room. Pulling her collar tight around her neck, she dissed herself for not packing a heavier coat.

Natalie knocked, the cold stinging her knuckles. "Ryleigh? You in there?" Another loud rap on the door. "Damn, damn, damn." She paused and rubbed her fingers, and then marched to the Inn's lobby.

The attendant assured her Mrs. Collins hadn't checked out. *Another crappy delay counting the minutes.* Slipping back inside the warm SUV, she leaned against a folded arm. Heavy weights pulled on her eyelids and the fog of weariness overtook her.

* * *

With a bare hand, Ryleigh touched each letter of the name engraved in the granite tombstone, scribing an indelible imprint on her fingertips. Her mind was numb, not from the bitter cold, but from the images of fragmented, disconnected dreams.

"I want to leave, Ambrose."

With his hands crossed over his walking stick, Ambrose stood quietly, peering over the graveyard. "I believe we shall return. The weather has been most disagreeable," he said, blinking away snowflakes.

"No, Ambrose. I want to go home. To Arizona. Where at least things are familiar and make some sort of sense. Here I'm this person who never existed and I'm listening to stories that don't belong to me."

"Ah, but they do, Miss Ryleigh, they do."

"It's not that." She hesitated. "Everything is inside *you,* and I've merely been eavesdropping. I don't even know you and I damn sure don't know how to deal with this." She lowered her head. "I don't want to deal with this."

"Come. We shall go. It will help clear the webs the spiders of truth tend to weave." Ambrose rested his hand in the small of her back, guiding her. They walked side by side, silent, back to the Jeep.

Once inside, Ryleigh rested her elbow on the armrest with her head in her palm. The snow had stopped, but the world outside blurred.

The Jeep warmed quickly. Ryleigh noted they took an even less traveled route back briefly following the railroad tracks.

By the time they returned to his house, the fire had died. Ryleigh rubbed her arms at the chill that had settled in her bones. Taking one last, long look around at the discriminating possessions and the doors behind which he sheltered a storied life, she couldn't help but wonder how her past had changed his life, and how his would change hers.

Tossing her jacket on the sofa, she turned to the woodstove. The heavy cast iron door uttered its lonely groan, the protest as loud as the reservations inside her heart. The embers had nearly died but, having grown up in the mountains, kindling a fire was second nature, and it didn't take long for the wood to spark into flame.

Ambrose emerged from the kitchen carrying a cast iron pot he placed on top of the woodstove. "Ah, Miss Ryleigh, my deepest thanks for resurrecting the fire." He turned his back to the stove. "I do hope you will join me when the soup is warm. You need something to eat, as do I."

"I haven't been very hungry lately."

"Ah, yes. Understandably so."

"I should go."

"Not quite yet."

Ryleigh shut her eyes tightly. "No, Ambrose. I'm done. I can't—"

"Please. A trifle longer. While the soup warms. This may be the last time we see each other."

A frown tightened her brow. "I can't come back?"

"Doubts plague you, Miss Ryleigh. I perceive you well enough."

She paused, unsure whether to let him continue or grab her things and go. Ambrose limped toward her, sparing her the decision.

"Megan is an extraordinary young woman. I have seen her along her rightful path, but that is neither here nor there."

Ryleigh hugged her middle and turned away, the weight of a suspended bubble following her. "Why do you keep insisting I know this Megan?"

"Your discretion is admirable, indeed. Now, if you will indulge me for a few moments longer."

Ryleigh swallowed any sort of remark and gave him a shallow nod of approval.

"I wish to impress upon you, Miss Ryleigh, when your mother lost Ryan and her son, a part of her died. Ben returned from Vietnam, his body whole but never truly the same, and he tried to fill the void and did so to some degree. Eleanor was happy…as happy as one could expect without the love denied her with Ryan and the son she would never know. I assumed she would lapse into depression. But she did not."

Ryleigh's eyebrows rose.

"She chose a path possibly worse. Instead of accepting her past and moving on, she chose to ignore it. And if you'll allow me to say so, I believe you inherited that trait from your mother."

She scowled. "What the hell do you mean by that?"

"Do not be offended. Consume it. Digest it," he counseled, pounding a fist on his heart. "Scars are merely the evidence—noble reminders, if you will—of our battles. Use what you know to be the truth of yourself and your past to your advantage. It is a part of you that cannot be ignored. You wear your heart openly. What you feel inside weeps on the outside, but you possess the strength of two honorable men and that of your mother. Use this, and it shall define your future."

"Ben is my past. He's the only father I ever knew. Ryan is a stranger," she said adamantly. "How can I ever love him as I loved my father?"

"This you shall process in time, Miss Ryleigh." Ambrose cradled her face in his large, misshapen hands and looked her intently in the eye. "Ryan's gift flows from you as it did him. Your future will be shaped by your words. Do not let another so gifted remain silent." His hands fell to his side. "Now if you will forgive me I must eat. The soup is bubbling, I am sure. Please, will you join me?"

"I'm exhausted and I want to go home."

"Indeed, you must go. Please do not forget your treasure chest."

"I don't know if that's what I would call it."

"It is a treasure chest—without a doubt."

"It's just an old cigar box."

"The treasures of family lay hidden inside. The letters they wrote to one another will turn the pages of the unknown. Compose your story as you uncover details I have forgotten or inadvertently omitted. Read the letters buried among your mother's things. Read your father's words. Understanding will surface as you do so. They reveal the innermost part of himself and shall live beyond death, and their strength will be yours and shall bind you as one. And when you write, a part of you is exposed."

"I was so taken with the journal I haven't looked through the letters yet." She sighed heavily. "Ambrose, I don't know how to process all of this."

"Take the box. You will uncover the treasures within," he said, scrutinizing her. "When someone you love becomes a memory, the memory becomes a treasure. You must learn to live with your past." He took both her hands and squeezed, the pressure assuring. "Do not ignore it. Embrace it. Release it to the wind and allow it to set you free. Love will be your guide and keep your heart safe."

Ryleigh paused, tucking her hair behind an ear. "You've never mentioned Chandler." His name stuck in her throat.

He looked down his crooked nose, his eyes searching one and then the other of hers. "The heart has expectations and some allow those expectations to become stale until the eyes no longer see the disappointment of reality. The one you first loved is now your past."

"Maybe."

"Indeed. He claims to love you still. Does he not?"

A deep furrow creased her brow. "I never dreamed he'd ever stop loving me."

"Perhaps knowing the choices one makes is not because of you, but is a decision they make in spite of you. You cannot know the strength of one's love, and perhaps knowing this will help sever the threads that bind you. Open your heart and allow yourself to let go."

Ryleigh tilted her head. "You sound as if you already know the outcome."

"Let me simply say, another shall be the source of your passions."

"That'll be the day."

"My dear Miss Ryleigh, you must set a match to the past in order to light the path of your future."

Holding the box to her chest, she turned to him. "May I come back someday?" Her cheeks flushed.

"Ah, yes. I see you are going to prove me wrong." He twisted the wiry hairs of his mustache. "The sun sets. A new day arrives," he said, showing her to the door. "There are other worlds to explore. New paths to follow."

Still clutching the cigar box, she reached up and hugged the lanky figure.

He hugged her in return and then held her at arm's length and gave her hands a tender squeeze. "Never forget, Ryleigh Endicott," he said, wagging a gnarled finger at her, "there will always be storms that rattle the foundation of your life and tear at your heart. The life you were comfortable in is over. Embrace your past. Use it to forge your future. Live and love for tomorrow. Trust me. You have survived the storm. Now you must learn to dance in the rain."

The gleam had returned to his liquid blue eyes, deep wells of memories as old as life itself. Or time, perhaps. Mysteries lurked there—carefully guarded questions with no answers, only belief. "Now, you must go. Natalie is waiting for you at the Inn."

* * *

Never having had much insight into her family history, Ryleigh wrestled with herself, teetering between laughter and tears as she drove back to the Inn. Missing years of her past tangled with the present, and she ached for normalcy, a mental library filled with ordinary memories like everyone else. Her tiny circle of relatives had expanded and imploded in the course of a single day.

Incomprehensible—the only way she could describe the last two days.

Despite a zealous curiosity about the world around her, it was odd how little consideration she had given her own past. She had quelled the desire to seek answers, not by conscious choice, but simply by loving a mother who had chosen to live a guarded, solitary life; a mother who had chosen to bury the past in the same way she had buried so many of those she loved.

A stranger, Wilford Langhorne D'Ambrose, knew fragments of her family history. No common blood flowed in their veins, but the bonds he shared with her family were not dissimilar to the bonds she shared with Evan. That, she understood. Perhaps someday the pieces would fit together, the dots of her personal timeline shuffled into place, as neat and tidy as a column of numbers.

Before entering the highway around the lake, she slowed to a stop. Reaching across the seat, she lifted the lid of the cigar box. The metal tinkled as she placed the chain around her neck and pressed the dog tag to her chest. A symbol of a father lay close to her heart. Closer now than the two would ever be.

She tucked the dog tag inside her hoodie and continued along the lake route. Her thoughts crisscrossed through the mesh of information Ambrose had given her, but she scoffed at the ridiculous idea Nat would be waiting for her as she pulled into the parking area of the Brook Hollow Inn. Ambrose was a lot of things (and he certainly saw more with one eye than most did with two) but psychic wasn't one of them.

Ryleigh got out of the Tahoe and headed for her room. A car door slammed. She looked up to see a tall, rather angry and very familiar woman stomping toward her.

"Ryleigh Michele Endicott Collins, where in hell have you been?"

"Nat!" Ryleigh gasped. "You scared the crap out of me. What're you doing here?"

Natalie's frustration matched her long strides. "I scared *you*?"

"I said not to worry."

"I wasn't the one sobbing." Outstretched hands slapped her thighs. "I wasn't the one who hung up without warning and wouldn't answer their phone. Worried, hell. I was frantic."

"I'm fine." *How did Ambrose know?*

They stood face to face. "Fine? You couldn't even talk to me. I had no clue what was happening. What was I supposed to do? Leave you here alone?" Natalie locked her in a hug, their faces pressed cheek to cheek. "You scared the shit out of me."

Complete resignation dissolved her defenses, and Ryleigh melted into the comforting embrace. Natalie had always had that effect on her, like a child who has fallen but feigns bravery and doesn't give in to tears until they see their mother. The tears began slowly, building to a crescendo of deep sobs, one by one falling onto the shoulders of the one person who could share the burden.

"Whatever it is, it's going to be okay."

They clung to each other, the wind whirling around them in stinging gusts.

"It's freezing." Ryleigh pulled away. "Let's go inside."

The two women, who shared everything from ice cream to cooties, crossed the threshold of a small room more than two thousand miles from home.

"Hey, you." Natalie opened her arms wide. Ryleigh stepped into them. "You look like hell."

"Thanks," she said, offering a halfhearted smile. "Nice to see you too."

Natalie brushed a windblown strand of hair from Ryleigh's face. "You're shivering. Go take a hot shower. I'll take in the view—it's gorgeous, by the way. Then we'll talk."

"Nat—"

"We'll talk after you shower."

NATALIE FLIPPED THE fireplace switch and flames danced in and out of make-believe logs. This was meant to be a fun getaway, a quest of sorts, not something that had added another scar to her friend's already embattled year.

The curtains were drawn, exposing the view of the lake. Natalie folded her arms, the day fading and as dreary as her mood. Ryleigh's safety was the lone bright spot—maybe not safe from whatever skeletons she'd dug up, but safe from physical harm. Nat sighed at the tiny ray of optimism poking its way through a whitewashed day.

Dressed in pajamas and towel-drying her hair, Ryleigh padded into the room in bare feet. "Quite a view, isn't it?"

Natalie turned. "It is," she said. "Be romantic when there's a pile of snow. This is a different cold than in Arizona, don't you think?"

"You have no idea. I can't wait to go home. I told Ambrose I might come back, but I don't know if I ever want to see this place again."

Natalie sat on the four-poster, bouncing once before settling. "Take it from the top."

Ryleigh propped the pillows in a heap. "Where do I begin?" she said, burying her head in a towel.

Nat kicked off her shoes and tossed a mountain of pillows on the bed. "We've got all night." Telling secrets to their pillow was a ritual started long ago—a place to muffle giggles or a soft landing for spilled tears.

Ryleigh lapsed into her storytelling voice, pausing awkwardly at times when emotion threatened to take over.

Natalie digested the story in silence as afternoon slipped quietly into dusk, a shaft of sunlight bathing the room in a warm glow before it winked and melted into the twilight.

Ryleigh rocked back and forth, pillow clutched in the folds of her arms, embracing a comfort neither she nor Nat could provide.

"What do I say?" Nat swiped at tears collecting on her cheeks. "I never dreamed—"

"Sometimes words get in the way." Ryleigh got to her feet and shook two sleeping pills from the vial. "I can't disappear like Frodo or Bilbo, or Ambrose for that matter, but I can escape into sleep."

Natalie knew the feeling—broken dreams could punch a hole in your heart so huge the wind seemed to whistle straight through it. When the doctors told her she would never carry a child, Ryleigh held her up when she'd been too devastated to stand alone. It had been Ryleigh who'd saved her from sinking into quicksand, gave her air, and helped stitch her wounds. Sometimes words weren't necessary. Knowing someone was there beside you, to offer the simple reassurance of a touch was enough. Mitch had been her rock, but he couldn't know the grief, the guilt and emptiness of a barren womb. Ryleigh never pretended to know; she simply helped absorb the pain. "Sleep is what you need right now, Riles. But first, can I have your plane ticket?"

"Why?"

"So we can fly back together."

"The sooner, the better." Ryleigh handed her the ticket and slipped beneath the blankets. "I'm glad you're here, Nat."

Without a word, Nat reached over and squeezed her best friend's hand.

"One redeeming thing has come from this whole ordeal," Ryleigh said as she yawned.

Nat drew her laptop from its case. "What's that?"

She yawned again. "I know how my book ends."

"Get some sleep. I'll take care of everything."

Ryleigh closed her eyes, her breaths slow and deep.

Nat air-pumped a fist. "Yes!" Clicking away at the keyboard, she turned to her friend. "It's about time, Riles. You're a writer. It's who you are." But her words fell on deaf ears.

Natalie's heart ached for the journey her friend would need to face. The climb would be as difficult as scaling the Grand Canyon with a hundred-pound backpack. And she'd help carry the load. But for now, she scanned the flight schedules and booked their flight. "Perfect."

She checked her e-mail and read a note about the opening of a resort her friend Rose managed in Colorado. Nestled at the base of the Rocky Mountains, the new owners wanted to attract the skiers, snow bunnies, and anyone else who thought frolicking in knee-deep snow was their idea of fun, and they were interested in incorporating Il Salotto's services as part of their amenities. The idea was intriguing. Accepting the invitation, she clicked the Send button and closed her laptop. She tucked the blankets around Ryleigh's shoulder and then sent Mitch a goodnight text. Setting her phone to vibrate, she leaned into the mound of pillows and considered Ambrose's story, now Ryleigh's story. Her past. If her best friend hadn't been thrown into a whirlwind of unfathomable emotion, it would have been a touching story of profound love. She pressed the phone to her heart. "Love you, Mitch, but Riles may kill me before I ever see you or Arizona again."

Chapter Twenty-One

"RISE AND SHINE, sleepyhead." Natalie's voice echoed from the bathroom.

Ryleigh groaned, pried one eye open, and poked her head from beneath the blankets. "Everything's fuzzy," she said, the words heavy with sleep. "I need caffeine."

"I brought coffee from the breakfast room."

"Thanks, Nat."

"Jet lag. Calls for desperate measures."

Ryleigh pressed her palms against her eyes.

"You slept okay?"

Ryleigh tossed the covers, set her feet on the floor, and aimed for the coffee. "No dreams," she said, the sleep hangover beginning to fade. "Double dose of artificial suspension of consciousness."

"We can get breakfast after you're dressed." Nat glanced at her watch and counted forward. "It's seven o'clock here. Our flight doesn't leave Albany until eleven thirty."

"Seems like I've been away for a lifetime. By the way, how's Kingsley?"

"As obnoxious as ever." Nat grinned. "I swear that cat hates me."

Ryleigh chuckled. Her companion through mishaps, nightmares, and dreamscapes, Kingsley never offered an opinion. Not an oral one anyway. "He doesn't hate anyone. He's just, different."

"Arrogant feline."

"Can't wait to see him. We should be back in Phoenix around five or so, right?"

"No," Nat said, adding the back to her earring. "I'll explain later. We have two rentals to return and a layover in D.C." She scrunched her nose. "Now get moving. It's early, but we've got a long day ahead of us. And I want to see Ballston Spa."

Ryleigh came fully awake and sat up. "What?"

* * *

On Nat's insistence and with time to spare, the women drove into Ballston Spa. Ryleigh had agreed, sputtering a few choice words under her breath as she tapped the navigation screen. Barnabas came to life.

Nat's eyes widened. "Step away from the dash, Barnabas Collins, vampire extraordinaire—and come to Mama," she said, waggling her fingers at the dash and then turned to Ryleigh. "And you thought you had no relatives."

Ryleigh slowed as they entered the village, Soldier's Monument looming directly in front of The Simmering Skillet. Ryleigh parked and together they walked to the window, but the sign indicated the restaurant didn't open until lunch.

"So much for breakfast here." Natalie rubbed her hands together. "We passed a place called The Koffee Kettle."

"That's where Megan works."

Nat smiled and skipped her long legs into high gear.

Ryleigh shook her head and hurried to keep in stride, their breath ahead of them in puffs of fog. "Sometimes you drive me nuts, Natalie Jo. I do not want to do this."

Christmas wreaths hung from streetlamps, and the storefronts competed for the best in holiday finery. Bells tinkled as shoppers moved in and out of the doorways, and the spicy aroma of gingerbread wafted through the brisk air.

The Koffee Kettle offered a welcomed retreat from the outside chill. Nat chose a table by the window.

The metallic clink of Megan's bracelet collection preceded her to the table. "Hell's bells, didn't think I'd see you again," she said, raising a studded eyebrow. "I see you brought reinforcements." She squinted an eye, clicked her tongue, and pointed to Natalie. "Now, what can I get for you two?"

Megan took their order and retreated behind the counter.

"She's exactly as you described, Riles."

"I'm extremely uncomfortable."

"Be good for you. You'll see."

Megan returned, steam rising from their mugs in lazy swirls. She set a caramel latte in front of Ryleigh, handed Natalie the white cloud mocha cappuccino and gave them each a bagel topped with egg and cheese. Ryleigh's taste buds awoke and her stomach sounded a pleased alarm. She raised her mug, sipped and wiped the foam from her lip.

Megan pulled up a chair between them, swung a leg over, and rested a hand and her chin on the backrest. "You can slurp the foam ya know," she said, waving her free hand at their mugs. "It's not forbidden, or even rude. It's a right of passage in a coffee house."

Natalie took a noisy sip. "Good to know."

Megan turned to Ryleigh. "So, did you find the old guy?" she asked, wiggling her eyebrows.

Ryleigh nearly choked. Her mug dropped to the table, the half-filled contents a coffee and caramel flavored tidal wave.

Megan flicked the feather earring off her shoulder. Her hair was darker and a purple streak had appeared over her left ear. "Sorry. Didn't mean to blindside you."

"Fine." Ryleigh swallowed. "I guess."

"He's a bit perplexing."

"That's an understatement."

Natalie's head bobbed from one to the other to keep up with the conversation.

Megan's dark eyes squinted. "And creepy," she whispered. Hiding behind a feigned grimace, she quickly brightened. "It's so cool to know someone who knows him like I do. So, what'd you guys talk about?" When Ryleigh didn't answer, Megan pursed her lips into a fine line. "Hey, I spilled my guts—it's only fair you spill yours."

With a mouth full of egg, Ryleigh glanced at Natalie, who nodded indiscernibly. She swallowed, giving herself another moment to collect her thoughts. "We talked about my mother."

"Way cool!" She straightened. "So he did know your mom. What else?"

"I was definitely born here."

"That's not so cool," she said, her face squinting as if she'd bitten into a lemon. "At least you escaped."

"And so will you. Ambrose assured me you'll do well for yourself."

Megan smiled briefly and her head ricocheted toward Natalie. "So, who's your friend?"

"Megan, this is Natalie. We've known each other for almost forty years."

"Boy, you have strange friends if they'd follow you to this dumpy town." Megan turned to Natalie. "Sorry. No offense meant." Nat smiled in response. "But I can't say there's anyone in this craphole I'd want to know that long, except the old guy." She leaned in. "Hey, did you ask him how old he is? I never did." She shrugged. "And he never volunteered." Her eyes sparkled, matching the glitter in her hair. "But my vote says he cast a ballot for Abraham Lincoln."

Natalie pressed her knuckles against her mouth, and Ryleigh bit her lip to contain a giggle.

"Nice to meet you, Megan." Natalie brushed her hand against a distressed pair of True Religion jeans and then offered her a crumb-free hand.

"Likewise," she said and turned to Ryleigh. "Guess you didn't ask either?"

Even though she had, Ryleigh shook her head, reluctant to go into details of his odd reply. Megan's head bobbed back to Natalie. "You from Arizona too? Cool place." The bell on the door tinkled. "Customers." Megan stood and returned the chair. "Gotta go." She bounded off, feather earring bouncing to the zip in her step.

"Good-bye, Megan. And good luck to you."

"Thanks," she said with a quick wave over her shoulder. Her bracelets plunged to her elbow, the chime of clinking metal following her to the counter.

Natalie swallowed the last bite of her bagel. "Was that so bad?"

"You were right." Ryleigh leaned into her palms. "As always."

"Better get going," Natalie said and took a hurried gulp of her mocha. "Airplanes wait for no one." She rose and left enough money to cover the bill and a generous tip. With a quick wave to Megan, they left the coffee shop.

"Nat, do you mind if we make a stop before we leave?"

"Need to make it quick."

"I'll only be a minute if you want to wait in the car."

Nat waved for her to go ahead and Ryleigh tossed her the keys.

Minutes later, Ryleigh returned and slipped into the driver's seat. She glanced down the road and turned onto Ballston Avenue.

Natalie frowned. "I don't remember this street."

"There's something I need to do."

The stone pillars guarding the Ballston Spa Village Cemetery entrance came into view. She turned in and followed the path Ambrose had taken. As the engine died, apprehension rose from somewhere deep in her belly with no less reservation than she'd had on her last visit here.

"Please come with me?"

Entwined among the leafless trees, evergreens stood statuesque despite the apathy of winter, but the great maple dominated the tiny grave. Ryleigh removed the wrapping from a simple Christmas wreath and placed it against the headstone. *Brother*, it said.

Kneeling alongside her twin, new words to an old verse spilled from her lips. *"I placed a piece of me today, alongside you as you rest—I placed my everlasting love, with you my brother, in whom I'm blessed."* Aware of an indescribable absence all these years, a quiet shiver found a path along her arm as her finger traced her brother's name, the bond complete—as if she'd reached out for him, and he for her.

* * *

The plane's tires kissed the asphalt with a screech and a bump. The aircraft landed safely, which was more than Ryleigh could say for the ride she'd taken over the last year. They disembarked quickly and Natalie hailed a cab. With a three-hour layover, why were they in such a rush? And why'd they need a cab? Nat traveled all over the world, so Ryleigh trusted her for the connection to Phoenix. Wouldn't be the first time she'd been kept in the dark.

After speaking briefly to the cabbie, Natalie scooted beside her, checked her watch and took a resigning breath. "Plenty of time."

"For what? And why're we leaving the airport?"

"A slight detour." Natalie raised her hand. "Don't ask."

"I'm really beginning to hate surprises, but whatever," she replied with a sidelong glance at her friend. "This has been a screwed up couple of days anyway; I might as well sit back and enjoy the ride. It's bound to get ugly."

Natalie raised a perfectly groomed eyebrow.

The havoc of the airport gave way to the busy streets of the nation's capital. Not unlike Phoenix freeways, the cabbie found every excuse to fume about everyone else's shoddy driving.

Delighted at the view from the cab's window, Ryleigh sat upright. "Natalie Jo, we're driving beside the Potomac River. Where're we going?"

"We're on George Washington Memorial Parkway and soon we'll cross the Potomac over the Arlington Memorial Bridge. It's quite a drive."

"You didn't answer my question." Distracted by the sights, Ryleigh allowed the question to fizzle.

"We're headed to Henry Bacon Drive, right?" Natalie asked the cabbie via the rearview mirror.

The cabbie nodded. "That's right."

"We aren't going to see much of D.C. in an hour," Ryleigh said.

"We haven't much time. It's a great trip, but for another visit. We only have one stop today."

"But this is D.C. So much to see. The Washington, Jefferson, and Lincoln Memorials, the Museum of Natural History, the White House, veterans memorials." Ryleigh turned and glared at her. "The Wall."

"Please don't be mad."

A response curdled in the back of her throat. Of course Natalie would put two and two together and assume if Ryan had been killed in Vietnam, his name would be permanently etched in the Vietnam Veteran's Memorial. And only Nat would think to fit it in on the return trip to Phoenix. How could she be angry? Natalie was one of those rare individuals who wore the shoes of compassion—for her, or for anyone who touched her life.

The cabbie pulled to the curb. "Here you go, ladies. It's straight ahead across the lawn." He stretched an arm across the seat, the marquee of a faded tattoo covered the spotted skin of his wrist. He turned to face them, the lines of a weathered face announcing his age. "Vietnam was a nasty war, the longest in history—until Afghanistan." His piercing eyes were the color of the D.C. sky. "The way the panels are set, from eight inches to over ten feet and then back to eight inches, signifies the beginning, middle and end to a long, unpopular war." The cabbie adjusted the bill of his hat. "It's constructed of black granite, signifying death and sadness, but it's highly polished, so it reflects life—trees, sky, friends. Family." He tipped his Redskins cap, his hairline hidden beneath the bill, and tufts of unkempt gray hair peeked from the bottom. He handed them each a small American flag. "It's a healing place."

"You know it well?" Ryleigh asked.

"I come here often. To visit friends."

They thanked him with a discriminate nod.

Natalie tapped the back of the cabbie's seat. "We won't be long."

"Take your time." The cabbie winked and tipped his cap. "I'm not going anywhere without you."

* * *

The solitude of The Wall surrounded her, the urgency of its embrace as intimate as a lover's caress. Vast slabs of polished black granite rose, peaked, and then narrowed again, as if born from, and given back to the earth. Ryleigh approached the monument, apprehension threatening to collapse her legs. Giving in to instinct, she closed her eyes. A breath of wind brushed her cheek. And she stood, silent, allowing the cold air to clear away everything except the moment before her.

She opened her eyes and glanced around at the other visitors. Some prayed. Some wept. Mementos, flowers, and flags were left at the foot of the stone in dried puddles of forgotten tears. But she watched young and old alike reach out to something beyond reality, lives linked with each touch of skin to stone.

Natalie withdrew a scribbled note from her purse. "Here. Let's find your father."

Ryleigh read the note and frowned. "Where'd you get this?"

"The Internet. There's a website," Nat said, pausing. "I looked him up after you fell asleep."

Ryleigh curled the paper around a finger as they searched the location. "When you changed the flights?"

Nat nodded. "He's a well-decorated soldier." She pointed ahead. "There."

Ryleigh's eyes fixed on the etched name honoring the soldier she knew only as the man who'd given her life. Her fingers curled around the dog tag that hung from her neck, the metal warm as if they shared something more than a name carved in a stone wall. Drawn by an unseen tether, she reached out, her fingers hesitantly meeting the cold stone. The icy sting dissipated into an odd warmth as she mapped the letters, each one a missing piece, each one a distinct reminder of a headstone that also bore his name, each one a footprint on her heart.

Natalie pulled a sheet of fine linen paper and a pencil from her purse, placed a hand on Ryleigh's shoulder, and handed her the items. The image formed with each unsteady stroke, consummate and palpable and undeniably real.

Natalie handed her a pair of white roses.

Ryleigh tilted her head. "Where—"

Nat put a finger to her lips. "Lobby of the Inn," she said and handed Ryleigh the tiny flags the cabbie had given them. And then she nodded, the faint smile a silent missive between the two, the message understood without the privilege of words.

Ryleigh placed the roses with stems crossed directly under Ryan's name at the base of the black granite, and then did the same with the flags. The flowers would wilt and die, the flags taken away, but her father's name would remain indelibly etched in the stone, a simple remembrance of a life given selflessly.

Ryleigh stepped back, her eyes mirrored in the polished granite at the spot where Ryan's name had been carved so long ago, and for a fleeting moment, her father's eyes (her eyes)—the color of the inside of an ocean wave—reflected from the black stone and held hers. And for that one moment, the past united with the present.

Afraid to blink, to move, to breathe, Ryleigh grabbed Nat's arm.

After forty-three years, father and daughter were together for the first time.

Chapter Twenty-Two

ACCEPTING THE JOB as general contractor for the expansion of Il Salotto Salon & Med Spa of Scottsdale amounted to a sizable commercial job Chandler hadn't attempted since Evan's birth. Remaining in Hidden Falls had been his main focus, and the lifestyle change afforded him the luxury of remaining close to home to raise his son, stick a pair of cold feet in the investment pool and solidify his reputation as a quality home builder.

When Evan left for college, his absence left a gaping hole in Chandler's heart. Then the housing industry crashed. Work was scarce. His wife had her job and her writing and found ways to satisfy the odd hours of emptiness. And eventually, so had he.

Chandler leaned back and exhaled a long breath. Building anything—from digging the footers to passing the final inspection and each step in between—was a piece of cake, but he'd never tried to fix something as broken as his life. His wife (he couldn't bring himself to use the *ex* word) plagued his thoughts. Every decision made was with her in mind. Pushing his hair back with both hands, he wondered if he could strip the nails from the hurt he'd caused and rebuild what he had lost.

Blueprints to the new spa were sprawled across a small dining table, the curled ends held down with mismatched mugs. He flipped the new elevations to the mechanical drawings, comparing them with the existing building plans. The job would be challenging, but manageable, and he considered the idea it might be worth taking on a project of this magnitude. Yet he struggled to wrap his mind around being so far from Hidden Falls and the one person tethering him here.

His jaw tightened and relaxed. Chandler concentrated on the details, and upon further inspection of the conversion of an empty office building to Tuscan-style med spa, he talked himself into taking the job on the chance it would be fulfilling (doubtful) and profitable (most likely).

Pushing the plans aside, he picked up his cell phone and dialed Mitch's cell.

"Hey, Chandler. We've been waiting for your call."

"I've been going over both sets of plans."

"And?"

"I'll take the job, but what time frame are we looking at?"

"We don't expect to have all the specs worked out for a few weeks, and escrow won't close for at least sixty days after signing. New regs."

"Red tape's a bitch."

"We hope to break ground in May."

"Great," Chandler said, "the coolest part of the year."

"But it's a dry heat," Mitch mocked. "Since I've got you on the phone, I need a favor—if you have time."

"What's up?"

"There's a duplicate set of blueprints and a file I need for a meeting with the finance company early in the morning. Think you could get them to Hidden Falls Packaging and overnight them to me? I'd come get them myself, but I'm meeting with Marc, our attorney, in a couple of hours."

Chandler hesitated. "The lumber package for Juniper Ridge won't be delivered until early tomorrow, so why don't I bring them to you?"

"You sure? I'll put you up in the hotel for your trouble."

"Thanks, but the trip has to be a turn-around so I can take inventory before they leave the site."

"I owe you one. And Chandler, you've made a wise decision taking the job. Our motto is to surround ourselves with the best and the business takes care of itself. It starts at groundbreaking. Welcome aboard."

"Thanks. I'll do my best," Chandler said. "I need to shower and change clothes. So where should I meet you?"

"We're at the FireSky Resort on Scottsdale Road. It's a little modern for my taste, but the lagoon reminds me of a jungle."

"Okay, Tarzan," Chandler said with a chuckle. "And thanks, Mitch."

"Like I said, we surround ourselves with the best."

* * *

The drive to the Scottsdale resort was a coagulated tangle of rush hour traffic. Chandler hated the city for its hurry-up attitude and standstill traffic, preferring the kicked-back nature of his one-horse town.

Entering the FireSky's tiled drive was like driving into a tropical rain forest. Though in the desert, the resort had a modern Mediterranean feel and was surrounded by lush greenery. Chandler tucked Mitch's blueprints under one arm, grabbed the file, and entered the lobby. Before he could inquire which room the Burstyns were in, the attendant handed him a keycard and a note with his name scrawled across the front.

"Mr. Collins? Mr. Burstyn asked that I give this to you."

Chandler unfolded the paper.

Chandler—hate to ask, but can you pick the girls up at the airport? US Airways, flight 3721, 8:12 arrival. Had to meet Marc earlier than expected. Drop plans off in the room—enjoy the lagoon until time to go—the girls are expecting you to meet them at baggage claim. Take the Beemer. Thanks —Mitch

Chandler reread the instructions to make sure he understood the reference to "the girls." That's what Mitch called his wife and Ryleigh. He wasn't exactly thrilled about going to the airport, but the reason was attractive. And he'd bet money only one was expecting him and neither would be overjoyed to see him.

"What happened to taking a cab?"

The attendant simply shrugged.

* * *

On his fourth trip around the baggage area pacing like an expectant father, Chandler noticed the uncomfortable stares from the security guards. He knew he wasn't a threat to airport security, but they didn't, and before he did something regrettably stupid that increased their suspicions, he shoved his hands in his pockets and headed for the gift shop on level three.

He decided against buying a rose (she'd probably tell him where to stick it, especially the thorns) and killed the time instead with a Sports Illustrated. He flipped the pages without thought and checked his watch. Close enough. He tossed the magazine in the trash and returned to baggage claim, thankful the security guards had taken up stalking some other would-be terrorist.

The buzzer clamored and the carousel churned into action. He tapped his watch. Their flight had landed early. He rolled up the sleeves of his shirt and stuffed his hands in his pockets, heart thumping perceptibly in his ears.

The girls were descending the escalator shoulder to shoulder when he spotted them, Nat with her overnight suitcase beside her, Ryleigh with her phone to her ear. It was obvious she was talking with Evan. Her smile was radiant.

Chandler approached the same time the women reached the baggage carousel. Nat nodded.

"Hello, ladies," he said with a courteous smile, "your taxi awaits."

Ryleigh turned to Natalie with a menacing glare.

Chandler stepped back. "I'm just a taxi service. Seems I was in the right place at the right time."

"You just happened to be in Phoenix," Ryleigh said, the deflated question rolling off her lips as a stiff statement.

"Yes."

"Right."

"Mitch needed blueprints, so I brought them."

She glared at Natalie. "Did you know about this?"

"Sorta."

"Figures," she mumbled. "Why am I always the last to know?" Ryleigh reached for her bag, but before she could extend the handle, Chandler took it from her. "I can manage," she said, reclaiming it.

Chandler raised his hands in surrender. "Just trying to help."

She squinted. "We could have taken a cab."

He knew that scornful face well—the one she wore when irritated. Though not particularly fun to be around when she was ticked, he missed it—and everything that went with it.

* * *

Mitch was waiting at the lobby entrance when they arrived at FireSky. Natalie scooted out of the Beemer, and before she had a chance to speak, Mitch lifted her off the ground. She wrapped her arms tightly around his neck and he kissed her enthusiastically, spinning in a lazy circle.

Ryleigh deliberately cleared her throat. "Excuse me, people, but can we dispense with the PDA and go home?"

Mitch released his wife and brushed her nose with his index finger. "Oh, right," Natalie said, a hand fixed on his chest. "There's a slight problem with that." She leaned into her husband. "I'm really sorry, Ryleigh, but we've got an early meeting, and if you want to go home tonight you'll have to go with Chandler."

"Wonderful," she said, emphasizing the word with as much sarcasm as she could muster.

"Sorry. But if he hadn't been here, you'd have to spend the night with us," she said, cupping Mitch's cheek. Her smile widened. "Now that would have been a problem."

"Great. I want to sleep in my own bed tonight with my independent cuss of a cat. Let's go, Chandler. I don't want to listen to any X-rated sounds coming from the next room."

Natalie hugged her.

"You are so dead meat," Ryleigh whispered through a set of tightly clenched teeth.

"I know. Sorry."

Natalie turned to Chandler. "Get her home safely, please."

"You have my word."

Ryleigh felt a low "humph" rising in her throat at the words. Since when did his word mean anything?

"Thanks for your help tonight, Chandler," Mitch said, shaking his hand. "You won't be sorry you took the job."

"Looking forward to the challenge."

It wasn't the first time in the past few days Ryleigh hadn't been privy to what was going on. Always in the dark it seemed, and now the Burstyns' sudden affability with her ex-husband was a little on the baffling side. She felt a keen kinship with mushrooms. Portabellas. The big ones.

A worm of irritation squirmed in her stomach. A trip home with Chandler wasn't how she had anticipated the last leg of this already convoluted few days, and she had no intention of making polite conversation. He would have to act like a cabbie and drive. In silence. Maybe she could sleep.

With a groan, Ryleigh lifted her suitcase to the bed of the pickup and held her breath as she struggled against the weight. Chandler reached around her and took hold of the bag, thighs flexing against hers as he maneuvered around her. He pressed the small of her back firmly. Without the least shred of desire and certainly without her consent, she hesitated, her body attuned to the gentle pressure marked with invisible ink in a diary of lost memories.

Ryleigh stiffened. "Sorry," she said, "it was too heavy."

He tightened his grip and turned to her, his face intimately close to hers. The air between them came alive with his clean, musky scent and an unpredictable flush threatened her balance.

"I just wanted to help."

She recovered quickly, slipped from his touch and climbed into the truck, avoiding a moment that would have proven to be both reckless and downright foolish.

Chandler started the engine and drove through town, and then north onto the highway toward Hidden Falls, the engine's purr the background music to the silence between them.

The truck's headlights pierced the night as the asphalt vanished beneath the tires. Ryleigh leaned into the headrest and stared out the window, the steady rhythm of passing bushes, trees, and occasional vehicle a pacifier to weary thoughts.

"What's with the blueprints?" she asked, chastising herself for starting a conversation. So much for sleeping.

"The new expansion. I suppose Natalie told you about it?"

She fixed him with a blank stare.

He glanced at her. "You didn't know?"

She shook her head.

"They're converting a two-story office building in Scottsdale into another spa. Construction starts in May."

Ryleigh punched herself in the thigh for breaking her own promise of no conversation, and when she finally spoke, she did so without inflection. "That's great. But what's Della got to say about it? You'll be gone when the baby comes."

Chandler squirmed. "Nat's been busy, so I guess she didn't tell you about that either?"

"I've been a little busy myself," she said, and brushed a nonexistent speck of dust from her sleeve. "Tell me about what?"

"She moved to Scottsdale."

"Gee, that's too bad."

"And she's not pregnant."

Ryleigh's head turned swiftly. Della seemed the type to do something unimaginably stupid, and her head swam with ugly thoughts. "What happened?"

"Nothing. She lied about it," he said, his words colored with self-reproach. "There never was a baby."

"Should I be sorry?" she asked with little emotion.

"I'm the one who's sorry," he said, hands clenched on the steering wheel. "I was a fool."

"Took you long enough to figure that one out."

"You sound like Evan."

She shot him a sideways glance. "God, all men seem to care about is sports and sex and not necessarily in that order. Their brains drop between their legs about the time they turn fifteen. And you're no exception. I was there."

"You're right. I don't know what I ever saw in her."

Was it guilt or perhaps embarrassment she heard in the sobered response? Did it matter?

"You saw a pretty face and store-bought boobs and followed your stiff prick. She's as transparent as those skanky nighties she probably wears."

"I'm sorry, Ryleigh."

"A little late."

"If I could turn back the clock, I would."

Ryleigh searched his face in the hushed light of the truck. Sincerity lurked behind his words, and it confused her. She quickly shook her head. "Chandler, it's not just about you. You think in straight lines, like the walls in your blueprints—a precise start and end point. But what about everything in between? So much more constitutes that wall; it's all jumbled up with wiring and switches, two-by-fours and plumbing," she said. "You can't simply apologize and forget about everything else attached along the line."

"I'd take it all back if I could."

"Hindsight. Pretty damn easy to go there, isn't it?"

"I know I can't—"

"You're right. The past can't be changed. Nor forgotten."

Tension poisoned the air with a stagnant pause. He plowed a hand through his hair. "How was New York?"

She was exhausted and much too close to the man who should have been with her through her mother's death, walking beside her on foreign sidewalks looking for a man she'd never met, and holding her through Ambrose's stories, protecting her, consoling her. His arm should have held her when she walked from her brother's grave and it should have been his hands helping her bridge the gap between past and present at The Wall. Caught somewhere between resentment and just plain pissed off, her eyes blurred. She blinked back the sudden moisture, but she couldn't fight the lone tear that gathered weight and spilled.

"I don't want to talk about New York." Ryleigh groped for the darkness beyond the window and with her head turned, she wiped at a moist cheek. "Or anything. Just drive."

* * *

They pulled into Ryleigh's drive, the remainder of the trip spent in silence. The light on the front stoop had sparked and died when she'd tried to replace the bulb, and the bronze carriage lights on either side of the garage did little to light the front door. Chandler set the suitcase down and fumbled with the key.

Her teeth chattered. "Why do you still have the house key?" she asked, folding her arms in front of her.

He shrugged. "You never asked for it back."

"I am now. Leave it on the counter before you go."

The lock released with a thump. Ryleigh flipped the light switch and tossed her denim jacket over the counter. Kingsley bounded into the room, winding himself around her legs.

"Hey, Kingsley," she cooed, and stooped to pet him. Purring loudly, he arched his back petitioning for more attention.

"Your key." Chandler slapped the key on the counter.

When she reached for it, Chandler put his hand over hers. "I'll let you have it when you tell me what's wrong."

"Not a chance in hell. You've done your good deed, now please go."

He tightened his grip. "Tell me and I'll leave." His voice was calm, yet his words echoed the same firm resolve his hand held on hers.

Subtle signs of endless days spent in the sun appeared at the corners of his eyes, the lines etched faintly into tanned skin. The contours of the man before her had changed, his smile seasoned. Though the lines had deepened, the edges had softened, become more thoughtful.

"Do you think it was easy for me to admit how foolish I've been?" His thumb stroked her palm. "I've had a long time to think about what's important. I miss you," he said and pulled her against him. "I miss us."

Ryleigh slipped into his arms with familiar ease, nothing between them but the air they breathed. A tendril of hair had fallen across his eye, his face unshaven. She'd begged him to let his hair grow and allow a few days scruff between shaves, but he never had. Until now.

His breathing quickened. This couldn't be happening. Not after she'd made the decision to move on and after what had happened over the past few days and weeks. Renewed tears stung her eyes, and she ground the bitter rancor between her teeth. He had defiled their marriage and the hurt and humiliation had gradually subsided. Revisiting what she'd put behind her would resurrect the pain and peel away the fragile layer that had begun to form over the wound. She'd been down that road and the experience wasn't high on her list of things she ever wished to repeat.

His voice softened. "Ryleigh, something happened in New York." Chandler took her face in his hands and stroked her cheek. "Tell me."

"It's none of your business."

"I know you better than anyone. Give me a chance."

She dug her teeth solidly into her lip. "You had your chance."

"I need you, Ryleigh Collins." He traced the hollow of her back. "Let me be a part of your life again."

She straightened and thrust her fists to his chest. "You gave up that right the moment the male part of your anatomy led you into another woman's bed."

An emotional air pocket bloated the space between them. Wads of his shirt twisted in her hands. "Say something, you bastard!"

"You're beautiful."

"Not what I meant."

"I know what you meant and I meant what I said." His sincerity was unwavering. "You're the girl I fell in love with, the one I want to be with. That hasn't changed."

The years had been kind to him; he was more handsome now, etched with the fine lines of age, than when they were kids, and with an instant's hesitation, she allowed the words to momentarily penetrate a thin bubble of restraint. Her fingers formed around the hard line of his chin and then briefly touched his cheek. The strong features were but a façade to the man inside, and she'd slipped easily into the role of commander in chief. Was it so selfish to want someone to take care of her for a change? She drew a cleansing breath. "You're right again. Nothing has changed, and yet everything has changed."

His eyes danced back and forth between hers. "I want to come home."

"God, Chandler, you aren't listening—"

He placed a finger to her lips. "Let me finish what I've wanted to say for a long time." He swallowed hard, the tiny muscles in his jaw tensing. "We belong together and I'll wait as long as it takes to be a part of your life again. I've never stopped loving you."

Chandler lifted her chin. Hesitantly, he leaned into her and kissed her tenderly, the familiar feel of him natural and easy. He pulled her close and the taste of his lips and the warmth of his tongue were shadow-memories of a dream, one she didn't know how to pull away from. He held her with an intensity she hadn't felt in a very long time.

He cradled the back of her neck with one hand, the rough stubble of his face newly stimulating against her skin, his touch ingrained. She responded, a feverish excitement as their tongues met and the past disappeared.

They broke apart but she remained pressed against him, his heart thumping against her cheek, the rhythm mercifully conciliate, yet her heart and her head hopped frantically between two different playing fields.

"Let me make love to you."

Desperately wanting to relinquish and give in, she grasped his shirt and pulled it loose, her hands beneath the soft cloth tracing the outline of muscle, the feel of his skin and his sigh a momentary relapse into the familiar. She breathed deeply. How many nights had she waited for the obnoxious sound of the diesel truck in the late night stillness? Even before Della, was he truly pounding nails and raising walls in the dark? Or was he raising himself and pounding someone else on the nights he'd left her alone? She forced the ugly thought to disintegrate. Her hands fell silent to her side, her forehead against his chest, and she stopped herself before the ridiculous idea that things could ever be the same took root and grew to something unstoppable.

Gently, he lifted her chin and leaned in to take possession of what dwindling resolve she had left.

Ryleigh's fingers blocked his advance. "This is a mistake, Chandler."

"Please," he murmured, "let me show you we can start over, be who we used to be."

What was it Ambrose had said? *'You cannot expect the truth not to exist simply by ignoring it.'* "Too much has happened." She shook her head. "Della may not be carrying your child, but it doesn't miraculously change the fact you slept with her. You lived with her for a year. An entire year." She squeezed her eyes to expel the pictures that trespassed across her mind. Paramount to the sickening image was the fact he had betrayed what they once shared as sacred.

Turmoil played across his paled face. "How can I convince you I would never hurt you again?"

A whisper of disquiet seeped into her heart, one she wished she could dispel—one she knew she couldn't. The truth settled over her in the soft clicking of a closing door inside her mind: the past and all its intrinsic threads had rewoven her path. The path to her future.

She raised her eyes to his and absorbed the grief hidden behind his eyes. "I'm sorry," she said and stepped away from what could have been a consequential mistake.

Before she could slip away, he traced her arms tenderly, ending at her fingertips. Holding both her hands in his, he squeezed lightly. "Marry me."

* * *

Every ounce of assurance Ryleigh had built faded with each of Chandler's footsteps as he left the house. Coupled with the sequence of events of the past few months, her scrambled emotions were a towering course of bricks, one nudge from toppling. Though utterly confused by his words, the memories and hurt, she savored how easy it had been within his arms.

His words echoed inside her head. Her heartbeat had taken up residence behind her eyes, and she couldn't shake the insidious feeling of free falling—spinning out of control—the ripcord jammed. The parachute wasn't going to open.

Part of her remained in the comfortable security of his embrace, and part of her flipped to the pages of the past. Taking him back would be the easy thing to do—a relapse into an addictive habit—easier to give in than try to break. Chandler would provide for her and give her a good life. This needed no contemplation. It was easy. And when life presented itself as a stormy battlefield, she preferred to run for shelter until the thunder passed and the clouds dissipated on their own.

Ryleigh took the journal from her suitcase pocket and retreated to her study. Kingsley followed eagerly, leaped into the chair, and curled up nose to tail beside her. With Ryan's journal in one hand, she stroked the cat with the other, the tomcat's purr motor in high gear.

She traced the watermarked smudges and skimmed her finger over the 'R' at the bottom of the page, the same way she had a few hours ago at her brother's gravesite and again at The Wall. It seemed an eternity. Surreal. With the story ingrained in her mind, she wondered whether the smudges were raindrops dripping from leaves in the jungles of Vietnam, or the silent tears of a soldier lost in the heady bubble of love halfway across the world.

Sinking into the comfort of the old blue chair, she escaped into the one world she was sure of. Words. She preferred their company, their comforting embrace. Words were constant. Solid. Dependable.

At random, she flipped the pages, holding to the words her father had written, the ones her daddy had read to her as a small child. "Rhythm of the Jungle" fell open, and in a whisper, she began to read aloud to drown the voices inside her head.

> *" 'Quiet swells her voice to a thick vicious roar*
> *and bellows heartbeats of cavernous fright—*
> *Bombs echo their thunder beyond the next rise*
> *and tracers splinter the black cover of night.*
>
> *Fire-lights flicker across boggy vine-laden trails*
> *and hushed boots trample a muddy virgin path—*
> *Spectral silence prowls through the murky haze*
> *and echoes the call of death's lonesome wrath.*
>
> *Mist's mournful shroud blankets dawn's early light*
> *and eyes ever watchful nurse bitter anguish unbled—*
> *Choirs of prayers croon the jungle's cruel lullaby*
> *and sing reverent melodies of unspoken dread.*
>
> *The rhythm of the jungle purrs poisoned rain*
> *and taps her lonely cadence, the drumbeat of fear—*
> *Days swallow dreams drowned in milky mists*
> *and imprison illusions in the cocoon of desire.*
>
> *Shadows embrace ghosts of fallen Eagles, my friends*
> *and pierce private dreams, memories held deep—*

'Till a whisper of wind holds hands with my dream
and your voice brushes my lips—a prelude to sleep.
~R~'67'"

Shadows of a soldier's fears littered the pages, and she read of the metaphor of jungle rain her father had used to describe the pelting of machine-gun rounds and of the impending rendezvous with destiny he sensed would take his life. As a child, she loved the drama and color of the words. Now she understood and loved them for what they were—love (fear/destiny/anger/loneliness/death) letters to her mother—written by a young man on a battlefield twelve thousand miles from home.

Closing the journal gently to preserve its integrity—for her lifetime and beyond—she closed her eyes and held the blood-stained leather next to her heart, as close an embrace as her father would ever give. Unlike the man who'd died a soldier's death, she wouldn't allow his words to die too.

Curled next to Kingsley, fatigue swallowed her and the words of an eccentric, white-haired old man swirled in her head.

'...you must learn to live with your past. Do not ignore it. Embrace it...you are your mother's daughter and of your father's loins...Ryan's gift flows from you as it did him. Use it. Do not let another so gifted with words remain silent...there will always be storms, Miss Ryleigh...you must learn to dance in the rain.'

Kingsley rolled from his back and glared at her, his eyes severe slits. Just to annoy him, she kissed him squarely between his golden eyes. The cat pulled away to avoid the intrusive contact and bounced off the chair. "Sorry. I shouldn't have done that." Ignoring the trite apology, he sauntered off.

Ryleigh got up and searched through every desk drawer until her fingers closed on a spiral notebook. Months ago (years now?) she'd purchased the notebook in anticipation of starting another novel, a place for notes and ideas. The pages were unspoiled, nothing hidden in the pockets. But this wasn't a new story. This was the ending to an old one. Her past had taken a twist, and so had the ending to the unfinished manuscript Evan had mercilessly stolen.

Curled again into the blue chair, she forced herself to purge troubled thoughts of Chandler from her mind, and the only sound in the makeshift study was the scratching of graphite across paper as the words spilled from her heart.

Chapter Twenty-Three

CHRISTMAS HAD COME and gone in a whisper, overshadowed by the looming prospect of Evan's internship in California and the final dissolution of a marriage. A few days after officially relinquishing her marital status, Ryleigh would lose her son again, this time to the quagmire of not just a big city, a monster city. Los Angeles wasn't Phoenix, and the air lying gray and motionless across the horizon wasn't the only thing she considered polluted. But she had to trust him and her instincts and let him go. His dreams and his future began with a small magazine publisher in California where he'd begin his dream of becoming an editor.

With Evan at his father's and only days until his departure, Ryleigh paced the small den, the contents of the old cigar box drawing her like a magnet to iron. She'd sorted the letters by postmark, and then stacked and tied each bundle with a length of ribbon. They begged to reveal their secrets, but she'd chosen to read them gradually over time. They were few, and the fear of finishing the last one elicited a sadness she paralleled to finishing the end of a novel. And losing her family again.

Sitting cross-legged on the floor of the den, she removed the ribbons and turned a stack from front to back, careful not to damage the timeworn envelopes, and then placed each one in order in front of her, like tiles in an unfinished mosaic. The same familiar scrawl of the journal graced Ryan's, the handwriting fluidly arched with a soft right slant, and at times barely legible—the similarities to her own remarkable. Her mother's letters were written in a beautiful flowing slant, her signature with an exaggerated swirl on the curl of the first "E". She lingered on it, mentally counting the years. Time had long passed from the girl who lived for these letters, to the woman who lay at rest. At the end, even her handwriting had been the victim of time.

She opened an envelope addressed to her mother. Ryan's letters were signed with a single 'R' and the year at the bottom of the page. She touched each word, the commas and watermarks, as if imprinting them on her skin, hesitating on the 'R' at the bottom. She shivered. The room was warm, but it wasn't the temperature that had caused her skin to rise in gooseflesh—but the feeling their fingers had somehow crossed the boundaries of time.

With her life in shambles and her son on the verge of leaving the state, she clung to the idea of family—embracing what she did have, and longing for what had been taken—and read the letters without intermission.

Ambrose had been right—he was uncanny that way. The letters unraveled the threads of three tightly woven lives.

Eleanor wrote of ordinary people oblivious to the war raging halfway across the planet, New York snowstorms, the pond, and a stray dog she had befriended and named Tareyton ("Us Tareyton smokers would rather fight than switch.") due to the perfect black spot over one eye. Summer nights in St. Louis watching the fireflies were at the heart of nearly every letter.

Despite the appalling way her family treated her, Eleanor's letters overflowed with happiness and her love for Ryan. Even at such a tender age it was evident theirs was the profound love few people experience. And her words filled the page with the overwhelming power of love she felt for the life growing inside her. Not once did she denounce her love for Ben. Though different, it rose from her words as insightful and as deep.

But one of her mother's letters proved more touching than all the others.

On a cold St. Louis night, Eleanor and Ryan lay huddled under heavy blankets in a farmer's old hayloft on the outskirts of the city. Surrounded by sweet alfalfa hay, cattle lowing, and the warmth and charm of a boy she adored, it was a Christmas Eve her mother would never forget. Although chastised for her actions, the consequence of a star-filled night had also given her the most precious gift anyone would ever give her. The gift of life.

Ryleigh loved her mother. (God knows she did.) But after reading the letters, the connection grew deeper, the empathy and loss stronger than she believed possible. If not for Ambrose, she never would have come to know her mother's immeasurable compassion, due in part, she assumed, to the losses her mother bore. Ryleigh knew her only as Mom, but in the span of a few short hours, she'd come to know her extraordinary courage—a woman who had sacrificed and lost more than most do in a lifetime. And if she could disconnect herself, it would be a poignant story—one worthy of telling the world.

Ryan's words were just as Ambrose had described. The jungle came alive—lush with palm trees, elephant grass and villagers farming acres of marshy rice paddies and then, like a chameleon, transformed. Hillsides drenched in blackened ash reeking of death and puddled with blood, decaying animals and corpses. Monkeys chattering, birds every color of the rainbow, and idle whispers squelched by sniper fire raining down from the very trees that offered cover. The aftermath of an ambush.

Ryleigh envisioned the place that took her father's life with awe at its inherent beauty and revulsion for the horrors of war. The scenes reverberated in the journal, the darkness, fear, and indisputable happiness woven intricately between the lines. Words could never convey the force of emotion, but the passion and pain bruised her as deeply as if a bullet had torn her flesh. She grieved for the baby boy—her brother. Ryan's son. Raw emotion overpowered her with an inexpressible emptiness for a family that had been stripped from her. Family she never knew she had. And she openly grieved for the family she'd been given, only to see it taken away.

Entranced in a surreal world created decades ago and spelled out on aged, brittle sheets of paper, Ryleigh retied the string around the letters with a renewed insight into the two men she referred to as "father" and an unequivocal deepened love for the woman who had given her life. It was then, in spite of the secrets, she felt closer to her mother in death than she had in life.

Ryleigh raised the ball chain that hung around her neck and rubbed a thumb across the raised metal letters of the dog tag. She held it against her heart and smiled, and then sifted through the old cigar box—her treasure chest.

A ragged envelope addressed to her mother lay mostly hidden in the bottom. She peeled back the flap and inside were government bonds amounting to several thousand dollars in today's market, her name neatly typed across the documents. Unable to absorb the reality, she set the certificates on her lap and removed another document, unfolding it with the same care she'd taken with the letters. Her original birth certificate trembled in her hands. She skimmed the information. Halfway through, she stopped on the space marked "twin."

"What's wrong, Mom?"

"Evan—you scared me. I didn't hear you come home."

"Sorry. I should have texted you. What's that?"

"God, you're nosy."

"Wonder which side of the family I inherited that intrinsic quality from."

"Very funny," she said, forcing back a growing unease. "How was your visit with your father?"

"You're changing the subject."

Ryleigh dropped her hands into her lap. "It's a long story," she said, noticing how his blue-green eyes were accentuated by dark hair, soft curls forming where it had grown past his ears. Until now, she hadn't realized how much he resembled the soldier in the photograph. Generations apart, yet time stood still and the past looked back at her from the same green eyes he'd inherited. All prejudices aside, her son was more handsome than the man he would someday know as grandfather.

"It's early."

"Some other time."

"You're stalling." Evan grabbed the side chair. He flipped it backward, straddled the seat, and folded his arms across the back. "I'm not going anywhere." He dropped his chin to his arms.

She had no reason not to tell him. If she could get through the story one more time, it would be over and she could go on with her life—if it was possible. Evan would see things differently. Didn't he always? He found the positive in any situation. But she couldn't tell him—not now—not when he was embarking on a new adventure.

Calling on every ounce of reserve, she forced a wide smile. "It's nothing. Really."

"Yeah, right," he said as Kingsley sauntered into the room, flicked his tail, and turned an abrupt about-face. "That cat hates me, I swear."

She wasn't good at lying, but she was good at being Mom. "It's nothing that can't wait until next time you're home. Now go—I have work to do. And Kingsley doesn't hate you."

Evan flipped the chair back with one hand. "Let me know when you change your mind."

"Evan," she said, her tone stern enough to turn him around. "I will tell you. Just not tonight."

"Okay," he said, "I can wait." He hesitated, and then leaned against the doorframe. "Oh, hey, have you seen the new house Dad's building?"

She shook her head, an unsettling tingle erupting in her stomach. Chandler hadn't been back since their last encounter, and she didn't know if he'd been untruthful with her again, or if he truly intended to wait. Or if she wanted him to.

"The framing's almost done and the roof's on. He designed this amazing floorplan and he's doing most of the work himself." Evan shrugged. "Then sometime this summer he's handling the remodel of an office building into another spa for Nat and Mitch."

"He'll do a good job for them."

"You should go see Dad's house."

"Where is it?"

"Juniper Ridge Road."

Ryleigh's stomach turned a nasty flip.

* * *

The trunk was already stuffed, so Evan shoved the last of his things into the backseat of the Civic. His eyes sparkled with the excitement of adventure, his smile infectious. Though January was half gone, Saturday broke with clear blue skies, and Ryleigh was thankful for the dry weather out of pure selfishness. Bad weather would have complicated her worries for Evan's trip to California.

"Please be careful, Son," Ryleigh said, wrapped in his bear hug. "Take your time and drive carefully."

"Mom, it's Los Angeles. It's only a couple hundred miles. I'll be fine."

"Four hundred and sixty…give or take."

Evan pushed his mother to arm's length.

"I Googled it."

"You did?"

"I did."

"Without help?"

"Bite me," she said, smacking his arm lightly. "I manage. When I have to." She wasn't about to tell him she had countless manuscript pages of handwritten material that needed to be transferred to the computer. He would've thought her insane.

"I'm impressed."

"Me too," Natalie added with a wink. "Come here, young man." Natalie and Mitch hugged their godson together. "Be safe and call your mother often."

"I will."

"Show that magazine they've got the best intern around. We'll take care of things here. Right Mitch?" Discreet tears hugged the edge of Natalie's eyes.

"Of course we will." Mitch slipped his arm around his wife's waist. "Give 'em hell, Evan. L.A. will be a better place with you in it." Mitch shook his hand, the gesture returned heartily.

"Guess Dad couldn't make it." He peered into the street. "I'd better hit the road."

"He's on his way," Ryleigh said. "I hear that obnoxious truck."

A few seconds later, Chandler pulled to the curb. Evan met him and the two men exchanged a long hug. With his arm draped loosely over his son's shoulder, they entered the garage.

Evan slid behind the wheel and the Honda engine came to life. With an animated wave and a smile that breached the darkened windows, he backed down the driveway and disappeared around the corner. Ryleigh's shoulders slumped, a symbolic wave into the empty street falling into her lap, and the ache squeezing her heart comparable to the divorce, the separation no less painful.

Natalie clapped her hands. "Coffee anyone?"

Ryleigh nodded. Tears trembled on the edge of her eyes as she stared into the distance, searching for the sound of the engine; postponing the last reminder that her son was gone and the house empty. And empty houses, empty marriages and empty hearts beat differently.

"I'll start a fresh pot." Nat dragged her husband by the sleeve. "You can help."

Chandler approached Ryleigh and without hesitation, pulled her into his embrace. "He'll be fine."

"I know he'll be fine," she said, struggling to free herself, but Chandler's grip was firm. Giving in to a flood of emotions, she relaxed into his embrace, unable to move. And didn't honestly know if she wanted to.

"I already miss him." She didn't look up. "And dammit, I miss you." She did miss him. That much she was sure of. Not the long hours away. Or the attention he flattered on baseball stars instead of her. But the way she'd settled into the comfort of knowing she belonged. "Damn you, Chandler!" Her fists pounded his chest, transferring her outrage to him. "I hate you for what you've done."

"I hate myself for what I've done to you."

"Not to me. To *us*. We were a family."

Chandler picked her up and set her on the counter that flanked one wall of the garage, the space where his tools hung in a former life. He'd built the counter taller than customary to fit his height, and she was inches from his sobering blue eyes.

"What the hell are you doing?"

Cradling the sides of her face in his hands, he brushed aside a strand of hair caught by the moisture of her tears. "I can't change what I've done." He searched her face. "But I can fix it. Tell me you want me to."

"I don't know what I want."

"I do."

"Chandler," she said, tracing a crack in the concrete with her eyes.

Their eyes met. "I want to come home." Chandler parted her legs so they hung discreetly beside his hips. She opened her mouth to speak, but he touched her lips with his fingers. "Don't answer now." He kissed her, his lips moist with the salt of her tears and eager with passion, his hands knowing and familiar over the curve of her waist, and then came to rest, solid and warm on her thighs. "I've never stopped loving you. And always will." With a gentle squeeze, he backed away. "I'll wait."

She stared after him into the empty street long after the drone of the diesel engine had died.

Natalie returned with steaming cups of coffee. "Aren't you cold?" She handed Ryleigh a mug, set hers down and then hoisted herself onto the counter.

"Not when you're wrapped in someone's arms and he's kissing you, confessing his screw ups, and how much he loves you and wants to come home."

"Oh, boy," Natalie said, turning to face her. "Should I say I'm happy? Or should I chase him down and beat the shit out of him?"

Although she smiled at Nat's remark, a tear spilled to her jeans. The dark stain spread to twice its size, as big as the confusion taking up too much real estate in her head. "I thought I was past this. Remember last month when he brought me home from the airport?"

"Oh, God. I'm dead meat, aren't I?"

"Charcoaled." She pushed her hair away from her forehead. "He told me the same things that night. He kissed me then too. And I shouldn't have kissed him back," she said, smiling demurely. "And then he asked if he could make love to me."

"Wow. When did chivalry return?" A perfectly groomed eyebrow arched dramatically. "Well, did you?"

She raised her eyes to the ceiling. "I wanted to. And badly," she said, her shoulders collapsing around her.

"What stopped you?"

"I'd like to think it was my incredible common sense."

"No?"

Ryleigh shook her head. "When I look at Chandler, I see him smiling at *her*." Would she ever be able to sidestep the anger the mere thought of Della caused? It had built inside her, an expanding balloon ready to burst. Yet each time, she'd allowed the balloon to collapse. Her hands curled into fists. "Every time I think of that bitch, I want to rip out every strand of her too-blond hair, puncture her store-bought boobs, and pluck her fake nails off with a pair of pliers."

Nat's legs swung freely. "That's my style, Riles. Not yours."

"Sometimes I wish it was."

"You're learning."

Ryleigh shrugged.

"You stood up to Chandler."

"Maybe." Ryleigh digested the words and nodded. "But I don't know if I can handle anymore crap in my life, Nat. How many times can I break before I shatter?"

"This last year has been more than anyone should have to bear."

"I'm spinning in circles and all I do is get dizzy." Ryleigh held her mug to her mouth with both hands. Steam rose in curls and disappeared. "He's changed, Nat. But he's still Chandler. The doorbell is dying, the porch light is dead and the cement walk needs to be exhumed. He didn't offer to replace, rewire or resurrect any of them. It's petty, but that's the Chandler I know. A long list of broken promises." She set the mug down. "And there's this teeny matter of trust," she said, pinching her thumb and first finger together.

"It's obvious he still loves you, Riles. But are you still in love with him?"

"A part of me will always love him. I could never abandon that. He's Evan's father. But there's a difference between loving someone and being *in* love with them."

Natalie nodded.

Ryleigh sat on her hands, her shoulders hunched between her ears. "And he's building the house I've always dreamed of." Beyond the garage, a cardinal pecked the winter grass for remnants of fall's crop of seeds, oblivious to the conversation, the cold, and the emptiness growing inside her.

"I know."

She raised her hands in resignation. "Welcome to my secret life as a Portobello," she mumbled. "Why am I always the last to know?"

"Stop feeling sorry for yourself and answer my question. Are you in love with him?"

"I don't think I know the answer."

"You have some hefty thinking to do, girlfriend."

"My son is gone. My ex-husband wants to come back, and the man I thought was my father, and my mom—" *Abandoned—from everyone and everything that defined her, that made her feel whole.* "I'm homesick, but I don't know where home is anymore. I just want to feel like I belong again. Somewhere. To someone."

Nat scooted off the bench. "I think I have a solution," she said, extending a helping hand.

"To which screwed up part?"

"The deep thinking part," she said. "Let's go inside. Your teeth are chattering since you don't have that hunky man crawling all over you. Oh, and just so you know, I love you, Ryleigh Collins, my best friend in the whole flippin' world, and I am also totally *in love* with you." Natalie swallowed her in a comforting embrace.

Inside, Mitch was rinsing his coffee cup. "So, ladies, is this my signal to hit the road?"

"Time to take a hike, big guy." Natalie reached around him from behind, slipped her hand precariously low on the front of his jeans, followed the zipper, and gently squeezed.

Ryleigh cleared her throat and turned away.

"You prepared to finish what you start?" Mitch whispered.

Natalie giggled and kissed him hard on the back. "Ryleigh and I are going for a run."

Ryleigh spun around. "Nat, I'm not in much of a mood to—"

"Tough," she said, turning to face her, "it'll take your mind off your worries. Besides, I have something to talk to you about." Turning to Mitch, she ran a perfectly manicured fingernail over his cheek. "And I'll see you later, Mister." Soft as suede, her eyes twinkled as the invitation rolled off her lips. "Wear a sweatshirt, Riles. We're running on the forest trail at the spa today."

* * *

The two women walked briskly to warm their muscles, their breath puffing ahead of them in disappearing clouds. Ryleigh gathered her hair into a ponytail and picked up the pace. The need to run overtook the reluctance, and she wanted to sprint, to outrun herself—to or from what she wasn't entirely sure.

"What did you want to talk to me about?" A tall stone fountain gurgled and the pungent scent of ponderosas and blue spruce reminded her of Christmas and for a fleeting moment, of Ballston Spa.

"I need a favor," Natalie replied between breaths. "Damn, girl, slow down. This isn't a race."

"Keep running and keep talking."

"I've been e-mailing a friend…in Estes Park…about adding my spa services at their resort," she said, the words coming in spurts. "Rose manages it. The owners are new…and want me to visit for the weekend to check things out." She paused, breathing deeply to soothe a side stitch. "Shit," she said under her breath. Ryleigh sprinted ahead.

Two miles went quickly. Ryleigh slowed to a walk, sweat trickling from her temples. Natalie joined her to walk the last lap.

"Estes Park. It's northwest of Denver, isn't it?"

"Yes," Natalie replied. "It's the entrance to the Rocky Mountain National Park. I was supposed to visit Whisper of the Pines Resort in two weeks. Go over the numbers. They set up a long weekend on a trial basis—investors mostly. The area around Fall River is filled with resorts and some stay open during the winter for the ski buffs—if it ever snows again. The owners want their investors happy with the renovations and amenities."

"Why're you telling me this?"

"Because I want you to go in my place."

"Yeah, right. I know nothing about opening or running a spa."

"You know my expectations and what appeals to my clientele. And you know me."

Ryleigh released the ponytail and let her hair fall loosely around her face. "Why can't you go?"

"Mitch and I are swamped with the preliminary plans for the expansion. The timing sucks, but I'm curious about this opportunity, and I really need you to do this for me. It's a complimentary trip, and you can take my laptop and work on your manuscript. Forget about life for a while. Relax. Evan will be settled in his new job."

Ryleigh glanced at her watch. He'd be on the outskirts of Phoenix by now. "The last time I went away I think the Azkaban dementors sucked out my soul."

"What?"

Ryleigh chuckled. "Never mind," she said as they entered the spa.

"And," Nat said, giving her a teasing jab to the arm, "the Stanley Hotel is in Estes Park."

Ryleigh grabbed her coat and purse. "Stephen King stayed there, and it was his inspiration for *The Shining*."

"They say it's haunted."

"I'd rather stay there than the resort. Room 237." The offer was intriguing. Though she didn't want to admit it, Nat's wiles had set the hook. She raised an eyebrow and grinned. "When do I leave?"

"Two weeks. End of January."

"Crap. That means more time off. Bernadette has no life outside *The Sentinel* and thinks no one else should either. I dread asking. I swear she inspired *Horrible Bosses*."

Natalie flashed her a mischievous grin. "I don't think she'll be much of a problem."

Ryleigh stopped dead. "What did you do?"

"Offered some incentives. A massage, pedicure and I threw in a facial." Natalie scrunched her face. "Quid pro quo."

"Gag me now," Ryleigh said, clapping her hand over her mouth. "That's bribery, Natalie Jo. I look good in pink, but I don't particularly relish the idea of spending time in Tent City in Sheriff Joe's infamous pink underwear. Besides, a facial won't do her any good."

Natalie chuckled. "Your boss will authorize the time. Trust me. And I guarantee she won't utter a peep."

"What did Mitch say about all this?"

Natalie swung her arm over Ryleigh's shoulder. "It was his idea."

A renewed energy forced a wide smile to spread across Ryleigh's face and her step lightened. Not quite the butterfly from the chrysalis, but just maybe…one step forward. This could be fun.

"Go pack your long johns, it's in the mountains. And cold. Oh, and these," she said, digging in her purse. She removed six foil packets.

Ryleigh's eyes widened. "What the hell do I need these for?"

"It's a resort." She shrugged. "With a boatload of male investors. You never know."

She shook her head. "Um, no."

"Know how to use one?"

Prickles of heat rose to the top of Ryleigh's head. "I was married a long time. Didn't have much need for…"

An impish smile played across Natalie's face and she regarded her from eyes gone devilishly dark. "They're flesh colored."

"What dif does that make?"

"Could be turquoise or pink. Or KFC. You know, finger-lickin' good?"

Her cheeks burned red hot. "You're hilarious, but I won't need them," Ryleigh said, pushing the condoms back at her as if they were contagious, "but if I ever do, I certainly hope I'm not stretching one over a fried chicken leg."

"I don't have any chicken legs handy." Nat laughed and tucked them into Ryleigh's purse. "But I do know where there's a cucumber."

Chapter Twenty-Four

DRIVING THE MOUNTAINOUS curves into Estes Park in the BMW X5 was the ultimate, but dwarfed in comparison when Ryleigh spied the conspicuous spire of the Stanley Hotel rising against the scabrous mountain backdrop. Nestled into the Rocky Mountain foothills, the hotel stood stark white against the gray mountains, its brick-red roof a bloody contrast to the evergreens.

Her spine tingled. "This is crazy cool," she muttered, recalling the Overlook Hotel from Stephen King's *The Shining*. And wasn't the second film shot there? The image shrank in the rearview mirror and she craned her neck for one last peek. "I must see this place close up."

As the miles passed, the snow deepened and the evergreens thickened. The majestic snow-capped peaks of the Rockies loomed around her, as if hand-painted against a cloud-studded blue canvas sky.

Ryleigh turned onto a narrow, snow-packed road, pulled over, and engaged the four-wheel drive. She wiped her palms on her jeans, cinched her fingers around the steering wheel, and then drove cautiously along the forest road.

Douglas fir, blue spruce and groves of leafless aspen draped the road in shadow. The first sight of the resort breached the palisade of trees, and for the first time since she left the asphalt, she allowed herself to relax. A wooden bridge crossed the rapids of Fall River and into a valley of provincial-style log cabins and one massive log-sided building she presumed to be the lobby. She pulled up and parked, wrapped her scarf around her neck, and stepped into the brisk mountain air. The river rippled to the energetic squeals of children caught in the crossfire of a snowball fight.

Ryleigh slipped, caught her balance, and then walked cautiously to the entrance. A rustic Whisper of the Pines sign hung over the entrance and images of the surrounding valley were carved into heavy oak doors. Inside, massive log beams laced themselves across a high cathedral ceiling, and windows rose floor to ceiling on one side.

"Welcome to Whisper of the Pines Resort," a boisterous voice rang out. "Your winter wonderland at the base of the Rockies."

Startled away from the view, Ryleigh turned. The woman's eyes sparkled amid an aged face that had seen too much sun over the years. "I'm Rose, your hostess for the weekend. What can I help you with today?"

Ryleigh recognized the name and smiled back. "Hello, Rose. I'm Ryleigh Collins," she said, pushing a wayward strand of hair behind an ear.

"Of course you are!" Rose extended a pair of robust arms and swallowed Ryleigh in a welcoming hug. "Natalie told me all about you. Welcome."

"She conned me into taking her place."

"We're thrilled to have you," she said, patting Ryleigh's hands enthusiastically, "and you'll be delighted you came."

"This place is gorgeous."

"It is, indeed. The new owners have made some marvelous improvements. It's amazing what the Cavanaughs—what Logan, I should say, does with his resorts. It's a Cinderella story—from ordinary to exquisite. He has quite an instinct. A Midas touch if you will."

"A lot like Nat and Mitch."

Rose threw her arms in the air. "Indeed they are, and now they're expanding. It's been her dream since we were in college." Rose chuckled. "Oh goodness, don't look so stunned. I'm a bit old, but better late than never they say." She spun around, glancing through the clusters of people. "Mr. Cavanaugh—the owner—is here somewhere. You must meet him." She grabbed Ryleigh by the hand. "Come. Let's get you checked in. Natalie reserved the best cabin for you."

"Of course she did." Ryleigh relaxed into a bright smile, the stress melting into the surroundings. Even the resort's name boasted of tranquility. "She's extremely generous. I wish I could reciprocate somehow."

"This is a tremendous favor you're doing for her," she said, wagging a finger back and forth. "Mr. Cavanaugh would have been extremely disappointed had she canceled. He feels the spa services are a much needed addition." She handed Ryleigh the keycard to cabin three. "Your visit is extremely important."

"Okay, then. I'll do my best. When would be a good time to show me the proposals?"

Rose glanced at the clock. "It's two now. What do you say after dinner? Around six?"

"Perfect." Ryleigh tilted her head slightly to one side. "Do you mind if I take in the view for a few minutes?"

"By all means." Rose beamed. "There's a wonderful Reading Room left of the lobby. You'll love it." She winked. "I understand you're a writer."

A shy smile curled the corners of her mouth. "That's a matter of opinion, but thank you, Rose." To dispute the notion Natalie had planted in Rose's head seemed futile. After this weekend she would probably never see Rose again. It seemed silly to refute it.

Ryleigh thanked her and glanced around the lobby, encased in glass and in the shape of the bow of a ship. The view wrapped itself around her. She drew a deep breath and followed her curious fascination to the Reading Room.

Ryleigh tossed her purse and coat on a leather chair, scanned the room and then paused at the section devoted to poetry. She breathed in the musty fragrance of newsprint and ink, the essence of familiarity. The essence of heaven. She ran her fingers along the spines and hesitated where the 'F's should be.

"Looking for a particular poet?"

"Crap." Ryleigh clutched her neck and turned abruptly. "You scared me."

A rather tall man with a black cashmere scarf hung loosely over broad shoulders stood at the entrance to the Reading Room stomping snow from his Sorels. Ryleigh raised an eyebrow, thankful a heavy throw rug caught the dribbles of mushy snow. "I'm sorry," he said and tucked wet leather gloves into his coat pockets. A coy smile erupted across an angular jaw. "I didn't mean to startle you. I was curious if I should see to adding another author."

She shrugged. "I favor Robert Frost's poetry, but I didn't see any of his."

"The collection isn't quite complete. Frost isn't among us."

"Not since the sixties, anyway." Heat prickled her cheeks as his mouth curled into a penetrating half-smile. "I enjoy his simplistic style," she said, wishing she could take back the silly remark. "But there's plenty to leaf through."

"Emily Dickinson…" he said with an awkward pause, as if he hadn't meant to say the name. "I find her work intriguing."

The hesitation caused her to look away. "I think I know what you mean." Ryleigh dragged her hand along the spines of Cummings, past Eliot and stopped at Stevenson. "Well, if you'll excuse me, I need to find my cabin. I have a date at six."

"You don't want to be late. Which cabin are you looking for?" He raised a hand. "I'm sorry, I didn't mean to be intrusive, but each of the cabins has its own history or bits of trivia and some have regular visitors. The wildlife in the Rockies is extraordinary."

"So, you work here?" she asked, noting the way his consummate smile accentuated perfectly matched dimples.

The man chuckled, his voice deep and rich. "You could say that."

* * *

Logan Cavanaugh shook his head to erase the picture from his mind. He'd been curious when one of his guests had entered the Reading Room, anxious to see if his mini library would lure anyone when the infinite winter playground of the Rocky Mountains lay just beyond the doors.

His father had been against the addition of the room, arguing it was a waste of resources. Contrary to his father's objections, he had the contractors add it anyway.

From across the room, he'd observed the woman, her enthusiasm for books and poetry apparent as she'd browsed the shelves. And he couldn't help but notice her shy smile and how it created a generous dimple in one cheek. The left. Up close, her green eyes sparkled in the firelight and her cheeks had blossomed to a warm shade of rose.

He hadn't meant to stare.

And he surely hadn't looked at a woman that way, or in any way, in more than three years.

As a pale winter sun sank below the craggy peaks of the Continental Divide, Logan pulled to the stop sign, turned onto the asphalt and drove toward town. He parked the Range Rover and walked the few blocks to the Estes Park Book Shop.

The sweet bouquet of lavender on Laurie's skin and her reserved smile were an integral part of him, and the mere thought of another woman brought about deep feelings of hypocrisy and betrayal. Her death had a way of sneaking past his rational side, even now. Logan's heart thundered inside his chest as if he had committed a sin, the desire to find a book for a woman he didn't know waging war with a deep-seated tug of guilt.

He didn't even know her name.

Assuming the book he wanted was one few people would ask for, he bypassed the shelves and went straight to customer service. He chose *Robert Frost, The Collected Poems, Complete and Unabridged*—hardback. He would be certain to have Frost's entire collection, insisting it arrive overnight no matter what the cost.

Logan thanked the cashier and stepped outside. The frigid air cooled the nervous perspiration on his brow, and he picked up his pace, desperate to leave the nefarious act of betrayal in his wake.

* * *

The hours flew by as Ryleigh settled into her cabin, and taking a last look in the mirror, left to find the dining room. Snow crunched under her boots. Encased entirely in glass, the dining room branched off the lobby and embraced the jagged outline of the Rockies. The delicate aromas of sautéed mushrooms and roasted garlic wafted over the tempting whispers of ripe strawberries and fresh cream. Ryleigh was escorted to her table and served a carefully personalized full-course meal.

Familiar with a good entrée and already spoiled by the Cavanaughs' exquisite taste in décor and food, future stays at the Days Inn would be nothing short of mundane.

Rose placed a hand on Ryleigh's shoulder and leaned in. "What do you think of your first meal at Whisper of the Pines, Ms. Collins?" She reached for a chair and sat across from her.

"A rare treat," Ryleigh said, placing her napkin alongside a square Mikasa china plate. "The cedar-plank salmon was seasoned to perfection and the citrus salad a superb blend of sweet and zesty flavors. And there's nothing to compare to fresh roasted vegetables in the middle of winter. Fresh asparagus this time of year is unheard of." She shook her head. "But the caramelized crème brûlée was to die for."

Rose beamed. "We have an extraordinary chef. Mr. Cavanaugh's choice, of course. And I see you know something about good food."

"A little." Ryleigh shrugged. "I'm impressed, and I'm dying to see what you have in store for the spa."

"It doesn't have the Tuscany theme Nat loves so much, but I have a feeling she will be pleased—on your recommendation, of course."

"I doubt there'll be a problem."

"If you're ready, I'll give you the full tour." The women rose and wove their way through the dining room. "Afterward, I've got to get home and help my husband bring in firewood. There's a storm coming. He's disabled and can't stack it himself."

"I'm sorry."

"Don't be." Rose shook her head. "We manage."

"There's a storm coming?"

"So they say. The clouds are building along the Divide. Isn't supposed to snow much, but things can change quickly along this fickle river valley. A storm can dump three times as much snow here as in town. It's odd, but it happens."

"Is it supposed to last long?"

"Don't be alarmed. It's been such a mild winter so far. Probably won't be anything more than a cookie-duster. Besides, weathermen are rarely right." Rose dismissed the statement with a wave of her hands, and then took Ryleigh's arm. "Look there," she whispered, "along the river." Rose pointed out the window. "You'll want to take in a sleigh ride. If the weather turns bad, Mr. Cavanaugh will have the horses put up for the duration of the storm."

Smiling guests bundled against the cold climbed into the horse-drawn sleigh. Old-fashioned lampposts bordered the winding path, diffused light radiating from them like a strand of pearls shimmering in the wake of incandescent moonlight. "Reminds me of a Thomas Kinkade painting," Ryleigh said under her breath, "and fairy tales." She turned to Rose. "What doesn't this place have?"

"Not much. Except a spa. And that's why you're here. If his resorts lack anything, Mr. Cavanaugh will see to acquiring it. I've never seen anything like it in this business, and I've managed a few resorts over the years." Rose leaned in closer to Ryleigh. "He's eligible, you know," she mused. "A bit on the solemn side but oh, goodness," she said, her hands clutching at her heart, "the man is as divine as the crème brûlée—a rare, sweet treat." Her face turned pink. "He's much too young for me and he is my boss—but you, my dear…"

"And you're married."

"That too," she said with a wink.

A prickle of warmth rose in Ryleigh's cheeks. "I'm here for the solitude and to get some work done. Nothing more."

Rose patted her arm. "Whatever you do during your stay will be splendid, I assure you."

Rose's enthusiasm bubbled at each point of the proposed spa facility. She fussed over the business proposals and latest asset and expenditure spreadsheets. Ryleigh jotted notes, leaving the business analysis to the Burstyns, but assured the astute woman there would be no question she'd give her blessing. She had already fallen in love with the quaint winter wonderland.

With a firm grip on the railing, Ryleigh waved to Rose and descended the lobby steps. A soft nicker echoed through the night stillness. Delighted they were still making rounds, she trudged carefully toward the sleigh hoping to catch a ride.

"Excuse me," she said, rubbing gloved hands together. "Am I too late?" Her breath puffed ahead of her in smoky clouds. The driver turned. A second man removed packed snow from the horse's hoof.

"No, ma'am." The driver tipped a black felt cowboy hat. "Which cabin?"

"Three, please."

The other man stood and stroked the big, black horse's nose. Ryleigh smiled at the familiar face. "I guess you know which cabin I'm in now."

"That I do," he said, studying her. "Three is special."

"Why is that?"

"When you wake in the morning, look for the large boulder across the river from your deck. You're likely to see Whistler, our resident bobcat. Cabin Three is named The Whistler, in her honor." He adjusted the horse's harness and then patted him on his withers. The horse chuffed and a fog of breath swirled around the tall man. He chuckled and patted the horse again.

"Why do you call her Whistler?"

"Whistle a tune to her," he said and spread a wool blanket across one of the sleigh's seats. "The sound seems to fascinate her, but she's skittish, so keep it soft. Any loud noise and she'll bolt." He offered his hand. "Watch your step." A large leather-gloved hand, firm and steady, grasped hers and assisted her into the seat. "I'd like to ride along, if you don't mind."

Not really a question, the statement puzzled her. Without offering an answer, she zipped the collar of her coat against the cold night air and cinched her scarf.

"I need to settle the horses for the night, and the barn is across the footbridge just beyond your cabin."

"Oh." The tension in her legs eased with the perfectly rational explanation.

He took a seat across from her, broad shoulders and dark hair dusted with snow. He nodded to the driver, who clicked his tongue and flipped the reins. Silver bells around the horse's necks jingled as they moved forward, their jet-black outline mere silhouettes in the soft light.

"The horses are beautiful. And so big. What kind are they? There's a footbridge?"

The man settled his arm over the back of the seat. "The horses are Percherons, to answer your first question. Draft horses. Windsor's on the right," he said, nodding in the horse's direction, "Apollo the left. Originally bred in France to carry knights into battle. They had to be quite substantial to transport the weight of a fully armored knight. In today's world, Percherons are bred by the Amish for plowing fields and pulling sleighs and carriages. There's not much call for knights in shining armor these days."

"You're not a woman." An awkward smile crept across her face, and she bit her lip in response to the silly remark she desperately wanted to take back.

"If you're inclined to require the services of a knight," he chuckled, "I'm afraid you're out of luck, shining armor or not. And yes, a footbridge crosses the river to answer your second question. Between cabins three and four."

The horses slowed, and then came to a stop outside cabin number three. He stepped from the sleigh and offered his hand, the strength of his grasp assurance she wouldn't fall. He reaffirmed her confidence by taking her waist, so close his musky scent overpowered the pines. Snowflakes as big as nickels had begun to fall.

"Good night, Miss…I'm sorry, but you haven't told me your name."

"You're right." She grasped her collar tightly. "I haven't." Snow rested quietly on her shoulders and tickled her lashes. "Nor have you offered yours." Ryleigh tilted her head shyly. "Good night, then, and thank you for the ride."

Ryleigh waved, privately noting the kindness behind the deep brown eyes of the man who seemed to be wherever she was. Gazing back at the winter wonderland, she couldn't help but wonder at the remote possibility of the existence of fairy tales.

And knights in shining armor.

LOGAN WAITED UNTIL she approached the door to cabin number three, the tingling warmth of her hand still residing in the palm of his. Her laugh echoed in his mind, the sound more brilliant than her smile. Her eyes glistened in the light from the lampposts and he need only close his eyes for full recollection.

"Let's put the horses up, Shep, before the skies unload."

"You got it, Mr. C." The driver dipped the brim of his Stetson and clicked his tongue. The sleigh lurched forward. The harness bells jingled, a crisp echo in the still night air.

Images of an old movie—Lara in the sleigh waving goodbye to Yuri—flashed across his mind as the woman slipped inside, a silhouette in the open cabin door. Though the compulsion to fix his eyes once more on the woman with the stormy green eyes tugged at his better judgment, the insurgent feeling he hoped to see her again tapped at the armor he'd wrapped around an empty spirit. Yet every rational part of him waged its own personal war against it.

Logan leaned into the cold leather seat. His hands trembled. He rubbed his temples, driving the images from his mind only to have them take shape and rise the way smoke swells into plumes from under the door.

RYLEIGH CLOSED THE door and leaned against the hard surface. A chill rushed over her; one that had nothing to do with the freezing temperature, but had everything to do with a snippet of memory: a shadow of beard, deep-set dimples, and if she watched closely (which she had) a solemn smile that softened his dark eyes.

Brushing snow from her shoulders, she hung her coat, pulled off her boots, and wiggled her emancipated toes. Instant warmth flooded the room as she flipped the switch to the gas fireplace and hesitantly skied across the room, thick fleece socks gliding easily over waxed planks of wood flooring. Set high above the floor, the queen bed yielded when she fell backward into the puffy down comforter. She laughed, a giddy sort of thing, and sat up. Grabbing her phone, she drew her legs to her chest and dialed Nat's number.

The connection was garbled and the call went straight to voicemail.

"Natalie Jo, this place is enchanting," she said, twirling her hair around an index finger. "You need to sign on with these guys, without a doubt. The amenities are impeccable and the scenery spectacular. People will love it, summer or winter. I'll send pictures if the connection clears up. By the way, between the Beemer and this place, I'm officially in love. Oh, hey—how's Kingsley? I miss that brat. Talk to you soon. Wait—one more thing. It's snowing," she sang. Her toes curled and her shoulders quirked up to meet her ears.

Ryleigh tossed her phone on the comforter and pulled Nat's laptop into her lap. "Crap. This'll be interesting," she said, cringing. Mastering technology was as simple to her as algebra—letters and numbers didn't belong together and neither did cookies and spam. But caffeine went with everything.

Soon, the bold aroma of gourmet coffee filled the cabin. She placed a full, piping hot mug on the nightstand, flopped on the bed, and lifted the computer into her lap. She clicked the icon. "Yes!" The document blossomed in front of her eyes and she made the final edits to both columns for *The Sentinel*, Bernadette's trade for time off. Smug with the results of the first document, she clicked the second folder and the title page of her manuscript appeared.

Armed with a mug of caffeine, she settled in to tweak one of her characters, an incessant fictional child—aka, hormonal male— begging for her attention. She recalled his features, confident stride, and shadowed face. Her hero emulated the spirited jawline and assured stature of the stranger on the sleigh, but a mountain of handwritten pages needed to be typed into the computer. She sighed at the prospect of a long night ahead.

Snow bathed the night in silence outside while the soft tapping of fingers on a keyboard resounded inside cabin number three. Ryleigh yawned. Transferring the last of the handwritten pages, she typed the word *Epilogue*, clicked Save, and closed the laptop.

Remnants of subdued light from the stone fireplace cast playful, soothing shadows across the log-sided cabin walls. Her tired limbs unfolded and she yawned so wide her eyes watered, the moisture cooling the burn. She shimmied out of her jeans and snuggled under fleece sheets and thick blankets. Firelight whirled behind her eyelids, and her fingers closed around the dog tag as sleep set the period at the end of a long day.

Outside, snow continued to fall.

Chapter Twenty-Five

RYLEIGH OPENED ONE eye and stretched languidly. Light poured through the glass doors, gray-white and blinding. In her haste to crawl into bed last night (or had it been morning?) she'd forgotten to close the blinds. Movement caught her eye beyond the back deck. She rose and tiptoed to the glass doors. *Could it be?*

Night had given way to a pristine blanket of snow, the wilderness quiescent. Directly across Fall River perched atop a large boulder sat the bobcat, legs buried in snow. Not much larger than Kingsley, its gray fur and black spots contrasted against the white backdrop. Careful not to disturb her, Ryleigh cracked the sliding glass door. A breath of air, cold and keenly virginal, showered her nose to ankle in gooseflesh. The cat flinched, every muscle on high alert. Slightly off-key and through chattering teeth, she whistled "Somewhere over the Rainbow," a tune she'd sang to Evan as a baby, before he could discern the fact she couldn't sing. The cat's ears twitched at the unseen notes floating over the river. The snap of a tree limb startled her and in two leaps, she'd disappeared. *What wasn't magical about this place?*

Fully awake, Ryleigh showered and dressed in jeans, minus any distressing—this was no place for natural air conditioning—and a turtleneck under a bold ecru fisherman's knit sweater, her father's dog tag nestled against her skin.

Bundled against the cold and the laptop secure, Ryleigh walked the short distance to the lobby. Snow parted in the wake of her knee-high snow boots, and icy wind bit her cheeks. The grounds bustled with activity. Knots of people milled about. Some loaded their vehicles. A child's shrill cry split the chaos.

Systematic commotion greeted her inside as she stomped snow from her boots. Across the lobby, Rose directed guests like an indoor traffic cop.

Ryleigh waved. "Good morning, Rose."

"Well, well, well, good morning, Ms. Collins." Rose beamed. "How was your evening? Did you sleep well?"

"No less than perfect, and I was greeted this morning by Whistler."

"You don't say?"

"Rose, what the heck is going on? Am I the only one left in the dark?" she asked, frowning.

"Oh my dear, it could get very dark around here."

"Seems to be the story of my life."

Bewilderment twinkled in Rose's eyes.

"Long story. What's going on?"

"Everyone's leaving due to the storm."

Ryleigh grinned. "A few inches of snow hardly constitute a storm."

"Oh, but there's a doozie coming." She leaned into Ryleigh and lowered her voice. "I swear those weathermen can't tell the difference between their *culo* and a hole in the ground sometimes." Frustration wrinkled Rose's brow. "We've advised everyone to leave just in case the forecasters get lucky this time." She patted Ryleigh's arm. "Otherwise you all might be stuck here longer than planned. This was a trial run for investors and we're not completely set up."

"Must we leave?"

"Of course not, if you don't mind being housebound for a few days."

"I have nothing else planned."

"If this storm hits like they say," she said with a note of caution, "the roads could be closed until Mr. Cavanaugh can arrange for the snowplows. I doubt he'll risk the horses if the snow's too deep."

"I could use the solitude."

"Couldn't we all?"

"Mind if I use the Reading Room?" An empty room to finish her story seemed indulgent. And wonderfully enticing.

"By all means. If I don't see you before I leave, enjoy the rest of your stay."

"You're leaving too?"

"My husband needs help preparing for the storm."

"Of course. It was nice meeting you, Rose. Be safe."

"It's been my pleasure, Ms. Collins. Give my best to Natalie when you return home."

Ryleigh turned to leave but turned back. "Rose, is Mr. Cavanaugh around? I'd like to meet him—to let Nat know I spoke with him."

"He should be back shortly. He's in his element flitting about town picking up supplies and all," she said, her smile on the wry side, "a ship in full sail, that one." Her hands rose in a wide circle, a feeble attempt to imitate a blustery sail.

Ryleigh smiled. "Thank you," she said, and headed for the quiet of the Reading Room.

With foot traffic at a peak, she zigzagged across the lobby. The knot of people had thinned. She slowed to a stop and gasped at the breathtaking view. Fall River, lined with boulders and prisms of ice, ran briskly through a blanket of white and she stood motionless to pin it to her memory.

She wasn't entirely surprised to see the Reading Room vacant. A fire crackled in the massive stone fireplace and subdued cove lighting encircled the room. Excited by the rows of books, she hadn't noticed the fireplace the previous day. An ample tree trunk, peeled and sawn flat on top, served as the mantel and stretched the eight-foot width of stone. A bronze bust of William Shakespeare sat on one end. Her eyes followed the river rock, naturally colored and worn smooth, to a log-beamed ceiling. The room had a masculine feel, but to her relief no animal heads hung on the walls.

She sat down and pulled off her boots. The flokati rug pooled under her feet and she wiggled her toes inside her socks against the long fibers. Ryleigh curled into the corner of the leather sofa and though not entirely convinced she wanted to work, she powered on the laptop. A leisurely nap, or curling up to read with the warmth of the fire at her back and the snowy landscape in front of her seemed more to her liking. Both sounded luxurious.

Ryleigh peeked over the top of the computer screen and did a subtle double-take at the man in the long tailored leather jacket standing at the entrance brushing snow from his shoulders. He nodded before entering and stopped short of the sofa, larger in both stature and presence than she remembered. The same black cashmere scarf hung casually over straight, broad shoulders, and she recognized the designer jeans—True Religion—the same brand Mitch and Nat wore. He looked as though he'd come from outside, but definitely not from the stables.

"We meet again, Cabin Number Three."

"Hello," she replied, setting the laptop aside. "You have a strange habit of finding me. Or following me, perhaps?" She pursed her lips. "And if you work here, you could have easily learned my name."

"That would be," he said, removing leather gloves from the large hands she keenly recalled steadying hers, "presumptuously rude. That," he paused, discarding brown paper and string from a small package, "could be considered stalking."

Ryleigh grinned, despite his sudden appearance.

He handed her the book. "This belongs between Emerson and Gibran, but since you're here, will you do the honor? Unless of course, you'd prefer to read from it first."

She stared at the book and then looked back at him. "You bought this because I mentioned Robert Frost?" She brushed her hand across the title.

"Yes."

"Why?"

"It's my job."

She opened the book to the index and ran her finger down the titles until she spotted "Stopping by Woods on a Snowy Evening" and then turned to the page and began to recite. She paused, surprised to see him reciting the words, his eyes fixed on hers. "You know this?"

"Yes."

"All the verses?"

"Yes." He glanced away. "If you'll excuse me, I have guests to attend to. There's a storm in the forecast and I must see they reach town safely. You should think about leaving soon."

"Rose assured me I could stay," she said, straightening. "I've been through my share of snowstorms."

Intense eyes the color of strong, bold coffee, held her gaze. "The resort will remain open. So whatever you decide is fine. However, Internet and cell service can be erratic during inclement weather in this river valley. You should advise your family."

"I intend to stay," she said, pinching her brow. "I have a lot of work to do and I need this time away."

He nodded politely. "Enjoy your afternoon, then. Be careful if you venture out," he said, retrieving the paper wrappings and then hesitated for quite an extended moment—but left the room without looking back.

Ryleigh stared after the puzzling man who tended horses in designer jeans, cashmere, and expensive leather. And knew poetry.

She captured one last glimpse as he strode confidently from the Reading Room, the sides of his stylish coat billowing with each long stride.

He intrigued her. Not only for the palpable display of thoughtfulness, but the way the story in his eyes seemed to emulate the turbulent emotion hidden behind hers. Part of her longed to step one foot into tomorrow and pursue the story, the other more stable, rational part tugged her back into the safety zone of today.

Summoning Rose with a wave, the stranger draped an arm across her shoulders and she disappeared beneath his arm, the man several inches taller and whose widespread shoulders were a generous shelter to the short, plump woman. They spoke briefly, the animated figures a silhouette against the white backdrop obscuring everything beyond a few feet from the window.

The storm had arrived with a vengeance.

Ryleigh sent texts to Natalie and Evan letting them know she would be staying on through the duration of an impending snowstorm. Both failed to deliver. "This thing is possessed." She tapped the screen as if doing so would inspire a cellular exorcism. Giving up on the texts, she sent each an e-mail. Surely the Internet would cooperate.

* * *

The hours passed slowly, but the snow accumulated quickly. The bustle had died and the only sounds were the occasional pop and hiss of hot pitch in the fireplace. Unable to focus, Ryleigh closed the laptop and turned back to the Frost poem and read it again, though the book acted merely as a prop, the words memorized years ago.

The developing snowstorm seemed the perfect end to a near perfect day. Ryleigh packed the computer and squeezed Robert Frost between the good company of Ralph Waldo Emerson and Khalil Gibran. She paused, and pulled a collection of poetry by Emily Dickinson from the shelf just as Rose's voice echoed across the room.

"Oh, Ms. Collins, I'm glad I caught you," she said, a buxom chest heaving in time to hurried breaths. "Everyone's gone. I wanted to make sure you still wanted to stay." She rolled her eyes. "They've upgraded the storm."

"Are you sure I should?"

"Mr. Cavanaugh insisted everyone go home to their families, but a portion of the staff is housed in the dormitories. Enough manpower to run the resort. And Mr. Cavanaugh will be here, of course. You'll be fine."

"It's settled, then. I'll stay."

"Mr. Cavanaugh will see to your needs." Rose patted her arm. "He knows this place better than anyone."

"Am I ever going to meet this mystery man?"

Footsteps echoed in the lobby.

Rose's eyes widened, and then disappeared in a wide grin. "I think that's him now. I'll introduce you and then I should leave before the snow gets any deeper, or it'll be melting down my *fondoshciena*." Rose cupped her hand to one side of her mouth. "My backside. God knows there's plenty of it," she whispered and darted to the lobby dragging the tall man back by the arm.

Ryleigh gasped, covertly adjusting her collar to hide the color surely rising in a steady stream of heat from her neck to the top of her head.

"Logan Cavanaugh, I'd like you to meet Ryleigh Collins. She's here to discuss the spa arrangements."

A furtive grin lightened his face. "Hello again, Cabin Number Three." He extended his hand.

Rose's round face pivoted between them. "You two have met?"

Ryleigh took his hand. A tingle startled her as their fingers touched. "You could say that."

Compassion and kindness emanated from watchful brown eyes and the same whisper of cologne tickled her nose.

Without the barrier of gloves, his touch sizzled with the energy of an impending lightning strike. Strong fingers closed around hers and his warm, chocolate eyes consumed her words before they could fall from her lips.

Rose glanced from one to the other. "Well, well, well." Dismissing herself, she gave a casual glance over her shoulder and left.

Chapter Twenty-Six

LOGAN RELEASED HER hand. "Dickinson?"

"Oh," she replied, holding the leather-bound book slightly away from her, "yes. I'm having trouble concentrating on work."

"Rose tells me you're a writer."

"Rose exaggerates."

"May I ask what you write?"

Ryleigh regarded him curiously, the sobering contour of a handsome face defined by lines that cut deeply beside a soft mouth. "Fantasies."

"Curiouser and curiouser?"

"No," she said, glancing away, "nothing like *Alice in Wonderland.*" She brushed a lock of hair behind an ear.

"Hobbits of the Shire or wizards of Hogwarts?"

"Neither." She lowered her eyes. "Romance."

"Not exactly what I consider the fantasy genre, Cabin Number Three."

"It is if you've lived my life lately." She raised her eyes to his, the pause no more than a mental stutter. He was smiling, but his dark eyes sheltered the emotion of the person they belonged to. "Love is a fantasy—an unrealistic dream created by the imagination."

"That's merely Webster's version." He motioned for her to sit. "Fairy tales and fantasy allow us a discernible way of escape."

"Fairy tales can also be mythical horror stories that would give Stephen King nightmares." She chose the corner of the sofa and drew her legs under her.

"Indeed," he said. "I take it you're a King fan?"

"No one knows the human psyche better than the Master of Horror."

A sly smile lifted one side of his mouth and he nodded at the book in her hands. "Do you know Dickinson's work?"

"Packs a walloping message in a short verse."

"She writes from within. Favored her solitude," he said.

"I can relate to that."

Logan's gaze remained fixed on her, and then he glanced away to check his watch. "If you'll excuse me, the horses need tending."

"I'm sorry. I didn't mean to keep you from your duties."

"It's early, but night falls quickly here and the snow is accumulating faster than I expected. I must see to feeding the horses."

Ryleigh nodded.

Logan slipped past her and disappeared through double doors at the far end of the Reading Room. For some time, she wondered where the doors led, and her eyes remained fixed on them. His imprint lingered there, a tall, masculine frame and handsome face revealing nothing but echoes of something much more intense beneath the calm demeanor. Emily Dickinson slipped from her grip and fell open in her lap, marked by some invisible bookmark. *"'I Shall Know Why—When Time is Over—,'"* she read the title silently. The poem was short, yet the despair settled heavily on her heart.

She flipped the page. Tucked neatly into the binding was a torn paper, lines handwritten in a fluid, distinguished script, but she didn't recognize the words. She read the poem, "Along the Road" twice, the weight of grief buried in each line.

In poetry and in music, Ryleigh believed something of yourself lay hidden in the words. Were these Logan's trademark poems? Ones he visited often to seek solace? Or remembrance? From what?

Logan returned minutes later in a heavy zippered sweatshirt, the Yale logo worn and faded. He crossed the room in wool socks and tossed a down jacket across the sofa, snow boots in one hand, scarf draped across the other.

"Snow's accumulating quickly, Cabin Number Three," he said, taking a seat to lace his Sorels. "We should see about returning you to your cabin."

"You know my name now, Mr. Cavanaugh. You can use it."

"The nickname suits you," he said, adjusting the lining in his boot. "And it's Logan, since we're on a first-name basis."

"I suppose a nickname could be considered a first name," she said with little regard to keeping the comment to herself.

Logan hesitated lacing his boots and the subtlety of a half-smile lifted one side of his mouth. "Did you find something from Dickinson you enjoy?"

"Not really." She shrugged. "The one about time being over seemed a bit morose."

"I see." Resting his arms on his thighs, he looked up from fully laced boots, and the intensity of his deep brown eyes seemed to burrow through hers. "And I see you've read Hamilton's work as well." He nodded at the paper she'd quite forgotten she held between her fingers.

"Ditto on the morose bit."

His jaw muscles tensed. Long fingers parted a thick tangle of hair as he raked a hand through a hint of easy curls lightly dusted with silver at the temples. They gently kissed his collar, glinting in the firelight when he moved just so. "You'll understand the true meaning of happiness when you've walked in sorrow's shoes," he said.

His voice was infused with a sedate undertone that suggested his own what? Sorrow? Regret? Confusion? An understanding sigh tugged at her heart. "I thought maybe you wrote it."

"Robert Browning Hamilton," he said in the same monotone. "I enjoy reading the written word in most any shape and form, but I leave the writing of literature to people like you."

Ryleigh leaned into her palm. "Rose exaggerates."

"Surely not our Rose," he said with the suggestion of a smirk. Logan stood. "You should return to your cabin."

Without regard for the sudden urge to disconnect from the close proximity of this intriguing man, she leapt into a capricious moment of impulse. "Need help with the horses?"

Logan momentarily froze. "You aren't quite dressed for the occasion, Cabin Number Three," he said, surveying her inadequate attire.

"I'll be fine. May I tag along?"

He rested his hands on his hips. "Put your boots on." He waited while she untangled her legs and pulled a boot over thick socks. "Penguins?"

Ryleigh wiggled her toes. "I have a thing for penguins." In truth, the little birds with Santa hats were the closest thing to Christmas festivities as she'd come this year.

"I'll save you a pebble."

"A pebble?"

Logan smiled. "Gather your things," he said and helped her to her feet. "We'll drop them at your cabin."

Without Rose's boisterous voice directing the constant flow of foot traffic, the resort had taken on an eerie quiet. The skies had turned a muddied gray, though sunset was still an hour away. Logan escorted her through the lobby and out the side doors. Snow fell relentlessly. "Better button up." Logan zipped his coat. "We're taking the snowmobiles."

She hesitated, and then hurried to keep up with his long strides. "We're not walking?"

"The Cats will be faster."

The idea was more than daunting. Exciting yes, but she knew nothing about snowmobiles or the man taking the controls and even less about his concern for safety—or lack of it. But Rose obviously trusted him. And Nat trusted Rose. She shrugged, tucked the messenger bag over her shoulder, and pulled on her gloves. As long as it was snowing, it couldn't be too terribly cold and the horses weren't far from her cabin. Were they? She swallowed an urge to recall the impulsive request.

A half-empty garage housed the Arctic Cats. Logan grabbed two helmets from a nearby shelf, pulled one over his head, and handed her a pink one. He settled into the seat of the nearest snowmobile, stretched his fingers into driving gloves, and turned the key. The engine purred. Grumbling, she pulled the helmet over her head and Logan motioned for her to sit behind him. Cold pierced through her jeans and then she could have kissed whoever invented heated seats, but wanted to stuff whoever invented helmets into the nearest snowbank.

"I'm ready." She looked around for handholds. "I think." She drew in a breath and hesitantly reached around his waist.

"Hang on."

The vehicle lurched into the storm and she tucked her head into his back to avoid the wind stinging every millimeter of exposed skin.

Barely a minute had passed when they pulled up to her cabin. Ryleigh jumped off and took only a second inside to drop off the computer and pull a knitted hat over her ears. When she returned to Logan, she tucked her scarf inside her coat and pulled the helmet back over her head. She straddled the seat and scooted next to Logan to block the cold. "Go, go, go!" A minute and a half and she was already a pro.

"Careful what you wish for."

Logan maneuvered the Arctic Cat slowly, gaining speed as he turned to cross over Fall River and follow the path to the barn.

Rounding a tight curve, he eased off the gas and drove into the forest.

Ryleigh stiffened, a trickle of panic seeping through the exhilaration. "Where are we going?" The whine of the engine muffled the bubble of apprehension in her voice.

"You'll see," he called back.

"Surprises," she grumbled. "Why can't people leave them to those who enjoy being sucker punched?" What words weren't lost in the faceplate of the helmet drowned in the drone of the engine.

The Cat skied effortlessly over the pristine landscape and careened around a cluster of aspens. Logan drove parallel to the edge of a shallow ravine and cut the engine. The air stilled and the earth held its breath. But life echoed all around them.

Tree limbs groaned beneath the weight of the snow. A flutter of wings dislodged a branch of snow that fell to the ground in a muffled thump. The lonesome bugle of a bull elk echoed through the canyon and Ryleigh leaned forward in the direction of the sound.

A herd of Rocky Mountain elk passed below the cliffs, their scruffy brown coats a vivid contrast against the white landscape. Snow rose in powdery clouds with each forward lunge, and vapor billowed from their nostrils as they passed in single file.

Ryleigh eased herself up, her weight teetering to one side to get a better view. "They're magnificent," she said with an airy whisper. She placed both hands on his shoulders and leaned into him, the breadth of him next to her as solid an anchor as the earth beneath her. "The view. It's incredible."

"Incredible doesn't come close to describing it, but the sun's not long on the horizon. We have to go. Ready?"

Ryleigh reseated herself and grabbed his waist. "Go!"

LOGAN RESTARTED THE engine and turned the Cat back toward the barn. More incredible than the scene playing out before his eyes was the feeling coursing through him as Ryleigh braced herself against him. Logan's senses churned, acutely aware of her body against him and her arms wrapped firmly around his waist. Despite his best efforts to toss the errant thoughts to the wind, he couldn't deny the sensation was pleasant, yet felt deceitfully wrong.

Right or wrong, he couldn't shake it, nor could he name it. The desolation he'd grown to accept as armor against the realities of a neatly packaged world wavered and then slipped. Even breathing could shatter what he'd only begun to feel. Disturbing the moment seemed inconceivable. But he dare not linger. Not here. Not ever. The horses needed tending.

Logan blew out a misty breath, and regained the upper hand of a careless rout of emotions, but resisted the urge to confess the handholds were below her.

Though the accumulating snow had nearly covered their tracks, Logan followed the trail without fault to the main road. Once back on course, he zigzagged around the clearing that surrounded the barn, the blinding snow a cool balm against the intrusion of misguided thoughts. Ryleigh's grip tightened, her laughter clear, her words a gentle sigh. He pulled to the barn doors, stepped off the Cat, and removed his helmet.

"This is crazy cool!" She grinned and removed the helmet, cheeks flushed from the cold air. "Can we go again sometime?"

"After the storm," he said, extending his hand to her. "The Rockies are breathtaking. Winter or summer."

RYLEIGH TUCKED HER hand securely in his and swung her leg over the Arctic Cat. Joy creased the corners of Logan's eyes, and they came alive as if the snowstorm had chiseled away some tiny piece of collateral damage.

He grasped her gloved hand, his grip a firm comfort to unsteady feet. "Watch your step. Ice forms under the snow here and it's—"

"Whoops!" Ryleigh's foot shot out from under her and she fell backward into the snow. Unable to break the fall, Logan slipped and fell beside her. Icy snow sneaked under the backside of her jacket and she inhaled sharply an instant before her laughter filled the muffled silence of falling snow.

"Cold-cold-cold," she said, barely able to squeeze the words between chattering teeth. "Help me up?" She reached for his hand.

Logan took her hand. Her fingers disappeared into the warm sheath and he tucked them both against his chest. He rolled to his side, mere inches from her face. The smile that played on her lips faltered and then collapsed altogether under the palpable desire to succumb to the consequence of shared closeness.

Logan gently wiped the snow from her cheeks, the sweet sigh of leather supple on her skin. He found the small of her back and eased her toward him, a gambol of unanswered questions sequestered behind eyes like deep pools of espresso. He leaned into her and cupped his hand to her cheek, the sting of cold skin evaporating with his touch. With a moment of subtle hesitation, he brushed his lips to hers.

Blood pulsed through her in animated gasps. Her heart stumbled. They drew breath as one, but her lungs refused to breathe as though he'd sucked the air from the world. In a moment of impulse, she reached around his neck and brought his mouth more firmly to hers; she was lost in the tentative, unwritten invitation.

The storm swallowed her voice, the silence a mere whisper of falling snowflakes and the far off whine of the wind through evergreen boughs. All around them the snow continued to fall, but she felt no sting, his body a shelter, a pledge of safety against the power of the storm.

"I'm sorry," he said, breaking apart.

"Are you always this enterprising toward your guests?"

"I'm sorry," he repeated, tucking a sodden strand of hair under her hat.

Short bristles of beard stubble glistened as snowflakes melted into tiny drops of dew.

"Don't be," she whispered, pressing her cheek into his touch. "I'm not."

"We need to get moving," he said, carefully standing, "or you'll be soaked."

"And the horses need tending."

"Yes. The horses."

Logan extended his hand to help her up. Holding her steady, he led her across the ice toward the barn's entrance. "Watch your step. The horses trample the snow and it's slick."

"I can manage—Oh!" she gasped, nearly tumbling to the ground again.

Logan gathered her around the waist, his grip unwavering, and held her upright. "I won't let you fall."

With the full strength of his body next to hers, she matched his long strides with two of her own into the barn. Logan flipped the light switch, dousing the barn with a mellow, dim light and muted hum of electric current. The horses acknowledged their visit with a chorus of chuffed nickers, and the sweet aroma of alfalfa mixed with the pungent odor from the stalls.

Four horses, two coal black and two dappled gray, stretched their necks expectantly. Their nostrils flared and ears twitched with anticipation of dinner.

"It's nice in here," she said, gazing around.

"Winters can be bitterly cold in the Rockies, so heaters were installed last fall."

Ryleigh stroked a black horse's velvety nose, his breaths materializing in warm chuffs against her hand. Long eyelashes drooped over kind eyes. "They look identical, Logan. How do you tell them apart?"

"Apollo has a faint star on his forehead. Windsor is jet black."

"And the grays? What are their names?"

"Sterling has knee-high dark gray socks and Lancelot—Lance—has more silver in his mane and tail."

"I see. I guess," she said, bending to check Sterling's legs for the so-called socks, but rose abruptly at the gratuitous display of equine affection she'd nearly come face to face with.

A deep, rumbling laugh came from the next stall as Logan tossed flakes of alfalfa into the cribs.

"Smart-ass," she mumbled. Sterling snorted in a spray of alfalfa and horse snot. "That goes for you too!"

Windsor's tail swished from side to side, dislodging the ghosts of summer flies as Logan threw the last flakes into the cribs. He moved beside her and leaned against the stall. "They're actually quite easy to tell apart."

"How—without inspecting their, umm…anatomy?" An embarrassing tickle crawled up her neck.

"Read their nametags," he chuckled, "on the stalls."

He was smirking. "Smart-ass," she sassed, this time loud enough that Apollo raised his head and bobbed it in what was surely an acknowledgement of the impish sense of humor.

Logan laughed openly, a deep, infectious timbre that accentuated the lines around his eyes, but the distance buried there refused to give way to complete joy. "I've been called worse."

Ryleigh turned and leaned against the stall, the spirited gift of his laughter still humming inside her. "Justifiably so."

Bits of chaff glinted in the dusty light as Logan brushed loose hay from his hands, the distance between them marked only by the brushing of fabric against fabric. She shivered, an involuntary reaction to the close proximity of this intriguing man.

"You're shivering." He removed his scarf, wrapped it around her neck, and held the ends.

"I don't know why I should be," she said. "It's not cold in here."

The inviting half-smile preceded a deep chuckle that tingled her flesh. A rich line framed his mouth on one side, a tenacious punctuation of what he kept hidden there.

"I find it rather warm myself," he said, and without warning, twined the scarf around his hands and pulled her against him.

Gentle eyes cradled hers in a tentative embrace, the power lurking there an anchor to restless avidity, and though his smile had dimmed, his face bore an inward tenderness ripe with compassion. He took her face in the broad span of both hands and brought his face to meet hers. He touched his lips to hers and following the absence of reservation, he kissed her.

His tongue met hers in an invitation as patient as it was longing, and then he deepened the kiss so completely and with such powerful gentleness, her body, her mind, and her resistance failed completely.

Logan dipped his forehead against hers. "I don't want to apologize this time, Cabin Number Three," he whispered. "But I will."

A rueful smile disappeared as quickly as it appeared.

Run.

A mirror reflection of her thoughts.

Stay.

A labyrinth of mixed emotions jammed inside her, clogging any rational course of escape.

Think.

She was powerless to move and as resignation set in, she allowed herself to let go, to be immersed in the solidity of his embrace. "Please don't apologize." She searched his discriminating features. For what? Answers? Answers to questions she didn't know how to voice. "Logan, I—"

"You're shivering. It's time to head back."

Ryleigh's teeth chattered, but she wasn't cold. Every ounce of her bathed in the steady flame of his warmth.

Obscured by the storm, the sun slipped below the mountains and dusk settled over Fall River Valley. Snow continued to fall, covering their tracks and concealing secrets. The lampposts sparked to life and snowflakes danced in the amber wake of light. No, she wasn't cold. A spark had kindled a sense of renewal in the aftermath of a malignant year.

* * *

On the return drive to Ryleigh's cabin, Logan wanted to believe she was holding on a little tighter. Compelled to free her of the awkward predicament in the snow, he found himself unable to pull away from the intensity that stared back at him over the faint suggestion of freckles scattered under extraordinary green eyes. The tethers that bound him had fallen victim to her infectious smile and warm, delightful laughter. Cheeks reddened from the cold and damp, errant strands of hair the color of caramel that peeked from beneath a knit cap had been more breathtaking nestled against the snow than any expanse of wilderness landscape. A December rose in bloom. A prism of colorful laughter. A sea of churning waves.

The wind numbed his face, but the whole of her had penetrated an invisible barrier—a safeguard nothing or no one in three years had come close to breaching.

An answer to a prayer.

One he hadn't asked for.

Something shifted in his memory and his throat tightened around some abstract thought he failed to drag from the recesses of a careless mind.

Or one he refused to expose.

Chapter Twenty-Seven

THE LAPTOP SAT idle on her lap. The cursor blinked, but didn't move. Concentration was useless. Gripped by the hypnotic trance of falling snow, Ryleigh stared out the window of her cabin confused and uneasy. The whisper of his touch lingered across her lips. Her head swam. The story in front of her had a tidy ending. But her story was chaotic. And messy.

Outside, snow fell in downy feathers, swallowed by the river and designing white top hats on the boulders lining the riverbank. Lost in thought, she barely heard the knock. She padded across the oak floor and peeked through the tiny peephole that turned humans into comically distorted aliens and saw nothing.

She took a useless swipe at the peephole. "Who's there?"

"I come bearing gifts."

She released the deadbolt and opened the door to Logan wiping the frozen peephole with a gloved finger. Snow dappled his ski bibs and settled on wet curls peeking from under a knit hat.

She shifted her weight. "You have a remarkable talent for scaring me," she said, the cold draft raising the hair on her arms in a ruffle of gooseflesh.

"I didn't mean to frighten you," he said and dusted the snow from his shoulders, "but I assumed you'd know who it was."

"I wasn't expecting anyone." She caught herself staring and quickly looked away.

"I brought the Arctic Cat," he said. "It's not exactly quiet."

"I was working. I barely heard the knock." Who was she kidding? She cleared her throat. "But why are you here?"

"I didn't want to disturb you, but with the storm in full swing it would be difficult for our guest to venture to the dining room, so I brought room service," he said, holding up an insulated food carrier.

Momentarily stunned, all she could do was stare.

"I'll leave the food," Logan said, turning toward the door, "so you can return to your work."

"Don't go," she replied so quickly she surprised herself. And from the look on his face, it surprised him too. "Please, come in."

Logan stepped inside, closed the door behind him, and removed his hat with a shower of melted snow. "Max, our chef, is staying through the storm. I don't know what he's prepared us, but it's hot and he hasn't disappointed me yet."

"Us?"

"Except for a skeleton staff, you and I are the only ones who remained behind."

Ryleigh set the carrier on the counter, the spicy balm of ginger and red peppers enticing as she removed the contents, the flush from his lingering gaze on her shoulders more pleasant than the fingers of heat from the fire. "Logan," she said, turning to face him.

"It's okay." He turned toward the door. "I wanted to make sure you had everything you need before I go."

"Please stay," she said, splaying her fingers. "Have dinner with me."

A smile matured across his face. "I'd be honored." He unzipped the front and legs of the ski bibs, muscled limbs tightening and relaxing as he stepped free.

The routine caused a pleasant tingle across her skin as she scanned his body, his jeans faded and worn smooth in all the places that fit him snugly. Turning away, she rubbed the back of her neck to choke the rising heat. "Hang the bibs, please. I wouldn't want the owner upset over water spots on the wood floors."

"You wouldn't want to cross him."

"And why is that?" she asked with a deliberate air of cynicism.

"I understand he's a smart-ass."

"Rumors precede him."

"First impressions based on rumor can be deceiving."

"I base my impressions solely on firsthand knowledge."

A flicker of humor crossed his face as she motioned for him to sit.

They talked through the meal, something Ryleigh hadn't done in an exceedingly long time. Prior to his liaison with Della, conversations with Chandler were scarce and the silence between them had risen to a deafening roar.

Keeping the conversation light, Logan mentioned how Wentworth-Cavanaugh had taken mediocre properties and transformed them into posh resorts, though he wasn't quite sure how it happened with the state of the economy. His father had been the pillar of the company with a shrewd mind for business, but an innocuous patriarch when it came to family. Logan spoke with undiluted pride about his daughters, Sophie and Abbey, now grown and gone, and how Sophie was to be married soon and Abbey would step into the family business after college. It was evident he cherished his mother and how it was her family's money—the Wentworths'—that started them in business. But his eyes confessed the softer side of his story—the admiration and abiding love he felt for his family.

Digesting every detail, Ryleigh considered how desperately she missed her mother and father, and in increasing measures the soldier who had given her life. As for her twin, she knew why she felt an immeasurable piece of her had been missing—it was the idea of family and the convoluted concept that fabricated hers—as she listened to Logan speak effortlessly of his. But he made no mention of a wife, or in her case, an ex.

"They're in their sixties now. I took the reins three years ago after…"

She studied the strong lines of a face turned suddenly pale under the dark smudge of an evening beard. "What happened three years ago?"

Logan lowered his eyes as if to break the connection and keep her from further inquiry. He leaned into his chair and an air of contemplation swept over his face. "Enough about me, I want to hear about you." A smile that failed to reach his eyes softened the traces of apprehension. "Your turn to share."

Ryleigh spoke warmly of Natalie, her childhood friend, confidante and savior, and sister she never had. She poked fun at her boss' pompousness, and he laughed openly when she told him about Kingsley—"Named after the wizard in *Harry Potter*, no doubt," he'd said. And he'd been right, though Kingsley behaved more like Garfield. But mostly she spoke proudly of Evan and how it killed her to have him so far away, of his uncanny ability with words, and his internship in California, purposely steering clear of any mention of Chandler.

"I miss him."

Logan's nod was one of complete understanding.

"More than I ever imagined. You must miss your daughters as much as I miss my son."

"I do." He didn't look up. "And what of Evan's father? You've never mentioned him."

The words stuck in her throat. "No, I haven't."

"You're not married."

"How do you know?" she asked, forcing herself to swallow the inevitable topic. "Maybe I'm the type who enjoys a weekend fling."

FROM YEARS OF trained experience, Logan noticed the momentary look of disquiet—an instant of recall maybe—that passed across her face. Instinct threatened to take over, the need to rescue, to protect. A somber bubble surrounded her and he wanted to break through the barrier and know her, to know the pieces she'd left behind and rescue her from whatever poison coursed through her veins. Foolish and nowhere near appropriate, he quickly dismissed the thoughts, his conscience pressing him to leave before things could progress any further. Caught in a vicious crossfire, he desperately wanted to stay—and urgently needed to leave.

"No," he said, placing his hand over hers. The simple touch sent his blood surging, betraying a catalogue of wayward thoughts. "I don't believe that." His finger traced the ghostly imprint of her wedding ring. "I see the evidence of what once was."

Ryleigh flinched and tried to pull her hand away. Logan tightened his grip and wrapped both hands around hers to secure the link between her story and the control by which he hung by a very thin thread. "Your story runs deeper than what you've revealed."

"I don't want to go there, Logan."

Having heard a multitude of stories through the years, Logan sensed when someone was holding back. She bore no visible marks, but the scars she didn't speak of, the ones on her heart, were another matter.

"You should." He hesitated, unsure whether he had opened a door to selfish need, or if he'd closed the door to his own story. "Please. Take me to those places you don't want to talk about."

THIS WASN'T A man easily swayed, and backing down wasn't an option. Perhaps she could skirt the edges. But why? The niggling compulsion to know the facets of this man endorsed the fact Ryleigh wanted (or was it some desperate need?) to let him in and she was acutely aware he sensed it. Though she stumbled over a wall of apprehension, this man's eyes were expressive and kind, and crossing over the edge of fear to tell her story felt natural.

And safe.

"My story's messy." She smiled to hide the shadow of fear clinging stubbornly to her heart. "It doesn't make much sense to me most of the time and it certainly isn't as interesting as yours. Just…messy."

"Try me. You might be surprised."

"I'm not a fan of surprises," she mumbled.

"No?"

"No. But you seem to have a gift for extracting unpredictable behavior from someone who has an extreme aversion to surprises."

A smile tucked itself into the corner of his mouth. "Why don't you care for surprises?"

She hesitated. "Clowns hide behind funny makeup and sometimes they hide in drains and grab and pull you into the sewer. So do surprises. They creep up on you, show their ugly teeth, then leave you to bandage the wounds while you're trying to figure out what the hell happened."

He scraped a hand over his chin and nodded. "Fair enough."

She hesitated, took a deep breath and before she could mentally talk herself out of it, tossed caution out the door. "*Reader's Digest* version?"

"It's still snowing. We have all night." His unwavering gaze held her fast. "But *Reader's Digest* it is."

Something remained hidden in his eyes, something deep and solid. Stepping inside felt safe, as though he could close his thoughts around her and protect her and safeguard her secrets. It puzzled her to feel so calm, when a few weeks ago she had disintegrated at the mere thought of retelling the story. Maybe it was as they say—easier with time. Or that time heals wounds. Or perhaps the way this man could peel away the layers, see past the invisible barriers and look directly into her soul.

She guessed it was the latter.

Her hand slipped from his. She stood and folded her arms beneath her breasts in a self-embrace, moved to the window seat, fluffed the cushions, and sat. The falling snow lulled her into deciding how—and where—to begin.

Starting with the end, she told her story backward—the way it happened.

LOGAN SAT BESIDE her with enough distance to afford her space, but close enough to catch her if he needed to. Compassion welled inside him when she described her mother's illness and subsequent death, and the weight of guilt pressed against his heart when she confided her absence at her mother's side to hold her hand while she passed from life.

Ambrose's story touched him deeply. The shock of gaining a father she never knew and then giving him up to death in the same breath tugged at the place in Logan's heart reserved for his own father and the father he himself had become. The triangle of love between her mother, Ben, and Ryan whirled through his mind, a carousel of restless thoughts. Anguish turned his stomach when she spoke of Chandler's infidelity and broken promises and of Della's lies. Over the years, he'd heard them all. The betrayals. The lies. Excuses. And though his training forced him into understanding, he was never able to tuck them away to be fully dismissed. The hurt would eventually subside, but the scars remained, the invisible wreckage of broken promises.

Logan laced his fingers and peered over them as he studied her. Infinite depth lurked behind her stormy eyes, and he yearned to unravel her story, to see through the window into her heart.

"Ambrose told me I have my father's eyes," Ryleigh said, leaning into the cushions. "The color of the inside of an ocean wave." She lowered her eyes.

The words she so carefully chose were steeped in emotion and each one touched him, a feathered kiss on his soul. "And deeper than any ocean on this earth."

She twirled a length of hair around her finger, and then her face softened. "I've only known Ambrose a few days, but I love the old guy." A frown inched across her brow. "But how can that happen?"

"It's easy."

"But I barely know him."

He nodded. "It's not for us to question, Cabin Number Three. The heart knows. We only need follow it."

"Good," she said, drawing her knees to her chest. "Because I do love him, even if he tends to brush elbows with the outlandish."

"He does seem to have a flare for the avant-garde."

A smile reached her eyes and widened. "That's putting it mildly."

"It sounds as though you wish to see him again someday."

"Wishes come true. Sometimes."

"And your husband? What do you wish for when it concerns him?"

"Ex." She picked randomly at her nails. "He wants to come back. To start over."

The implication hung like a dark shadow that had swallowed the light. Logan spread his fingers and pushed them through his hair in a slow, useless act initiated solely to suffocate the image. "Is this what you want also? To start over, I mean?"

She shrugged and looked directly at him. "It would be the easy thing to do."

His lungs refused to breathe. "I see."

"It's the coward's way. Scared to go back. Terrified to take a step forward."

"When pushed to our limits, we assume there is nowhere to go but backward. But each of us possess an inner strength that goes beyond what we think we're capable of."

She smiled and looked away. "There's a difference between curiosity and strength. I seem to be curious to a fault, but when it comes to strength, I'm a wimp."

"So tell me," he said, reaching to lift her chin. Emotion swam in her eyes. "Is it your wish to start over with Evan's father?"

"It's true," she said, and looked directly at him, "it would be the easy thing to do. But not the right thing."

Until his shoulders relaxed, he hadn't noticed the tension.

THE STRENGTH HIS presence assured kept Ryleigh from collapsing. Retelling the story was emancipating, as if an invisible barrier had encapsulated them, protecting her from the heartache of reopening the wounds she'd so carefully sewn closed.

She rose, picked up the journal, returned to the window seat and handed it to him.

He hesitated. "May I?"

She nodded.

Logan flipped carefully through the pages. "These are extraordinary." He closed the book gently. "No wonder you were awestruck as a child."

A winsome smile swept over him when she mentioned the fireflies and how deeply their presence affected her mother. And how they both loved white roses, though until recently she hadn't known of their significance.

"My father—Ryan—was gifted," she said, the name still foreign as it rolled off her tongue. She still hadn't fully processed the story, unsure where all the pieces belonged. And she was tired of dredging up the past—one decades old, but one so fresh she had yet to consider it a memory.

"God won't give you any more than you can handle, Cabin Number Three."

The wind gusted. Snow lashed against the window. "My mother said that to me when Chandler left."

"I see."

"I'm sorry, Logan."

"You've no reason to apologize. You have an anomalous history and an extraordinary life ahead. Never abandon your past, your memories." He inched closer and placed a hand on her thigh, his thumb stroking the denim above her knee. "No one is exempt from the shadows that cross our paths. Even the hearts of saints and sinners bleed, Cabin Number Three, and rain falls on the innocent and the condemned alike. Your secrets—your past—mold you into the person you are and the pieces knitted together are what make you special. It's what makes scraps of unmatched cloth a quilt." Empathy sheltered an inward smile. "'*Let love and faithfulness never leave you: bind them around your neck, write them on the table of your heart,*'" he said, tightening the grip on her thigh. "Some safeguard the past, some run from it. Don't let it steal the person you can become."

At the sound of his words, Ryleigh's heart opened like a flower exposing its petals to the sun. Where once there had been but one man who had opened the door to her heart, Logan Cavanaugh was inching his way in slowly, unquestionably. He knew her secrets yet remained beside her, his compassion, his solidity unwavering.

Ryleigh placed her hand on Logan's cheek. Tears clung to her lashes. Not sad tears, but tears for that which she'd hidden, gradually rising to the surface after a long drought.

"You're amazing," she whispered.

"And you amaze me." He gathered her into his arms, a human shield protecting her from the pain of a broken past. "And incredibly beautiful, Ryleigh Collins."

It was the first time he had spoken her name, the sound a sigh against her skin. The way he'd said it and the way he'd looked at her suggested there could be more. And yet, she didn't know if she possessed the courage, or if she would know how to take the next step, and it certainly wasn't one she could, or would take lightly. Plenty of opportunities presented themselves while she'd been married, but she had never crossed the line.

The security of his embrace seemed natural—and so close her skin leapt toward his, the sensitive hairs on her arms singing in rhythm to his song, the melody comfortably pleasant. Like coming home after a long absence.

Cradling his face in her hands, she stroked the day's shadowy stubble and closed the distance between them. She touched his lips with soft brushes of hers. His mouth parted. Every pore opened to the musky scent of him, the kiss of his breath a warm massage on willing lips.

He lowered her hands to her side and claimed her mouth as his own, his tongue possessive and sweet and tangled with hers. What little reserve she clung to vanished in the wake of the gentle authority with which he claimed her. Assured of the promises his embrace foretold, she melted into the overwhelming power of his kiss.

Chapter Twenty-Eight

EVERY INCH OF him had wanted to stay, to be with the woman who had begun to chisel at the stone that had become his heart, but the reluctance to act on mounting desire had forced him to return to his suite.

Logan wasn't surprised often, but when she had kissed him—as a lover would—it unnerved him, and he'd responded with a terrifying passion he couldn't explain. She was vulnerable. And he was fighting an irrefutable battle with himself. The mental anguish was as sharp and painful as an exposed, gaping wound.

The storm raged on. Thunder echoed in the distance. Alone and unable to sleep, Logan extended his hand over cold, empty sheets. As an ardent desire grew within him to be with a woman he barely knew, the struggle to purge the torment of betraying a promise mounted, a love he'd treasured most of his adult life.

The fireplace and cove lighting cast muted shadows and Logan watched them mingle and flow in silence across the room. The cove lights sputtered, then settled briefly. But a moment later they failed completely. Logan sat up, listening. If the power failed, the generators would supply minimal power to the kitchen and main complex, but the cabins would be dark and without heat. If asleep, his only guest would awake freezing.

The telltale hum sounded in the distance and the cove lights trembled, and then once again burned steady.

Urgent raps rattled the door to his suite. Reaching for his jeans, he hobbled to the door as he pulled them on one leg at a time.

"*Se fue la luz, señor*! The power is out, sir!"

"Hang on, I hear you," Logan shouted back. He reached the entrance in several long strides and opened the door to all five feet four inches of his right-hand man sprinkled with snow and fidgeting like an anxious jockey.

"Mr. Cavanaugh, sir. Our guest," he said with obvious panic, "she will have no power. The generators for the cabins and barn have not arrived. *Tenemos que rescatarla, señor*."

"Slow down, Carlos," he said, motioning with a hand, "and speak English, please."

"We must rescue her, sir!"

Logan couldn't help but chuckle. "Yes, Carlos," he said, patting him on the shoulder. "I'll take care of it. You go back to bed."

"Carlos will be happy to assist, Mr. Cavanaugh."

"Your concern is admirable, but I'll take the Arctic Cat and retrieve Ms. Collins. She can stay here tonight until the power returns."

"Sir?" Carlos' eyes widened and he glanced around. "In here? But the staff quarters are very nice. She can stay with my Karina." His chest noticeably puffed.

"Ms. Collins will be fine in the extra room, but thank you."

"*Ay caray.*" Carlos left, sputtering a string of Spanish expletives as he hurried across the lobby.

Logan dressed and grabbed an extra set of ski bibs and followed Carlos' path out the door, small footprints already filling with snow. The generator had successfully powered the security lights, casting the perimeter and short distance to the garage in suffused light. Snow fell in wicked sheets, silent and relentless in their mission. He hesitated, allowing his eyes to adjust.

The entire periphery of cabins was dark, the lampposts unlit, but the snowmobile's headlight cut through the snow and darkness as he inched his way to The Whistler.

Logan rapped loudly on the door. Pain shot through his knuckles. In his haste, he'd forgotten his gloves, and he blew a string of breaths over his hands to warm them.

The door opened immediately. Ryleigh grabbed his arm and pulled him inside, and then stared at him with her lip clenched between her teeth as though she had unintentionally dragged in a stray. Without weighing her intentions, she hugged him and then stepped quickly back.

"I normally don't receive quite this warm a welcome from my guests," he said, waving a flashlight.

Ryleigh shivered. "I don't care to be alone in the dark."

"I thought you enjoyed scary stories."

"In theory. In the daylight. And never alone."

"It is dark, but you're not alone."

She peered around him, as if expecting someone else to appear.

"There's only the two of us, but you've nothing to be afraid of."

"I knew someone would come for me," she said, wrapping her arms around herself.

"I had to. Or risk terrible embarrassment," he said, the wake of the flashlight dancing around their feet. "Even the horse barns have heat."

"Smart-ass," she said, her teeth chattering. "Wait…Logan, the horses—"

"As long as it continues to snow, the temperature will remain steady in the barn even without heat," he assured her. "Get your things. Just the necessities. I'll send someone for the rest tomorrow," he said, brandishing the flashlight through the cabin. "I brought you a set of bibs. You'll stay warm until we get back to my place."

She took a step and froze. "Your place?"

"The family suite."

"Oh." With only a pale beam of light from his flashlight, she shimmied into the snowsuit. Long, slim legs stepped first, and then her entire body wiggled as she pushed one and then the other arm through the bulky sleeves, and finally zipped the front and leg openings.

"All our resorts have a family suite," he said, and swallowed a sharp breath as the short zing of the zipper came to a quiet end. "You're coming with me."

"I, uh…"

"You'll be safe. However, Carlos thinks you need rescuing."

"Who's Carlos? And rescued from what? Or whom?" Her sheepish grin looked mischievous in the flashlight's wake. "Never mind. I can take care of myself."

How could he not smile? "I have no doubt."

* * *

When they returned to the lobby, Logan escorted her into the Reading Room.

"So, do I have the honor of sleeping on the sofa?"

"No."

"Then what are we doing in the Reading Room?"

"I thought you might enjoy a bedtime story."

"God, you really are a smart-ass," she sputtered. "I'm serious."

"So am I." He grabbed her hand and led her to the double doors of the owner's suite.

She tried to pull her hand free, but his grip tightened.

"You can let go, I can find my way."

"No."

"Your extensive vocabulary is astounding."

"I don't want you to trip. As I recall, your footing isn't the most sound."

"And yours is?" she asked.

"Better than yours, apparently."

"I distinctly recall where your butt landed."

Logan smiled at the recollection.

"Where are you taking me?"

"My place. Now keep it down."

"No one's around." She looked behind them. "Why do I have to be quiet?"

"Carlos sleeps lightly. You wouldn't want to wake him."

"Why? Does he bite?"

"No, but he can be quite insufferable if roused from sleep."

"Oh, Edward Cullen vampire tendencies. I must meet this Carlos."

"You read too much junk," he said, shaking his head. "Vampires are one thing, but you won't find the incredulous works of Ms. Meyers in my house."

Ryleigh smirked. "Books—the delight of the soul."

He turned and brushed his finger across her nose. "Vampires have no soul, Cabin Number Three."

The feel of her skin left his finger and settled in a deep hollow somewhere beyond the farthest reaches of his gut—somewhere unreached, untouched—for longer than he cared to think. "Welcome to my place."

INNOCENTLY PLACED, HIS touch aroused a quiver in her belly—something unnamed or perhaps a whisper of something lost, yearning to escape the confines of suppressed memory. In a feeble attempt to shake the feeling, Ryleigh gazed around the suite.

The room was a mirror of the Reading Room with a smaller version of the bookshelves and stone fireplace visible on one side of the room, the ceilings as high, the beams as massive. She discovered a small collection of books lining the mahogany shelves and scrutinized the titles. She picked one, opened the cover, returned it carefully and then opened another. She stared at him. "These are signed first editions."

"Yes."

Ryleigh dragged her finger over the spines as she read. "Hemingway, LaHaye and Jenkins, Zane Grey, Steinbeck. Tolkien?" She looked up at him. "And these are all signed Grant editions of the Dark Tower series? It's a rare set if you have *The Gunslinger*."

"Collecting signed firsts has become a sort of hobby. I have most of Mr. King's at my home in Chicago. *The Shining* is a favorite. I meant to bring it."

"How?"

"By packing it in my suitcase."

"You're such a smart-ass." She pulled her lips in on themselves, failing miserably to control the teasing declaration she had come to identify with this man's droll remarks. "So, you're partial to a story about a resort in a snowstorm with a psychopathic caretaker?"

"I am."

"Should I be worried?"

Logan chuckled and pulled *The Gunslinger* from its spot. "In answer to the 'how,' Mr. King is a regular guest at our resort on the coast of Maine," he said, showing her the autograph and then returning the book. "You're perfectly safe here. You have my word and my protection, to answer your second. I'll be sleeping on the sofa just outside the suite."

Ryleigh gaped at him. "Sweet hobby."

"Sleeping on the sofa? Or bedtime stories?"

"Stories, smart-ass. Comfort-food for bookworms." She carefully returned *The Fellowship of the Ring* to the shelf. Her excitement again flared. "Have you been to The Stanley Hotel? It's close by, in Estes Park," she said, pointing out the window.

"Yes," Logan said, stepping next to her. He placed one hand around her waist, took her hand, and pointed it in the opposite direction. "And town is that way."

Ryleigh rolled her eyes. "Okay, smart-ass," she said and stepped back.

"Checking out The Stanley was one of the first things I did when we looked into this resort. It's a grand hotel. My first choice had it been for sale."

She shook her head in staggered disbelief. "Crazy cool."

"Like your host," he said, holding up his hands to ward off the riposte. "No need to say it."

Ryleigh simply mouthed the words instead.

He took her hand and led her to her bedroom, opened the door, and showed her inside. Flames danced in a smaller stone fireplace, the room awash with subdued light. A warm shiver radiated along her arms as he turned to face her.

"Good night, Cabin Number Three. I'll be just beyond the double doors." He dipped his head. "Help yourself to a bedtime story."

The words tumbled free before she could stop them. "You can't stay out there. There's no heat." She swallowed hard, scrunching her eyes shut stupidly. The generator was running. Of course there'd be heat. "This place has to have another bedroom. Besides, you promised I'd be safe. Please," she pleaded, unsure of where the words were coming from, "I'd feel terrible dislodging you from your own bed."

"The other master suite is across the sitting room."

"Then it's settled."

"Are you sure you'll be comfortable with the arrangement?"

The lone cry of a wolf rose above the crackle of the fire and her head spun to the window. "Quite sure," she said, biting her lip.

"You needn't be afraid. The wolves have never wandered close to the resort. You're safe here."

Ryleigh nodded, the assurance teetering on the edge of her mind.

"My room is off the kitchen if you need anything." He turned again to leave.

"Logan, wait—there is something."

He turned slowly.

"I forgot to bring something to sleep in. Do you have an extra shirt I could borrow?"

"Right," he said, and raked a hand through thick waves of dark hair. "Be right back."

Logan returned with a neatly folded, long-sleeved chambray shirt and handed it to her. Dark eyes rested on hers, tiny flickers of copper firelight reflecting back at her. "Good night again, Cabin Number Three," he said, and turned to leave.

"Good night," she called after him, disappointed in his quick departure, yet pleased with what seemed a rare sense of valor.

She arranged the few items she'd brought with her on the edge of the bed and sat next to them with a plop; just as quickly, her purse fell, spewing its contents. "Great," she said, and shoved the contents back. She paused on the packets Natalie had given her, raised her eyebrows, and then stuck them in the drawer of the nightstand. "Even if they are flesh colored, I won't be needing these. Maybe the next guest will."

Ryleigh set her cosmetic case on the bathroom counter and pressed her palms to the cool surface of the granite. As she stood in front of the mirror, a generous amount of doubt sprouted and rallied against the incredulity of her actions.

Have you lost your mind?

The wife she'd been, the mother, nurturer, and journalist were the solid pieces of the woman who stared back at her, not the one shielding a fragmented past, the wreckage of which she had yet to clear away.

Ryleigh doused her face with warm water, caught the drops spilling off her nose with a thick terry towel, straightened, and drew a long, deep breath.

She undressed, and standing in her panties, raised the shirt to her face and breathed the freshness of laundry detergent, and then the faint recollection of his scent, musk and earth that somehow matched the deep tone that voiced his words. Her stomach fluttered. Lacing her arms through the sleeves, she hugged the fabric to her body, the soft chambray a pleasant sigh against bare skin. With the top two buttons left undone, she climbed into bed and slipped beneath a pile of blankets, their weight and the steady glow of the fire a comforting shelter.

She lay awake, reliving his lips against hers, allowing the pleasure of his touch to wash over her, and wondered why he hadn't touched her or kissed her again, the urgency palpable, the distance between them mere steps across a solid hardwood floor. Maybe in some valiant way, he was allowing her to set the pace. Both satisfied and remotely disappointed with the idea, she closed her eyes, a private, content smile ushering her into sleep.

HALFWAY ACROSS THE suite, Logan raked a hand through his hair. He turned around, and then stopped—seeking some obstacle, anything to deter the misguided intentions that crept through his mind. Abject desire tore at him, but a lifetime of convictions won the battle of wills.

Firelight danced beneath the closed door of her room. He cursed himself for not kissing her and chastised himself for thinking he should have. If he had—and God knows he wanted to—would he have been able to control the desire lurking so close to the surface? Her mere touch kindled some small fire and once fanned to life, would surely burn the ragged threads of control he desperately clung to. He allowed himself to breathe, and forced himself to continue across the sitting room to his room.

Unable to chase the echoes of her laughter and eyes the intensity of viridian crystals from his mind, Logan crawled into an empty bed. Sleep beckoned him. There in the darkness, in the suspension of consciousness, he could avert the torment of guilt and fear and escape the turmoil of being pulled apart at the seams as if being dragged through a keyhole one limb at a time.

He stared into the shadows, fully awake. Few steps separated them, and the inherent desire to be with her raged its inner battle, both sides seeking to plunge the other into a cavernous abyss, a challenge for decisions hastily made.

Sleep escaped him as he contemplated how close he had come to violating the oath he had made to his wife, who slept peacefully in a grave halfway across the continent.

Chapter Twenty-Nine

RYLEIGH WOKE SATURDAY morning with no clue what time it was and a twinge in her stomach she couldn't identify, but the soft cotton shirt against her skin intensified the feeling. She tucked her nose into the collar and breathed the subtle scent. His scent. His autograph written in her senses.

The room was quiet except for the exaggerated thump of her heart. Hearing nothing from beyond the door, she rose, grateful the shirt fell just above her knees. She yawned, rolled the sleeves of Logan's shirt to her elbows and opened the bedroom door to a neat pile of her belongings. Her bare feet padded lightly across the wood floors as she crossed the space to the sitting room. Light spilled into the room through a bank of glass doors.

"Good morning, Cabin Number Three."

Ryleigh turned sharply. "You scared me."

Mug in hand, Logan leaned against the granite counter. "It's part of my repertoire of remarkable talents."

"Do you always sneak up on people like that?"

"Only beautiful women who sleep in my shirt," he replied, nursing his coffee. "And I recall you entered the room after I did." He raised his mug in mock salute.

"Smart-ass," she mumbled, processing his words through a mental sieve. She wrinkled her nose. *Women? As in plural?* Though he didn't fit the stereotypical playboy type, she didn't truly want to know the answer. Surprises, especially ones that hovered on the edge of unwelcomed information, stunk.

Logan chuckled, the mug muffling the deep timbre of his voice. "Care for some coffee? I hope lattes are acceptable."

"What?" The question slipped out of her mouth before she could stop it. Was her affinity for lattes first place on some secret Google search?

"It's the only thing Rose taught me how to make in the Jura. And Max brought his specialty—yesterday's freshly baked croissants."

Ryleigh raised an eyebrow and her grin grew wide.

"And there's fruit."

"Lattes are my weakness." She took the steaming mug from him, her fingers grazing his. A tingle raced down her legs. And he was staring. "What? Haven't you ever seen a girl with no makeup and frumpy hair?"

"Not one that looks this good in my shirt." Logan's eyes dropped to the hollow of her neck.

His heated gaze was unnerving, yet her body responded with sudden warmth, his words an encompassing blanket folding around her. Fully aware she wore nothing but her panties under his shirt, she bunched the gaping collar together. "I need a shower," she said, clearing her throat. She turned but felt his eyes follow her across the room.

"Dress warm."

"Why?" she asked, walking backward.

"You're decidedly nosy."

"I don't care for surprises."

"You're still nosy."

"And you're still a smart-ass."

"Probably so, but you had best turn around."

"Why?" With the question barely out of her mouth, she backed into the wall and grabbed her mug with both hands in a successful, albeit awkward, attempt to keep from spilling her coffee.

"Because your sense of direction is a little off, Cabin Number Three."

"Smart-ass," she mumbled, whirled, and closed the bedroom door behind her.

LOGAN COULDN'T HELP but laugh. Hundreds of beautiful women graced his travels with Wentworth-Cavanaugh. Countless heartbroken women sat opposite him over the years. But never had he met a woman who bore the scars of fresh sorrow, yet radiated such inner strength. She was enchanting and a little crazy. And more than beautiful. She was also scared to death of herself, and didn't see any of it. He wanted nothing more than to take her in his arms, to protect her from the pain and shadows that haunted her; to be there for her in all ways, always.

He wrapped his fingers around his mug and downed the last of his coffee. His eyes remained on the door long after she'd disappeared behind it, the image of her bare legs stretched long and lean beneath a shirt that belonged to him permanently ingrained in his mind.

She was delightful.

And she terrified him.

* * *

A long shower helped erase the nervous tension. Ryleigh dressed in a hurry but took extra time to apply her makeup, easy on the eyeliner and mascara and then added a touch of lip gloss. She reached for the blush but put it back. The chilly mountain air had kissed her cheeks with a natural glow and she decided against adding any more color. She took a deep breath and tried hard to remember the last time it mattered how she looked.

Logan was gone when she entered the main sitting room. The door to his bedroom stood ajar, but not wide enough to peek inside. Even on tiptoes and stretching her neck it was impossible to see more than a few feet in either direction, or whether he made his bed or tossed his clothes on the floor—as if it mattered—and abandoned the nosy exploit. She returned to the kitchen, poured herself another latte, and stepped to the sliding doors.

Lazy snowflakes as fine as powder fell in intermittent waves—the last cough of a storm that covered the landscape with a deep, downy blanket—a winter wonderland, untouched and unspoiled, reminding her of Narnia after the White Witch had cast her spell.

She stepped outside. Funnels of snow swirled across the wooden planks, but the covered deck remained free of snow. Several feet below, Fall River rumbled past. The frigid water undercut the ice, forming undetectable shelves of ice. A panorama lay before her, a colorless prism of sight, sound, and smell. Crisp air stung her lungs, but she inhaled a long breath, examining the core of crumpled emotions rippling through her. As if the storm had cleansed her thoughts like the snow had cleansed the world around her, her feelings had surfaced and run over, too late to turn off. Cold winter air calmed the flame that both warmed her insides and pebbled her skin with gooseflesh. Nothing remotely similar had stirred within her in a very long time.

Grasping the mug of hot liquid in both hands, Ryleigh stood alone on the deck, vulnerable and exposed.

LOGAN RETURNED FROM a quick storm damage assessment to find Ryleigh alone on the deck. Afraid he'd startle her again, he stepped quietly to the glass door content to merely watch. Warm puffs of breath fanned out in front of her in wispy clouds.

The majestic tips of the Rockies punched through the clouds. Pools of orange and pink sunlight seeped through a gap in the clouds outlining her silhouette, as if a halo had formed around her. A perfect landscape. A perfect woman. Both painted by the hand of God. And through no conscious effort of his own, he felt a gentle nudge lift his spirit: a resurrected conviction absent for three years.

Every inch of his physical being rooted him to the spot with an insatiable desire to remain here in the quiet of a perfect moment, yet every mental fragment fought the transgression.

THE DOOR SLID open with barely a sound. Ryleigh set her mug on the deck rail, but didn't turn around.

Logan stepped to the deck and stood behind her, the magnitude of his presence unwavering, his body a shield. "Good morning, Cabin Number Three."

"Hello, Logan Wentworth Cavanaugh."

He stepped closer. "Is this spot taken?"

"It is now."

"I don't want to intrude."

"You're not. I was just taking in the view."

"In stocking feet?"

She looked down, straightened her toes, and looked beyond the deck. "It's beautiful."

"It is, indeed."

"Nothing compares to the solitude after a heavy snow."

"Earth's quiet time. Can you hear it?"

She nodded.

"What do you hear?"

"Sometimes words get in the way. Of the stillness, I mean. The beauty. Feelings."

"Please. Tell me what you hear."

"I hear the river's lullaby. Trees whispering. The psalm the wind sings." She breathed a cold, deep breath and smiled. "The glitter of sunlight on the snow."

"You hear sunlight?"

"It's like…" She paused, tilted her head, and then started again. "It's like the tinkle of bells. Thousands of bells. A chorus of high-pitched chimes sprinkled across the snow, each tiny sparkle a heavenly note."

Logan reached his arms around her and more by instinct than conscious thought, she leaned against him and closed her hands over his, afraid to move, afraid the moment—the quiet stillness that embraced the world and held her captive—would collapse and shatter. "What do you hear?"

"You have a gift. One I cannot match in words."

"Fair is fair."

His heart beat against her back, the steady rhythm a parallel to the quiet pulse of the earth. "I hear only you." His chest rose and fell, the motion gentle, yet as palpable as his body beside her. And then he took her arm and turned her to face him.

"I hear you breathe and my own breath ceases." He took her hand and pressed it to his chest, near his heart. "I hear the joy in your smile and I never want that smile to fade." Then he brushed her cheek with the back of his other hand. "And when I hear your voice, I wish only to memorize the lyrics." And then his thumb traced her lips.

With a sharp breath, she drew in the moment to seal it inside her, to keep the echo of his words safe from leaking out and fading away. Simple. Complex. Deep. She closed her eyes, the silence impenetrable as two people stood together, witnessing the end of a snowstorm in a sequestered world, their fragmented worlds infinitely and prodigiously colliding into one.

Though huddled together, Ryleigh's teeth chattered. "The storm's breaking."

"It's cold and night falls early this time of year. Time to get moving."

She took a step back. "There's over two feet of snow on the ground. Where are we going? And how?"

"The snowmobiles can go most anywhere. Let's have some fun."

"Where to?"

Amusement curled one corner of his mouth and reached the humor in his dark eyes. "Dress warm."

"I'm not particularly fond of surprises."

"Wear the snow bibs."

* * *

Though packed with snow, the roads were nothing a snowmobile couldn't handle and the Arctic Cat skimmed the vague layout of the road with little effort. Logan followed it into Estes Park.

Leaning forward as close as the helmet would allow, she wrapped her arms around his waist—a little tighter than before—and spoke over the drone of the engine. "Logan, is it legal to drive on the highway with these things?"

His muscles tensed as he laughed. "Haven't got a clue."

"What do you mean you haven't got a clue?"

"Never asked. The machines were delivered a few days before the storm."

"Sweet," she mumbled.

"You worried?"

"Just slightly."

"I can pull over and you can walk."

"Not on your life, smart-ass."

His laughter, rich and deep, carried over the drum of the engine, the pleasure of it rippling over her arms.

Ryleigh spent the remainder of the ride with her helmet tucked into his back. It would definitely be a surprise where they were going, because she had no intention of being first to see the flashing red and blue strobes of a police car.

The engine slowed and Logan drove into a partially cleared parking lot. The Stanley Hotel loomed directly in front of them, snow drifted in heaps against the sides and piled high atop the roof.

"The Stanley," she said, stepping off the Arctic Cat. "Animal topiaries and Jack Torrance's insane eyes. And Halloran. *Redrum,*" she groaned, mimicking Danny's creepy voice from the movie. "How'd you know?"

"Every Stephen King fan should see this hotel."

Ryleigh stepped to him and laced her arms around his neck. "This is crazy cool."

Though the ski bibs restricted contact, she savored the closeness. A shiver feathered her spine as he tightened his grip around her waist and pulled her close.

"Let's go inside," she said after an embarrassingly long pause. "I can't wait any longer."

Logan took her hand. "The ghosts of The Stanley await you."

The hotel was deserted and the staff fawned over them. Ryleigh browsed through the abundance of souvenirs and picked up a T-shirt with the word '*redrum*' scrawled across the back. She held it up.

"What do you think?"

"Beautiful."

A blush of pleasure tickled the back of her neck. "Murder—psychopathic or not—isn't usually something I would consider beautiful," she said, planting her hands on her hips.

"Oh," he said, raising an eyebrow. "You were talking about the shirt?"

"Smart-ass," she mumbled and refolded the shirt.

She'd no more set it back on the shelf when Logan took it and tucked it under his arm. "My gift for a beautiful scaredy-cat."

* * *

After spending over an hour pouring over every aspect of the hotel and asking countless questions (she certainly was a curious one) they said their good-byes to the ghosts of The Stanley.

On their way back to the resort, they passed a policeman driving cautiously slow along the slick highway. Ryleigh tightened her grip. Logan waved. The policeman nodded. With virtually no traffic, if it wasn't legal to ride on the highway, it was one of those times where rules were graciously—and gratefully—overlooked.

When they returned to the resort, Logan left the motor running and stepped off the Cat. Ryleigh started to follow.

"Wait here. I'll only be a minute."

"Where to now?" she insisted.

He grinned.

"Surprises are for the birds."

"You'll need better pictures than those taken with a phone. Even a writer can't describe this place."

Logan returned with a camera and secured it in a compartment on the Cat. "By the way," he said, "the handholds are below your seat."

"Now you tell me?"

"Thought you might need them."

She raised an eyebrow. "For your information, Mr. Cavanaugh, I figured out where they were quite a while ago."

As he gathered speed, her arms tightened around his waist and he smiled at the gentle pressure.

Not far from the cabins, an open meadow begged to be spoiled. The winter playground was ripe for spinning doughnuts, the exhilaration of a little extra speed and teaching Ryleigh how to drive. Eager as a sixteen-year-old with their first car, she caught on fast and drove as such and seemed just as disappointed when Logan took the keys from a woman who sported a pout with amazing sincerity.

It had been a long time since he'd seen such simple gestures cause such a reaction. Ordinary things were fresh and exciting and she delighted in the simplest of pleasures. Her enthusiasm was contagious. Showing her The Stanley Hotel had been effortless and he wondered how she would react to seeing the wonders the world had to offer.

RYLEIGH REMOVED HER helmet and set it on the seat. Her first step sank into the snow above her knees. "Oomph." She laughed and toppled over as she tried to take a second step. "Help," she said, realizing she was now quite stuck. "Help me up!"

Logan set his helmet beside hers. God, was he smirking again at the impossible situation she was in? He reached for her hand and then drew it back, crossed his arms, and laughed.

"What're you doing?"

"Taking in the view."

"Are you going to leave me here?"

"Yes." He paused. "I've got you exactly where I want you."

Eager anticipation gleamed from his eyes as he dropped beside her.

"Don't you dare apologize," she said with a knowing smile.

"I don't plan to, Cabin Number Three."

He took her face in his hands. Acutely aware of his hesitation, or prelude to his next move, she reached around his neck and pulled herself to him, his mouth warm and moist against hers. A day's growth of beard brushed her cheek with tantalizing softness. With a deepened hunger and without apology, he pulled her over him and out of the snow, his kiss fervent and hesitant, and as untamed as the wilderness around them.

His arms moved easily around her and drew her close, the snowsuits the only barrier between them, and the tip of his tongue found hers, exploring, discovering. Everything around her disappeared in a hazy fog. The forest stillness, the rush of the river, the murmur of the wind through the pines, gone—lost in the silence of the unspoken.

Their eyes met, locked as tight as their embrace.

"Looking in your eyes is like falling into the ocean," he whispered, kissing them gently, one and then the other, "so deep I feel as though I'm drowning."

She pressed her weight fully against him. "Hold me."

He surrendered to her simple request, holding her against him, his penetrating warmth a sharp contrast to the cool wave that shivered her spine.

"It's close to sunset," he said, glancing at the horizon, "and I have something to show you."

"I'm enjoying the view from here."

"I can find no argument with that, but I have promises to keep," he said, rolling to his side. He took her hand, lifting her from the shelter of his embrace and out of the snow. "And we've many miles to go before we sleep."

* * *

Logan maneuvered the Arctic Cat around tightly knit evergreens and clumps of bare aspen. Tiny footprints dotted the snow where small critters had ventured into the broken sunlight. The ride hadn't taken long. The engine slowed and the forest opened its arms to a wide section of Fall River. Shiny black with icy silver ripples, the water rushed angrily—not the whispered sigh near the cabins—and plunged from a rugged cliff into a deep pool. The river fell sharply between snow-covered boulders and layers of ice, thick as stalactites, hung between the jumbles of rock glistening in the patchwork of early afternoon sun.

"It's breathtaking." Ryleigh removed her helmet. "You were right, I need pictures."

He grabbed her hand. "Don't get too close to the water."

She nodded and he let her slip free, and then he reached to take the camera from its case. He raised his voice over the rush of swift-moving water. "The river undercuts the ice—" He looked up. "Ryleigh!" Panic burned his throat. "Don't move!"

She'd already trudged dangerously close. "What's wrong? The water is still a long way off."

His heart thundered in his ears. "Get back!" The strength drained from his legs.

"I'm just going to the rock."

The ice groaned.

Logan's instincts leapt into full panic mode. "Back up!"

The unmistakable groan of the ice sliced through the air, the sound magnified to a deafening growl. He bolted, his legs heavy and useless against the drag of knee-deep snow.

Ryleigh froze. "Logan—?"

The terror in her voice crippled his heart. So close. Two more steps. Adrenaline flooded his veins as he reached for her outstretched hand. "Don't move!" And then as though an invisible barrier had crumbled, he prayed.

The ice shattered. She screamed. The sound ripped through his body as the river dragged her under.

"NO!" Panic erupted inside him and he lunged. Logan's fingers tightened around her wrist. He pulled. Every muscle screamed. He bit down hard. "GOD!" Spit flew from between clenched teeth. "Don't do this to me again." His grip slipped, and then failed, and the river swallowed her.

He scrambled closer to the edge. "I won't let you take her," he screamed and reared his head to the sky. "USE ME, damn you!"

Logan plunged his arm into the water and groped blindly. A finger. A hand. Her wrist. Adrenaline pumped his muscles to action and they exploded into hot, violent tremors. He braced his feet against the slick rocks and grabbed hold.

A HAND TIGHTENED around her wrist. Then there was nothing and the current dragged her under. Her sinuses burned. Panic screamed from every pore. The serrated blades of arctic cold ripped at her skin. Still, Ryleigh sank.

Her arms floated beside her in some weightless water dance, yet one hand stretched in a mindless effort toward the surface but grasped nothing but water.

Bubbles tickled her nose and cheeks and clung to unblinking lashes, and then drifted upward through ripples of clear, cold water. Eerie, muffled sounds gurgled above her, *echoes of him*, and surrounded her in a peaceful, liquid bubble. Fatigue weighed her down as if her feet were tied to the rocks beneath them. Her lungs screamed for a breath and tiny bursts of white and pink and blue popped on and off behind her eyes, a kaleidoscope of color. *Beautiful*. Her eyes closed, the cold skin of her eyelids heavy. *Peaceful*. She longed to give in to the guise of sleep…

...a muffled sound. From where? She opened her eyes. A shapeless form rippled the surface. She reached out, but sank further down. Pain screamed from her lungs. Then, her foot struck something solid.

She bent her knees and pushed.

WITH A FINAL BURST of adrenalin set loose by a harrowing scream, Logan seized her wrists with both hands. Lightning hot bolts of pain shot through every muscle, every tissue. Rooted in desperation, he hooked his elbows under her arms.

Shards of broken ice bobbed around them as he dragged her from the river. Her weight slid easily across the snow to solid ground, but her body shook in convulsive waves, her lips and skin blue. She flinched as sunlight struck her eyes.

Logan pinched her nose and breathed into her mouth, forcing air into her lungs. "C'mon. C'mon, breathe for me." He counted the seconds.

Her eyes flew wide. She gasped, a gurgled intake that raised her chest off the snow. Logan turned her head and she retched and then coughed, clearing her lungs.

"There you are." Mere seconds had elapsed; it seemed like hours. He held her, his body for hers. "You're mine now."

Ryleigh gulped air and stared blankly up at him.

"Talk to me. What's your name?"

She tried to sit. He held her down.

"C'mon, baby, talk to me. Who are you?"

"If you don't know..." The words formed around vicious shudders. "It's a little late to ask." She forced a smile.

Logan's eyes blurred. "Who am I?"

"Too easy." Her body convulsed in shivers. "Smart-ass."

He buried her head in his arms. "Can you walk?"

"So cold." With his assistance, she struggled but failed to stand.

Logan carried her to the snowmobile, ignoring the pain ripping through his exhausted muscles. Stripping out of his snow bibs, he wrapped them around her and placed her in front of him, but there was nothing he could do to stop the wind from blasting her with cold air, lowering her temperature further. He had to get her out of the cold and warm her body.

With one arm around her waist, he gripped her tightly to keep her limp body upright on the Cat and leaned his body into hers, her body starved for warmth.

Long before they reached the resort, Logan blasted the horn in several short bursts.

Carlos met them in the breezeway.

"Mr. Cavanaugh, sir, what has happened?" Carlos frantically steadied Ryleigh's shivering body.

"The Falls. She fell through the ice. Go get Karina. I need her NOW!"

Carlos ran.

Logan carried her inside.

Water dripped from every thread of the snow bibs as he unzipped and pulled them off her shoulders to the meager tank top and shorts underneath—just as soaked, just as cold. "God," he said, "my fault, *mia bella*."

Logan set her in a chair in the sitting room and carefully pulled her boots and socks off, her skin as cold and gray as death in his hands. *Her hands.* Vivid memories paralyzed him and the hair on his arms rose in a wave of gooseflesh. Then, as if slapped back to reality, he tugged the blanket from the sofa, draped it around her and wrapped himself around them both.

Still, she shivered in his arms.

"I'm sorry," he said, and tucked her hand under the blanket.

"I told you," she said, her lips quivering, "not to apologize."

Logan wanted to smile, but his muscles refused to obey. He gently wiped the dripping hair from her eyes. "Forgive me."

She smiled.

"Karina's on her way."

"Who's Karina?"

"Carlos' daughter. She's an EMT."

"I don't need help," she said, squirming. Logan tightened his embrace and she collapsed against his shoulder the same time Karina entered the room and knelt beside her.

"Let's take a look, Miss Ryleigh."

Ryleigh shivered. "I'm okay."

Logan rose to allow Karina room to work. Ryleigh tightened the blanket and straightened. "I can dress myself."

Karina turned to Logan, her brows knitted together. "We need privacy. Please, sir, carry her to the bedroom."

Logan nodded and did as he was instructed. Karina went to work removing the blanket from one shoulder and taking Ryleigh's hand in both of hers in a practiced movement.

"Pulse is a little weak, Mr. Cavanaugh, but not dangerous." Ryleigh pulled her arm free. Karina took it back, gently inspecting the skin. "Skin looks good and her breathing is normal." She turned back to Logan. "She's lucky. As far as I can tell, she's in no immediate danger."

Logan relaxed. "What can I do to help?"

Karina smiled. "Fix something warm to drink. No alcohol or caffeine. A warm drink won't hurt either one of you, and I'll help her get out of these wet clothes."

"I can dress myself." Ryleigh closed the blanket around her.

"The effects can last for some time, Miss Ryleigh."

Ryleigh suffocated a shiver. "I'm fine."

Karina pursed her lips and tossed Logan a sharp look. Logan shrugged off the silent inquisition. "If anything changes, come for me immediately."

Ryleigh forced a smile between involuntary shudders. "I'm sure we can manage."

Karina covered her mouth, smiled, and unleashed a torrent of rapid-fire Spanish. She crossed the room and tugged at her father's sleeve to follow.

"*Ay caray!*" The two stepped through the doorway. "*No quiero saber.*" Carlos raised his chin in a mock salute to his boss.

Logan scratched his head and then sat next to her. "Why didn't you let Karina help you get into dry clothes?"

"I'm fine," she said, throwing the blanket aside. "Really. I just want a hot shower."

"Not until you're thoroughly warm. Basic first aid for hypothermia. Does funny things, Cabin Number Three."

"I flunked first aid."

"Now who's being smart?" Logan rose and eyed her with guarded concern. "No shower. Get out of those wet clothes and come sit by the fire until I'm sure your blood has thoroughly warmed. There's a bathrobe next to the towels. I'll be in the sitting room if you need me," he said, and then shut the door behind him.

RYLEIGH STEPPED INTO the bathroom and turned the faucet. Water pattered against the tiles. She stepped into the steaming shower, tank top and panties clinging to her skin. Warm, soothing water flowed over her as if she stood in a downpour of summer rain, washing away the fear. Life was short. Hadn't the river shown her that? Chandler had been the only man she had ever been with, but she had no room left for doubt. The water spiraled down the drain and took with it any lingering thoughts of returning to that part of her life—a part that had slowly withered and died. She felt no remorse, no guilt, nor any regret with its passing.

The flow of warming blood pushed the chill from her skin in a wave of prickles, the challenge of desire battling with inherent need. But a lifetime of shared intimacy first absent, then broken, did nothing to quench the desire for the pleasure of a man's touch. His touch. Dark eyes filled with unpretentious compassion. The gentle strength of his embrace. Her body molded to his, unfamiliar, yet with an unexplained sense of belonging.

"You shouldn't be in there." Logan's words penetrated the cadence of the water, more a statement than command.

She held her breath and waited, afraid to move, and terrified not to.

"Ryleigh?" Restlessness seasoned his words. "Answer me!" Bare feet padded across the tiled floor. "Obstinate woman," he muttered and burst around the corner and into the shower, eyes averted to the floor. Twin showerheads sprayed at his feet and soaked his clothes. "Are you okay?"

"Yes." It was her turn to play the one-word game.

"You sure?"

"No."

"What's wrong?"

"Nothing."

He rubbed his hand across the back of his neck, eyes moving slowly from his feet to her bare toes and stopped. Slowly, he raised his eyes upward until they met the hem of her top. Only then did he breathe. Only then did he reach out and take her hand. "You okay?"

"Quite."

"Then what is it?"

Drops of water blurred her vision. She blinked them away. The words she had planned in her head drowned in his immediate presence. "I need…some help."

"I'm here." With unspoken permission, Logan stepped under the spray. "And I won't let you fall." He took her shoulders in his firm grip.

Ryleigh raised her eyes to his, circled his wrists with her hands and held them tightly, an anchor in a sea of turbulent emotions. She eased her grip and skimmed her hands over his chest, his shirt clinging to his body as black and sleek as seal's skin. The swell of muscle and rise of his chest beneath her fingertips a liquid memory purling in her belly. Freeing the hem, she leaned into him, her hands resting in the soft nestle of hair beneath his shirt, his heartbeat a rapid tickle against her palm.

Logan grabbed her hands. Brown eyes burned into hers with questions she had no answers for, but with a coveted hesitation wavering on the crest of uncertainty.

His breathing quickened. "Ryleigh—"

She pressed a finger to his lips.

He curled his hand around hers and held it tightly to his chest. "Whatever you need, it's yours."

"I need you."

His features softened from confusion to one of empathy. "This isn't...." He swallowed the remainder of his words with a slight shake of the head.

The deliberate silence swept over her in a liquid wave.

He pulled her against him, two layers of wet cloth the only distance between them, his firm embrace the quiet to the deafening chatter of trembling limbs. "My God, *mia bella*, if only it were so." He stroked her hair, fanning the dripping locks between his fingers. "Trauma speaks a foreign language."

Unchecked emotion rose and spilled from her eyes, the shower of warm water masking the evidence.

"You're trembling." The words rumbled against her cheek. "You shouldn't be in here. It's the hypothermia speaking."

She closed her eyes, the realization of how foolishly she'd written the ending to a story that didn't exist taking hold until every ounce of strength she possessed drained from her.

Logan circled an arm around her waist, braced her firmly against his body, and together they stepped from the shower. He wrapped the bathrobe around her and wiped her hair and face with a towel gently, as a father would a child. He tucked one arm under her knees and lifted her into his arms, his hold strong and sure, and clearly embarrassing. Leaving a puddle of wet footprints, he carried her to her room.

With a solid hold around her waist to steady her he set her down, his interest surprisingly apparent on the back of her legs and as confusing in her mind. A rise of blood heated her face.

"Good sign." He cleared his throat, and wiggled a finger at her face. "The color's returning in your cheeks, so I assume I can trust you by yourself for a few minutes?"

She grabbed his arms, welcoming the assistance while her legs decided if they'd stand on their own or send her crashing to the floor, unsure whether to blame her instability on trembling legs, an icy bath, or a terribly stupid notion. He cupped her elbow firmly and directed her to the bed, the mattress giving slightly under her weight.

With the bed solidly under her, she scooted back. "You're leaving?"

"I have some things to check on."

"Better check on a mop," she said, nodding toward the floor.

Logan lowered his eyes to the growing puddle of water at his feet, mumbled something very similar to a bullfrog in complete distress, and turned to leave. He smacked the doorframe and faced her, fingers drumming on the oak trim. "No shower." His penetrating gaze spoke deeper than his words. "When you're ready, come sit by the fire."

Ryleigh pulled the bathrobe tightly around her. "Where're you going?"

"There's still no power and we need to eat. I'll see if Max can throw something together."

"Good. I'm starving."

He tucked his chin to his chest and looked up at her, a grin curling one side of his mouth. "Classic."

"What's classic?"

"If you're going to play in the snow, you should brush up on your first aid. Hunger's another classic symptom of hypothermia."

She stood and tightened the belt around the bathrobe. "I'm fairly certain it's a classic symptom of not having eaten in a very long time."

"I won't be long." Logan stepped into the hall. "And stay put." The authority in his voice didn't match the gleam in his eye. "I think trout is on the menu."

"Sounds good."

"You're quite the fisherman."

"Me?"

"Found a rainbow trout stuck in the pocket of your ski bibs." He turned briskly and walked away.

She flopped on the bed, arms sprawled above her head and the full force of her body weight the catalyst for an ailing squeak from a set of stiff but comfortable springs. "Smart-ass," she said and stared at the line of deep notches in the beams overhead. Whether hand hewn by a farmer in need of a barn a hundred years ago or manufactured to pass as an antique she didn't know. Nor did she particularly care. She locked her hands behind her head and took some comfort in knowing her embarrassing and altogether stupid charade in the shower had been shrugged off as the aftereffects of nearly drowning in an icy river.

* * *

Lemon zest and garlic with the slightest hint of a dry white wine mingled with the sweet redolence of shrimp. A far cry from trout. And if she had to be perfectly honest, Ryleigh was grateful for an exoskeleton and paper-thin tail instead of a plate teaming with tiny bones, no matter how fresh the catch.

The door shut behind her with a faint click. She swallowed the last bit of reservation that hadn't dried up while blow-drying her hair and headed to the sitting room. The fire crackled brightly, glowing bits of ash rising with the heat and winking out as they disappeared up the chimney.

Logan was nowhere to be seen, though she knew he'd been here by the wonderful smells of what she assumed to be dinner. Her mouth watered. And since he wasn't here, she slipped around the sofa to the bookshelf to steal another look at his collection of first editions.

She pulled *The Gunslinger* from the shelf and carefully opened the cover as if the creatures inside would jump off the page. The binding creaked. The pages lay before her, as pristine on the inside as the dust jacket outside. Her fingers gravitated to the author's signature and settled for a moment on the angled scrawl. "Crazy cool," she murmured and then turned and ran headlong into the engulfing chest of her host. She let out a squeak and the book flew from her hand. Logan caught the book in his right hand and her with his left in a favorable attempt to keep both from crashing to the floor.

"Another bedtime story?"

Crushed against his chest and eye level with a tangle of hair peeking through the vee of an obviously dry shirt, she unraveled herself from his grip. "You scared the crap out of me. Again."

A grin spread over Logan's face that ended with a laugh, the deep rumble taking root in the lower region of her belly. To quell the imprudence, she crossed her arms over the invisible web of jumbled nerves.

"My apologies, Cabin Number Three, but I believe the illusions Stephen King creates are far more alarming than anything I could come up with," he said, handing the book back to her.

She pointed the book at him. "This is fiction." She placed her hand on the cover of the book. "You aren't. And you have a very real, very disquieting infatuation with a rather sinister resort caretaker," she said, returning *The Gunslinger* to its proper space on the shelf.

Logan's deep laugh echoed in her bones, and she turned to see the amusement mirrored in his eyes before it flickered and died. "And speaking of books, I have a lot of work to do on mine. I should get back to it."

"Please," he said, and offered the sofa with a wave of his hand, "sit with me by the fire for a while. Besides, Max has thrown together something that smells quite good and I've brought an Italian Pinot Grigio to complement."

Ryleigh followed her nose and Logan to the kitchen. "Shrimp Scampi?"

"Yes," he said, and glanced at her. "And you know this, because?"

"I know my way around a kitchen."

"Good to know," he said, and poured two glasses of the wine.

"Why?"

"Might come in handy when the power comes on."

"I see."

"Do you?"

"Clear as day. I'll be helping Max to earn my keep."

An artful expression of amusement slowly spread across Logan's face and met the corners of watchful eyes, the brown as deep as molten chocolate, yet as soft as the down on a doe's nose.

"Interesting thought," he said and touched the rim of his glass to hers.

Chapter Thirty

THE EARTH HELD its breath. And so did she. Ryleigh rubbed her arms, the frozen landscape beyond the glass door a vivid reminder of the manner in which the mindless acts of fools mimicked the unpredictability of nature, and how—for the most part—neither could be controlled.

Save for the occasional hiss of pitch from the fire, the room remained quiet. No one to remind her how silly she'd been. No one to emphasize her uncanny ability to create fiction from nothing more than an indiscriminate kiss and an overactive imagination, a talent that should have remained an imaginary scene on a disconnected flash drive.

The wilderness lay in full dark, the membrane of the night a cloak to all but a freckle of stars, and here and there a slice of moonlight cut through the pines. Ryleigh drew the collar of the chambray shirt into her fists, pulled her elbows to her sides, and prayed the power would return to shed light on a distorted sense of reality.

She sensed his approach before his shadow flickered in the glow of firelight, his presence as visceral as the man who stood beside her.

"Couldn't sleep?"

She shook her head.

He handed her a glass. "Neither could I," he said, his voice rich with sleep. "A glass of wine might help."

"I'm sorry if I woke you."

"You didn't."

"I couldn't concentrate on writing. What's your excuse?"

Logan drained the wine, set the glass aside and stepped toward the door. He dragged a hand slowly through his hair and placed both hands on his hips. "You."

She took his arm and turned him toward her. "I don't understand."

"I'm not sure I do either." The smile hidden in the corner of his mouth defied the salient uneasiness in his voice.

"I thought," she said, biting her lip, "never mind. It doesn't matter."

"It matters." Logan reached a hand to her face and stroked her cheek. "You matter."

She shoved his hand away. "Don't touch me," she said, and took a step back. "I don't make a habit of humiliating myself more than once a day."

Logan turned away and scrubbed a hand over his face, the day's growth a harsh rasp in contrast to the ambiance of the room. "I don't suppose you'd care to explain?"

"No," she snapped. "I learn quickly from my mistakes and don't particularly care to repeat them."

He frowned, the lines cutting deeply into his brow. "I was…mistaken?" He dragged a hand through disheveled curls. "Or have I done something I shouldn't have?"

"No. Of course not." The tension bled from her shoulders. "You've been nothing but a perfect gentleman."

"And, is that a problem?"

"Today," she said, facing him directly, "in the shower."

"Ah." He cleared his throat.

"An explanation would be helpful," she said, crossing her arms against the air of embarrassment surrounding them, "so I don't make the same mistake the next time I throw myself at a man."

"I see."

"I'm glad somebody does."

He released a long, slow breath. "I couldn't allow myself to take advantage of the situation. Of you."

The rush of intimacy the first time his lips had brushed hers lingered as unquestionably lucid now as it had been then. Hadn't he taken full advantage then? She pulled her lips in on themselves and bit down hard to counter the effect. She raised a hand and rubbed her neck. "Seems it didn't stop you before."

"Under the circumstances—"

"What circumstances?"

"Nearly drowning. You couldn't control your actions any more than you could control how badly you were shaking."

"You thought I was delirious?"

"It's common in times of severe trauma."

"I knew exactly what I was doing." Her spine stiffened. "I practically raped you of my own free will and for your information,

Logan Cavanaugh, the only thing that has permanently traumatized me is you."

With a hesitant smile that held as much pain as it did joy, Logan reached for her hand. This time she allowed him to take it, or maybe it was the intensity with which he held her gaze that rendered every muscle in her body useless. He gently cradled her hand to his chest, and as he tightened his grip and pulled her close she felt the movement—not of her body instinctively drawn to him—but the inescapable tug of her heart.

The lines on Logan's brow deepened. "I can't deny the wanting, the need," he said, his jaw clenching and unclenching. "It's like standing at the threshold of a hurricane."

She reclaimed her hands. "I'm not very good at this." Uninvited emotion clogged her throat. "Fiction," she said with a disconcerted shrug, "is easy. Comes with a delete key. But you aren't a character in a novel."

"No. This isn't fiction." He turned to face the window. "You're as real to me in my sleep as you are standing here. I feel you with me everywhere. And I shouldn't."

She followed his eyes as he steadied his gaze on the landscape outside. The moon shone brightly, a luminescent brooch pinned to a pearl-black dress, casting a blue wake over the gentle slopes of the meadow. The snow glistened like thousands of tiny diamonds scattered with a breath of wind.

"Then what is it?" Though the room was warm, the hairs rose on her skin, a silent warning of the distance growing between them. Her knees trembled. "You're scaring me, Logan."

"Don't be frightened, Cabin Number Three." A hushed lapse hung between them. "You've faced enough fear and pain to last a lifetime."

"I'm not afraid. Not of you, or of taking a chance even if it cracks and sucks me under. You've shown me how to trust again— to step beyond the boundaries I built around myself."

He released a long breath but remained silent.

She shook her head. "I wasn't afraid when I fell through the ice because I knew you'd be there. The way I knew you'd come for me when the power failed." She lowered her head. "And that scares the hell out of me."

"Please," Logan said and took her face in his hands, "trust me one more time, Ryleigh Collins. I won't let you fall."

The sound of her name resonated through her, the syllables flowing together in a fluid dance as though he'd spoken it in a foreign language. Though his brief touch fell eager and warm against her cheeks, his words held nothing but the voice of reason.

He lowered his hands. "I'm the one who's afraid," he said, studying each finger. "And that's not exactly true." He turned to her. "I'm terrified."

Ryleigh swallowed to force the bile rising in her throat. "I've kept no secrets from you." She placed her hand on his arm, a reminder there was no room for doubt. "What happened three years ago, Logan?"

He pulled her against him and held her securely in his embrace. "You're trembling."

"Don't let go," she whispered, afraid he would. Knowing he should. Either would collapse what little resolve she clung to.

Logan held her against him, the air around them as raw and tender as their emotions. He lifted the hair from her neck, his breath a whisper as he called her name. Yet hesitation rippled across her skin. "I would hold you like this forever if I could."

She closed her eyes to the simple phrase burdened with implication.

Sliding a hand along her arm, he took her hand and led her to the sofa. They sat facing the fire, his eyes hooded in thought. He leaned forward, draped his arms over his knees and drew restless hands together kneading his palms in a slow, methodical rhythm. The dim glow of the flames played across his face. But her eyes settled on his hands. Compassionate and tender, yet the veins pulsed with authority and competence, the marked aggregate of his strength and the poise of vulnerability.

He stared into the fire. "Three years ago as my youngest daughter was choosing a college," he said, pausing to swallow and then drawing a long breath, "God took my wife."

The loss in his voice was staggering and as deafening as the silence before a clap of thunder. She placed her hand on his arm, a hallmark of her trust. His muscles tensed beneath her touch.

"Pancreatic cancer." He cleared his throat. "The devil's plague."

"Oh, God—"

"I begged the Lord to spare her." The quiet plea strangled his voice, yet remained so sonorous she couldn't breathe. "Nothing the doctors did—nothing I did—could free her from a living hell."

"Logan—"

"The illness ate at her body until she no longer resembled the woman I knew." His jaw clenched and unclenched. "I watched her draw closer to death every day, every minute. Every breath I feared would be her last."

In the deepest recesses of her mind, Ryleigh begged for him to stop—and pleaded for him to continue despite the shattering of her heart.

"I watched her wither to nothing before my eyes. The cancer consumed her and destroyed me," he said, bitterness overpowering the grief. "Six months after the diagnosis, her body failed. God knows the number of your days, but I was selfish and I begged for a miracle. I would have given my life for hers. To take her pain." The lines in his face softened, but his eyes remained distant, as if frozen in the memory. "Day and night I prayed. And waited for a miracle that never came."

A deep, unforgiving ache penetrated her gut and she took it along with his. One secret had been explained, yet the mystery of him deepened. She tightened her grip. He covered her hand and squeezed, his grasp the tether that bound their grief, and she answered, leaning into him, her assurance she would safeguard his words—his pain—as her own.

"I knew her time was near, and that morning as the sun rose, I promised to meet her in heaven with a warm wet kiss. It's a line from a Keith Urban song. She would cry every time she heard it," he said with a wistful smile that faded as quickly as it had appeared. "And she opened her eyes and smiled at me, like she used to. And I knew." Tears welled in his eyes. "So I held her and rocked her, and it was then she took her last breath and crossed the threshold. And I closed her eyes to this world." He turned away. "God claimed her pain. And her. And I felt nothing—as if I had died with her and I cursed myself for closing her eyes." He shook his head. "I tried, but I couldn't remember." Logan dragged his hand across a deeply furrowed brow as if to remove the pain of the memory. "I can't remember her eyes. I can't remember what color they were."

Logan rose and stood by the fire, the distance an open, raw wound. Broad shoulders rose and then fell, grabbing at whatever loose thread he could to climb from his mental grave as she watched from hers. "I could ease anyone through the devastation of losing someone. But no one could help me through Laurie's death." He took a deep breath, swiped an arm across his face and continued to stare into the fire. "The nights were unbearable. I eventually found the numbing eraser I needed. But I found I was no better off drunk than sober, so I prayed I would fall asleep and never wake."

Logan turned to face her. In the pale light, she witnessed the return of the solemn loneliness that overshadowed the strong lines of his features. It couldn't be denied, nor could it be disguised, and it somehow matched hers. She rose and taking his hand, allowed him to assuage his grief as he pulled her close, their bodies molding into one.

"Everything in me belonged to God," he said, the words drawn harshly through his teeth, "but it wasn't enough. He took my girl too. And part of me died with her."

Uncertainty played across his face in a road map plagued with grief, jaw muscles pulsing between memories too painful to reveal. "I dream of her…like she was before the illness, and it wakes me." His voice echoed the acuity of his pain and he drew his eyes to hers, his expression one of exposed secrets—a naked profession of truth that touched raw nerves. She knew it well, that feeling, for she too sometimes woke from dreams of ghosts who walked the halls of her past. And of Chandler.

Sorrow and pain lay cached behind a smokescreen, but the distance in his eyes spoke of truths that had been denied to her, but mostly to himself. His soul was no longer hidden, exposed through one who has experienced indescribable grief, a grief that paled in comparison to hers. The resurgence of a nightmare rose its ugly tentacles, one she thought had been put to rest, and her own scars stung with the pain of a freshly opened wound. Her heart ached on the inside for him, and tears fell on the outside for her.

"After her death, I became an expert at fooling everyone— including myself—and I was nothing but an incomplete version of the man I used to be. I became intimately acquainted with a bottle." He plowed both hands through his hair several times as if he could grab the memories and drive them away. "Alcohol is the devil's prescription for pain. My father forced me to look at myself, dragged me from the bottom of the bottle and into the family business, and when I sobered up and took the reins of Wentworth-Cavanaugh, the business flourished."

"When God closes one door, He opens another," she whispered, and for the first time since her mother had recited the words to her, she understood.

"Laurie was all I ever needed. Or wanted. I believe once married, you're married forever. In life and in death." As he stepped back, the distance between them grew to a deafening measure.

The words stung as if he had poured salt in an open wound. But worse was the emotional withdrawal, and a feral chill burrowed into her heart. Her strength dissolved. She didn't feel her legs give way, only Logan's arms around her, his grip steady, his face inches from hers, and she took hold and clung to him like the sole piece of driftwood in a restless sea. The pain buried in his eyes refused to give way. And in hers, he searched for something she didn't know if she had the strength to let go of.

"I've not looked at another woman since the day I met my wife, nor any day after her death. Until you." His voice was hoarse, but he spoke the words searching her eyes as if branding them on her heart. "I stopped believing in miracles three years ago. But when I saw you on the deck I knew God sent you to me, to witness His majesty again," he said pensively. "I prayed then. And again today at the falls. It's been years since I've done so, and I begged God not to take you. This time, my prayers were answered." She wadded his shirt in her fists and held fast. "I've seen the hand of God for the first time in more days than I can count. I don't know what it means, but there's one thing I'm certain of," he said with a deliberate pause. "I'm falling for you, Ryleigh Collins, and it scares the hell out of me."

A bubble of joy rose amid the chaos of emotions. She would have given her soul as comfort for his pain, but what she could give needed no persuasion and called for no words, simply the reassurance of human touch. Ryleigh buried the last whisper of hesitation and twined her fingers through thick curls, allowing a measure of time to sweep the pieces of shattered memories into place and lock them away. Alone, yet together, two lost souls joined in the knowledge of each other, a barrier against the shadows—not of darkness but those of troubled memories.

She rose on her toes and wrapped her arms around his neck. The brine of poignant tears, empathy's sweet tang, and the keen ache of need collided in shifting patterns of sensation as she took his mouth. With a breath of wine still sweet on his tongue, he responded in an urgent, soul-searching kiss, fusing their undeniable connection as if he'd found something lost and wouldn't let go.

And in a secret place of her heart, she knew it to be so.

Encompassed in his embrace, she closed her eyes and resigned herself to the man who touched a place so deep, who'd carved a piece from her only his lifeblood could fill. Compassion, honesty and trust were but a fragment of what lay beneath the rugged exterior. And he shared it selflessly. He knew no other way. And she allowed herself to be drawn fully into his protective cocoon.

He raised her hand in his and kissed each finger. Her skin shivered, each touch a moist, tender caress that settled on her heart. When each had been served, he pressed her palm to his cheek, the day's stubble both shadow and comfort, an intimation of the man within.

Tentative hands sought the curves of her waist and hips, the need to feel the whole of her clearly written in eyes gone dark as sable mink. Delicate kisses bathed the hollow of her neck, his touch simmering in places reserved for the most intimate of embraces, and her skin met the kindled burn of his fingers as he worked the buttons of her shirt.

When the last button came free, he slid the cloth over her shoulders and it pooled around her bare feet, her panties a transparent whisper of cloth between them. Dark eyes stroked her from forehead to toe. Her nipples peaked under his scrutiny and waves of desire pooled in her belly.

Ryleigh pulled the T-shirt loose from his sweats and with her unspoken guidance, he raised it over his head and let it drop. His chest lay open before her, a mat of dark curls. She pressed a palm over each nipple, the muscle tensing under her touch and he winced as her fingertips skimmed the smooth indentation of a scar. She raised her eyes to meet his. With a gentle tug, the laces of his sweats loosened. They fell in a puddle around his ankles and her hands took no pause in sliding over the firm muscle of thigh and hip, and then reaching around, exploring in the flesh the profile of muscle that so nicely shaped the backside of his jeans. Gooseflesh rose in the wake of her touch and Logan drew a short breath between his teeth. A smile curled her mouth and she dug her fingers into the firm flesh and drew him against her, wanting—needing—the close intimacy, the bond of skin against skin in the joining of need. Her breath caught and she cooled the urge to lose herself as his arms folded around her.

Hands seasoned in gentleness lifted her face and he took her mouth with eager passion. The gentle power of his tongue parted her lips and slipped inside. Every nerve sang in response, emptying her mind to all thought to fill again with only those of skilled hands sweeping over her body. His heart thundered against her ribs and her breasts grew heavy with desire.

Warm breath tickled her skin. "Is this truly what you want?"

"More than you know," she whispered.

"Once we take that step—"

"I'm sure." She traced the outline of his jaw, the lines beautifully carved over time by the propensity of wisdom, sorrow and compassion.

He cupped her face, tenderness colliding with urgency in his dark eyes. "God knows I want you," he said, his breath warm and moist and tasting sweetly of wine and husky spice uniquely his. "But—"

She intercepted the thought with her mouth. "Sometimes words get in the way."

Apprehension slipped from his face. He kissed her deeply, lifted the chain over her head, and let the dog tag slip through his fingers to the floor. The urgency with which he laid claim rose in her, the desire absolute.

WITH THE TASTE of her mouth still heavy on his tongue, Logan took her hands and lowered his eyes to hers, seeking the solace in her eyes, searching the cool green pools for something to break the undeniable connection, to calm the emotions flooding through him. Tears clung to her lashes like tiny drops of dew, and the need trembling in the wake of her fingertips stared back at him through eyes a verdant sea of passion. With an inherent desire to ease the remnants of her emotion, he kissed her eyes, first one and then the other, the delicate skin a cool balm to the fire burning inside him. A faint whisper of a summer breeze rose from her skin and hair and settled in every fiber of memory.

Her arms circled his neck. With both hands cupped to her bottom, he scooped her up, long legs wrapping around his waist. Logan crushed her against him, the proof of his desire pressed hard against the cleft of her legs, silk panties the last barrier to a crumbling defense.

With her fastened in his arms, he carried her to her bed and held her in his lap. Every muscle trembled, every nerve thrummed where her skin met his. A wisp of hair drifted across her face and clung to moist lashes. "There's still time," he whispered, brushing the hair aside.

She shook her head.

Logan matched her hesitant smile with one of his own, her answer as quiet yet as palpable as snow falling on pine boughs. He ached to pull her closer. To mold his body around her. To fuse the very air that separated them. "If we take this step—"

She pressed her fingers to his lips. "I want this. I want you."

He swallowed hard. "If you honor me by giving me your body—"

"You already know my answer."

The lines between his eyes deepened. "It's not something I take lightly."

"Nor do I." She smiled, one of hesitance that faded quickly. "There is one thing…" She leaned over and tugged the drawer open, placed a foil package on the nightstand (mentally thanking her wickedly perceptive friend), and wiggled back into his lap. "I'm sorry, but—"

"I understand."

"It's not you. Or me. It's an unfaithful ex-husband. I don't know—"

He took her face in his hands and kissed her. And she kissed him back, her consent as sweet and deep as he'd imagined, as sure as if she'd written it on his heart.

"If you're sure," he said, brushing the tops of her breasts with the back of his hand. "You're so beautiful. I don't know if I'll be able to control myself."

In answer to his unspoken plea, she reached behind his neck and pulled him down beside her. "Then please, don't stop."

With both hands, Logan slid the thin barrier of silk from her hips and allowed a moment to fully embrace the miracle that lay before him, and as if blinded to everything except the woman before him, his senses took over and every ounce of willpower failed.

Harnessing his own desire, he explored the delicate skin on the inside of her thighs and took her breast with his mouth, a firm peak rising to meet his tongue. Pebbles of gooseflesh rose on his skin, her subtle movements and rousing sighs as pleasing as her moist, bare skin beneath his fingers. A short breath hissed through his teeth as she traced the dark line from his navel and her hand closed around him, the ache peaking beneath her capable hands. With a longing that drowned all sense of reason, he pulled her against the testimony of his need.

THE EVIDENCE OF his pleasure pressed hard against her, the flesh beneath her fingertips smooth and slick and eager. Ryleigh reached for the packet on the nightstand, tore it open, and covered him first with her hand and then the thin shield of protection. With a needful groan, he pulled her against him, and with his hips fitted firmly to hers, she surrendered fully, the pleasure of her smile nestled in the softly curled mat of chest hair.

Logan's heart beat strong and fast against her cheek and echoed her own pulse humming in places intimately roused from a long, dormant spell. Hands seasoned in intimacy rounded her shoulders and possessed her breasts with such eager tenderness, sensitive peaks rose in the wake of his touch. Fully awakened, her body molded itself to the curve of his, the touch of his hands nourishing her as his pleasure became hers.

His hands lingered over the hollow of her back and then lowered to the swell of her bottom and with patient assurance, pulled her firmly against the undeniable proof of shared desire. The hunger of a deep sigh rumbled in his chest, and when his mouth found hers, she guided him into her, warm, wet and eager to accept his unspoken invitation. He entered her with such tenderness she drew in a breath and he answered, his presence deep and intimate, filling not only her body, but the empty spaces of heart and soul.

In the refuge of heightened sensation they became as one flesh, their movements as slow and easy as the words of a lullaby. As they moved as one, the world dissolved around them, and took with it the reservation of doubt, burying the painful ghosts of haunted memories, their bond complete.

* * *

The moon rose above the mountains and bathed the room in subtle light. Ryleigh's head lay in the crook of Logan's arm as she dozed, her breath a whisper on his skin, and the feel of her against him natural, as if born by innate design. He raised himself to one elbow, content to simply watch her dark eyelashes kiss the faint suggestion of freckles above the delicate slope of cheekbone, the placid smile buried in the corners of her mouth, and with each breath, the peaceful rise and fall of her breasts beneath the sheet. But it was the curl of moist lips, the echo of her laugh, and the sparkle of green eyes that tugged at the places in his heart he thought dead.

Her eyelids fluttered, the intimation of dreams hidden in the surf of those passionate green eyes. Dreams he wanted to know. Eyes he could be lost in forever and never grow tired of the infinite passion that lurked behind them. *"Dormi, la mia tresorina preziosa,"* he whispered, touched the tip of her nose with his finger, and slipped away to clean up.

Moments later, Logan slid quietly back beside her and covered her shoulder with the sheet. As if shielding her and refusing to concede to the dissonance infringing its way into his thoughts, he pulled her closer—covering her with his body, his own blanket of protection.

Ryleigh stirred, her toes a cool flutter against his ankle. The glow of lovemaking had blushed her cheeks and he tightened his embrace. But even skin touching skin would never be close enough. Traces of amber highlighted her light brown hair and he let the fibers slide through his fingers. She opened her eyes, the color as deep and paralyzing as a cabochon emerald, her drowsy smile a tempting simper against his skin. This woman wore passion like he'd never known, and God it looked good on her. She had branded his soul with the whole of her, and without a doubt had staked her claim. And he'd given it freely, and without pardon.

WITH A LEISURELY sigh, she traced the lines of his jaw to the cleft of his chin. Soft stubbles with a dusting of silver aroused the ache to sink into the safe haven of his embrace with nothing more absolute than their bodies joined as one.

Logan closed what little distance lay between them and she welcomed an intimately lazy kiss. Intensely aware of the desire stirring in him again, she nurtured every exploratory touch with a selfless one of her own. And as she reacquainted him with the pleasure of applying protection, his restless sighs matched the touch of her hands. No words were exchanged; there was no need. Their needs, their desires, their movements, were written in silent song.

With the memory of him still fresh on her skin, she immersed herself around him, threaded her fingers through his hair and eased him inside her.

They made love again as the quiet stillness of a winter storm lay perfect and untouched just beyond their world.

Chapter Thirty-One

SUNLIGHT PLAYED OVER her eyes, rousing her to the blissful pleasure of half sleep. Ryleigh stretched an arm across a jumble of blankets, the bed still warm where he'd slept beside her. During the night she had reached out only to find him waiting, his body a warm, solid fortress and eyes pleasuring her in the same way his hands had. And he had reached for her, pulling her to him, the rhythm of his heartbeat a lullaby against her skin.

With the sheet curled under her nose, she breathed in. The masculine, heady spice stirred the recollection of his touch and the intimacy of giving wholly, not only of the body, but mind and spirit and the consummate relinquishing of her dreams.

Reluctantly, she pushed back the blankets, rose, tied his robe around her, and followed the aroma of coffee to the kitchen. The sight of him wrapped only in a towel teased something deep inside her. She paused to cherish the sensation and the view.

Logan's back and arms tensed with each tap, tap, tap as he made a fierce attempt to obliterate whatever was on the counter. She approached from behind and skimmed her hands over his chest. He turned and pulled her against him.

"Good morning, Cabin Number Three," he said, and brushed her nose with his index finger. She warmed under the pleasure of his concentrated gaze, memories of the night clearly written in his.

"It's a grand morning, Mr. Cavanaugh," she said, peeking around him and then raising an eyebrow at the remnants of strawberries and mango that looked as if Jack Torrance had taken his infamous ax to them. She scrutinized a strawberry slice carefully before popping it into her mouth. "You haven't been to The Stanley Hotel this morning, have you?"

Logan bent to her ear and dropped his voice to an ominous tone. "Heeeere's Johnny!"

"Smart-ass," she said and smacked him lightly on the arm. "I'm quite impressed you're fixing breakfast, even if you are using a rather sinister-looking butcher knife."

Logan laughed. "Not so much fixing as mutilating, perhaps."

The sound of his laughter purled in her belly and spread its warmth over her body. "Well then, you're using the appropriate knife."

"Max put together what he could, but the power hasn't returned and the kitchen has minimal usage. No croissants today. Fresh or otherwise. But there's plenty of fruit."

"Someday I'll show you what I can do with fruit."

As if pondering the implications of her words, a slow smile settled in one corner of his mouth and met the mischievous glint in his dark eyes. "If it's anything close to what you do to me, Cabin Number Three, it will be a most painful wait to find out."

She tucked her lip between her teeth. "Do I smell coffee?"

"I can't boil water, but lattes are one thing I'm good at."

He handed her a steaming mug. "Only one?" She sipped the latte, her eyes fixed on his. "I can think of a couple of things you're pretty good at."

"Oh?"

She cocked an eyebrow. "Smart-ass remarks for one."

"And the other?"

"That's for show. Not tell."

Logan's sly half-smile tickled that place low in her belly and she buried a smile in her mug. "How are the roads?"

"Snowplow has been through. They're passable."

"Too bad." She smiled playfully. "I favor having the place to ourselves. Except for Rose and Max, of course. They're handy to have around."

He gathered her into his arms and rested his chin on top of her head. "And I'm not?"

"Eminently," she said, nestling herself into his chest, the mat of curls a soft landing against her cheek. "Your hands are extraordinarily nice."

The deep timbre of his laugh rumbled through her and her heart leapt at the sound. She immersed herself in the power of his embrace as his hands moved over her with gentle assurance, sequestered memories tucked safely between them.

Inside the Rocky Mountain resort suite, their souls had been adrift, yet they'd weathered the storm, a palette of turbulent color in the hands of a skilled artist whose brushstrokes had blended them together into the subtle hues of a watercolor landscape.

* * *

The day blossomed brightly, spilling sunlight over the sofa where they sat together, the warmth of the fire still a welcomed necessity in the absence of power.

Ryleigh stretched her legs across Logan's lap, nearly spilling his coffee. She was so absorbed in her work that she didn't look up, and he grinned at the inadvertent simper she made when his fingers crept under her fleece socks and stroked her ankles. He fought the niggling urge to continue his path up the back of her leg.

The lights above the fireplace flickered indecisively, and then settled for good. Logan's iPhone chirped. "Power and cell service are back." He tossed the phone to the end of the sofa.

"I prefer moonlight and the sounds of silence," she said, brushing a palm against his clean-shaven face, "even without fresh croissants."

"I can find no fault in your observation." Logan closed her laptop, set it on the flokati, and pulled her under him. "But I fear Rose's wrath after being cooped up for two days not knowing what's going on, the nosy old woman."

"Surely not our Rose?"

He laughed and kissed the palm of her hand. "And if I don't leave now, she'll think we got buried in an avalanche."

"It's not far from the truth. When you're near me, I seem to forget to breathe."

"I'm sorry."

"I told you not to apologize."

"I'm sorry." He leaned in, her face a breath away. "Breathe, *mia bella*, breathe," he said, and kissed her hard on the mouth.

"Indisputable smart-ass," she said, the words mingled with their combined laughter.

Disentangling himself, Logan tugged at the collar of his shirt and mumbled something in a futile attempt to straighten the wrinkles as he disappeared through the double doors.

Logan's laughter echoed in that place deep inside where all the feelings, all the pleasures, the whole of him dwelled, and for a long time she stared at the double doors, twirling a strand of hair between her fingers. He was an accomplished businessman, extraordinary employer, and consummate, sensual lover, and she pushed thoughts of leaving him—of leaving this place—out of her mind. She cringed at the thought of facing Chandler to tell him there could be nothing more between them except their mutual love for their son. It seemed ages ago now, but she had once loved him deeply. Feelings didn't switch on and off, but their passion, their love, had dimmed—imperceptibly fading to a cool ember and then like a puff of air on a candle flame, extinguished. She would always love him—the father of her son would always hold a special place in her heart—but she hadn't been in love with Chandler for quite some time.

The difference was palpable.

Ready to work on the epilogue of her story, she took a deep breath and settled in. A few hours of quiet and an absurd amount of coffee and her fantasy would be complete, the ending as tragically sweet as any love story. As for her real life, starting over seemed an incredible adventure. Like dreaming awake. Her eyes blurred, thinking how this could be the beginning of her own personal Neverland.

* * *

In the short time since the roads had been cleared, the resort flurried with activity. The remainder of the staff had arrived and everyone bustled about. Carlos barked orders and Rose had returned as boisterous as ever with a renewed disdain for weathermen. And snow. Nestled at the base of the Rockies, Whisper of the Pines was fast becoming Logan's favored resort with its sheer beauty and laid-back nature. But it was eminently due to a certain writer who had wandered into his life and placed a bookmark in the center of his heart.

As a sense of normalcy returned, Logan spent most of the day in the office under a never-ending flood of paperwork with his iPhone stuck to his ear. Carlos wasted no time insisting—in emphatic Spanish—that the generators be delivered pronto, and at Logan's request, he procured six more snowmobiles (they were "crazy cool").

Karina passed by his office with a furtive glance inside and plastered her hand to her mouth, unsuccessfully covering a giggle. Logan winked and nodded back as if they shared a secret. By this time, he was sure it wasn't.

"Well, well, well. Looks like you made it unscathed through the storm."

Logan leaned back in his chair and smiled. "Welcome back, Rose."

Rose parked her hands on a pair of over-abundant hips. "Welcome back my foot! Snow is piled up past my *chiappa*, there are no tomatoes for Max's marinara sauce, Shepherd is out of oats for the horses, and the automatic watering thingies," she said through puffed cheeks and waving her arms, "on the north side of the barn froze and are spewing water like Old Faithful."

Logan opened his mouth to speak, but she beat him to it. "And what's this?" The invoice for the snowmobiles fluttered to the desk and came to rest at his elbow. "And there's a shipment of books for the Reading Room waiting in Estes Park, and what the heck did you do with Ms. Collins? She's not in her cabin and no one seems to know where she is." Her face was now the color of one of Max's ripe tomatoes with the skin about to pop. "What went on around here during the storm?" She raised her arms, let them fall to her side, and shook her head. "For the love of Moses, how I despise snow."

Fully aware of Rose's distaste for chaos and even greater capacity to unleash her aversion to snow, Logan rubbed his hand from nose to chin to suppress his amusement and allowed her to pacify her temper before she completely imploded in front of him. "Are you quite finished?"

"Of course I am. Now, fill me in before I come uncorked and get angry."

Logan chuckled. Rose glared. "The power failed," he said, "and there wasn't much we could do until early this morning."

"We?" Her scowl morphed into curiosity.

Logan leaned over his desk and steepled his fingers as he considered Rose's meddlesome inquisition. He hedged on his answer, or whether he should answer at all. The recollection of their night together stirred the pleasure he'd felt in Ryleigh's arms. Their bodies as one. Her skin against his and the passion in a pair of ocean green eyes. He cleared his throat and looked away, and his eyes caught the glint of sun on glass. The photograph. Laurie's photograph.

The spasm of pain was instant, staggering drunkenly through his gut. Though beads of sweat erupted on his brow, he turned back to Rose and answered calmly. "No need to worry, Rose," he said, and dragged his fingers across his forehead to dispel the worm of turmoil from snaking through his insides. "I've taken the liberty in your absence to personally take care of the problems. I assure you, there's plenty of alfalfa for the horses, and I haven't seen one starve without oats, which are scheduled for delivery tomorrow. Shep is taking care of the leak as we speak and I've sent Carlos after the necessities for the kitchen. Tomatoes aren't all we're short of."

"Hmph. And the books?"

"The books won't freeze or sprout leaks, and last time I checked they don't need tomatoes or hay for sustenance. They'll wait."

Rose visibly relaxed and a challenging smile rounded her cheeks. Curiosity twinkled in her steel-gray eyes. "And?"

Logan stood, placed his hands flat on his desk, and leaned heavily into them. "And as for the snowmobiles, I think the guests will enjoy renting them." He quirked an eyebrow. "Any thoughts?"

"That's not what—or rather, *who*—I meant."

With two long strides, Logan rounded the desk, wrapped an arm over Rose's shoulder and ushered her—albeit reluctantly—from the office. "Please have the details of the Il Salotto deal on my desk before morning."

"One e-mail shy of being finished." Rose planted her feet at the doorway and raised her chin. "And you didn't answer my question."

Logan dragged a hand through his hair. "She's safe."

"Well, it's about frigging time," she mumbled and waddled out the door.

With his manager back to directing the staff as if it was an entire battalion of marines, Logan closed the door and took the few steps to the bookshelf. He picked up the photograph and carefully brushed a thin layer of dust from the glass.

Years vanished. Shattered lives and broken promises stared back at him. A shiver took root and climbed from inside to outside in beads of cold sweat. His shoulders tensed. Unspilled emotion blurred his eyes, and he grabbed hold of the bookshelf to steady the shifting axis beneath his feet. He squeezed his eyes shut, desperate to keep the memories buried, but they gathered strength and pushed back. The frame slipped from his grip—falling, falling, falling—a slow-motion eternity of anguish. The crash split her photo in two and the guilt of his transgressions hit him. He squeezed his head in his hands as if to keep the torment from erupting and claiming its prey. He'd used a night of pleasure to blind the pain and the silent predator of regret seized him in an agonizing wave, one not only rooted in remorse and fear—but of remembrance.

"Blue," he whispered, his voice hoarse with the weight of her memory. "Her eyes were sapphire blue."

* * *

Ryleigh's fingers lay poised over the keyboard, the cursor mocking her with an idle blink, blink, blink. The handle of the double doors rattled, startling her from her trance, and Logan stepped into the room scraping away the last bit of insulation surrounding her fragile soap bubble world.

Logan moved the laptop, sank to his knees beside her, and buried her head in his chest. He combed his fingers through her hair, his heartbeat as pronounced as the desperation with which he held her.

She wiggled free and tucked a disarray of curls behind his ears. Dread snaked its way around her middle. "What's wrong, Logan?"

"Take a break, Cabin Number Three." The chill in his eyes defied the warmth in his words.

"Seems I'll have to. Someone has thoroughly broken my concentration." And his, she thought, pushing the unsettling assumption aside. "Besides, I'm stumped."

He situated himself beside her with his head on her lap. "What has you stumped?"

"It's just a scene," she said, her fingers flirting with the peppered curls that fell just above his ears, "but I can't do it justice."

"What's it about?"

"Fireflies."

"Why is that so difficult?"

"Well…if you've never seen one."

"You've never seen a firefly?"

"I suppose you have?"

"Hasn't everyone seen," he said, toying with a smile, "mosquitos with flashlights?"

"Okay, smart-ass," she laughed, "not everyone. At least I haven't. And they're not mosquitos. They're beetles." Logan raised his eyes, the questions residing there as evident as the reflection of the fire. "I've done the research, I've just never seen one."

"They're so predominant in Chicago, we use them as streetlamps."

Ryleigh rolled her eyes playfully.

"There should be images on the Internet."

"It's not the same." She dipped a finger into the cleft of his chin. "When I first saw the mountains, the landscape drenched in snow, the Reading Room and rock-faced fireplace, and you, I memorized them. They're effortless to recall."

He nodded. "Did you know a local artist hand-picked the rock for the fireplaces from the rivers in the area? Each one placed according to color and size."

"Really?" Ryleigh stared at him. "And how did you come across this tidbit of trivia?"

He smiled, but the spark in his eyes had dimmed. "There's a plaque next to the stonework. Spells out the artisan and the history."

"I fell right into that one," she said, ruffling his hair.

"And you'll create something for the fireflies. How's it going otherwise?"

"Almost finished."

"It will be amazing. As is the author." He touched his finger to her nose and returned her smile with one that failed to meet his eyes. "You've been given a rare gift. All you need is the courage to show the world," he said, rising to leave. "I have work to do." He paused at the double doors. "Besides, Karina needs something to giggle about."

"Why is she giggling?"

"She thinks you and I are having an affair," he said with a wink.

"That poor girl. You're such a smart-ass, Logan Cavanaugh."

Logan's laugh tickled the hollow part of her belly, and she sank into the cushions to enjoy the pleasure. She had an idea to finish the scene and was lost once again in the throes of her imaginary world.

With no more interruptions, Ryleigh worked nonstop into late afternoon, and now it was time to let it go. She attached the manuscript to an e-mail to Evan, reiterating the fact she didn't want anyone else to read it. Someone else reading her fantasies seemed intimidating and a whole lot terrifying. Dodging the inevitable, she e-mailed the completed newspaper columns instead.

And then she sat idle and so did the cursor, blinking in time with her stuttering heartbeat. Her hands shook. Then, digging deep for an ounce of courage, she closed her eyes and clicked.

Ping.

Swoosh.

Gone.

Evan didn't respond.

But Natalie did, anxious for details. Ryleigh shot her a short reply, but she couldn't fill in the details, only how this place had stolen her heart.

* * *

Logan returned to the suite with dinner (compliments of Max and fully restored services), two bottles of wine that he set on the coffee table by the fire, and four white roses wrapped in cellophane. Logan handed her one bottle and dug the point of the bottle opener in the other.

"Poetry in a bottle," she said with a thorough inspection of the label. "Orma Toscana." The printing was Italian, evident by the shape of the map. "A breath of Siena."

"I take it you know something about wine?"

"Not really."

With an inquisitive turn of the head he caught her eyes.

"There's a map of Italy on the label."

He smiled, but it lacked the enthusiasm to reach his eyes. "These are from the Tuscany Valley region near Siena. One of the finest in Europe," he said, twisting the opener. "The Orma Toscana was Max's suggestion." The cork popped free, a spire of mist rising from the neck. He poured two glasses.

Ryleigh inhaled and sipped slowly. With the aroma of red chilies, plums, and a hint of chocolate ripe on her tongue, she swallowed, the liquid spreading a small fire of warmth in her stomach. "Italy is on my bucket list." Their glasses clinked as glass kissed glass. "And fireflies."

"Italy's rustic charm will pale in comparison to your presence."

Her cheeks warmed.

"And I have faith you'll see fireflies in all their glory."

"I'd rather see you in all your glory."

He smiled and handed her the roses.

"White roses." She caressed his cheek, the soft prickle of his beard sensual and enticing.

"In remembrance of your mother, father, baby brother and the soldier who gave you life."

Her stomach fluttered. This man was smart, witty and fun. He loved books, words, and poetry, and was honest and sincere. She had sensed the compassion behind his deep brown eyes the first time she'd set eyes on him. Now he was proving it, presenting her with symbols of what it means to truly care about another's feelings. He listened on every conscious level and was attentive. And he remembered. It was as simple as a child's puzzle—he seemed to understand every facet of who she was.

"I don't know what to say," she said, fighting back a rush of emotion.

Logan turned her chin toward him. "Sometimes words get in the way."

She slid into the crook of his arm and almost indiscernibly, the muscles in his arm tensed. *Probably business.*

"Tomorrow's Monday," she said, the wine tickling the back of her tongue. "I hate the thought of leaving."

His expression turned in on itself, and an awkward hitch accompanied his words. "And I don't want you to leave."

The stirrings of fear tumbled in her gut, and the compulsion to curl into his chest and disappear was hindered only by the tight grip of his hand on her shoulder.

"But you must. And so must I."

Despite the warmth of the fire, a shiver feathered her skin. "I guess I've known all along," she said, biting her lip to keep her emotions in check, "since you told me about your wife."

"Promises aren't meant to be broken."

"You don't need to explain," she said with a fierce effort to keep her voice from trembling.

"I've chastised myself because of what I'm feeling for you, and it's killing me inside." The longing in his eyes defied the avalanche of remorse spilling from his words. "I need time."

Ryleigh stood and walked to the sliding doors. His words rose between them, an invisible barrier, a wary shadow. He had secrets. Most people do, carrying the baggage through life. God knows she had her own baggage, but his—his was an inconceivable burden. She contemplated the silent landscape before her and felt the echoes of her past rebound.

An oppressive silence swallowed her, the quiet of the world beyond the glass cold and stark, but the woman she knew herself to be fought the cold fingers of disappointment clawing their way into her heart. The burn of tears threatened, but she kept her emotions in check.

He came into her life unexpectedly, a sudden mutual attraction, but his was marked by respect and not the usual intents of a man. Content to simply stand beside her, he'd let her set the pace. She'd been the one to make the move. The one who shattered his convictions. Overwhelmed and sickened with grief and heartache had been a constant in her life, and she felt its ugly head rearing again. She shuddered—as if the river had swallowed her again.

Logan came to stand next to her. "I'm sorry."

"Don't apologize for what we shared. I'm not sorry." She turned to face him. "But I am scared." She swallowed a growing lump in her throat. "Scared to let go. Terrified to stay."

Stars winked acutely against a black velvet sky and the snow glistened in the amber wake of the moon. Logan wrapped her in his arms, and she leaned her head against his chest. It seemed a magical shift of time and space, and she groped for words to tell him how he felt against her, afraid if she said it out loud the spell would shatter into a million pieces. A discreet tear stained his shirt.

Logan lifted her face, the implication of unspoken words as clear as the night sky. She resigned herself to the inevitable and tried to pull away. "I'll get my things."

"Please." He tightened his embrace. "Stay with me tonight."

She pushed him away, shaking her head. "One minute you want me to leave, the next you want me to stay."

"I never wanted you to leave."

"Then what do you want?"

"Don't leave. Not tonight."

"You're confusing me."

"I want to be with you."

"It doesn't seem that way."

"I betrayed a promise." Ryleigh felt the pause as much as heard it. "And I'm caught in the middle of a battle I don't know how to fight."

"Everyone struggles with their past," she said, touched by the anguish in his voice. "You can't undo what's been done and you damn sure can't outrun it. And why tell me to embrace my past and not let it steal the person I can become, when you don't trust or even believe it yourself?" She threw his words back at him.

The pause was as paramount as the insinuation. "Please," he whispered, taking her hands. "Fall asleep with me tonight."

Ignoring or making sense of the incredulous reservations clashing in her head was useless. But in the quiet of her heart, she heard a whisper.

And she stayed.

They undressed each other in silence and slipped beneath the sheets, their secrets as exposed and naked as their skin. She closed her eyes, but sleep did not come, overshadowed by the feel of him curled into her back, the gentle sigh of his breath on her bare shoulder and the desperate longing to mold herself into him. With his knees fitted into the back of hers, Logan cradled her against him, and through the night—illusive yet soothing in the hollow of the mountains—they clung to each other and the fragments of recent memory, content in the quiet intimacy of each other's embrace.

* * *

Ryleigh's arm fell across an empty bed. She longed for a few more hours of night, for a few more hours of his body next to hers. Tightening the sheet around her, she curled into a ball to fill the empty space. To be alone with this man was to be fully embraced in a protective joy. To be alone without him was nothing more than being alone. Beyond the bed lay too many empty days, too many lonely nights and too much empty space.

Knowing she had to leave and not knowing what their conversation meant for their future—if there was a future—left her numb, the uncertainty a heavy weight pressing on every fiber of her being. A casual affair had never crossed her mind and for her it wasn't. She was crazy about a man who rarely called her by her name and who had inadvertently saved her from more than the shattered ice.

She showered, dressed for the flight home, and set her things by the double doors. Max had fixed a breakfast fit for a queen, but even the yeasty aroma of fresh croissants soured her stomach. The deep rumble of his laugh echoed through the empty chambers of her heart, and the thought of leaving here—of leaving Logan—buckled her knees. Tears threatened to overtake her composure and maybe they would have spilled, but a moment later, he walked into the room.

Logan met her at the door and wrapped her securely in his embrace, so close she could hear him breathe, yet to truly reach out and touch him, all the parts that made him whole, seemed as remote as touching stars.

Her fingers trembled as she adjusted his lapel and smoothed his shirt, a light gray, opened loosely at the neck. A tangle of chest hair poked over the top button, and she resisted the urge to touch the wiry curls. Waves of dark hair touched with silver and still damp from his shower kissed the tops of his ears, and her fingers traced the shadows of a smooth face.

She thought him tactfully gorgeous.

"Nice suit," she said, her words masking the ache attached to her heart. "Where're you headed?"

"Chicago." He raked her into his arms again, his solid warmth molding them into one—for one last time. Comfortably whole and safe, she gave freely what strength she had left, and her body went soft and liquid as she clung to him, afraid to let go—afraid if she did so, she would collapse under the insurmountable weight of losing someone she cared for deeply. Again.

Though she smiled, tears blurred her eyes. "I need to go or I'll miss my flight."

"Carlos will take care of your things and he insisted on bringing your car around."

"He probably thinks I'm an incredibly bad influence on his daughter and wants me out of here."

"Bad influence? No. Incredible? There's no question."

"Logan, please," she said, resting her palms on his chest. "Don't make this any harder."

With his finger, Logan lifted her chin and kissed her eagerly, one rooted in passion and longing for what could be, not the restrained sigh of a good-bye kiss. And when his lips left hers, she felt their absence, an ache for the loss of time and space and of his being, and the evidence of that absence stained his jacket. This time, he kissed her cheeks as if to erase the pain leaking from her eyes, but nothing he did could shield the cry of her heart.

She drew away.

Logan answered by closing the distance between them, his arms around her a shelter to the pain of letting go.

Ryleigh tried again to step away. "I need to go."

He tightened his embrace.

"What are you doing?

Moisture gathered in his eyes. "Crying with you, Cabin Number Three."

And they did.

Words clogged her throat, words she needed to say but couldn't form, ones left unsaid with each passing moment. Her body turned liquid, for it seemed more than she could bear. And she prayed for one more ounce of strength to let go. And to let him go.

He took her hand, the connection between them like the draw of magnets thrown together at opposite ends. He stroked her cheek, her neck and let her hair fall through his fingers. And he looked past her eyes and touched the places only he knew, the feeling as feral yet as intimate as mink on bare skin.

"I won't let you fall." With a forefinger, he brushed her nose and then he squeezed her hand and she let his fingers slip from hers. And let him go.

She watched him leave as she had done with another man. Unlike that day, she felt no bitterness, no anger—only the indescribable pain of the moment; the moment her heart would surely break as the man she'd fallen in love with disappeared around the corner without a backward glance.

The emptiness was staggering. She grabbed the doorframe to steady a world slowly tilting in all the wrong directions. Every nerve cried in protest. Every bone ached as his last words echoed in her mind. *I won't let you fall.* "It's too late, Logan Cavanaugh." Tears blurred her eyes and the ache touched her heart. "I already have."

* * *

After reapplying her makeup to hide the telltale signs of her emotion, Ryleigh battled the compulsion to look back but refused to give in and walked straight to the lobby.

Rose greeted her with open arms and a smile that could melt a mountain of snow. "It's good to see you again, Ms. Collins," she said with a stifling hug. "How was your stay?"

"Magical, Rose. A fantasy."

Rose dipped her chin and raised her eyes. "*Magico come l'amore nuovo?*"

"You sound like Mr. Cavanaugh."

Rose lifted her arms. "Oh my goodness," she cackled, raising an ample bosom. "His Italian is, well, a bit lacking yet."

Ryleigh frowned.

"He's a quick study, but he's got a long way to go. He's looking into purchasing a vineyard in Italy. Maybe as early as summer. It's quite the buzz."

"I see."

"It's a beautiful language. My husband seems to get his jollies out of seducing me in his native tongue. Last name's Corleone, you know," she said, winking, "just like in the movie."

Ryleigh smiled.

Rose shrugged and released a long sigh. "Of course, now that Mr. Cavanaugh is leaving," she said with a sly smile and let the notion die on her lips.

Ryleigh glanced around. "Is Logan—Mr. Cavanaugh around? I'd like to say good-bye before he leaves." *To see him once more...*

"Oh, I'm sorry, dear. He left a few minutes ago for Chicago. And for some reason beyond me," she said, raising her hands in resignation, "he mentioned returning to his ministry as well."

The impact of the words threatened to buckle her knees and she prayed it didn't show.

"Oh, dear," Rose said, "of course you wouldn't know." She patted Ryleigh's shoulder. "Besides being one hell of a businessman, he's a minister. And a damn good one."

A shadow crossed over Ryleigh's heart as the pieces fell together in complete understanding.

"I certainly hope he changes his mind," Rose said, visibly distressed. "He's proven he's the cog that keeps Wentworth-Cavanaugh Properties turning. He'll be sorely missed."

"Yes," she said, looking away. "Sorely missed."

* * *

The silhouette of the Rocky Mountains shrank in Ryleigh's rearview mirror, and the harder she pressed the accelerator, the deeper the ache became. Not only was she leaving a place that had left an indelible imprint but one where she had reluctantly opened her heart only to lose it under a blanket of snow.

The road unfurled behind her, the resort and her memories a shrinking blip in the mirror. "Crossfire" played on the radio, the lyrics a trigger to an avalanche of memories—dark clouds and storms, secrets, and of heartache, and it stirred her flesh as if the man she let slip away had touched her skin. The keen sensation opened a cavern in her heart, and a chill settled inside her, deeper and more intimate than she thought possible.

* * *

Across the lobby, Logan stood transfixed in front of the window, the silver SUV leaving the parking area.

"Mr. Cavanaugh," Rose said, waving. "I thought you'd left." She hurried toward him, holding a picture frame. "I reframed Laurie's picture for you," she said with a shrug, "and you just missed Ms. Collins. She wanted to say goodbye...."

Goodbye. The thought froze in Logan's mind and he nodded, unwilling to shift his attention and miss the last glimpse.

"You never did tell me how you fared through the storm, Logan."

"It was magical, Rose. The storm of the century."

"I see," she said, faking a cough. "Clearly. You didn't come through unscathed after all, did you?"

Logan leaned against the window and turned to her. Rose pursed her lips and held the frame to her chest. She followed his eyes to the window and watched him straighten as the silver SUV passed over the bridge and out of sight.

"You can't bring her back, Logan."

"Yes, I know."

"I'm not talking about the woman who just left," she said, approaching him.

Logan's eyes landed on the woman nearly a foot shorter, but who stood stalwart before him.

"I meant the one who left you three years ago."

He glared at her.

"Laurie's gone." She placed her hand on his arm. "And Ryleigh is right in front of you." Rose straightened. "Don't be a fool," she whispered with a hard, challenging gaze and then squared her shoulders and handed him the newly framed photograph. "Your memories will always be there, to call upon. But it's time to live again. To make new memories." She squeezed his arm and walked away.

The trail of her words hung in the air.

Nothing could have prepared him for the devastating loss that threatened to split him in two. Living without the woman who had shown him he could love again blinded him from the past and sheltered the future. But guilt had won, overshadowing any rational thought of a future beyond his transgressions.

With his thoughts in an upheaval of confusion, he would have sold his soul to the devil for an answer.

Chapter Thirty-Two

RYLEIGH CLOSED FROST'S book of poetry and bunched her knees to her chest. A fleece throw warmed her outside, but her insides were as cold as the icicles hanging from the eaves. Reading the words only reopened the scar left on her heart.

The sky had turned from gloomy to angry and dusted the lawn with snow. Kingsley jumped to the sofa mercifully disrupting her thoughts and curled himself at her side. She massaged her fingers behind his ears and the cat settled into a noisy purr. "This is the first snowstorm since…" Emotion tangled her words as she watched the snow accumulate, as did recollections of another snowstorm not long past.

"Earth to Ryleigh? Are you in there or somewhere fabulous with your gorgeous imaginary hunks?"

"Hey, Nat." Ryleigh quickly tucked the book beside her, patting the cushion for Natalie to sit. "I didn't hear you knock."

"I have a key, remember?"

"Remind me to change the locks," she said, and forced a smile.

Natalie sat next to her, the movement jostling the cat. "You wouldn't dare. Who'd take care of this mangy cat when you're away? Right, Kingsley?" At the sound of his name, the cat rose, leered at Natalie, and sauntered off. "I swear that cat hates me." Natalie rested her chin on her knees. "Your eyes aren't smiling. Time to fess up, my friend. Besides, you won't answer your phone. And when you act like this, I launch into rescue mode."

"I don't need rescuing."

"Maybe. Maybe not." Natalie shrugged. "But whatever's going on, maybe I need to be here?"

Ryleigh faced her, the need to be upfront more important to herself than her best friend. "It's the first snowstorm since Whisper of the Pines."

Natalie nodded.

"I should have heard something by now."

"About what? Your publishing date?"

"No, those dates are set. PrestWood fast-tracked publication. The book will be out in mid-May."

"You don't sound too excited about it."

"I'm thrilled—if I don't go to jail first for killing my son," she said, and shot Natalie a conspiratorial glare. "I thought I could trust him *and* my friend with my manuscript."

Natalie squirmed. "You wouldn't be cashing a fat check and getting ready for book signings if Evan and Demi hadn't sneaked it to the publisher."

"I'm teasing. I'm extremely grateful."

"So, if not your book, what is it?"

Ryleigh retrieved the Frost book and handed it to her. Only weeks old, the cover already showed signs of wear.

"Frost. Your fave."

"Open it."

Natalie opened the book, removed the bookmark and read aloud.

"'Dear Cabin Number Three,

These last few days have opened my eyes in more ways than you will ever know. Three years ago, I stopped believing in miracles. Three days ago, you were my miracle. The moment I saw you standing on the deck in the storm, I witnessed an angel with a halo as pure as gold surrounding her and God's promises stirred in my heart. I thought I'd fallen in love again with God, but I was mistaken. I already loved Him. It was you I'd fallen in love with.

I will not know a night's sleep without reaching for your touch. I will not take a breath without your delicate scent a reminder of your flesh against mine. I will not open my eyes to the night without beholding the purr of moonlight on your skin. I will not hear the rush of a river without hearing your laughter in its lullaby, and I will not speak without the whisper of your name escaping on the wind. I will not seek the warmth of a fire without the memory of flames dancing in your ocean green eyes. And my heart froze as surely as the ice when you slipped from my grasp.

I can't quiet the resounding unrest I feel without you, nor can I deny the irrevocable truth of a betrayed promise. My transgressions weigh heavily upon me, yet how can I feel regret for what we shared? As I try to remember everything about you, the memory is nothing compared to your flesh as one with mine. Until the day the Lord calls me home, you will forever be a part of me, Cabin Number

Three—the woman with the eyes the color of the inside of an ocean wave. Believe me when I tell you I never meant to hurt you. Ti prego, perdonami. Please forgive me.

'Fireflies hover out of fingertip's reach, just beyond capture they flutter and sway—so close I can feel them as I feel you, your tender embrace though we're oceans away.'

Eternally,
~ Logan '"

Natalie's mouth gaped.

A soft blush warmed Ryleigh's cheeks. "We met in the Reading Room at the resort. I told him I favored Robert Frost's poetry but didn't see anything by him, so he brought this for the library the next day," she said, nodding at the book in Nat's hand. "He must have slipped it in my suitcase the day I left."

Natalie sighed, flipping the bookmark between her fingers.

"The first evening we ended up in the sleigh together and he dropped me off at my cabin. I didn't offer my name, so he called me 'Cabin Number Three.' He rarely called me anything else."

"Holy shit! How romantic."

"I warned you this place was magical."

"It's a fairytale come to life."

"More like fiction." Ryleigh sighed. "I haven't heard from him since."

"What're you gonna do?"

"Nothing. Stupidity is one of those things we see clearly after the fact. Silly me," she said, rolling her eyes. "I took a chance and it didn't work out. And now I feel like my heart is being ripped apart."

"Why didn't you call him?"

"I made the first move. I won't make that mistake again."

"There's nothing wrong with taking a chance. Sometimes it needs no consideration, it's just…right."

Ryleigh picked at her nails.

"Second thoughts?"

"Plenty. But I knew the risks." She blew a breath through puffed cheeks. "I started a fire I don't know how to put out."

"Maybe it's just supposed to simmer."

"Maybe," she said, pleating the fleece between her fingers, "but it's hard, you know? To wait for something you know won't happen."

"You sure about that?"

"Oh, yeah," she said with a definitive nod. "What's even harder is letting go completely, when what you're giving up is everything you've ever dreamed of."

"What's your next step?"

She took a deep breath. "Being with him proved I can love again. Move on. And," she said and then hesitated, "I know Chandler can't be part of my life."

"It's about time," Natalie said, glancing sideways at her. "But it won't be easy telling him."

"I haven't had the courage to face him. So far it's just a bold statement from the mouth of a coward."

"Umm, Riles?" The bookmark settled in Nat's hand. "This isn't a bookmark. It's a business card," she said, confusion settling into a grin. "Logan Cavanaugh's business card."

"I didn't know who he was at first."

"Wait a sec," Natalie frowned, "the inscription in the book—his?" She stabbed a finger at the book. "*My* Logan? Well, not *my* Logan."

"Yes, *your* Logan." Ryleigh smiled hesitantly. "And yes, his words. Except for the last verse. He must have memorized it from one of Ryan's poems."

"Okay," Natalie settled firmly into the cushions, "from the beginning."

Ryleigh told her the story, minus a few details. "When I left, Rose told me he was going back to the church."

"Excuse me?"

"He's a minister."

Nat's eyes widened. "No way," she said, fanning herself.

"He betrayed his promise he made to his dying wife. And it's my fault." Her chin fell to her knees. "Of all the people in the world, I fell for someone I can't have."

Nat scrunched her nose. "I have a feeling there's a lot more to this story."

"He rescued me that weekend, Nat." She smiled at the recollection. "Twice." A breath of cold swept over her and the tiny hairs on her arms rose in silent reminder.

"I'm listening."

"I don't know how spending three days with someone can change your entire perspective. Your life. Your future. He made me feel whole again. Like I belonged with him." She frowned. "I've never known anyone so attentive to what I said or did." She rubbed her hands in quiet contemplation and then twirled her hair around her finger. "And he saved me when I fell through the ice—"

Natalie sat upright. "What?"

"I didn't drown."

"Unless I'm talking to a ghost, I figured that much out on my own."

She told Nat how she had wandered too close to the water's edge and the ice had given way. And though she'd never been reluctant to tell her friend about anything, she couldn't bring herself to reveal the intimate secrets shared with only one person. Even being the wordsmith she was, she couldn't find words. Nor did she want to.

"Do you have a picture of this knight in shining armor?"

Ryleigh swiped a moist cheek with the back of her hand. "The camera fell into two feet of snow. Or maybe the river. I went swimming before we'd had a chance to take any pictures."

"Jesus, Ryleigh. Do I want to know how he saved you the second time?"

"He taught me to love again. It's as if I've been sleepwalking through life and I didn't know how to start over. I never knew how close," she said, clenching her hands to her chest, "how intimately into someone you can become so quickly. It's as though I was born to be with him. Does that make any sense?"

"I found Mitch, didn't I?"

Ryleigh nodded. "Logan awoke a part of me I didn't know was dormant. Loving him felt so right." Recalling the memory struck her hard, but she forced herself to swallow past the pain of remembrance. "Somehow he saw through me, the lost me, and showed me the courage to believe in myself and accept my past— not following in someone's footsteps, but my own path. I'd become someone I thought I was supposed to be, instead of just me. And who knew a pastor could be so sensual and so damn sexy?" Her eyes sparkled. "That part doesn't seem right somehow."

"Remember *The Thorn Birds*?"

"That's fiction."

"The point is, Riles, he may be a man of God, but he's a man first."

She sighed. "I may have lost him, but to experience what we had comes once in a lifetime and if this was my chance, then I consider myself lucky. Even if it was only one intimately long weekend." She rested her head on her knees. "I never had that kind of passion with Chandler," she said, picking specks of lint from the throw.

Tears stained the knees of Nat's jeans and she pressed a finger to the spots. "It's reassuring to be so well-protected and cared for by someone you adore, and when you give your heart and expect nothing in return, love takes root and grows into something indescribable."

"Yeah, well, it seems all I nurture is a crop of weeds and a lopsided set of morals."

Natalie laughed. "Your so-called whacked out moral dogmas got you laid, didn't they?"

"Only from the mouth of my smart-ass friend."

"Told you those weenie wraps might come in handy."

Natalie's pixie-like grin made her smile too.

Outside, snow fell in lazy curtains, a quiet world draped in white. "God, I miss him," Ryleigh whispered and opened the Frost book, "and I'm scared I'll forget his smile and the taste of his kiss." *Moist and sweet with Italian wine.* With her finger, she traced the words written in a strong right slant, the ink beneath her fingertips drawing him from the page as if their skin had touched. "I never want to forget the deep timbre of his laugh or the way he says my name, it's the whisper on my pillow that carries me through my dreams." *The warmth and security of his body next to mine.* "The only thing I have to remember him by is a T-shirt from The Stanley Hotel. The book. A shirt of his that I slept in and a bowl overflowing with green M&M's."

"Your mom saved the green ones too."

Ryleigh nodded.

"You okay?"

"I have to be. Logan's not coming back." Ryleigh bunched her shoulders to her ears. "But I have a life to live, a book to promote and another to write. I've said goodnight to one life and hello to another. My characters can't keep me warm, but they're pretty good company."

"Another book?"

Ryleigh sighed. "I finished the manuscript just to say I did it. Now PrestWood Publishing wants two more."

"That's awesome!" Nat said, squeezing her arm.

"And Evan's magazine wants to use Ryan's poems and letters for a series on Vietnam. But I can't decide whether to share the letters. Seems like an invasion of their privacy."

"How'd they find out about the journal and the letters?"

Ryleigh glared at her. "Evidently keeping secrets isn't one of my son's finer qualities. Or my best friend's."

Natalie's eyes grew wide and she put her hand over a sneaky grin.

"I've decided to donate the proceeds from Ryan's poems to the Vietnam Veterans memorial fund. I've already spoken to Marc about some things too. He's your attorney, but I hope you don't mind."

"Of course not. And I think the memorial fund is a wonderful idea."

"I've asked Marc to transfer Ryan's bonds to Evan. I think Mom would approve." She paused. "And I've given the construction business back to Chandler, along with half the investments."

"Riles, are you sure?"

"Without a doubt."

"You've been busy since Colorado."

"I left my heart buried under three feet of snow, so I had to stay busy. I didn't want to think."

Natalie scooted beside her, their silent reassurance as vocal as spoken words.

"I know I'll be okay without him, Nat. But I don't know if I want to be." She drew in a deep breath. "But it's time to stop sulking and get on with my life." Ryleigh stood and went to the window, mesmerized by the falling snow. Natalie followed. "Why'd I fall for a guy with strings?"

"What strings? He's not married."

"He's married to God. And a ghost." She shrugged. "And I can't compete with either one."

Natalie looped an arm around her waist. "He was a fool to let you go."

"I seem to be a magnet for fools—and I'm the biggest fool for trying to hold onto something I never truly had. Hearts don't physically break, but it would be a damn sight easier if they did."

Ryleigh rubbed her arms. "I'm going to see Chandler tomorrow afternoon. I need to convince him it's truly over between us. And has been for a long time."

"He's not going to take it well."

"He doesn't have a choice in the matter. I love him, Nat. I do. But I'm no longer in love with him. I knew long before Logan, but I didn't want to admit it, not even to myself. It would have been so easy to take him back, to go back to the way things were." Ryleigh inhaled deeply, shook her head and let it out slowly. "But it became different somehow. I missed being in love. I missed the comfort. The feelings and special moments more than I missed him."

Natalie tightened her grip.

"How the hell do you realize you're not in love with one, only to fall totally in love with another all in the span of three days?"

Streetlamps popped to life, throwing an amber wake over a deepening blanket of snow, earth's secrets safely hidden beneath the white coverlet. A violet-pink haze bloomed across the western sky, glinting in the icicles that hung from the eaves, and her eyes followed the slow drip into the snow below. Tiny pillows of snow gathered on the edge of a birdhouse that only last spring had brimmed with the promise of new life.

"It's beautiful, isn't it?" Ryleigh's thoughts sank back to another snowstorm that not only covered the landscape, but had opened her heart and upended her world.

"Yes, it is. I can see why you write romance."

"Fantasy, Nat. Nothing but pure fantasy. Knights in shining armor don't exist."

Ryleigh closed her eyes to her memories, her heart bursting with love for the woman who stood next to her and like her own shadow, knew her every step. But she ached for a man who had drifted into her life on the heels of a snowstorm and held her captive in the safe haven of his embrace. He had rescued her—not only from the fragments of a tormented, broken heart—but from herself.

"Nat?" Ryleigh laid her head on Nat's shoulder. "What happens when it hurts so bad you can no longer cry?"

Chapter Thirty-Three

THE CORD SLIPPED through Chandler's hand as he lowered the drill to the floor. He hiked his tool belt back into place, swept an arm across his forehead, and checked from the bay window to see who had stopped by. His heart rate doubled as Ryleigh stepped into a patch of snow left in the unfinished drive.

He brushed the sawdust from his shirt as she made her way up the walk and into the courtyard. Early afternoon light bounced off the sidelights of the oak doors, dragonflies and sunflowers etched in the glass. He opened the double doors to the warm smile he genuinely missed.

"Hey," he said, motioning her to step inside.

"It's good to see you, Chandler," she said. He bent to kiss her, but his welcome kiss landed on her cheek, and though she'd stepped into his arms, she responded as though she'd been lured into an awkward snare. He tightened his arms around her and took a moment to recall how good she felt against him.

"You look great." She was radiant, but he sensed a pronounced change. Not only sun kissed cheeks, or the brightness in her eyes. Something new. "Your new lifestyle agrees with you."

"Thanks," she said. "I'm enjoying it very much."

"Congratulations on your book, by the way."

She pushed her hair behind an ear covering a shy smile. "May I see the rest of the house or are we going to stand here exchanging pleasantries all afternoon?"

"Be done by spring." He smiled and stepped aside. "In time to see the trees leaf out from the bay window."

Ryleigh slipped past him. She gasped and brought her hands to her chest. "Chandler, this is gorgeous." She turned in his direction. "Please show me the rest."

Explaining the unique features, Chandler walked her through each room before concluding the tour in the den.

"You've always had a discriminating eye for what people want in a home. The layout is incredible, high ceilings, crown molding.

You've outdone yourself," she said, placing her hand on his arm. "This house is a work of art."

"I built it for you." He took her hand and pulled her toward him.

"Chandler—"

"Look around, Riles. It's your den. A place for you to write."

"You don't understand."

"It's your dream house."

"No," she said, backing away. "This is your dream now. Not mine."

Her words sucked a hollow cavern of emptiness in the place where rational thought lived.

"You don't have to explain," he said, adjusting his sleeves. "It's written all over your face."

"Excuse me?"

"You wear the look well." He stared at the floor.

"What look?"

"The first time we made love. Our wedding day. The day you told me you were pregnant. It's the same look you're wearing now. Who is he, Ryleigh?" His jaw clenched. "Anyone I know?"

"Chandler, please. This isn't necessary."

"Who is he?" Anger fueled his words.

"It doesn't matter," she said, taking his arm and turning him to her. "What does matter is you know I love you."

His anger calmed to a feeling of relief at the simple words.

"And I always will. You're Evan's father and I won't deny our connection because of that. You'll always be an important part of my life."

"We can be a family again. Right here. In this house."

She shook her head. "That's not why I came."

Her words crawled through his gut. "Let me prove to you it can be like it was."

RYLEIGH TURNED TO the window. The sun had begun its descent, casting golden rays across a rocky cliff. A bald eagle soared along its edge. "I'm sorry, Chandler," she said, turning to face him. "Too many things have changed for us to go back to the way things were. I'm happy. You and I weren't happy together long before Della entered the picture."

He stuffed his hands in his pockets. "Does he make you happy?"

"If you must know, yes," she said, and raised her chin. "He talks to me. And he listens."

"I listen," he said, his brow pinched. "I hate it when you say I don't listen."

"Then why are dragonflies etched in the sidelights instead of fireflies?"

"I'll change them if that's what you want."

She shook her head slowly as she lowered her eyes.

"Then what do you want? I gave you everything, Ryleigh," he said, jaw muscles pulsing. "Everything."

"But not what I needed most." She blinked back tears she had no intention of allowing to fall. "Your time. Love. Attention. Your trust. There was always something more important, more interesting—a baseball game, a job. Della."

He dragged a hand restlessly along the bookshelves and then stopped and kicked at the nails in the plywood subfloor. "I would have given you whatever you wanted." His voice softened. "All you had to do was ask."

"I shouldn't have to ask. It should have been a part of who we were together. Things we did for each other. Love should be shown and felt. Not spoken with meaningless words."

He approached her and took her in his arms. He nuzzled her neck, his breath warm against her skin. She stood resolute in an awkward embrace. "Don't do this, Chandler, please."

"Does he hold you," he said, tightening his embrace, "like I used to?"

His voice was low and husky and warm on her neck. She closed her eyes, a recent memory flooding over her. He pulled her closer, his scent familiar, but not the one she clung to on nights sleep failed to overcome the memories. It wasn't the chiseled body or calloused hands of the carpenter she longed for, but the tenderness of a man forged by compassion, sorrow and wisdom, whose knowing touch nourished every facet of who she was, and whose mere presence offered a safe haven to entrust her dreams, her sorrows, herself.

"Tell me, Riles. Does he hold you like this when you cry?"

And it was Logan who pushed his way through her dreams— steady and strong and real and whose scent crowded her thoughts at unexpected times. "Yes." She bit the inside of her lip to steady the tremble there. "He holds me when I cry." A hollow ache pulled itself fully forward as she recalled Logan's arms wrapped around her, her lips swollen and yearning for the taste and promise of his kiss. "He holds me all the time."

She closed her eyes and allowed the sliver of what was left between her and Chandler to die in his arms.

"And you're happy?"

"Yes."

"I can't let you go again," he said, turning to face her, "and I never will."

"Chandler—"

"I need you, Ryleigh."

"I hope you find someone who makes you happy."

"I already have. Marry me, Ryleigh Michele Endicott. Take back my name."

"You know that would be a mistake."

"Some of my biggest mistakes I've turned into my best accomplishments."

She clenched her teeth. "I'm not a bunch of two-by-fours you can cut and nail into a replica of lines drawn on blue paper."

"That's not what I meant."

"God, Chandler." She leaned her forehead against his chest and kissed him there, and then placing her hands just below the vee of his shirt, absently adjusted a button, the flannel so familiar against her palm. "I should go."

Chandler held her at arm's length, his hands covering hers. Pain showered his face. "Ryleigh, please don't throw away what we had."

"I didn't throw it away," she said, reclaiming her hands. "You did." She turned, and with the click of the latch the dim shadow of what once had been vanished behind the closed door.

Ryleigh left without a second thought of looking back.

EACH FOOTSTEP TORE the hole in his heart a little wider, and though hushed and spoken gently, her words echoed off the walls of the unfinished den. Chandler scrubbed a hand over his face as if to erase the memory, yet a deep emptiness settled in its place. The room collapsed around him—an inaccessible aperture. Without her, this house was nothing more than an empty shell.

She had changed. Maybe it was selling her book and living her dream. Hell, maybe it was the fucking guy. He didn't know. He only knew pain—a grievous ache cinched around his heart.

As the last shaft of sunlight collapsed behind the cliff, Chandler left Juniper Ridge Road.

He cranked the radio volume trying to drown the echo of her words, but remorse, fueled by an anger he couldn't define nor control coursed through his blood and fed his temper.

"You're a fool!" He hit the steering wheel hard several times. "A fucking fool!"

Chapter Thirty-Four

THE DOORBELL COUGHED twice, a sure sign of its impending demise. Ryleigh opened the door to a UPS delivery. She wasn't expecting anything, and unexpected deliveries were a close second to unexpected phone calls in the middle of the night—a surprise both unwanted and unnerving.

Early June air smelled of jasmine and held the promise of a long, warm summer. She smiled, returned the driver's greeting and signed for the small package postmarked from New York.

The name on the return address was spelled out with no hint of the alias he insisted on using. Dread prickled the back of her neck. She examined it, turning the package over several times before finally snipping the tape. The wrapping fell to the floor.

The leather journal was identical to the one her father had filled so many years ago, yet no blood stained the cover. The pages were stark white and empty except for a single sheet of yellow legal paper, edges precisely aligned. The letter was penned in the same scrawl she'd seen in a note handwritten to her mother. The paper quivered in her hands.

My Dear Miss Ryleigh—
I hope you find words enough to fill these pages for the man you desire—yes, I know of Mr. Cavanaugh.

Her mouth went dry. How did he know? A shiver of warmth crept over her at the sight of Logan's name, the pleasure of his touch and her body curled next to him more real than memory. Afraid her legs would crumple, she entered the den, fell into the old blue chair and continued:

The desires of the heart are rarely an obstacle for those who treasure love. He is one who truly deserves a place inside your heart, inside your treasure chest. Kindle his love with your words. Write to him often, in here. He is an insightful man. Trust me.

I am pleased to hear of the success of your book and plans for Ryan's journal. Words flow from you as they did your father, a true and rare gift, indeed. Words are your destiny. You see the world from the eyes he gave you: eyes the color of the inside of an ocean wave.

You should receive this package about the time you learn of my leaving this realm. Please do not mourn—I am ready to pursue a new adventure! I do not leave much behind, nor do I have anything to offer save the wisdom of my indiscretions.

Most importantly—write what your heart reveals to you in this journal. Write to the man who desires your heart and whom you so desire. He will hear you, for love is ageless and knows not the boundary of time.

You have dismissed the complacent routes along your path and have embarked in a new direction, indeed. You have dug deeper than I ever imagined. I am well pleased. You will always hold a special place in my treasure chest, but I beg you never forget—it is not how you weather the storms of life, Miss Ryleigh, but that you learn to dance in the rain.

Most affectionately,
Ambrose

Surrounded by ghosts, she allowed the longing to take hold and breed. Tears splashed across his words as the old man—whose compassion and love spoke through a grizzled exterior—came fully to life. Pale, twinkling eyes. Knotted knuckles. A roadmap of memories etched across an aged face. The chipped mug, a souvenir of the jagged pieces of memory he'd given her. His arm around her shoulders.

Moisture puckered the page. The ink ran, leaving the mark of her emotion, yet renewed optimism tapped at her heart. Did he truly sense her with Logan? Surely too much time had passed. No, it was best to think of this as an old man's dying wish. Yet, it would be easy to do as he suggested. Her heart overflowed with things to say and she needed to write her story—if only for herself—to help her understand and let loose the grief.

She set the letter aside and opened the journal. The words flowed effortlessly across the empty page.

under protection, murky darkness of dusk
a wake of light, a path, a way—
awaken from sleep; a calloused heart
convictions lost in winter's snowy quay

broken promises, dispirited heart
severed dreams shattered in transgression—
disclosed secrets, silent ones lost
assuaged under cover of winter's confession

solitary souls in solemn solitude
surrender as one, a sheltered egress—
calmed fears, forged of queried faiths
lost souls found within winter's embrace
~RME~

The words came easily as did her tears, branding her journal as her father had done decades ago in the jungles of Vietnam.

* * *

It can't pop out of nowhere. Ryleigh checked the e-mail address again. Clueless to the inner workings of computers and things as romantically idealistic as the Internet, she thought surely there must be some way—

The buzz from her cell phone broke her concentration and she slapped a hand to her back pocket to quiet the intrusion, but the swoon of "California Dreamin'" had her racing to answer.

"I'm glad you called, Evan."

"I thought you were always glad when I call."

"I am," she said, stuttering on the words, "but…" Even though she couldn't see his face, she knew Evan's eyes had narrowed and he'd already formulated questions. "I was just wondering how, I mean, do you know…? Crap. I can't figure out where this e-mail came from. There's no address." She slapped her hand to her thigh.

"Send it to me and I'll take a look." A heavy silence fell over the line and she envisioned his exaggerated eye roll. "Send it from your Mac, Mom. Not your phone."

"I knew that."

"Yeah, right," he said, and laughed, the infectious sound deeper than when he'd left, she was sure. The dead space in their conversation seemed to last an eternity.

"Wow."

"Wow, what?"

"Means I've never seen anything like this web interface, and actually—"

"Never mind, I wouldn't understand it anyway. I just wanted to know where it came from."

"Cyberspace. Hey, this is from Ambrose, that guy you visited in New York, right?"

"Yes."

"Does the subject line, 'My adventure begins' mean anything to you?"

"He's gone, Evan."

"I'm sorry, Mom. He was Gram's friend."

"Mine too. I knew this was coming, but I didn't think it would happen so soon. It's only been two days since I received his letter." She bit her lip to suffocate the rising emotion, prior to the subsequent interrogation from her son.

"I think you owe me some details. About your trip to New York."

She groped for a reasonable explanation, or better yet, a quick way out. "I didn't want to say anything when I got back because of the internship. And then came Colorado, the book, now the journal—"

"Wait. That's been months ago. And what's Colorado got to do with this?"

"Five months since New York." *Four since Colorado.* "Of course you're confused."

"I'm waiting."

"I'm flying into L.A. tomorrow to see my publisher and go over the details with your editor on the Vietnam spread. We can talk then. I have to be in Scottsdale for a book signing afterward, so I can't stay."

"You've kept it from me, so it must be bad."

"You'll find it interesting, I'm sure, and you'll look at the whole picture as a bump in the road of life."

"You make me sound heartless."

"Optimistic."

"Hmph." He paused. "Have you started your new book?"

"I have."

"Cool. Can't wait to hear what this one's about."

She chuckled. "I write fantasies, Evan."

"Yeah, romance. How about an evil corporate takeover-slash-murder plot, or vampires this time?"

Chapter Thirty-Five

REMINISCENT OF KING Arthur's days, stone replicas of noble knights poised atop battle-ready horses guarded the entrance to Camelot Gardens Resort on the outskirts of Chicago. Horse-drawn carriages clip-clopped along cobblestone drives and the distant plink of guitars readied the band. A setting typical of a Wentworth-Cavanaugh property, Camelot Gardens posed as the ideal spot for a fairy tale June wedding.

Shoulders squared, Logan stood in a white tux amid the wedding party, men in matching tuxedos to his left, women in breezy lavender gowns to his right. He clutched a worn Bible, the spine tucked firmly into crossed hands. One thumb worried the top of his hand while he waited to deliver the vows that would unite his oldest daughter in marriage.

A flourish of small lavender and white hand fans waved rhythmically among the sea of guests, the air moist and heavy with the perfume of wisteria and freshly mown grass. And for the father of the bride, incredibly hard to breathe.

Guitars meshed into a soft intro. He looked up. Straightened. The crowd hushed. The volume rose as the band launched into the "Wedding March." Heads careened backward. The grip on his Bible tightened and without warning, his knees faltered. He had single-handedly transformed the grounds into a stunning landscape, but nothing compared to the sight before him, a stunning, priceless gem he hadn't created alone, nor took any credit for her beauty.

Glowing as if she'd been dipped in sunlight, Sophie walked arm in arm alongside her grandfather through an arbor of lush English ivy and Wisteria vines heavily laden with lavender blossoms. She caught his eye and smiled with sparkling blue eyes that put sapphires to shame. Dark hair cascaded over her bare shoulders, contrasting against a jeweled white gown—one that had taken the Cavanaugh women weeks to choose and nipped a rather large chunk from Logan's wallet. He smiled at the recollection—he'd have gladly given his last dollar to see her eyes sparkle like they did today.

Logan shifted his weight and rubbed a knuckle under his nose. Since the first time he'd held her in his arms he'd been the one to tuck her in and read her fairy tales at bedtime, and he'd prayed she would find a man worthy of her, one who would take up the role as protector, become one with her as lover and be her prince in her own fairy tale.

Sophie's radiance outshone the Chicago summer sun, so much like her mother, Laurie, he had to bite back a growing lump as Sophie's grandfather placed her in the hands of Logan's very soon to be son-in-law.

As he recited the words and listened to his daughter and son-in-law share their vows, Logan's heart swelled, the pleasure slowly churning up a fountain of emotions awakened during a snowstorm in the Rocky Mountains. Fleeting recollections of tender passion flooded his veins with ardent heat, incomparable to the late-morning temperatures, and he prayed his daughter shared the same feelings with the man who vowed to love and protect her always. In all ways. A handsome, tall, and effectual entrepreneur, Reese Davenport seemed the perfect son-in-law, but so help him God if he wasn't respectful of his little girl.

* * *

"C'mon, Daddy," Sophie begged, pulling Logan to the dance floor. "They're playing our song." Long, dark hair with a touch of natural curl and deep-set dimples (thanks to the Cavanaugh genes) flashed below vivid blue eyes (compliments of her mother) as she fell into his arms for the traditional father-daughter dance.

All eyes turned to them as the band transitioned into Heartland's "I Loved Her First." With grace and eloquence, he led her around the parquet floor to the country song, their steps gracefully synced and her head nestled into the curve of his shoulder.

Sophie looked up at her father. "Daddy, what's bothering you?"

"What makes you say that, *mia bel figliola*?"

"Abbey has your eyes and I can tell when she's hiding something. You're a million miles away."

"Nonsense."

"You haven't been the same since you came back from Colorado."

Logan's heart stumbled and though competent on the dance floor he missed a step. "This is your day, Sophie. Celebrate your new life and save your worries about anyone else." He twirled his daughter under his arm and back around. "Embrace your happiness."

"I'm extremely happy right now."

Logan smiled and hugged her tightly.

"But I'd be much happier if you'd find someone too."

"Sophie, please. Not today."

"You said yourself this is my day. And the best wedding present you could give me is your happiness." The music changed. They joined the line and two-stepped around the floor. "Something happened in Colorado."

"Sophie—"

"Don't say anything. Just listen." Sophie demanded your attention, a trait Logan concluded had skipped a generation and she'd inherited from her grandfather. "Your real smile was back. Your eyes sparkled and you laughed like you did before Mom died. Whatever happened in Colorado, my daddy came home. Now he's gone again and I want him back."

"A bit overdramatic, don't you think?"

"Don't patronize me! You're obviously blind to the truth."

As the words spilled from her mouth, her grandfather tapped him on the shoulder, demanding his time with the bride. Logan pulled a lavender-tipped white rose from his lapel and placed it in her hair. "Always my baby girl," he whispered, cheek to cheek, "*ti amo così tanto.*" I do so love you."

"I love you too, Daddy," she whispered in return. "And I'm impressed—your Italian is heart-stopping sexy in that husky voice of yours."

Logan winked and handed his daughter to his father, pushed his hands in his pockets, and strolled to the table set aside for family. Serving himself a glass of champagne from the fountain, he sat next to his mother, who for the first time today was alone.

Audrey patted her son's hand. "It's hard to imagine your little girl so grown up." She glanced from Logan to Sophie. "And she's right, you know."

He downed half the champagne in one long drink. "About what, Mom?"

She twisted her bracelet. "I shouldn't think I need to spell it out for you," she said, sunlight dancing off the diamonds. "You're a smart man, but you can be as bullheaded as your father."

"I think you and Sophie are conspiring against me."

"No one is conspiring against you, Logan Wentworth Cavanaugh," she said, shifting her broad-rimmed summer hat and waving a hand fan. "You're doing an acceptable job of it all by yourself."

"Not you too?" he scowled, and rubbed a hand across his chin, the stubble rough against his palm. "Less than an hour ago, I married my daughter to a man I hardly know. I have a right to be somewhat discrepant."

"Your daughter's radiant. And Reese is a wonderful man. Very much like you."

Logan shot her a critical glance.

"Sophie's happy and in capable hands. And she wants to see her father happy. As do I. There's no such thing as a safe passage through this life and it's time you put the past where it belongs."

"This isn't the time or place for this, Mom." Logan clenched his jaw and looked away, struggling to bury the need for a woman he shouldn't, and rebuking himself for betraying a promise.

"You were a changed man when you came back from Whisper of the Pines. What happened to that man?"

Green eyes. The Mediterranean Sea on a stormy day. Passion. A broken promise. A good-bye kiss that touched the places no one ever had. No one. "I don't think I need to explain myself—"

"I want my son back."

Logan straightened. "What is it with the Cavanaugh women today? Do they have eyes that can pierce my soul, or is it they enjoy seeing me flounder?" He downed the rest of the champagne and took another from the passing waiter.

"We're sensitive, intuitive women and your daughter sees what I see. You've distanced yourself again," she said, scooting her chair next to his. She took his arm. "You love the Lord, Logan. But something's not right. Whatever happened changed you, and you have to accept the fact you don't have to pastor a church to live your life for God."

"What's that got to do with anything?"

"Sometimes God uses our circumstances to change us, and my son found something that affected him deeply and he doesn't know how to deal with it." She brushed invisible lint from the bodice of her lavender dress. "Guilt shows up like a radioactive biohazard on your face, Logan. Has since you were a little boy caught with your hand in the cookie jar. And don't try to tell me you're happy behind that counterfeit smile. You're a damned wind-up toy trying to pass your existence off as part of the living."

Her words touched a raw nerve and his first thought was to distance himself from her insinuating remarks. But his mother's voice had been gentle, and her words somehow rang true. He found no need to force himself to stay.

"You'll always carry the past with you, Logan. It can't be changed. But you can change the path you choose now."

"Haven't I already done that?"

"You've compromised." Audrey leaned into her chair. "I think you were sent an angel and you let her go because you can't honor a promise you can't possibly keep."

"I don't make promises lightly." Logan glared at her. "And it's not your concern if I choose to honor one or not." He turned away from her, raising his glass to a passing guest.

"I may be meddling where I'm not welcome. But I love you, Logan. I want what's best for my son and right now Chicago is not the place for you. Nor is the pastorate."

"It's my calling." He leaned forward, resting his arms across his knees.

"Perhaps," she said with a shrug, "but life's too short to surrender yourself to something you aren't meant for. Life happens. People change. Pray about it, Son. God listens." Audrey leaned closer. "He's tapped into souls like Nixon was to Watergate," she whispered, and then patted his arm.

"Sometimes I think you have a direct line to my mind."

She shook her head. "A mother knows her son."

An artful smile lurked in the corners of her mouth. A pragmatic woman by nature, Audrey Cavanaugh wasn't one to ordinarily make light of a serious situation, but an instant later the knowing expression reached her eyes in a firework of joyous lines. Logan's chuckle gave way to an inward smile, one steeped in remembrance.

"There's my son's precious half-smile."

With a deep sigh, Logan lowered his head, the champagne easing his reservations. "You know me well," he said with a sidelong glance.

Audrey swiveled in her chair, raising her glass to guests as he had done moments ago.

"You made a promise to a woman you loved, but she's gone, Logan."

Logan rubbed his hands together in an effort to dislodge words that rang in his head as truth. "I feel like I've been sucked inside the belly of a ship that can't break from the storm."

"Perhaps you need to get off that ship."

"I don't know if I can. I can't go back. Or change anything."

"Stop torturing yourself and whoever this woman is, find her. Love her. Don't turn her away."

The words simmered and slowly burned through the façade of denial. "She's more than a memory." He lowered his head and spoke in a ruffled whisper. "I can't put her out of my mind. To let go. Of her, or the memories."

"Then don't be a fool. Find her. Don't let that passion smolder and burn out."

Rooted in truth, her words consumed him. Truths he'd fought to deny. Ones he'd quietly swept behind the masquerade of duplicity. And he bore the weight of their brutality, cruel and restless, unable to deny the solidity of their power. "How did you know?"

Audrey cradled her son's hands in hers. "I'm your mother. I can see it in your eyes. I'm also a woman. I'm old, Son. Not dead."

Logan squinted in the bright light as he surveyed the crowd. "I made a promise…to Laurie. And I betrayed that promise."

Audrey raised an eyebrow and gave a shallow nod of understanding.

A lump rose in Logan's throat. "There's a war going on inside me and I don't know how to fight it."

"Don't."

"What if I make the wrong decision?"

"You might," she responded without hesitation. "But I have faith that if you saw enough in her to let her in, even for a moment, then it's right. Besides, it's not your decision to make, and I think you've already been given the answer."

He sighed, raking a hand through his hair. "I've got one hand in hers, the Devil's got the other, and I'm caught in the crossfire of heaven and hell."

"It's not love that hurts, Logan, but the heartache and loneliness of losing someone. You've known that kind of love. Never forget how it feels," she said. "Whoever this woman is, her absence is causing your heart to break, and if it wasn't right, it damn sure wouldn't hurt. Find her. Go to her." Her face brightened. "And when you do, bring her home. She's a woman of impeccable taste," she added, nodding, "and I want to meet the amazing woman who has stolen my son's heart."

"I was a coward to leave her," he whispered, "and I didn't mean to fall...."

Audrey stood. "I know," she said and placed a hand on her son's shoulder.

Logan covered her hand and drew a breath. "I'm in love with her." The thought turned warm and yearning inside him, and with sudden clarity he knew it to be true.

"Love always finds its way home, Logan."

"It's too late. I left her."

"You're a Cavanaugh, and Cavanaugh men fight for what they want and know is right." Audrey smiled and adjusted the line of her dress with both hands. "Yes, well, now that I've convinced one Cavanaugh male to think straight, I believe I shall rescue your father. He looks far too giddy dancing with that perky young woman."

Logan sat alone, his hands clasped before him. Snowbound in the Rocky Mountains, he'd felt an ingrained desire to rescue a woman from the pain of her past, from herself and from the river. Looking back, it had been the woman with the paralyzing ocean-green eyes who had rescued him.

After taking a few steps, Audrey turned back. "And I think you need to disentangle your youngest. Judging by her behavior, she's celebrating a bit too intimately."

Logan smiled and rose to find Abbey.

* * *

Always the entertainer, Abbey kept things colorfully spirited with the same natural exuberance her mother had. High on the euphoria of her sister's wedding, the bubbly elation of champagne, and a throng of friends hanging on her every word, the sparkle in her eyes matched the animated wave over a sea of bobbing heads.

"Dance with me, Daddy," she giggled. "Only I'm not a little girl anymore, I'm not going to stand on your shoes." Alive with mischief, her brown eyes smiled and the button nose her mother bequeathed her scrunched into a little knot.

The lavender maid of honor dress her sister had chosen for her illuminated her porcelain skin, and burnished light brown curls kissed her shoulders, the resemblance to her mother uncanny. Her image struck him unexpectedly, not as a bitter reminder of what he'd lost, but of the amazing young woman she'd become, and whose petite frame bounced on tiptoes.

"Fair enough," he said, and bent his head to her upturned face, "but I don't want to step on your bare feet."

Abbey wiggled her toes. Logan threw his head back and laughed, grasped her tightly, and two-stepped across the dance floor to "I'm In," a lively Keith Urban tune.

"You seem happier than I've seen you in awhile," she said, smiling up at him. "It's nice."

Though she favored her mother, her eyes were his, and the illustration of her joy shimmered in their tawny depths.

"It's good to hear you laugh again. It makes me all funny inside."

"I believe that has something to do with the champagne."

"No, sir," she pouted. "I'm serious." And she placed her hand over her father's heart. "It comes from here."

"What do you expect? I'm surrounded by beautiful Cavanaugh women."

Abbey hugged her father selfishly. "I love you, Daddy," she whispered and nestled herself against him, just below the shoulder in the shallow crook of his chest, a safe haven for sleep-weary heads of little girls, exhausted brides, and maids of honor. And one woman.

His daughters would always be his little girls and they rarely passed an opportunity to wrap themselves around his finger or melt his heart.

"I do so love you, my baby girl." Logan kissed her on the forehead just as a handsome young man approached—his unruly hair a bit on the long side—waiting for her to turn around. "I believe this gentleman desires your attention, Abbey," he said, regarding the lanky young man whose hesitance seemed engendered by Logan's presence, easily a head taller and shoulders twice as broad.

"Jason," she squealed, arms open wide.

She truly was the spitting image of her mother.

The band changed pace and a slow, haunting tune drifted across the gardens. Logan's father grasped Audrey's hand and held it securely against his chest. Sophie, nestled against Reese's shoulder shared a quiet moment with her new husband. And Abbey, one arm waving wilding about, the other resting lightly on the young man's shoulder, swayed to the music. The tiny knot of people teased one corner of his mouth that tugged an invisible string tied to his heart. His family—a reflection of the past and a vision of the future.

Urgency swept through him as if the last four months had suddenly caught up, threatening to consume the very air he breathed. Logan slipped away, retreating to a corner of the garden where an aged willow spread her leafy umbrella of cool shade across the pond. Birds hidden in the branches chattered away or splashed about in the waterfall. He leaned against a boulder, pulled his iPhone from his pocket, and scrolled to her picture, a solitary moment he'd stolen in the still of the morning without waking her.

The fire had bathed her shoulder in a warm glow and her cheeks wore the soft blush of their lovemaking, the memory as vivid in his mind as her touch on his skin. Passionate green eyes stared back at him each time he closed his. Tangled legs, skin against skin. Hair like silk between his fingers. Her tears, tiny diamonds clinging to her lashes and cheeks wet beneath his thumb. The purr of moonlight on her breasts, peaked and eager for his touch. His heart stumbled. And he yearned for her; to touch her and put to flesh those things his mind couldn't let go. And his dreams of her so real he need but reach out to feel her skin and breathe her scent only to awaken alone and restless in a tangle of sheets, empty arms, and an unsatisfied need.

Four months had passed, yet he never tired of the memory of her beside him. Leaves stirred, and he shivered as if the breeze had whispered her name across his skin, afraid to move, afraid the ghost of her touch would fade. He pressed his fingers to his lips then gently touched the screen, a picture perfect memory. Like the sigh of a prayer, the remnants of her kiss lingered on his lips. "Need You Now" played softly in the background and he wondered if he ever crossed her mind.

"*Mi dispiace*," he whispered. "*Perdonami*."

Four months ago he hadn't known why God placed her in his life at that time and place, but he knew exactly where he wanted her for the rest of it. "*Dormi, la mia tresorina preziosa*," he whispered, the breeze lifting his words. "Sleep, my precious treasure."

Logan scrolled through a multitude of numbers and selected Rose's cell. With the summer season in full swing she'd be on the fly, but he didn't think she'd hesitate to help him.

Rose answered on the second ring, immediately peppering him with questions. "Mr. Cavanaugh! It's so good to hear from you. This place is booming, which is nothing new. Are you coming for a visit?

How are your folks? And Sophie and the wedding? Ohhh, I bet the bride is stunning, am I right? And Abbey? As bubbly as the champagne I imagine. You wouldn't recognize this place without all the snow, the meadows are filled with wildflowers—"

"Take a breath, Rose," Logan said with a warm laugh, "your enthusiasm is exhausting."

"It's just so darn good to hear from you. We've missed you."

"I've missed you too."

"Are you coming back to the business? Please say you are."

"I never really left, but with obligations in the ministry I haven't had time to make the rounds as often as I used to."

"Is that a yes? Please say you're coming back."

"I am."

Rose let out a high-pitched squeal comparable to a bull elk at the height of the rut. "Will you be coming to visit soon?"

"Soon. But right now I need your help."

"You name it."

"The arrangements for the addition of Il Salotto's spa services— do you still have the contact information?"

"I do. Natalie and I are old friends."

"I'll be in Phoenix tomorrow and I need to get in touch with her."

"Of course. Can I ask what this is about?"

"Let's just say I have some unfinished business to attend to. I promised no business today, but this can't wait. I need to fly out early tomorrow."

For an unusual moment, the line was silent. "If you'll give me the details, I'd be more than happy to take care of everything. Do you have your flight booked?"

"I wanted to talk to you first."

"Consider it done. I'll contact Natalie, book your flight, and you'll be free to spend the rest of the day with your family."

"You're amazing, Rose. I don't know how to thank you."

"A raise would be nice."

"I've got some pull with the boss. I'll see what I can do."

"Just tell me you're going to see Ms. Collins. That'll be thanks enough."

Logan poked a hand in his pocket and glanced over both shoulders. "Rose, how—"

"Natalie and I are old friends, remember? And Ryleigh is her best friend."

The reason Ryleigh had gone to the resort had slipped his mind. "Well?"

* * *

Unrelenting heat met her when Ryleigh arrived at Sky Harbor Airport. Although jeans and a light cotton three-quarter sleeved top had been appropriate for the ocean breezes of L.A., a gauzy sundress from QB Designs seemed more agreeable for Phoenix in June. A bead of sweat trickled down her temple, a sure sign of an impending hair disaster if she didn't find air conditioning soon. With a quick check of the parking ticket, she headed to her Tahoe.

Standing alongside the vehicle, she cranked the AC to max and dialed Nat's number. With the renovations for the Scottsdale spa in full swing she hoped they were in town.

Nat picked up on the first ring. "Welcome back, stranger. You in town?"

Natalie's energy never seemed to wane, and Ryleigh sensed the bounce in her step despite the triple-digit temperature. "I'm at the airport waiting for the steering wheel to cool so it doesn't brand my fingers." She sighed. "I really don't care for this place in the summer."

"I think you'll like it better tomorrow…uh," Natalie sighed, "…after you cool off a bit and get your book signings over with."

"I'm ready to go home to the mountains, but my first signing is in a couple of hours." She glanced at her watch. "Think you guys can break away around nine for a late dinner?"

"Nine-thirty sound okay? There's an Italian place at the FireSky. That'll give Mitch time to clean up. He's with Chandler and well, he thinks he's 'working,'" Nat scoffed. "Chandler gives him a hammer and tells him which nails to pound. Makes him feel studly. All it really does is make him sweat. And stink." Her voice deepened. "The showers can be quite fun, though."

Despite the heat, Ryleigh smiled at the insinuation. "See you at nine-thirty."

"I'm glad you're back, Riles. I'm so excited for tomorrow."

"It's just a book signing."

"Uh…well, if you don't mind, Mitch and I are going to hang out at the bookstore for a while."

"Wonderful," she said, the sarcasm thick. "You can tease me about the long line of people who don't show up."

"They'll come."

"Yeah, right."

"They will. We offered free spa passes."

"You're such a smart-ass." The sudden reminder skittered across her stomach in a whorl of butterflies. "See you soon."

Smart-ass. Her brand for the man who'd upended her world but like so many of the people she loved, had left her too. With the Tahoe cooled to a respectable temperature, she slid behind the wheel. In the stillness of the moment she closed her eyes, the light brush of Logan's lips against hers as real as if he were there, the heat of the desert no comparison to the fever of his body against hers. *God, I miss you.* Though the AC was cool, tingling warmth spread from the tips of her fingers to the inside of her thighs—a fiery reminder—pleasure fused with pain.

She adjusted the radio, desperate to drown her thoughts, and then turned down the terminal's spiral exit. Instead of something upbeat, the familiar piano intro to "Need You Now" flooded the Tahoe. Great. Just what she didn't need. Why couldn't she purge the emotional connection she felt in music and words and just listen like everyone else? The lyrics unleashed a fresh ache of longing and she wondered if she ever crossed his mind.

She changed the station and headed to the FireSky.

* * *

The clip-clop of hooves faded with the last carriage of wedding guests. Logan lengthened his stride and found Abbey on a bench massaging her feet.

"There you are, baby girl. It's time to wind down," he said, his arms extended to greet her.

Abbey stood and curled into his embrace, the straps of her heels hanging from one hand. "You look like you're in a hurry, Daddy. Are you leaving?"

"I have business to attend to in the morning," he said, loosening his tie.

"On Sunday?" She scrunched her nose. "What about your sermon?"

Logan slipped his arm around his daughter's waist and they followed the cobblestone path to the section of the resort reserved for family. "I spoke to Pastor Forsythe and he's taking over the congregation until they can find a replacement. I'm stepping down."

"So I take it you're going back to Wentworth-Cavanaugh full time?" Her dimples framed a buoyant smile.

"I am."

"It's about time. You made the company what it is," she said, animating the words with her hands. "It's where you belong. Besides, when I get my degree I want you to teach me the business."

"I'd be honored, baby girl."

"And you have to stop calling me that."

He paused and turned to her, enjoying the coy smile that widened from her mouth and sparkled in her eyes. "For as long as God allows me to grace this earth, Abbey Cavanaugh, you and your sister will always be my baby girls."

Logan escorted his daughter to her suite with her tucked securely under his arm. He hugged her and she returned his token of love with a squeeze that left him breathless. "I love you so much, Daddy," she said. "I don't know where you went for all those months, but I knew you'd come back. I just had to be patient."

"I'll always be here for you, Abbey."

"That's not what I meant." She looked up at him and smiled. "You're happy again."

Intuitive and smart—and slightly tipsy—Abbey's words struck the chords of truth. And it had taken a gaggle of Cavanaugh women to expose the charade. The only person he'd managed to fool was himself. For one intimate weekend, he'd been truly happy. And the hunger to find the woman who'd given her heart freely and who had opened his smoldered in his veins.

"I do so love you," he said, and Abbey relaxed in his arms.

Eric and Audrey approached them hand in hand, looking both exuberant and exhausted. Logan escorted Abbey inside, kissed his daughter on the forehead, and touched his finger to her nose in a gesture they'd shared since she was a baby. *"Dormi bene, cucciola,"* he said, and then closed the door behind him. He turned to his parents. "I'm not staying. I hope you don't mind."

"I had hopes you wouldn't." Audrey kissed her son lightly on both cheeks. Logan hugged her in return. "When do you expect to be back?"

"I don't know. I have the Tuscany property to look into—you do want me to pursue it, don't you, Dad?"

Eric nodded. "If a vineyard in Tuscany is what you want for our next venture, run the figures and see what resources it'll take." He rubbed his forehead. "Check with the lawyers about purchasing abroad. I trust your instincts. You know this business better than I do."

"Thanks, Dad."

"Welcome back, Son."

Logan embraced his father and then turned to leave.

"Oh, and Logan?"

Walking backward, Logan lifted his head in acknowledgement.

"Is she pretty?"

He stuffed his hands in his pockets. "Her eyes," he said, pausing to let the memory fully blossom, "are the color of the inside of an ocean wave." Eric's brows rose. "No, Pop, she's not just pretty. She's extraordinary."

Never again would he let loose of the memory. Transparent blue-green eyes had seen past the armor, and she'd held out her hand and touched his soul. Turning back around, Logan broke into a jog and waved a hand in the air bidding them good night.

One stop remained before his flight to Phoenix.

* * *

A bouquet of purple hyacinths (forgive me) among a spray of baby's breath (everlasting love) trembled in his hand. Leaning on one knee, Logan placed the flowers at the foot of Laurie's headstone. One at a time he absorbed each letter of her name—the name she'd taken willingly so many years ago—and closed his eyes to pray. The letters blazed white behind his eyes until one by one, they faded into the hallways of memory—not to be forgotten, but covered with love and tucked safely away where they belonged. His muscles relaxed. Every nerve steadied until the trembling subsided and his breaths came easy.

Logan raised his head. A breath of lavender brushed his face as if she were here, in the wind, in the rustle of leaves, in the chatter of birds, but no longer a prisoner of his heart. The invisible bindings that held him captive loosened and fell away, as if Laurie had finally let him go. In reality, it was he who had let her go.

And for the first time in three years, he didn't weep.

Chapter Thirty-Six

RYLEIGH ARRIVED AT the bookstore on Sunday a few minutes ahead of the scheduled nine o'clock opening. Wanda met her at the door and the two women went straight to the table they'd set up for Ryleigh the night before. Together they straightened the remaining books into neat stacks and set them at an angle to best showcase the striking hardbound cover.

Wanda clapped her hands together. "Ready?"

"We wouldn't want to keep anyone waiting, would we?" Ryleigh nodded toward the empty entrance.

Wanda laughed, a spirited snigger that matched her smile. "Well, this isn't American Idol, hon, but don't worry, they'll come."

Although yesterday evening hadn't produced much of a crowd, people stopped intermittently to chat or to ask her to sign their copy of *Firefly Pond*, and today's crowd did much the same, wandering in and out in a slow but steady stream.

The door opened and an older woman walked by the table. Spying the modest stack of books, she turned to address Ryleigh.

"Excuse me, are you the author?"

"I am."

"Oh," the woman said, scrutinizing her. Then she broke into a smile. "Your picture doesn't do you justice. You're much lovelier in person."

Ryleigh's cheeks flushed warmly. "Thank you," she said and pushed a strand of hair behind her ear. "You're much too kind."

"I read my sister's copy of this charming story and I came to buy a book, so I'll buy yours and have you sign it. How exotic," she said without taking a breath, her smile as crooked as Wanda's was perfect. "Will you be reading?" Ryleigh's heart jumped into her throat at the thought as she reached for the closest copy. The binding creaked, the spice of newsprint and fresh ink a comforting balm. "Make it to Millie, please."

Ryleigh handed her the signed book. "I'll be reading shortly." Her feet rearranged themselves and she pinched her toes into curls.

"Chapter thirteen? When Landon takes Reena to the pond?" Millie reared her head back and clutched her heart. "So lovely. Oh, Ms. Endicott, it's been a pleasure, and my sister Lottie will be green with envy." The woman walked away, hand still resting over her heart.

Ryleigh checked her watch, surprised at how much time had passed and then made her way to the nook at the back of the store. Wanda had placed chairs in a semicircle around the fireplace, and a wave of heads turned in her direction. *Where'd all these people come from?* Another surprise she could do without. She picked her way to the stool, a sea of eyes following her. The fireplace showed no signs of life, yet her skin prickled with heat.

Ryleigh sat with one leg over the stool, one planted firmly on the floor. "Good morning, Scottsdale." Her voice wavered. *So many people.* The crowd responded with smiles and muffled greetings. "I'm honored to be reading for you today from my novel, *Firefly Pond.*" She couldn't afford the luxury of giving in to anxiety and swallowed past the words competing with the heartbeat in her throat. "I've been asked to read from chapter thirteen." She winked at Millie, who'd taken a front row seat. *People who love to read.* Millie scrunched her bony shoulders to her ears, smiled, and winked back. Ryleigh's quivering stomach eased at the cordial gesture.

A ribbon marked a previously chosen place, but she turned to chapter thirteen instead. *People who enjoyed her work.* Ryleigh cleared her throat, and her voice steadied. *"Every ounce of willpower he possessed failed. Landon took her hand and kissed each of her fingers sequentially, the spark of his skin against hers reignited..."* Ryleigh immersed herself and became one with the words. The crowd smiled. The pleasure on their faces spread inside her and she returned it with a generous smile of her own. This was where she belonged—in a fantasy world created for others to enjoy.

Ryleigh closed the book to a round of applause. The crowd mingled for a few minutes and then gradually dispersed. She returned to the front of the store in time to see a short, paunchy man in shorts and shirt lumber through the door, red cheeks huffing. He raised his clipboard to Wanda, who signed for the delivery and pointed to Ryleigh.

"For you," he said, placing a dozen white roses on the table.

"Me?"

"Are you R. M. Endicott?"

"Last time I checked."

He smiled. "Then they're for you." He returned a moment later with another dozen roses. Ryleigh stared at them and then at him. He returned twice more—four dozen in all, each pure white, each without flaw.

"Wanda, did it say who they're from?"

"Nope." Wanda's face bloomed into a brilliant smile. "You must have one devoted fan."

"I guess so." She cringed. Chandler was in town. Flowers weren't his style, but given the talent her life had for throwing curveballs, she wouldn't put it past him to show up unannounced. With flowers. Two surprises too many. Both of which she could do without.

Not many people knew of her passion for white roses. This was something Ambrose might have done, but that was preposterous. Psychic? Possibly. Omniscient? Maybe. But not to the point of ordering flowers from the grave.

People milled in and out of the bookstore. A few knew of her; most didn't, but seemed eager to chat. Some even bought her book. But the roses were distracting. The only other explanation—she shook her head and pushed the ridiculous thought from her mind.

Near noon, Natalie and Mitch sidestepped through the clogged doorway, generous smiles pasted to their faces. They waved. She waved back and then froze. A silver-haired man wove among the people leaving, the disheveled copse of hair bobbing as if he bore the weight of a limp. *Ambrose?* No, the mere idea seemed silly. She was used to creating fantasy, but this was absurd. Keeping her eye on the door, she backed away and nearly knocked over a stack of books. In the instant it took to regain her balance, the man had vanished, but her wits refused to settle.

By straight-up noon, the small crowd had fast become no crowd. Wanda locked the door and Ryleigh bent to gather her things.

A customer approached the table and placed his book on the table in front of her. "I would be honored if you would sign your book for me," he said, his voice deep and even. "I collect signed first editions."

His voice resonated inside her as surely as if he'd stroked her skin, the sound as deep as a ripple of thunder, yet as gentle as the sough of the wind, and it swelled inside her until she couldn't breathe. Her heart leapt, but her stomach turned a buffet of somersaults. Her legs faltered and she sat. Afraid she was imagining the voice, she dared not look up. "Who would you like me to address it to?"

"I've been called a lot of things, but 'smart-ass' will do."

Her knees trembled. Thoughts collided in a wave of desire and disbelief.

"With a capital 'S.'"

Unsteady hands fumbled to open the book. Two items fell from inside the cover. Moisture blurred her vision and she tucked the items between the pages.

"And I prefer you sign it 'the girl with eyes the color of the inside of an ocean wave.'"

"Logan," she whispered and scraped enough courage together to look up. Wanda slipped quietly past and turned the sign in the window to 'Closed' and stepped into the back room. Mitch and Natalie followed.

"I'm here, Cabin Number Three."

His voice, deep and strong and mellow, pulsed inside her and he stood before her, solid and as absolute as the first time he'd held her. Still, she raised caution around her heart, but the same heart defied her and leapt at the image before her.

Ryleigh stood, the chair grating across the floor. Logan stepped around the table. She stepped back, and then grabbed the table to stop the floor from shifting under her feet. He reached for her, the distance between them weighted in hesitation, yet rife with the need to draw near. She held up a hand to his imminent touch—one she both wanted and cursed but hadn't the courage to reach for.

Dark eyes held hers, their expression one of longing and joy and hesitation, yet guarded in fear. He stepped closer, empathy allowing the distance between them to simmer and she touched the lines of his face with her eyes the way she'd once touched them with her hands.

"I so want to hate you right now," she said, unable to mask the pain beneath the words.

"Do you want me to leave?"

She shook her head.

"May I approach you?"

Again, she shook her head.

"I'm not leaving," he said, his words gentle, yet spoken with conviction.

"That's what terrifies me."

"You've nothing to be afraid of. Trust me."

"I trusted you once." The memory burned in her throat, bitterness fused with longing. "You took my trust and my heart and left."

"I will never again leave you."

She leaned into the table. "Don't make promises you can't keep," she said, clutching the edge of the table. "Breaking them is too painful to bear."

"For either one of us."

The implication of his words reached beyond the distance, and she tamed the need to reach out, to touch him, to comfort the invisible scars and soothe her own.

"I can't promise the memories will never haunt me, as I expect they will," he said, his voice husky with emotion, "for I bear the scars of the life I have lived, ones I fear may never completely fade. I can't guarantee there will be no pain or sorrow, for life promises both." He raked a hand over a day's growth of beard. "But I will promise your heart will never know emptiness, or want, or need, and I will protect your heart and your soul with everything that is in me. You'll not stand alone without me by your side, and the fire you kindle within me will forever warm your bed."

He stepped toward her, tall and resolute and of solid flesh before her, the distance between them no more than a breath. And that was enough for now.

"The first time I touched you, I felt your blood flow through me as my own." He wrapped her hands in his, and bent his head to her upturned face. "At that moment, my heart became yours. And if you'll have me, Cabin Number Three, I'll give life to your dreams, bear your sorrows, and I swear," he said, his eyes dark with the joy of concession, "I'll never let you fall."

With only the sound of his breathing as background noise, she stood weighted by eyes that held her as tightly as his hands, ones that saw only with his heart. And she tucked his words inside her heart, the need to preserve them, to stop time and safeguard this moment overwhelming.

"It's too late, Logan," she said, tears filling her eyes. "I already have."

Memories were shaken free but none could compare to his presence and promise of his words, prying open a heart once tightly sealed. This man gave all of himself or nothing at all. Of that, she was sure. Yet, she had let him go. A decision she cared not to repeat. And never would again.

Ryleigh stepped into his arms, his response as solid and strong around her as she remembered. She fitted against the hollow of his chest, a place both newly acquainted and comfortably familiar and she took title to all of him, the inside and the out, both broken and whole. And in her next breath, she relinquished her fears back to him.

Logan held her in trembling arms and kissed the trail of tears, absorbing each silent cry of her heart, filling the cavern of empty space his absence had left. Her tears fell warm and wet against him, a soothing ointment for two lost souls. They remained quiet in each other's arms, the pieces of their world falling back together.

The moisture on his cheek echoed hers, and she touched them, fear and sadness shifting beneath her fingers. A hesitant smile rose with her touch. She traced the lines anchoring his dimples down to the cleft in his chin and then sketched the outline of his lips as if she had been blind and was seeing him for the first time.

"God, I've missed you," she whispered. "You have no idea."

Relief softened his eyes and erased the remaining apprehension written in the lines of his face. "I've held priceless treasures in my hands only to see them slip away and I believed I could never love again. Then you came to me, and I let you slip away too. But you never let go. Awake or in sleep, you never left me. Yes, *amore mio*, I think I know."

Logan took her face in his hands and brushed his lips to hers. When his mouth covered hers, the room disappeared in a fog, and she gave way to the weeks lost in one restless kiss, one whose uncertainty spoke of gentleness, but one whose promise gave way to the power of complete affirmation.

"No," Natalie said, "wait—"

Ryleigh turned. Chandler yanked his arm from Natalie's grasp, his eyes narrowed.

"Oh, God," she said.

In a few long strides, Chandler reached the door and pulled. The locks rattled. Natalie straightened a pile of children's books.

"Chandler," Ryleigh whispered into Logan's chest.

Logan shifted one foot between hers, hips set firmly against hers.

"I have to talk to him."

His eyes pleaded. "Let him go."

Ryleigh placed her hand on his cheek, the stubble awakening sensations nearly lost over time. "I love you, Logan Cavanaugh," she said, searching his face, "but I loved him first and I need to talk to him."

He hesitated and then let her go.

Ryleigh approached the man she'd spent over half her life with. "I'm sorry you had to witness this, Chandler." She took no pleasure in the pain written on his face, and took his arm to lessen it. "I never meant to hurt you."

"By kissing another man? You're my wife!"

"I was. A lifetime ago." Ryleigh lowered her head, and then raised it to meet his eyes. "I told you months ago we can't be together."

"I didn't believe you." Bitterness dripped from his words. "I couldn't."

"I don't say things I don't mean."

"I thought you'd come around," he said, reaching into his pocket. "I've carried this with me, hoping…" His voice trailed and he closed her hand around the mate to her wedding ring.

Logan took two steps forward. Ryleigh sensed the movement, caught his eye and then shook her head.

"You should go, Chandler. Wanda will see you out."

"Riles," he said, and touched her face. "Can I kiss you goodbye?" With his thumb, he kneaded her cheek. "It doesn't have to mean anything to you, but it would to me. Sort of the beginning of the end."

"I'm sorry." Ryleigh removed his hand and stepped back. "But you put the period at the end of us a long time ago."

Logan closed the space between them and stood beside her, one foot in front of her, his presence a shield against the irascible climate. He eyed Chandler with cool wariness and straightened, his shoulders broader and several inches over Chandler's, not a small man himself. Ryleigh glanced from one to the other, the air restless and percolating with tension. Yet despite the serious nature of the situation she held her breath and bit her lip to keep from laughing.

Chandler rose to full height, which reminded her of a somewhat underinflated puffer fish, took several steps back, and made a clean swipe at a stack of books that sent them crashing to the floor. He pushed the hair from his face and left through the back of the store.

Logan gathered her into his arms. "You all right?"

Ryleigh let go a breath and slapped a hand over her nose and mouth to stop the air from maturing into an unrestrained snicker.

"Am I to assume a rumble in a bookshop is amusing?"

"No, of course not. Well, maybe a little," she said, and laughed. "It's just…I've never had anyone fight over me before. It's kind of barbaric. And cute."

"Barbaric I can handle." He raised an eyebrow. "But cute?" He winced unconvincingly, the amusement deepening the creases around his eyes.

She leaned into him. "I thought it was cute you stood ready for battle," she said, and tucked her lips at the bubbling humor.

"*Sei mia, mia dolce cara. La mia vita per la tua.*"

"What'd you say?"

"I'm not quite sure I know myself, but it's neither barbaric nor cute. I hope." Sincerity softened the amusement on his face. "But I know what I meant to say."

"Tell me, please?"

He stared back at her, his eyes purposeful and selfless and somehow reckless. "You are mine, my dearest sweetheart," he said, inky brown discs never wavering from hers. "My life for yours."

The words to any sort of suitable reply beat its wings hopelessly against her stomach. She studied his face, one carved by the magic of time, the one that held her spellbound to the man it belonged to. His smile, tawny eyes, and handsome lines carved from the beautifully knitted scars of a broken heart—all a comfortable reminder of the sum of him. "The roses. From you?"

"A rose each for the ones you've lost," he said, "and for each of the twelve weeks we have lost."

"Ambrose." She swallowed hard. "Two months ago." Surely it wasn't him she glimpsed among the crowd? As impossible as it seemed, she'd carry that glimpse—that small ray of hope—with her forever. But how did he know? The man truly had been carved from the ages of time and as he had told her, love is ageless. Somehow she thought he might be, too.

"I'm sorry." Logan brushed a strand of hair caught in the moisture of her tears. "I should have been there for you. To ease the pain of loss."

"Please don't apologize." Joy softened her features. "My pain stopped the moment you took me in your arms."

Logan held her as if letting go would cause her to slip away again. "The tickets," he said, pointing to his yet unsigned copy of *Firefly Pond*. "We have a flight to catch."

"Today?" She scrunched her nose. "Where are you taking me?"

"St. Louis."

"Why St. Louis?"

"It's a surprise," he said, a hint of the mischievous boy he must have been peered from beneath eyes gone bright as copper pennies.

"I don't care much for surprises."

Logan raised her hand and kissed the back, long and purposeful. "There's one more thing you can count on, Cabin Number Three," he said with decisive amusement. "You'll grow to love my surprises. And that's a promise."

She answered with a wide smile.

Natalie cleared her throat and dragged Mitch from their perch. Wanda followed, restacking the toppled pile of books. Wiping the residue of her tears, Natalie pulled Ryleigh away from Logan and hugged her best friend.

Introductions were made, though none were needed.

"You knew about this, didn't you?"

Natalie and Logan exchanged a knowing smile.

Chapter Thirty-Seven

"WHERE ARE WE?"

"Near the Zahorsky Woods."

"Are we still in Missouri?"

"We are," he grinned, "Near Steeleville at the base of the Ozarks."

The road narrowed. The Z4 convertible roadster hugged the asphalt as they drove farther into the dense overhangs of sycamore and silver maple. Logan slowed and turned on a neatly maintained road, tires spitting gravel behind them. A vine-covered stone villa emerged through a copse of trees.

Ryleigh straightened. "You sure this isn't Italy?"

Logan set the brake and Ryleigh clambered from the car. He opened his door and leaned against it, the tap of the cooling engine a soothing rhythm to an eager heartbeat. Moist air, heavy with the balm of pitch and chatter of birds carried in the breeze, and Ryleigh spun in a lazy circle a few yards away absorbing every detail. With his eyes, he followed her legs, long and lean and draped in denim, and drifted down the line of buttons on her white cotton top and over soft, round shoulders, bringing to life the feminine curves of his memories. And whose voice was like an angel's sigh. "*Il mio angelo.* My angel. In blue jeans." And he marveled at how she celebrated things most took for granted. He'd show her all of God's majesty, if she would let him. But the light that shined within her he cherished above all.

"It's gorgeous," she said, settling into the crook of his arm.

He tucked her close. The sun, an exaggerated orange ball, hung near the horizon against the canvas of a sun-bleached blue sky, merging their shadows into one dark pool. "Welcome to Dolomite Falls Resort, Cabin Number Three. A touch of Italy tucked into the Ozarks."

"Don't tell me this is one of your resorts too?"

"Okay. I won't."

"Smart-ass," she mumbled and jabbed him playfully in the ribs. "Do you own anything that isn't knock-out gorgeous?"

He lifted her chin, his thumb gently stroking her ear. "I have discerning taste, so the answer is no. Sometimes it's obvious. The breathtaking beauty..." he said, glancing around. "Sometimes it's hidden beneath the surface. The first time I looked in your gentle eyes," he said, "I saw both." Logan brushed his lips against them, kissing them softly, one and then the other.

"Gentle?"

"Gentle heart. Gentle soul." He smiled. "Mirrored in your eyes."

"You haven't seen me angry."

"I've seen enough to want to know all that's hidden there," he whispered, smoothing her hair from her face. "The verdant green ones that smile, the storm clouds that brew in the angry ones, and the passion of the deepest ocean, the ones that say 'yes.'"

"Yes."

He touched her mouth with his fingers. "And I want to know your smile. The pouty one and the one that warns me to tread lightly. But mostly the happy one, the one that says 'yes.'"

"Yes, yes, and yes."

Her words formed around a brilliant smile, the steady rhythm of her heartbeat the melody to a song he prayed would not end until life no longer coursed through his body. "Then I'll put them together—those everyone sees, the ones unseen, and those reserved only for me."

He was met with puzzlement and he smiled down at her. "I see things most don't, Cabin Number Three. It's the reason I'm good at what I do, choosing locations with endless possibilities for our resorts, as I did this one. And as I see in you."

"It's truly beautiful here."

"It's not Italy, but it'll do. For now. It's more secluded than some of our other resorts, and I know how much you value solitude."

"Emily Dickinson and I."

"Both purveyors of words, lovers of solitude."

She leaned against him. "Sometimes words get in the way."

He felt the words as if she'd whispered them against his skin. "You say it best when you say nothing at all." Ryleigh turned to him, her response clearly written in the quirk of her smile and reflection in her eyes. He took her hand and gestured toward the house. "This is the family villa, secluded from the resort."

They walked arm in arm, but before they reached the entrance a young man emerged whistling to the melody of a jangle of keys. "Mr. Cavanaugh," he choked, extending his hand.

Logan shook his hand. "Good to see you, Nathan."

"I didn't expect you and Ms. Collins this early."

Logan nodded toward the Beemer. "Fully loaded street rocket," he mused. "It's not easy maintaining the speed limit."

Nathan whistled.

Ryleigh nudged Logan in the ribs. "He thinks the speed limit's a guideline, and certainly not for him."

"Look who's talking, leadfoot," Logan said, and laughed. "Remember the snowmobiles?"

Ryleigh rolled her eyes.

Logan planted a hand on his hip and pulled Ryleigh close with the other. "Has everything been taken care of?"

"Yes, sir."

Logan felt rather than heard the hesitation. "Is there something you're hesitant to tell me?"

"The wine delivery was late and I had to put pressure on the vintner. But she came through and everything is as you requested."

Logan smiled at the young man's guile. "Nothing less than I would have done, Nathan."

Nathan raised his chin and nodded. "Enjoy your stay, Ms. Collins. Mr. Cavanaugh." He turned and walked away and then turned back, grinning widely. "Oh, and by the way, Mr. Cavanaugh, it's good to have you back."

"It's good to be back."

Logan led Ryleigh inside.

"He's a keeper. Knows the ins and outs of keeping the family residences stocked. And if I have anything to say about it, he'll be as good as Rose someday."

VINES CLUNG TO the exterior of the villa, its red tiled roof the instrument a hard rain would use to strum its melody, but the crumbled plaster inside revealed the brick bones of the wall beneath and massive rough-hewn beams stretched across the ceilings. Though designed with modern amenities, the stone building could have been tucked into the hills of Tuscany time had overlooked.

Ryleigh spun a pirouette around the room. Everywhere she looked was another testament to this man's attention to detail and her eyes settled on a stone vase filled with five white roses. She touched each one reflectively, each one a gentle reminder of those she'd lost. A jardinière of green M&M's sat next to the roses, a white "R" stamped on each one. For her? For her father? Without question, she knew it to be both.

Several bottles of Italian wine were nestled in a metal basket on the counter. Logan chose a bottle and twisted the opener until the cork popped free, the familiar aroma of red chilies, plums, and the subtle hint of chocolate rising in a wisp as he poured their glasses. He flipped a switch and music filled the villa.

He hadn't forgotten anything, every detail a memory clothed in the compassion of the man who watched her with a quiet sense of pleasure.

She picked things up and put them down, the intrinsic ability and discernment of Logan's talent—or Midas touch, perhaps—for transforming something from mediocre to exquisite seemed the trademark of the Cavanaugh name. The effects of his influence and charm grew unmistakably apparent as she dragged her fingers along the cracked, crumbling walls, a metaphor to her own recent past.

Ryleigh stepped through the French doors to an arbor shading a full-length patio. The canopy of vines had given way to a burst of new life and the arbor dripped with unopened purple wisteria clusters. The air had that moist heaviness about it when spring opens its arms to summer and comes alive with the perfume of damp moss, fertile earth, and sun-warmed pine. She leaned against the railing, Logan's footsteps light across the hardwood floors. He handed her a goblet. The wine slid down her throat and settled in her belly, a tiny fire of warmth. He set his down and cradled her, the power of his arms around her and his thighs against hers the security and solidity of purpose she knew him to be.

Whether the influence of the wine, the music or simply his presence next to her, the feeling of belonging grew and settled over her and around her and in all the empty spaces within.

A light breeze lifted her hair, the subtle movement adrift with his musky scent. "I need you, Logan Cavanaugh," she said, reflections of afternoon light playing on the soft curls that caressed the tops of his ears. She touched the curls, wanting—needing—to know the stories behind the silver, ghostly reminders hidden in the same way the past had taken the color. "You became my strength when I needed it most."

A quiet moment passed. "And you, my weakness. You held my heart in your hands and I fell apart only to see the one who could hold me together slip away."

His hands moved over her like the gentle roll of waves on a summer lake. She closed her eyes, his touch slowly shifting, rearranging her inner core, and with a contented sigh, gave herself wholly—her dreams and her fears—for him to safeguard in his heart. "Breathe" played quietly in the background. "It's peaceful here, Logan."

Brushing her hair aside, he leaned in and kissed her neck, his tongue light on her skin. "I couldn't agree with you more, Cabin Number Three."

She turned her face to meet his. Raw emotion emanated from his gaze, a message conveyed without words.

Logan took her face in his hands and kissed her with unresolved passion, a kiss profoundly physical and meant to recapture the weeks lost, one she hungered to deepen and surrender completely to its power.

Her hands loosened his shirt from his jeans, but Logan took them and gripped them tightly to his chest. His gaze drifted over her, awakening her body as if he'd touched her with his hands.

An artful smile lifted one side of his mouth. "I can take it from here."

And he claimed her, his kiss soft and moist and laden with the sweet ruffle of wine. "*Ti amo così tanto*, Ryleigh Collins. I do so love you." The words drifted over her, spoken as if in prayer.

"Logan—"

Logan pressed his fingers to her mouth and then swept an arm under her knees and lifted her against him. "Sometimes words get in the way," he said, and carried her inside.

Sunlight filtered through the bedroom windows, bathing him in a pool of amber light. He set her down, the air alive with promise. His fingers brushed the hollow of her neck with such seasoned tenderness, she felt only the whisper of cloth as he lifted her top over her head. He unfastened her bra and it fell unhindered, exposing her breasts, heavy with the unspoken invitation. And he took them, the desire in his eyes naked, yet reposeful, his breath a sigh on her bare skin. Blood pulsed through her, rousing her in places hungry for his touch. Everything she offered, he claimed with no hesitation in his need, and the whole of her went liquid as he nourished her with the touch of his hands.

In answer, she fumbled with the buttons of his shirt, and when the last gave way, the tangle of chest hair flowed dark and soft between her fingers, and then she gave the ripple of muscle a gentle squeeze. A hard nub rose beneath her palm and desire rose in her own nipples as if he'd stroked them. A moan rumbled in his throat, his male spice rich and heady. Her memories shifted and became real—constant and solid and unquestionable.

With discreet abandon, she unfastened his jeans and traced the dark line from navel to groin. She met his eyes and tucked her arms around him and urged him closer, the need to be one with him absolute, a bond she had refused to relinquish in his absence, nor would she today or any day after.

"Is this okay?" Her eyes sought the confirmation of her thoughts. "What we're doing, I mean?"

Logan took her head in his hands, "Your body is a treasure, your pleasure my gift," he whispered, his thumb stroking her chin, "and I do not intend for either one to be taken lightly. I say 'I love you' and my words come not from my mouth, but from the blood and bones and heart that sustain me, the soul and spirit that are me. You are not the first I have spoken these words to." And then he moved his thumb to her lips, each stroke a caress of words softly spoken. "And though a first love cannot truly be forgotten, love is a priceless treasure to be guarded. And I shall do so, with my heart and mind, and with my life. And you shall be my last love. I'm just a man, *amore mio*," he said, his smile linked to hers, "a man who's wanted you from the first time I saw you, whose heart has been scribed with your name before the beginning of time, and who will spend the rest of his days pleasing you, and worshiping your body the way a man should, if you'll allow me the honor."

His words tugged at something so deep inside her, the tiny cracks in her heart came together as if he'd used the fiber of his words to mend it. Ryleigh tucked her lips between her teeth and bit down to keep a rein on the emotion stirred by his words and penetrating gaze. "Yes," was all she managed to say through a blur of unspilled tears. Logan took her hands, guiding her until his jeans slipped past his hips and fell in a heap. He did the same with hers until nothing remained between them but the bond of skin against skin, his heartbeat matching hers as if their hearts beat as one.

With one hand cradled on her bottom, he reached into the drawer and removed a foil package. "I made sure the villa came well-stocked."

"Smart-ass," she said, took the package and peeked at him through lowered lashes. "I can take it from here." She tore the package and slid the condom over his length. A breath hissed through his teeth and he pulled her tight against him, the urgency of his need hard and restless against her belly.

Logan laid her down, the featherbed an airy cushion beneath her, his body a cradling shield of strength and power, of compassion and tenderness above her. And she welcomed the whole of him as she molded her body to his. With a kiss that left no doubt he'd claimed the whole of her, he eased himself inside her, the pleasure deep with promise. They joined as one, the intimacy as slow and easy as fine wine: ripe with passion, yet mellow in the arms of empathy, the bond complete.

Like a feather caught in the current of a stream, the haunting memories drifted away in silence—a language with no need of words. In the subtle glow of the waning afternoon, they returned to the place where two lost souls had collided into one under the cover of a Rocky Mountain snowstorm.

* * *

The clock ticked and blood pulsed in his veins, but time seemed irrelevant. Propped on one elbow, Logan watched her doze—every breath, every rise and fall of her chest an unspoken answer to a prayer. Emotion crashed through him, something so deep, so compelling, there wasn't enough of her to fill the void each time he took a breath. And when he'd taken her mouth, her answer had been so deeply rooted the sheer depth unhinged the last of his resolve, and left no doubt her dreams were his to bring to life and her fears were his to heal—now and every day after.

Bubbles of moisture still clung to her lashes and he smiled at the hint of freckles sprinkled just below her eyes, an unconsumed keepsake to the little girl. In the stillness of the moment he traced the outline of her face, the touch so light she didn't wake, memorizing her sleepy smile and the feel of her flesh beneath his fingers. And he'd use the rest of his lifetime to please her and keep her safe. In the moments before she stirred, he breathed the faint notes of her perfume and tucked them away to recall at will, and bathed in the languor of their lovemaking.

"Hey," she said with a sigh and then reached to meet his leisurely kiss.

"Tell me your eyes will be the last I see when I close mine and the first I wake up to."

"Always," she said with a sheepish smile, "unless you surprise me with a puppy."

"Sei mia, mia cucciola."

RYLEIGH LAY BESIDE him, secure in his arms and the rumble of his laugh a soothing melody to the intensity of his words. A day's stubble rasped against her cheek, a contradiction to the man beneath and his breaths a reminder of the life beside her. And if she stopped breathing—this day, this moment would be enough. "I love you, and I want to know the stories behind every silver hair," she said and wrapped a curl around her finger.

His voice shook with impish pleasure. "The title would be, 'Two Daughters and Forty-Six Years Under My Belt.'"

"Okay, smart-ass, I'm trying to be seriously charming and you're making jokes."

"You're already seriously charming."

"And I happen to enjoy what's under your belt." She tucked her lip between her teeth and studied him—the bold chin and eyes that spoke without words—and her belly fluttered at how deeply she had fallen under his spell. Logan brushed her nose with his finger and winked, and the tug of these simple acts curled her toes. With her arm around his waist, she snuggled closer, a finger tracing the smooth indentation of the scar below his ribs.

He flinched and pushed her hand away.

"I'm sorry," she said, frowning, "does it still hurt?"

"It tickles."

"I'm sure it didn't tickle at the time."

"No, it didn't. In fact," he said with a deep noise in his throat that might have passed for a chuckle, "that day's a little hazy, but I was told I was rather vocal." He did chuckle this time. "Guess I was somewhat insolent while they tried to dig a cannonball out of my side."

"Cannonball?"

"Felt like one. Before the magic of drugs took hold." Logan rolled on his back and she curled beside him, her head nestled against his shoulder. One hand stroked his chest. He drew a deep breath. "Pink Lady .38 Special. We were serving dinner at a local soup kitchen on Christmas Eve. I watched her pull the gun—"

Ryleigh raised up on an elbow. "A woman?"

"She aimed, fired five rounds, and all I could think of was why'd she need a pink gun to tell us she wasn't fond of turkey?"

"A woman? With a pink gun?"

"And lousy aim." He raked a hand over his chin. "It was a long time ago. No one was seriously hurt."

"Besides you?"

"And the pot of gravy," he said, making a rather dubious imitation of an explosion.

"And you?"

"A bit messy, but it wasn't serious. Gravy pot bled more than I did."

"Smart-ass." She took his hands in hers and pressed them to her cheek, humor relaxing from her face. The weight of him next to her satisfied the doubt of his physical presence, but what she needed now was to know all the pieces that made him one. Besides what she did know—the consummate partner, sensual lover, compassionate minister and devoted father she knew him to be, she sensed the other, more discreet layers of this fascinating man. And she hungered to peel those layers away, to uncover the whole of the man within, to hold his hand through the dark places he wanted to forget, and to know his thoughts through the weeks that had separated them. "I wish I could take your memories—the painful ones—and erase them."

"I wouldn't want you to, Cabin Number Three. Scars are proof we fought through our battles. And made it through."

"I want to know them. The good ones and the painful ones. Your secrets."

"*Amore mio*," Logan said and pulled her close, "there are secrets meant to be shared and some that aren't. I'll never lie to you and I'll share those that are meant for you. To keep safe. As I will do with yours." Logan tightened his embrace and kissed her forehead. "Our past is what makes us who we are, but without pain, we never know true joy. Joy like you've given me."

"You told me once you didn't have a gift for words."

"I don't," he said, brushing her nose with a finger. "But when I look at you, you become my words and it's a story I wish to write until I no longer walk this earth."

Her face erupted in a brilliant smile at the implication. With his help, she ran her finger over the scar again, evidence of the past hidden in a ticklish grin. But the invisible scars remained. The ones on his heart she could never truly mend. Over time, she hoped those too would be as remote and as smooth as the one beneath her touch, knitted together with the fabric of her love in the same way his body had closed a gaping wound into a fine line of remembrance, but no longer painful.

"I'm happy, Logan Cavanaugh," she said, and though the ghosts of the past would forever lurk in the untouchable places where nightmares roamed, they would share them as one flesh, solid and truth and protection in physical form. She dared anyone or anything to take him from her again.

"And I too, share a happy heart. Because of you." Logan squeezed her bottom. "Time to get moving, Cabin Number Three."

"Why?"

"Stop asking so many questions and get dressed."

"I don't care much for surprises."

"So you keep reminding me," he said in the mischievous tone she adored.

"Bite me!"

Logan grabbed her and rolled on top of her, and she giggled as the sheet tangled around them. "Gladly," he said and nipped her neck.

Her skin tingled. "Thought you had no use for vampires."

"Depends on who they've claimed as victim." Logan kissed her on the nose, disentangled the sheet and got out of bed.

Ryleigh watched him with attentive eyes. She pulled the sheet over her mouth to cover a snicker. "Your butt is ghostly."

"Ghostly or ghastly?"

"White. As in snow. You own all these resorts and you've no time to tan your hide?"

"None of my resorts are devoted to nudists. Now get dressed."

"Can I shower first?"

He gave her a lopsided grin. "Need help?" He paused. "I would enjoy seeing you with nothing on but a smile."

"Haven't we already done that?" She turned on her side, dragging the sheet with her. "Do I need to push your rewind button?"

"You can push my buttons anytime." Logan chuckled and pulled on his jeans. "I'll start dinner while you shower."

"When are you going to let me cook for you? I'm pretty good at it, you know."

"There's no hurry." Logan raised an eyebrow. "You've a lifetime to show me all your talents."

Ryleigh smiled genuinely, but inside, her heart leapt at the repeat of the insinuation that they would be together for a very long time. "Man of my dreams." The sight of the man before her stilled her thoughts—how his bare chest narrowed at the waist and the way his shoulders tensed as he fastened his jeans, displaying the strong lines of his thighs and rear in perfect definition. "One who can cook and makes love like the men in my books." Ryleigh chuckled, slipped into a robe and headed for the shower.

"I've been taking lessons."

"Oh?" She stopped abruptly. "From whom?"

"You."

"Me?"

"I've read your book."

She hugged the robe around her. "You're such a smart-ass, Logan Cavanaugh," she mumbled. She let the robe drop and stepped into the shower. The hot spray washed over her, dissolving the weeks of doubt and sending them swirling down the drain.

* * *

By the time they'd finished dinner the sun had vanished. The sky settled into the pale violet of dusk and the air was heavy with the bouquet of a pregnant forest. Pines breathed their fragrant sigh and maple leaves fluttered in the stir of the wind. Logan leaned against the deck railing and Ryleigh huddled against him.

A stone stairway led to the creek where the water had scooped its path, moss and low-growing creeper carpeting the earth between stones. Water spilled over jagged outcrops of mossy dolomite rock and cascaded several feet before tumbling into a shallow pool. Crickets chirped their nightly songs.

"Are there waterfalls at all your resorts?"

Logan increased the intensity of his embrace. "I will never let that happen again."

Sensing the magnitude of his promise, she squeezed his thigh.

Logan stroked her arms, his touch raising pebbles of gooseflesh. "Unbreak" played softly in the background, the strum of guitars mimicking the rhythm of the splashing water.

"I wish I could say I wrote these words for you," he whispered. "I don't have the gift you or your father have. Songwriters are modern-day poets, and I think this was written for me, about you."

She closed her eyes. The lyrics scrolled through her mind, the message purposeful and as stirring as his touch and she couldn't help wonder how he knew her so well, how he could separate every facet of who she was and nourish her with exactly what she needed. "Your words are honest and pure. They're spoken from the heart and written forever on mine."

"I'm no Ryan Star, but I will comfort your broken dreams and bring life to new ones until the stars rain down from the heavens."

She let the words warm her from inside to out and then she kissed his cheek with her palm. "Wait here."

Ryleigh considered the journal Ambrose had given her an extension of herself, filled with poems and song lyrics, her emotions set to words—letters to a man she adored and knew without a doubt she loved. Guessing it was the profound emotion of the last few months that had seasoned her pen, the passion had flowed effortlessly from her heart and into her words.

"Ambrose said the poems Ryan wrote were his love letters to my mother," she said, tucking a strand of hair behind an ear. "He sent this to me before he…died… and told me to write to you and you would hear the words."

She handed him the journal.

* * *

Logan took his time reading and when he finally looked up, he smiled and then turned the page to the last entry and read aloud:

" 'Who winked and set the stars ablaze
and hung the moon between the peaks?
Who sprinkled the earth with fairy dust
and cast the meadows in moonlit wakes?

Who draped the trees in blankets deep
and sent wild creatures into flight?
Who whispered and asked the wind to still
and calmed the fears on a thunderous night?

Who sent an angel to save a soul
and open a heart once more to grace?
Who wrapped this frozen world in warmth?
Surely God, and your embrace.
~RME~'"

He closed the journal and tucked her into his shoulder. "Poetry is when emotion, thoughts, and pieces of your soul become your words. You have a gift, and I consider myself blessed to be a part of it."

"I write words in pencil. But you're written across my heart in indelible ink," she said, stroking his chin.

"God has blessed you with an extraordinary gift," he said to her as "My Heart is Open," played softly in the background. He paused before he spoke again. "I have a confession to make."

She tensed. "Confessions are first cousins to surprises."

"I have a contact in St. Louis. He's an historian of sorts and helped me locate the cemetery where Ryan is buried."

An unpleasant shift turned Ryleigh's stomach.

"We don't have to go, but the option is there if you wish."

Ryleigh leaned her back against his chest. She couldn't rewrite the past and the last thing she wanted was to complicate things. But most of her past remained a mystery, as did a family she wanted to know—had fantasized about. "Mom shared few details about Daddy, fewer about his death, and none about my father or my twin brother. I understand why now, and I've given this a lot of thought."

"You won't have to do this alone. I've taken your body as my own and I'll hold your hand as well. I'll be there with you, every step and I'll never let go."

She wiggled around to face him. "When I'm ready, I'll go. To find the rest of the missing pieces to my past. My family."

"I want to know everything about you, Cabin Number Three, including your past." He stroked her arms. "And your family. I don't want to go through life as an 'I' any longer. You're better at seclusion than I am and I'm ready to be a 'we.'"

She lowered her head and swallowed. "What about your ministry, Logan? You've never mentioned it."

He let out a long breath. "You know about that?"

"Rose mentioned it."

Logan chuckled. "You women bounce off each other like rogue balls in a pinball machine." His expression turned serious. "My prayers have been answered, Ryleigh. That part of my life is over. 'There is a time for everything, and a season for every activity under heaven:'"

"You won't miss it?"

Deep-set dimples accentuated his thoughtful smile. "I'm not giving up anything I'm not supposed to, nor relinquishing anything I don't want to. God's fingerprints are everywhere—in your words, the laughter of the birds, and the redolence of the wine. On us." He kissed her hand. "He isn't just a part of me, God is a part of everyone. And everything. Besides, I speak to Him daily. He's speed-dial number one, right above the lawyers and accountants."

She punched him playfully on the arm. "Logan Cavanaugh, you are the biggest smart-ass I've ever had the pleasure to know." She gasped and slapped her hand to her mouth. "Is it okay to say that to a minister? And while we're on the subject, you never answered my question. Before, you know, I asked if it was okay…to do what we were doing?"

Logan's laugh echoed through the still evening air. "*That's* what you meant?"

She nodded, heat rising in her cheeks.

"Come here," he said, tightening his arms around her. "I'm a man who used to be a pastor. Now I'm just an ordinary man who loves the Lord, and ordinary men laugh, we cry and we become angry as much as anyone does. We fall in love. And I believe love, and making love, are to be shared for a lifetime. Not simply for pleasure or when convenient. When you honored me with your body, you gave me your soul, and mine I gave willingly to you. We're one in my eyes and for all it's worth, I'm yours until God calls me home."

The promise of his words soothed her, and she allowed herself to rest in their assurance, words not read from a book but from a heart seasoned in love. To reside in the intimacy with which he gave so selflessly was to relinquish herself. And she had.

"Don't be afraid, *un dolce*. It's only love we're falling in. Not an icy river." And with a one-sided smile still playing across his lips, he kissed her deeply.

"God," she said, resting her head on his chest, "your kiss is deadly."

"I can't give God the credit, Cabin Number Three," he said with a laugh. "I spent four years at Yale."

"Classic answer for a smart-ass."

"Let's take a walk."

"Now where?"

"I know—you can do without surprises."

Her mind drifted back less than twenty-four hours, and a flirty smile preceded a shrug. "Depends on the surprise."

"That's my girl," he said and kissed her nose. "I'm taking you to the footbridge over the Wauwatosa." He slipped his hand in hers and led her off the deck.

"The wa-wa what?"

"Wauwatosa. It's the name of the creek."

Dusk slipped into the cool azure of twilight, the lazy space before nightfall consumes the light. Hand in hand, they made their way along a narrow cobblestone path illuminated by the iridescent splinter of the moon. Crickets chirped. An owl hooted her evening lullaby and summer thunder rumbled in the distance.

The footbridge wasn't far. The rocks along the edge of the creek were smooth and colorful, not the jagged spires that formed around the waterfall. The water gurgled peacefully beneath them, inconsequential matters washing away in its flow. Logan stooped, picked through the smallest pebbles along the creek, came up with a smooth white one, and then closed her fingers around it.

Ryleigh looked up and caught the glimmer of a smile in his eyes. "You're giving me a rock?"

"You once told me you had a thing for penguins."

"I love penguins, but what does that have to do with rocks?"

"It's not a rock, it's a pebble."

"A pebble, then. Why?"

Logan smiled, his eyes bright with interest. "Male penguins find the perfect pebble for their chosen mate. It's up to the female to accept it and if she does, she tucks it in her nest."

The recollection came tumbling back. The resort. Fleece penguin socks. His remark about the pebble. She tucked the pebble in her pocket. Logan smiled, took her hand and led her to the center of the footbridge.

She nestled herself against his chest, the pungent summer air a soothing breath of pine and moss. And him. "Crickets and owls, but no stars tonight."

"There will always be stars, Cabin Number Three," he said, lifting her chin. "They're God's creation and He won't let them die. But if they should, there will be fireflies to fill the darkest nights," he said, tracing the faded splash of freckles under her eyes. "But you've never seen stars as brilliant as those under the Tuscan moon." Mischief danced in his eyes. "Come with me to the Tuscany Valley."

Ryleigh gasped. "Italy," she said, more a statement than question.

He nodded.

Excitement swallowed her normal voice. "The country shaped like a boot? Across the Atlantic?"

"Where the true Dolomite Mountains rise on the horizon." He paused. "I'm contemplating the purchase of a property with a small vineyard I think would make a fine addition to Wentworth-Cavanaugh Properties. Please say you'll come with me. I'll need help testing the wine the vineyard produces."

"Logan, I can't. I've never been out of the country. I don't have a passport."

Logan chuckled. "I have connections."

"Of course you do. Speed dial three? Or four? Legal? Or not so much?"

Logan laughed again and pulled her close, her head buried in his chest.

As if written into the perfect script, everything seemed to fall into place and there wasn't a trickle of doubt she loved him. Maybe it was the way she knew he would always be there in subtle ways—presenting her with a shiny pebble or a book of poetry simply because he knew she adored Frost, or in obvious ways—the day he'd saved her from the river. To trust someone so immediately and completely, yes, she knew. Maybe it was the answer she'd longed for while trying to sidestep a malignant past. Maybe the answers to prayers aren't exactly what you ask for, but what is destined. Memories filtered through her mind with refined intricacy and would always be there—not as the haunted memories that made up so much of her past, but cherished and treasured—the kind belonging in a treasure chest.

After a long pause, she answered. "Eighteen months ago, I wandered through the days as if in shadow. Now the only shadow I want to see is yours. Next to mine." She paused. "How can I say no? Besides, we can't let Rose's Italian lessons go to waste."

Logan laughed aloud, lightly stroking her back. "Did you know Longfellow mentions the word wauwatosa in 'Hiawatha'?"

"What's it mean?"

"It's Chippewa for lightning bug." Taking her arms, he slowly turned her around. "Fireflies, Cabin Number Three."

The evening came alive as hundreds of fireflies lit up the creek bed, a twinkling myriad of silent song, a trail of yellow-green ribbons in their wake.

She glanced at Logan. He laughed quietly. Leaning into the bridge rail, she reached for them, luminescent teardrops just beyond her reach. "Fairy lights, Logan, magical fairy lights. I never dreamed…tiny falling stars. The essence of dreams." She reached to touch one and its light blinked, as if they were winking, relaying some magical language of secrets.

THE REFLECTION IN her eyes was as wondrous as a child's, and he would never tire of the feeling it gave him. Beautiful and talented, gentle and passionate, she had captured him with her unsophisticated innocence and natural charm. He'd been drawn to her as a moth would a light and had fallen for every inch of her, an angel God had surely blessed him with.

'Even in darkness light dawns for the upright.'

Sometimes choices aren't choices at all.

He watched as she marveled at the fireflies; he simply marveled at her.

"Your dreams are my dreams now, Cabin Number Three. To keep safe, to treasure and to ensure every one comes true. If I do nothing but fulfill my promise to love you for the rest of my life, I promise you fireflies for the rest of yours."

Ryleigh leaned into his embrace. The hunger to please her, to fulfill her dreams deepened. The air hung heavy. Birds and crickets stilled. Even the wind paused and held its breath, and his world fell into balance.

Raindrops pattered on the bridge. A smattering at first and then as the fireflies winked and disappeared, fell in a light drizzle.

"It's raining, Logan."

"That it is."

"Shouldn't we go?"

"Soon, Cabin Number Three." And he took her in his arms. "Dance with me first."

And they did.

As the rain soaked their clothes, they danced to the rhythm of the falling rain.

"You must learn to dance in the rain," she said, raindrops clinging to her lashes.

"Always." Logan brushed rain-soaked hair from her face. "I do so love you, Miss Ryleigh. You've captured half my heart here among the fireflies."

"Only half?"

"I lost the other half in the Rocky Mountains beneath a blanket of snow."

RAINDROPS BLURRED HER vision. They gathered on Logan's cheeks and trickled from the curls of his hair. He had come into her life unexpectedly, his attraction deliberate yet slow, content to stand beside her, to let her set the pace. Though she thought he'd been lost to her, he had come for her and she saw none of the loneliness, none of the sadness behind his soulful eyes. There she saw the man complete and beautifully made, the one who understood her with all her secrets and still chose her. Like the reflection witnessed in a granite wall, the past had merged with the present and their memories were simply that. Memories. Defining who they were, but no longer haunting them.

The drizzle lightened and then let up for good. The air stirred with cricket-song. A host of fireflies emerged from the banks of the creek, their beacons shining through the mist. Logan took her in his arms and kissed her sweetly. She disappeared into his shoulder, where she belonged—not somewhere, but to someone—in the sanctuary of his kiss and the safe haven of his embrace.

Comfortable.

Safe.

Home.

ACKNOWLEDGEMENTS

One Writer's Confessions

I believe in fairy tales, so when Ryleigh and Logan popped into my dream in a sleigh drawn by two very large horses, I knew I had to write their story. I need to thank them first and foremost for not abandoning me, and for their ever-present (and sometimes annoying) banter inside my head. With their story complete, maybe they'll allow me to get some sleep.

Now, to answer your questions concerning Ambrose—yes, he's a puzzling character, and no, I'm not going to reveal his secrets. Not yet. But if you happen to catch a glimpse of a tall, lanky man with frowzy hair who walks with a decided limp, do say hello. You never know where or when he'll show up.

No story would ever be told without those who help along the way. To my husband, Bruce, I owe you. Big time. Without you, the dust bunnies would have morphed into dinosaurs, Mercedes would have signed herself into a shelter for abandoned dogs, and doubt and fear would have completely consumed me. You're the constant in my life. My rock. And I love you. To my son, Adam—I wish I had a smidgeon of your ambition and courage. Watching you exhibit yours has kept me reaching for my dream and for that, I admire you. My love for you is a given. Always. And to my friends—thank you for tolerating my reclusive tendencies over the life of this project. And by the way, I'm free this Friday—if you haven't given up on me.

As I was writing the final draft, Logan informed me he intended to purchase a vineyard in Italy (now you tell me) and I soon discovered Google couldn't translate the foreign phrases into the dialects I needed. So, to Tyana Bennett, for translating them into Italian the way they should be, and to my niece, Jessica Nagy, for her help with the Spanish phrases—I thank you both for your efforts. I take full responsibility for any discrepancies that may have occurred.

Some of the locations used in this book are real, but I've taken liberties to create the necessary elements of the world where my characters live and love. You may be familiar with these locations, but perhaps not the buildings, businesses, streets, etc., within their boundaries because they are products of my imagination. It's the best of both worlds!

And I raise my glass to these incredible individuals:

To my editor, Michelle Kowalski, who took her red pen to my love affair with the comma and turned my words around. To Anne Pisacano, beta reader/critique partner and traveling buddy extraordinaire, and my proofreaders, Arlene Hittle and Karen Phylow, who found the discrepancies, dots and dashes I missed.

To Elizabeth Mackey—you took my flimsy ideas and turned them into an extraordinary cover. You're a brilliant graphic designer and I can't wait to see what you have in store for future projects.

To the members of Northern Arizona RWA—what can I say? You opened your arms to a terrified newbie and with your warm welcome, guidance, and unfailing encouragement, I left my comfort zone and got 'er done. You guys ROCK! And to the members of the Women's Fiction Writers Association—you're my tribe—I love you guys.

To EMT Laurie Lindell, a huge applause for walking me through the symptoms, stages, and recovery for hypothermia. Sorry, Laurie, some rubbing of cold flesh did occur. For once in her life, Ryleigh chose not to follow the rules.

To Shawn Haught, attorney extraordinaire (and one crazy relative I'll claim any old day) for your expertise on copyright laws, even though it wasn't what I wanted to hear. Sigh.

To Alice Crosbie for sharing her stories of Ballston Spa, NY. It didn't take long to know I wanted to set part of my story in this quaint village. And to the Ballston Spa Town Historian for sending me the details of your visit in the Village Cemetery. The cemetery scenes came to life because of your assistance.

And to D'Elen McClain. My mentor. My confidante. My "person". Without you, the fireflies in my world would never have taken wing to shine their light. I believe people come into our lives at precisely the right time and I'm grateful you entered mine and took me under your wing. I love you, you crazy blond. Your next slice of Starbucks' lemon loaf is on me.

To songwriters everywhere—you are indeed, modern day poets. Your words offer both comfort and inspiration on a daily basis.

And finally to you, cherished reader—you'll forever be a part of my treasure chest. I hope you enjoyed Ryleigh and Logan's journeys as much as I did writing them, and remember always—

Love is Ageless and has the power to change lives—
one step, one touch, one kiss at a time.
~ Susan